A WARHAMMER 40,000 NOVEL

RAVENOR

ROGUE

Dan Abnett

For Andy Lanning, the 'A' of DnA, and about time too

A BLACK LIBRARY PUBLICATION

First published in Great Britain in 2007.
Paperback edition published in 2008 by BL Publishing,
Games Workshop Ltd.,
Willow Road, Nottingham,
NG7 2WS, UK.

10 9 8 7 6 5 4 3 2 1

Cover illustration by Wayne England.
Map by Ralph Horsley.

A CIP record for this book is available from the British Library.

ISBN 13: 978 1 84416 461 5
ISBN 10: 1 84416 461 6

Distributed in the US by Simon & Schuster
1230 Avenue of the Americas, New York, NY 10020, US.

See the Black Library on the Internet at
www.blacklibrary.com

Find out more about Games Workshop
and the world of Warhammer 40,000 at
www.games-workshop.com

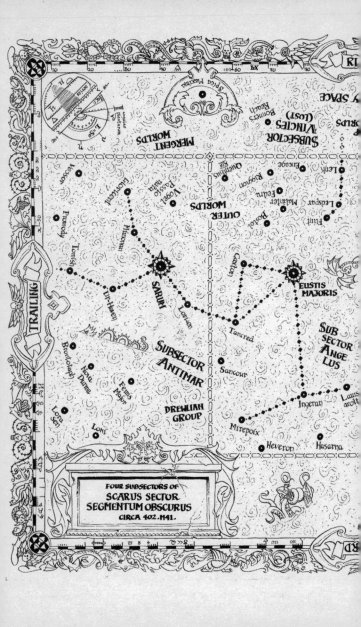

FOUR SUBSECTORS OF
SCARUS SECTOR
SEGMENTUM OBSCURUS
CIRCA 402.M41.

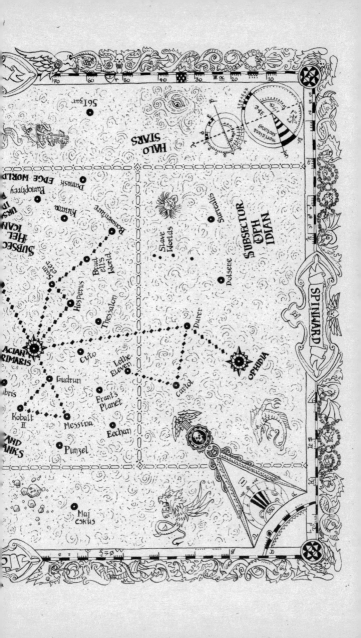

IT IS THE 41st millennium. For more than a hundred centuries the Emperor has sat immobile on the Golden Throne of Earth. He is the master of mankind by the will of the gods, and master of a million worlds by the might of his inexhaustible armies. He is a rotting carcass writhing invisibly with power from the Dark Age of Technology. He is the Carrion Lord of the Imperium for whom a thousand souls are sacrificed every day, so that he may never truly die.

YET EVEN IN his deathless state, the Emperor continues his eternal vigilance. Mighty battlefleets cross the daemon-infested miasma of the warp, the only route between distant stars, their way lit by the Astronomican, the psychic manifestation of the Emperor's will. Vast armies give battle in His name on uncounted worlds. Greatest amongst his soldiers are the Adeptus Astartes, the Space Marines, bio-engineered super-warriors. Their comrades in arms are legion: the Imperial Guard and countless planetary defence forces, the ever-vigilant Inquisition and the tech-priests of the Adeptus Mechanicus to name only a few. But for all their multitudes, they are barely enough to hold off the ever-present threat from aliens, heretics, mutants – and worse.

TO BE A man in such times is to be one amongst untold billions. It is to live in the cruellest and most bloody regime imaginable. These are the tales of those times. Forget the power of technology and science, for so much has been forgotten, never to be re-learned. Forget the promise of progress and understanding, for in the grim dark future there is only war. There is no peace amongst the stars, only an eternity of carnage and slaughter, and the laughter of thirsting gods.

'To have faith is to have purpose, and purpose in life is what defines a man, and makes him steadfast and resolute. Faith keeps him true and, even in the darkest hours, illuminates him like a candle flame. Faith guides him surely, from birth to the grave. It shows him the path, and prevents him from straying into the lightless thickets where insanity awaits. To lose faith is to lose purpose, and to be bereft of guidance. For a man without faith will no longer be true, and a mind without purpose will walk in dark places.'

– *The Spheres of Longing*, II. ix. 31.

'Keep your friends close, and your enemies closer.'

– Ancient human adage.

THEN

Sleef Outworld, 336.M41

IT WAS ALL over. Ordion's scheme was in tatters. All that mattered now was survival.

'Don't make me kill you,' the bounty hunter ordered. He was standing ten metres away, and had a gun aimed at Zygmunt Molotch's face. The bounty hunter was formidably large and shaven-headed. His powerful body was packed into a matt-black bodyglove. He had been sent to watch the back steps into the upper vents.

'Oh, please! Don't!' Molotch cried, and sank to his knees in the sulphurous dust. *Loki*, he decided instantly. That was the man's accent. Loki, the freeze-world. That meant tough, no quarter. Best of the best.

No surprise that their opponent would employ the best of the best.

Keeping the big handgun aimed at Molotch's head, the bounty hunter came forward. Molotch could hear his approaching footsteps crunching the sand. *That's it, close the distance. Ten metres is no use to me. Arm's length will make us equal, gun or no gun.*

13

'Identify yourself,' the bounty hunter commanded.

'My name is Satis,' Molotch replied. He dropped his voice a tone and a half, and affected the nasal twang of southshore Sameter. 'I'm a flier, just a flier, sir!' He whimpered slightly, for effect, trusting that the Fliers' Guild jacket he had dragged off a corpse five minutes earlier would back up his story.

'Are you armed?'

'No, sir, indeed I am not!'

The edge of the bounty hunter's shadow fell across him, cast by the lurid flames spewing up out of the vents. *One step closer, just another step.*

'Nayl?' a voice called out; a woman's voice, thickly accented.

Molotch tensed. Peering up, he saw a second person approaching. Saw her feet, anyway. Leather armour, tight-lashed. A particular loop-in-loop detailing to the hide work decoration. That and the accent added together to make a Carthaen swordswoman. Best of the best, once again.

'Just kill him,' said the woman.

'Wait,' replied the bounty hunter. Molotch heard him adjust his vox-link. 'Iron wishes Thorn, by heartbeat, dark after dusk. Petals scattered, abundant. Teal sky. Closed shells, whispering dogs adjacent. Pattern delta?'

'Query adjacent dogs. The centre of the ripple, spreading.'

'A thaw. Idiot mouths,' the bounty hunter replied. 'Pattern delta?' he asked again.

'Pattern denied. Pattern silver.'

Some informal code. It was fascinating to hear. Molotch divined the principles quickly. He'd always had a talent for languages. His opponent was instructing the bounty hunter to keep Molotch alive, pending interview. The bounty hunter – Nayl, it seemed his name was – was leaning towards Molotch's claim to be just a hapless accomplice to the day's events.

'Pattern confirmed.'

'Look at me,' the woman said. Molotch eagerly wanted to, but he was in character, and his character was timid and scared. He kept his head bowed and mewed a sob.

The bounty hunter hoisted Molotch back onto his feet. His grip was astonishingly strong. Molotch found himself facing the bounty hunter – Nayl – and the swordswoman. She was typical of her breed: taller than most grown men, almost Astartes height, but slender, her hair tight braided, her body cased in leather armour, a tasselled cloak flapping out like wings in the wind. Every centimetre of her tight armour and her cloak was ritually decorated with scrollwork, knotting and bronze studs.

She was the most beautiful thing Molotch had ever seen, and he instantly decided he had to kill her.

She had a sword in her hands, clenched firmly as if it was feather light and about to fly away on the mountain wind. It was a sabre of extraordinary length, two-thirds as tall as she was. The blue cast of the metal told Molotch it had been folded eighteen or nineteen times, which was typical of ancient Carthaen metalwork, and indicated it was a masterpiece weapon, a priceless antique and, very likely, a psychic blade. The oldest Carthaen steels all were. That meant the woman and the sword were united in sentience. Yes, he could see it quiver ever so slightly in time with her breathing.

'You are a flier?' she asked, staring down at him.

Molotch made sure the fear remained in his eyes, even though all that was really there was desire. He was captivated. She was extraordinary, a goddess. He wanted to possess her. He wanted to hear her cry out his name in that delicious outworld accent as she died.

'I am a flier, indeed,' he replied. Tone and accent. Tone and accent.

'You were hired?'

'Just for conveyance. It was a legal contract of hire.'

'Leave him alone,' the bounty hunter said. 'There'll be time for that later.' He was studying the vents above them, watching the glow of the plasma fires light up the sky.

The woman's brow furrowed. 'Barbarisater thirsts,' she said. 'He is not what he seems.'

She was good. She'd seen something, or the sword had smelled something. He longed to know what it was, so he could correct it next time. Accent? Body language? It wasn't the time to ask. The bounty hunter was turning back to face him. Molotch knew he was about to be afforded a one or possibly two-second window of opportunity, and that was all, and if he missed it, he would be dead. He had to swerve the initiative, quickly.

'Who are you?' he asked suddenly. The bounty hunter blinked in surprise.

'I need to know who you are,' Molotch said, more urgently.

'Shut it!' Nayl said.

'I just don't know what's going on,' Molotch whined.

'Better you don't,' Nayl replied and glanced at the woman. 'Cover him while I search him for weapons, Arianhrod.'

Arianhrod. Nayl. Now he had both their names.

The woman nodded, and swept the sword around in a high guard that Molotch was fairly sure was called the *ehn kulsar*. She held it there. Over her shoulder, the vents boomed again.

Nayl reached forward. When he'd been down on his knees, Molotch had picked one of the heavy brass buttons off the cuff of the flier's coat and palmed it. He fired it with a flick of his index finger up into Nayl's left eye.

Nayl cursed and jerked backwards. Molotch sprang past him, hooking his toe behind the bounty hunter's calf to turn the stagger into an outright fall. The woman was already moving, the sabre lunging.

'Arianhrod,' Molotch said, using the tone of command.

She hesitated. A hesitation was all he was ever going to get out of a Carthaen swordswoman, especially as he didn't know her full clan name. But it was enough. A momentary wrong-foot. He chopped the edge of his hand into her neck between the lip of her armour's collar and her braided hair. The muscles in her left shoulder went into involuntary spasm. As she recoiled in surprise, he lifted the sabre out of her hands.

It was like taking hold of the choke chain of an attack dog. The sabre fought him. It didn't want his touch. It pulled like the reins of a bolting steed. Molotch knew he had absolutely no hope of mastering it. Instead, he let it pull away from him like a kite in a gale.

Straight into the bounty hunter.

Nayl had just recovered from his stumble, and was pouncing to snap Molotch's neck. The Carthaen sabre impaled itself through his belly before he even saw it.

The bounty hunter made a soft sound, like a *tut* of disappointment. There was surprisingly little blood, even when he slid off the blade. It was so sharp that the lips of the wounds it had cut through flesh and bodyglove closed tight again, sealed along perfect incisions.

Nayl hit the dust, and lay there, one knee bent, his back arched. Molotch let go of the sabre and set it free. It flew away as if he'd thrown it. He didn't bother to see where it fell. The woman was a more pressing concern.

She uttered no words or curses as she came at him, which seemed remarkably restrained. Molotch wondered just how many tenets of the *Ewl Wyla Scryi* he had just dishonoured by taking her blade from her and using it on her comrade. A seven-fold shame, he estimated. He'd spare her the drudge of penance and mortification by killing her.

Someone had trained her well. He barely avoided a two-finger jab that came at him like the blade of a chisel, and deflected the iron-hard edge of her other hand with a brush of his forearm. She pivoted, and swept around with her left leg – so long and shapely! – and he had to swing out with his hips, arms raised like a dancer, in order to miss it. Her weight came over onto her left leg as it landed, and she swung the right leg out after it, backwards, wheeling herself into the air.

This time, the flying right toecap almost connected. Molotch flopped right back at the waist, dropping his chin into his collarbone to minimise the profile of his face, and converted his body's downward progress into a spring off his right hand that flipped him behind her as she landed.

Aware of him, she back-jabbed with her right elbow to crack his jaw. He stopped her elbow with the cup of his right hand – an impact hard enough to sting his palm – and drove his left fist in under her armpit with the middle finger extended like a beak.

She yowled and lurched away. He'd been studying her intricate body armour, the patterns of bronze studs, the leather ridges, the knot work. All designed to deflect a blade. Simple, very effective. When you fought a sword, the last thing you wanted to take was a scratch that would bleed you to weakness or death. All but the truest killing thrusts could be turned by her armour's complex surface.

But a fist wasn't a blade edge. A hand wasn't a sword. A cluster of bronze studs placed perfectly to glance away a cut to the ribs simply provided a target for a beaked fist. They as good as marked out the mid axillery line, and that governed the autonomic supply to the heart.

She tried to turn, but she was hurt and, besides, he was enjoying himself too much. He kicked her in the back of the left knee, and met her falling body with the heel of his left hand, striking the sacral plexus and flaring pain through her pelvis and legs.

She screamed. She was strong, three or four times as strong as him. She tore away and tried to roll clear. Having exploited the disadvantages of her armour, Molotch turned his attention to her cloak. Who but a barbarian fought in a cloak?

He grabbed it, and pulled with both arms as he simultaneously raised his left leg in a sidekick. Arianhrod snapped backwards, throttled by her cloak-clasp, and the back of her head slammed into his kicking foot.

She was done.

The urge to linger and kill her was immense, but there was no time to relish it. No time to explore a truly complex death. Pleasure could wait. All that mattered was survival.

Molotch started up the rock-cut stairs into the cliff. The smell of the vents was pungent. Clouds of miasmal gas fogged the air. It was hot. He began to move more quickly, and took off the borrowed jacket, throwing it aside.

He was already making mental notes and annotations. The Cognitae trained a man to recognise defeat or failure the moment it happened, and to be empowered by that knowledge. Men are often crippled or undone by the prospect of defeat, and that makes them vulnerable. A Cognitae was never vulnerable unless he chose to make himself so.

A defeat was something to be identified, analysed and used. A defeat was a springboard to launch a man onwards. That was what Madam Chase had taught them. Schemes failed. Plans came apart. Nothing happened with dead certainty. But men only perished when they allowed themselves the weakness of disappointment or maudlin regret.

A waste of effort, when the effort expended on regret could be put to much better use.

Clinical, precise, his mind calculated. Next time, he would plan scrupulously, because next time, he would be in charge. Ordion had been a flawed choice as leader. Molotch had only gone along with it because there was a matter of seniority to be respected. Ordion was twelve years his senior; Molotch a new, unproven graduate. No matter his extraordinary achievements as a student – extraordinary even in a school of extraordinarily able souls – Molotch was still obliged to wait his turn. He fancied Chase had appointed him to Ordion's team to keep an eye on the venture.

In which case, he had failed. The plan was ruined and Ordion was dead. The others too, as far as Molotch knew. He should have acted the moment Ordion started to lose perspective. Those little decisions, for instance, early on, that Molotch had disagreed with. He should have acted. He should have taken the initiative and confronted Ordion. If necessary, he should have killed Ordion and replaced him.

These things he was now learning. Do not rely on a leader. Be your own leader. And, as leader, do not rely on your subordinates to check your actions, for they may well be guilty of the first sin.

Next time, these things would be corrected.

All that remained to do was to make sure there was a next time.

He reached the upper levels of the crags. The limestone cliffs curved away beneath him like old, yellow bone. Far below, in the gnarled landscape of the lower vents, he could see the smudgy outline of their base camp. The gnosis engines were down there still, unless the inquisitors had smashed them; so tantalisingly within reach, so precious, even though they had barely half-loaded them to capacity. The vents had spoken much more slowly than Ordion had predicted. Two weeks, Ordion had estimated, followed by a return trip to Sarum with at least two if not three engines ripe and ready for use. But they had been on Sleef three months, more than enough time for the agencies of the Throne to track them, corner them, and bring them down.

The pale blue air shimmered with heat haze. The vents erupted periodically, boiling vast tides of super-hot plasmatic flow up from the planet's ugly heart. They'd timed their visit to coincide with an eruptive period. The voices were said to be louder and more talkative at such times. Now, it seemed as if the plasma vents were booming and lighting up the sky in sympathy with the afternoon's violence.

Yellow smoke trickled back across the cliff top. Rock waste from the last surge pattered off the crags and skittered down the steeper drops. He could taste the hot stench in his mouth.

He paused by a large, ovoid boulder and took his link out of his pocket.

'Are you still there?' he asked.

'Who is this? Ordion?'

'It's Molotch. Everyone's dead. It's time to leave, *Oktober Country*, before they find you in parking orbit.'

'We appreciate the tip.'

'Don't think you're going without me,' Molotch said.

'Of course.' A pause. 'We'll do our best. Are you near transport?'

'No. Fire up the teleport and lock onto my signal.'

'The teleport's too valuable to risk—'

'I'm too valuable to leave here, you bastards. Fire it up.'

'Molotch, I'm telling you, the vents are in flare. That activity is going to play hell with the teleport. Maybe even fry it, and that's if we get a fix.'

'That's why I headed for high ground, to make it easy for you. I'm right up on the cliffs. Lock onto my signal.'

'Move around. Into the open. Hurry.'

Molotch moved out from beside the rock. Plasma heat and the sunlight stung his face. The wind caught his hair. Holding the link out, he clambered up the rocks until he was overlooking two of the main vents. He walked to the edge of one. Plasma bloomed in bright clouds from the crags a couple of kilometres west. It would be another five minutes until a surge came here again.

He looked down. The drop was immense. The terror was stimulating. Such a long way down, a long drop, it seemed, into the bowels of hell. The vent was forty metres in diameter, its walls scorched black and smoking, and it fell away for thousands of metres, straight down. Far below, there was a glimmer of light as the flames began to rise again.

'Hurry up,' Molotch said.

'We're getting it,' the vox crackled.

Hot, sulphurous gas billowed up out of the vent, and Molotch turned aside, wrinkling his nose. The rock underneath him was rumbling, vibrating with the deep subterranean pressure. The boom and flash of venting lit up along the far crags.

'Come on!'

'Getting a fix now. We've fixed your signal. We're just...'

'*Oktober Country?*'

A hesitation. 'Molotch, confirm which bio-sign you are.'

Molotch didn't answer. He swept around. The man facing him had almost got the drop on him. Very stealthy, very clever.

But he'd made one crucial mistake. He'd tried to take Molotch alive.

Molotch made a flicking gesture with his right arm. It was unexpected and subliminally fast, but so ridiculously obvious, it shouldn't have worked. Except that, as with all things, Molotch had practised it to the point of obsession.

The flick knocked the man's laspistol up out of his hand into the air. The man looked honestly surprised to be disarmed so foolishly, but he was far from defenceless. He was a psyker, a strong one. Molotch could feel it. Only the hexagrammic wards tattooed on Molotch's scalp under the hairline were keeping the man's mind at bay.

Molotch threw himself full length and caught the tumbling laspistol in his outstretched hand. He rolled on the rock to fire it, but the man had landed on top of him, forcing the hand holding the gun up and to the side. They were face to face, like lovers, for a moment. Molotch saw the man's sculptural, high cheek-boned face, his long black hair tied back, the set to his eyes that was noble and faintly reminiscent of the eldar.

With supreme effort, the veins in his neck bulging, Molotch slowly dragged the hand holding the gun back towards the man's head. The man grunted, trying to keep the arm bent away. Molotch pushed harder.

The man head butted Molotch squarely in the face and broke his nose. Molotch winced in pain, and felt the

blood stream down his cheeks. His effort relaxed involuntarily. The man clubbed Molotch's hand against the
ground until the fingers broke and the gun fell out of
them. Molotch gasped, hurt and furious. He threw a
hasty left-hand jab that caught his adversary in the neck.
It shifted the man's weight off Molotch's legs, but in
delivering the jab, Molotch lost his grip on his link. The
small, flat, golden device clattered away across the ivory
rocks.

He could hear the shipmaster's tinny voice croaking
from the speaker. 'Molotch? Molotch?'

Molotch pulled himself away from his foe, scrambling
after the link. It was right on the rim of the vent. Gas was
jetting up from the chasm. The ground was shaking more
than before.

Sprawling on his belly, Molotch stretched for the link,
but the hand his enemy had smashed against the rocks
was useless and the fingers refused to close or grip.
Molotch rolled, grabbing at the link with his left hand.

His scalp began to smoulder. The oppressive weight of
psychic power was burning out the tattooed wards, turning them into bloody welts. In another few seconds, they
would be gone and he would be open to the man's mind.

He grabbed the link, and struggled to his feet, shouting
into it. 'Now. *Now!*'

His back was to the vent. The man was facing him.
He'd retrieved his pistol and was aiming it at Molotch.
No chances this time, no mistakes. The aim was square,
the distance between them too great for Molotch to
repeat his flicking trick.

'Enough,' the man said. 'Drop the link. I want you
alive, but not that much.'

Molotch raised his hands slowly, but he did not drop
the link. He smiled at the man and shook his head.

'Now!'

He stepped backwards off the rim.

He heard the man cry out in dismay. Then he was falling, head over heels, down and down into the deep, blackened pit, into the exhaling heat, into hell.

He screamed the shipmaster's name one final time, fighting to keep his grip on the link.

He saw the plasma flare surging up to meet him. A rising fireball of blossoming yellow and green. He felt his hair singe. He was falling into it and it was rising to engulf him, to devour him, a searing, white wall of–

THE PLASMA FLARE boomed up out of the vents, and trembled the rocks. Heat wash licked back across the crag top. The inferno withdrew, and revealed the man, standing beside the rim. He had encased himself in a cone of frigid air, and held it there as the flare erupted around him. He had no wish to be burned away to nothing.

It had been close. If the flare had lasted a few moments longer, his psychic shield would have failed.

He turned. Arianhrod Esw Sweydyr was limping towards him. There was pain in her face. The man embraced her and kissed her mouth.

'Nayl?' he asked.

'He's bad. I don't think–'.

The man activated his link. 'Talon wishes thorn, the colour of winter. Supplicant idol, with grace, reclining.'

'Commencing.'

A moment later, they both heard the rising whine of the gun cutter's engines echoing around the valley. 'It's all right, they're on their way,' the man told Arianhrod. 'Besides, we got the last of them. The one who did it.'

'Are you sure?' she asked.

Gideon Ravenor glanced at the smoking vent. 'Pretty damn sure,' he said.

NOW

Tancred, Angelus subsector, 404.M41

I CAN'T IGNORE them much longer. I'll have to speak to them. I've been blanking their polite messages for six months, and their stern demands for two. It is tiresome, but if I intend to carry on as an inquisitor of the holy Inquisition, I must make time for them. One can be on Special Condition for only so long.

I sit by the window and look out across the towers and high walls of Basteen, Tancred's principal city. I do not need the window to see it. I feel it. I am much less than a man and much more.

My mind inhales the city. Basteen is basking under a lazy yellow sky. The sun is a molten ball. Red stone, red brick, and red tiles soak in the heat. I feel the sunlight on my soul. I smell the enduring, intricate, feudal character of Basteen: ink and steel pins, silk, wax, obscura smoke, veils and screens, jet shadows and scalding light. The city is rambling and convoluted, a Byzantine network of streets, alleys and buildings wound around and over one

25

another with no discernable pattern or plan, no symmetry or scheme. Cadizky would have abhorred it.

My mind wanders the winding lanes, passing between the cool shadows of overhung alleys into small courts and squares where the sunlight lies on the flagstones in glaring white panels. A trader, in the shaded gloom of his premises, clacks an abacus as he makes up his ledger. A food vendor snores under his stove barrow. The barrow's oven is unlit. No one purchases hot pastries in the heat of noon. It is time to rest before the brisk business of the evening.

Over here, a housekeeper steps home to her master's mansion from the washhouse, a basket of damp linen on her head. She is wondering if she dares stop to take a glass of caffeine, but is fearful that the sun will dry the linen stale and creased if she does not get it hung up. Passing her, coming up the street, are two boys with a pet simivulpa on a string. They are laughing at a joke that I analyse but fail to understand. Here, a servitor paints a door. The servitor's mind is empty, like an unused attic. Over there, an inker hurries to his next appointment, his wooden case of dyes and pens knocking against his hip. He is tired from a morning transcribing deeds that covered an entire shoulder blade.

Behind that wall, a cook dices root vegetables for a slow-braised stew. On a nearby chopping board, the three fish she bought at the dawn market lie, waiting to be cleaned and portioned. They look like three silver ingots. Behind that wall, a secret garden of fig trees, just four metres by four, a tiny pocket of green between high walled residences. Its owner looks down on it from his unshuttered windows, and covets it, and knows that no one else knows it is there. On a roof terrace, a young man plays a viol in the sun while his lover, another young man, sits in the shade of an awning and learns lines for his part in a play. In a cool basement lounge, a woman hesitantly questions a visiting physician about her aunt's dementia.

There, a girl and a boy make love for the first time. There, an ageing thief wakes up and takes a drink to steady his nerves. There, an ecclesiarch's servant scrapes wax from the temple candlesticks. There, a visiting businessman, late for his appointment, realises he has taken a wrong turn, and hurries back down the street the way he came. There, a woman sews. There, a man wonders how he's going to explain it to his wife.

There, a man worries how the meeting to renew his employment contract will go at five, not realising that he won't make the meeting because a heart attack is going to kill him, quite suddenly, in twenty-six minutes.

And somewhere out there...

I cast my mind wider. Forty streets, fifty, a radius of two kilometres... five. Thousands of minds, thousands of lives, twittering on, en masse but individual, lit up to me like the stars in the heavens: some hot, some cool, some clever, some stupid, some promising, some doomed, all contained within the warren of red stone, red brick and red tiles, soaking in the heat.

And not one of them Zygmunt Molotch.

I know he's here. I can't taste him, or breathe him, or sense even an afterthought of him, but I know. I can't say why. I won't be able to tell the envoys why either, when I finally decide to stop ignoring them. But this is where he's hiding. Six months, faint leads, false trails, and here is where I'm drawn to. I have been a servant of the Inquisition since 332, and an autonomous inquisitor since 346. A long time. Long enough to be confident that I am good at what I do. I have faith.

Or am I just obsessing?

The nagging idea that I have been fooling myself has come and gone with increasing regularity these last few weeks. The others feel it, I know. I see it in their faces. They're tired and frustrated with my quest.

I rein back my mind, and pull it in like a trawler's nets until it covers only the house around me. A leased residence, red brick built, well made. Three floors, a grand walled courtyard, a well. There's Patience Kys, my telekine, reclining on a stone bench in the covered walk. She has the plays of Clokus open on her lap, a first folio, but inside it is a copy of my early work, *The Mirror of Smoke*. She doesn't want me to know that she's been reading it. She is too embarrassed to admit she likes what I composed. I am too embarrassed to admit I know, and that I am flattered.

In the yard, there's Sholto Unwerth, my erstwhile shipmaster, and his elquon manhound, Fyflank. Fyflank is throwing a ball for the little man to chase. Shouldn't that be the other way around?

Overlooking the yard, Harlon Nayl thinks the same thing. He's laughing at the antics as he cleans the mechanism of an autopistol on a small desk. I hear him call out 'Look at this, now!' to Maud Plyton, and she gets up from the bowl of salad she was eating and comes to join him, munching, wiping her mouth. She laughs too. It's a deep, dirty snort. I like Maud. I'm glad she left the Magistratum of Eustis Majoris to come with me in the service of the ordos. I have hopes for her. She's as canny as Kara and, I suspect, every bit as tough as Nayl.

Where's Kara? Not in the library. That's Carl Thonius's domain. He's working at his cogitator, winnowing down the latest crop of leads I fed him. He's changed a lot, these last few years. Since Flint, I suppose. The prissiness has gone. He's hard now, like glass, almost unreadable in his determination and reserve. He's dressing differently, behaving differently. He looks Kys and Nayl in the eye these days, and gives as good as he gets. I doubt it will be long before Interrogator Thonius is ready for his next career step. I'll sponsor him, without question. Inquisitor Thonius. It will suit him. I will miss him.

I find Kara Swole, in the rear bedroom. I look away again instantly. Belknap is with her. The moment they are sharing is... intimate. I have no wish or right to intrude.

Belknap, the medicae, is a useful addition to my party, though his manner of joining was improvised. He's a good man, fiercely religious, wonderfully skilled. He came to us when we needed a doctor to tend Kara, and stayed, I think, through love for her. They make a pretty pair. He makes her happy. I question his resolve: such a devout, centred man might not condone some of the things that an inquisitor and his party are forced to do.

I worry about Kara. There is a guarded quality to her, a guarded quality and an unspoken need, and it's been there since we were billeted in the house called Miserimus, in the ninth ward of Formal E, Petropolis. She was hurt and we needed a doctor to save her. I don't like to pry, and I don't like to rifle through the minds of my friends without their consent, but she's hiding something from me. A heavy secret.

I can guess what it is. She wants to leave. An inquisitor can only hold on to his followers for so long. Death is the most usual end to service, I'm sorry to say, but there are other circumstances: disenchantment, incompatibility, fatigue. With Kara, it's fatigue. Kara Swole has served me loyally for a long time and, before that, served my master, Gregor. She has been nothing but a credit, and has nothing left to prove. Tchaikov's vampiric blade almost killed her, and that gave her pause. Then Patrik Belknap came along, her literal saviour, and brought the prospect of a viably different lifetime commitment with him. She wants to live. She wants to live a life where hazard is not a daily expectation. She wants to step back from the duty, her duty done, and embrace the ordinary, miraculous world of love and parenting and, I wager, grandparenting.

I don't resent that. In moments of private despair, I yearn hopelessly for the same thing myself, truth be told. She's done her part, done more than the Emperor himself could have expected of a no-prospects dancer-acrobat from Bonaventure. I wish her that happiness, and delight in the fact that now, for a brief moment, she has the opportunity to seize it. That opportunity won't last, once we get going again. It's now, or, I fear, never. I just wish she'd decide. I wish she'd pluck up the courage and tell me. I won't rant or sulk or try to change her mind. She knows me better. I will give her my blessing, heartfelt. An inquisitor seldom gets that privilege.

That said, I won't suggest it to her either. She's too good to lose. She has to tell me herself, in her own time. This is, I suppose, petulant and controlling of me. I make no apologies. I am an Imperial inquisitor. Gregor Eisenhorn taught me this control, and I can't change the way I am.

Emperor knows, I'd love to.

There are two other people in the house with us.

I roll my support chair away from the window and coast across the floor of the room. The armoured chair is dark-matt, ominous, sleek, suspended and propelled by the ever-turning grav hoop's whispering hum. I have lived inside it, essentially bodiless, for almost seventy years, since that day at the Spatian Gate, that day of hideous alchemy when triumph changed to atrocity, and I changed from an able, upright young man to a fused mass of burned flesh that required an armoured support chair to allow me to function. It's not much, but I call it home.

I slide, frictionless, down the hallway to the room where Zael sleeps. Zael is one of the other two people in the house. Wystan Frauka is the other. Wystan is sitting at

Zael's bedside, his customary place. Wystan is my blunter, my untouchable, leadenly impervious to any and all psychic operation. He smokes lho-sticks incessantly, affects a disdainful manner, and amuses himself by reading lurid erotica.

He's quite wonderful. The disdain is an act. I can read that despite Wystan's unreadability. He has looked after Zael since the boy fell into his fugue state, his coma, his trance... whatever it is. He has carried him, washed him, read to him, watched him.

And he has promised me that he will kill Zael the moment he wakes up. If Zael is what we fear he is.

Zael Efferneti. Zael Sleet. A low-hab stack-runt from Petropolis, a vagabond kid, and also a nascent psyker, undetected by the periodic sweeps and examinations. Not just a psyker, a mirror psyker, that rarest of rare beasts.

And – and this is the big 'and' – potentially the most dangerous being in the sector. There exists a complex and involved series of predictions that concern the manifestation of a daemon in our reality, a daemon called Sleet or Slyte or some such variation. It was reckoned that Slyte would incarnate because of me, or because of one of the people close to me, on Eustis Majoris, between the years 400 and 403.M41. Hundreds, perhaps millions, were predicted to perish if Slyte got loose. So I was warned. I took precautions. Fate can be changed, predictions denied.

At Miserimus, during the attack that took Zeph Mathuin from us, Zael collapsed under psychic assault. At the time, the psykers bombarding him shrieked the name Slyte. Zael has been catatonic ever since. Perhaps his mind couldn't take it. Perhaps his fugue state is a result of him being too weak a vessel to host a daemon.

When he wakes, we will know. He will wake as Zael, or he will wake as a daemon clothed in flesh. If the latter is the case, then my untouchable is standing by to blunt the power of the waking daemon. There is also an autopistol in Wystan's coat pocket, so he can kill the host before it's too late.

Many of my fellow inquisitors, including my beloved ex-master, would chastise me for this. They would say I am being too lenient. They would say I am a fool, and I should take no chances whatsoever. I should extinguish Zael's life, right now, while he is helpless.

I choose not to. For one thing I cannot predict how such a course of action might provoke a sleeping daemon.

For the other, I cannot, in all conscience, murder a teenage boy in his sleep. Zael may not be possessed. Zael may not be Slyte. While there is still a chance, I will not be party to his execution.

Does that make me weak? Charitable? Foolish? Sentimental? Perhaps. Does it make me a radical? Yes, I think it does, though not in the way the term is usually used. I cannot, *will* not, sanction Zael's death on the basis of 'what if?'; I will give him the benefit of the doubt. Throne help me.

If I'm wrong, pray Terra I can contain the damage. If I'm right... it begs the question 'Where is the real Slyte?' Have we aborted his birth? Is his threat passed? It's 404, and that puts us outside the time span of the prophecy. Far enough outside? I don't know. Does Slyte lurk somewhere else, beyond my knowing? Like Molotch? I don't know that either.

I just have to go with what I have.

Wystan looks up as I enter the room. We do this every day. I give him a break from his steadfast vigil.

'All right?' he asks, nodding to my sleek metal chair.

'I'm all right. Were you reading to him?'

'A bedtime story.'

'About people at bedtime?'

He sniggers, and switches off his data-slate. 'The boy doesn't care what I read.'

'And if he does?'

'It's educational.'

'Go for a walk,' I tell him. 'Take a nap.'

Wystan nods and leaves the room. The scent of his last lho-stick lingers after him.

I bring my chair to a halt at the side of Zael's cot. His flesh is pale, his eyelids dark and sunken. He has been away a long time.

Zael, I begin. *Zael, it's me, Ravenor. Just checking in. Are you well?*

No response. Not even a flutter of muffled sentience. We've done this every day, so many times now.

If you can hear me, here's how things are. We won. On Eustis Majoris, we won. It was a hard fight, and the battle was costly, but we won. It was my old, old nemesis, Zygmunt Molotch, Zael. Dead twice at my hands, so I believed. He has a habit of coming back. He had taken the identity of the Lord Subsector, and was intent on using the arcane geography of Petropolis to reawaken an ancient language.

I imagine Zael chuckling, and looking confused. Even as I explain it, I realise it's such an odd story.

Enuncia, Zael. A primaeval language that grants the speaker the power of creation, the power to speak a word, and have that word make or destroy. He'd been years planning it. The city was the mechanism to bring it to life. And we stopped him. That's good. Thousands of people died, but that's preferable to billions. We couldn't have allowed him to walk free, empowered like a god.

I turn my chair slightly, kill the field, and drop onto the struts. The hooves of the struts sink into the carpet.

The bad part is, Molotch escaped. Hurt but alive, and in company with several dangerous individuals. Chief amongst them is a cult facilitator named Orfeo Culzean. Culzean is enormously pernicious. So is Molotch. Together...

Zael does not move. He does not react in any way. He sleeps like death is his sleep.

It's my duty to find them, to hunt down Molotch before he can regroup and try another scheme. That's the way he works, you see. Long term plans. He doesn't think twice about embarking on a scheme that might take years, decades, to reach fruition. This I know about him. I've been sparring with him for more than seventy years. I dearly wish he'd stay dead.

There was a school, Zael, an academy: private, esoteric, long since closed down. It existed about a century ago. It was run by a renegade called Lilean Chase, now long dead. Its aim was to develop, by means psychic, eugenic and noetic, a generation of people who would work to further the cause of Chaos in this sector. Every one of them was a genius, a devil, a monster. They, and their handiwork, have plagued the Inquisition for decades. A secret society. A weapons-grade secret society. Molotch was one of the academy's graduates, one of Chase's star pupils. His intellect was astonishing, and it was tempered with extraordinary noetic training. Zygmunt Molotch, you see, is one of the Inquisition's most wanted. He is abominably malicious. He is Cognitae.

So, that's why I'm chasing him. It's not enough we thwarted him on Eustis Majoris. He's still alive, and we have to track him down and finish him before he can rise again. Nothing in my career is more important or vital than this. Not the Gomek Violation, or even the Cervan-Holman Affair on Sarum which, incidentally, I'm sure Molotch had a hand in. Tracking and executing Zygmunt Molotch is the single most important thing I can ever do with my curious life.

I regarded his so-innocently sleeping form.

Zael Sleet. Or is that Slyte?

The single most important thing, I hope. Anyway, we're close. I think we have him. He's here. By which I mean he's where we are. Tancred. One jump stop down from your home-world, Eustis Majoris. The trouble is, the ordos want to reel me back in. I left Eustis Majoris in a mess. They want a report, and my explanation. They won't wait any longer. I risk losing my warrant and being denounced as a rogue element.

I don't like it, Zael, but I have to stop and answer to my masters. I just hope I can find and finish Molotch before they take away my rosette.

I pause.

Well, that's me. How are you? Zael?

He doesn't respond. I don't expect him to. I hear the door open behind me and presume it's Wystan.

It's not. It's Carl.

'The envoys have arrived,' he says.

+Have they? Very well. I'll be down directly.+

Zael sleeps on, unperturbed.

I engage my chair's lift field, turn, and follow Carl out of the room.

To face, as they say, the music.

PART ONE

A matter of the most pleasant fraternal confidence

ONE

IT TOOK A certain sort of man to perform eight ritual killings in three hours, and he was, without doubt, that sort of man.

Each killing was random, opportunistic, each one carried out with wildly different methods and weapons. The first, with a purloined knife, looked like a back street mugging. The second, a strangulation, was made to seem like a sex crime. The third and fourth, together, would later appear to be a drunken argument over cards that ended with both parties shooting one another simultaneously. The fifth, a poisoning, would have any medicae examiner blaming poorly preserved shellfish. The sixth and seventh, also simultaneous, were electrocutions, and made faulty hab wiring seem responsible. The eighth, the most grisly, was staged to resemble a robbery gone wrong.

She finally caught up with him during the eighth murder. A local moneylender, and part-time fence, owned a house on the lower pavements behind the Basillica Mechanicus. He had slipped in through the back kitchen, found the moneylender alone in a shuttered study, and bludgeoned him to death with a votive statue of Saint Kiodrus.

Then he'd removed some paper money orders and gold bars from the moneylender's floor safe to cement the notion of a robbery.

'What are you doing?' she asked, cautiously entering the gloomy room behind him. The rank, metallic stink of blood choked the close air.

Bent over the body, he glanced at her. 'What needs to be done.'

He reached down and did something to the blood-stained corpse.

'You don't need that,' he added.

She kept the snub-nosed Hostec 5 aimed at the back of his head. 'I'll be the judge of what I need,' she replied.

'Really, you don't need that,' he repeated, using the tone of command this time.

She lowered her aim, but she was strong and well trained. She didn't put the gun away.

'This is madness,' she said. 'You were told to stay in the exclave. Secrecy is paramount. To walk abroad invites discovery. And this... this killing...'

Her voice caught on the word. Leyla Slade was not a squeamish woman. She'd done her fair share of killing, but it had always been professional work. She'd never killed for pleasure, or to appease some mental deviation.

She was disappointed with him, he could tell. He didn't really care, because Leyla Slade wasn't very important in the grand sweep of things. But, for the moment, there were good reasons for keeping her on his side. She was one of his few friends in the cosmos. He could see the disgust on her face, as if she was being asked to babysit some sociopath. She didn't understand. He decided it was time she did.

If nothing else, he didn't like the idea that she considered him to be a homicidal pervert.

'You think I'm killing for kicks?' he asked.

Leyla shrugged. 'It looks like what it looks like. I don't care what kind of animal you are. I just get paid to mind you. In this case, that means dragging your psycho arse back to the exclave.'

He rose to his feet, facing her. The body on the floor lay in an undignified heap, one slipper off, one stockinged toe turned at right angles. The clothes had been ruffled and disarrayed by the fury of the attack. The votive statue of Saint Kiodrus had made a pink pulp of the moneylender's face.

'And if I don't want to go back to the exclave?' he asked.

'Well, I'm not sure I can force you. I have no doubt of your abilities. At the very least, though, we'll hurt each other. A lot.'

He nodded, and smiled. The smile was genuine. 'Yes, I believe we would. I like you because you're honest about these things. We would hurt each other. Let's not.'

'Let's not. Agreed. Now, are you coming back?'

'Soon. Let's talk first, Leyla.'

She raised the gun. 'No. No negotiation. We're going back.'

He nodded, half turned, and made some kind of quick, flicking gesture with his right arm. She flinched, felt a slight impact against her wrist, and then the Hostec 5 was in his right hand.

He aimed it at her. He expected anger, dismay, perhaps even a futile attempt to retake possession of the weapon.

Instead she said, 'Teach me to do that.'

THEY CLEANED THE moneylender's house of incriminating traces, and left the victim on the floor of his study, beside the open floor safe. He stood patiently while she dabbed the specks of impact-spatter blood from his face and neck with a wet cloth. His clothes were black, and the rest wouldn't show.

'A robber would set a fire to cover the body, if a burglary had gone wrong,' she suggested. 'Oh...'

He had already overturned a lamp bowl, and small, blue flames were dancing along the edge of the rug.

FIVE STREETS FROM the moneylender's hab, they entered a small eating house, and took a table at the back. Leyla selected the place because of the low light levels and the fact they could sit away from the street. She ordered a pitcher of petal water, sweetmeats, a *cauldro* of lemon and tchail rice, and a carafe of the local red wine.

'This is nice,' he said.

'It's not. You still have my gun.'

He displayed his hands, open. They were very pale, very expressive.

She frowned, reached inside her jacket, and found her Hostec 5 secure in its rig.

'You can teach me how to do that, too.'

'If you like. Are you eager to learn?'

'Some things. I have skills, and they earn me a market price. My skills are good enough to please my master. And he teaches me some of his skills too.'

'I'm sure he does.'

'But a girl always wants to learn new things. From a man like you–'

'Like me? My dear Leyla, not so many minutes past, you characterised me as a deviant killer. A psycho.'

She shrugged. 'With skills,' she said.

He laughed. She was a piece of work. When the time came, he might even spare her. Or at least, kill her mercifully.

The food arrived. The waitress gave them no more than a passing look. A couple, taking a late lunch. An off-worlder girl, tall, built like a swimmer, with short fair hair and a hard, unforgiving face and what? Her lover? Her employer? A slender man, dignified, dressed in black, with a hairless face that, though handsome, seemed uncomfortably asymmetrical.

Leyla picked at the rice. 'You wanted to talk.'

He poured some wine. 'Six months since we left Eustis Majoris,' he said. 'All that while, you've sheltered me. Kept me hidden, in your custody.'

'For safety.'

'I understand. I appreciate that. I also appreciate, if I haven't told you, the efforts you and the others have made to secure my safety.'

'It doesn't look that way. The first opportunity you get, you slip away from us, and go off into a strange city, killing.'

'There's that,' he nodded.

'So?' She had no desire to tell him the truth. No need to let him in on the fact that her master had told her to allow his escape, and to monitor it.

'Our principal is getting stir crazy, Ley,' Orfeo Culzean had said. 'He's kicking his heels, pacing the cage. Let him out for a while. Let him think he's given us the slip. Give him his head for an hour or two, but tail him and bring him back before he, oh, I don't know, tries to undermine the planetary government or something.'

Leyla Slade had laughed. 'I'll watch him,' she'd promised. 'If all he wants is a bit of fresh air...'

Molotch took a finger pinch of rice, added a sweetmeat, and slid the load into his mouth. He munched and then washed it down with a sip of petal water.

'I needed to get out,' he said. 'I have been handled for too long. By you, and, before that, by my Secretists at Petropolis. My life has been lived according to the timetables of others. I needed to walk, free.'

'If you'd asked, it could have been arranged.'

'If it had been arranged, then it wouldn't have been freedom, would it?'

'Point,' she conceded.

He sat back. 'On Eustis Majoris, Leyla, I came so close. I came so close to doing something extraordinary, something that would have changed the Imperium forever. Ended it, probably. But I was thwarted, and I failed, and you and your master were on hand to pull me out of the fire and bundle me away. Now, your master and I work on new schemes.'

'But?'

'Do you know who I serve, Leyla?'

'Yourself? The deep-time plans of the Cognitae?'

'Yes, and before all of those things?'

She shrugged.

'I won't speak their names aloud, or all the food in this emporium will spoil and all the wine turn to vinegar. They are Ruinous Powers.'

'I understand.'

'Good. So, you see, I had to give thanks. Though my mission to Eustis Majoris failed, I escaped with my life, to continue my work. I had to give thanks for that.'

'Orfeo would–'

'Dear Orfeo doesn't really understand. I don't know what he tells you he is, Leyla, but he's a mercenary. A prostitute. Brilliant, skilled, talented... but he works for money. I don't do what I do for money, or even power, as power is understood by the grandees of this Imperium of Man. I am, I suppose, a man of quite strong religious beliefs.'

'You needed to give thanks?' she asked, drinking a sip of water.

'To the old gods I serve. I had to make appeasement, benediction. I had to make a sacrifice of thanks for deliverance, even though that meant risking discovery. A sacrifice must honour the eight, for eight is the symbol, eight-pointed. A common follower might have killed eight at the eighth house on the eighth street in the eighth enclave, at eight in the evening, but I eschew such crudity. The agents of the Throne would have recognised the occult significance in a moment. Even they are not that stupid. So I made eight subtle sacrifices that, according to inspection, would seem random and unconnected.'

'But they still had ritual purpose?'

He nodded. He ate some more, and drank some wine. She refilled his glass. 'The beggar in the alley. I made eight incisions with a knife that weighed eight ounces. I did this at eight minutes to the hour. The housemaid had eight moles on her left thigh, and took eight minutes to suffocate. I was very particular. The gamblers both held double eights in their hands, and eight shots were discharged. And so on. The moneylender, killed at eight minutes past the hour, was slain with eight primary blows, no more, no less, and had been busy accounting the books for the eighth trading month. I anointed all the bodies with certain marks and runes, all made in water now long evaporated. It was ritual, Leyla. It was worship. It was not the act of a psychopath.'

'I see that now,' she said.

He felt her remark was perhaps sardonic. He half-smiled anyway and drank some water.

'Such an extraordinary level of detail,' she added, scooping up more rice. 'To plan it like that...'

'I was taught to improvise. Leyla, I don't mean to be rude, but I don't think like you think. My mind doesn't work like yours does.'

'Really?'

'I was trained from birth to utilise the full dynamic of my mind. Trained in noetic techniques that give me an edge. More than an edge. What would take another man a week to plan, I can do in a moment.'

'Really?' she repeated.

He enjoyed the hauteur in her voice. The scorn. She was tolerating him.

'Really. Leyla, I'm not boasting or showing off. This is
what the Cognitae does to a mind. Acute observation, for a
start. The ability to read low-level, passive body language.
The ability to notice and compare. To analyse. To predict.'

'Prove it.'

He lifted his glass and smiled. 'Where would you like
me to start?' he asked.

'Oh, you go right ahead.'

'How many buttons did the waitress have on her
bodice?'

Leyla hunched her shoulders. 'Six.'

'Six. Correct. Good. How many were undone?'

'Two,' she said.

'Well noticed. The top two?'

'No, the top one and the bottom one. Her hips were
wide.'

'Again, excellent. Are you sure you haven't had Cognitae training, Leyla?'

She snorted. 'All you've proved is we both like to look
at pretty girls.'

'Dressed in?'

'What?'

'Dressed in?'

'A bodice?'

'The silk from?'

'Hesperus.'

'Good, but no. Sameter. The weave is tighter, and there
is a rumpled quality, a rouching, to Sameter silk. And the
buttons were made on Gudrun.'

'Really?'

'They were gold, and had a hallmark. As she leaned
over...'

Leyla put down her glass. 'You're making this up.'

'Am I? The man at the booth next to us. We passed him
on the way in. Rogue trader, armed. Where was his concealed weapon?'

'Left armpit. I saw the bulge. Got a blade in his right boot too, under the hem of the trouser.'

'You are sharp.'

'It's my business to know.'

'Was his moustache longer on the left or right?'

'I... why does that matter?'

'Shorter on the right, because he smokes an obscura pipe, and the hairs don't grow so fast on the side he sucks the mouthpiece. You could see it in his mannerisms, with the lho-stick. A habitual rise and draw. Which means?'

'He'll be unpredictable. And jumpy. Obscura does that.'

'Now you're learning.'

'It means nothing,' she laughed.

'The man by the window. Left- or right-handed?'

'Right. He's drumming the fingers of his right hand on the table top beside his cup of caffeine.'

'Wrong. He's watching the street crowd, because he's waiting for a business partner he doesn't know. His left hand is under the table, on the butt of his weapon. A Hecuter model, badly stowed. The right hand is a distraction.'

Leyla shook her head. 'Should I go over and ask him to prove it?'

'If you want to get shot. The barman. 19th Gudrunite Irregulars. A Guard veteran.'

'Why?'

'Tattoo on his left wrist. "Company of Angels". The vets of the 19th took that as a tat after Latislaw Heights.'

'You can see that?'

'Not from here. But on the way in. And you–'

'Me?'

'You've eaten enough, you're full. But you like the rice, so you keep picking at it, even though you don't want it.'

'It's good rice.'

'And you haven't touched your wine in thirteen minutes. You keep playing with the glass, but you don't drink, because you're afraid that if you get merry, you'll lose control of this situation. But you play with the glass all the same, so as not to draw attention to the fact you're not drinking.'

'That's just nonsense.'

'Is it?' He looked at her. 'You sit slightly sidelong to me, favouring your left buttock, because your right hip gives you pain. Old wound? An augmetic?'

She breathed out. 'An augmetic.'

Molotch clapped his hands. 'You dearly want to go back now, but you're afraid of goading me, or having to force me. You want to make it seem like my idea.'

'Now, look–'

'You're quite certain I don't know that Orfeo instructed you to let me loose for a few hours. Orfeo thinks I'm going stir crazy. The idea was to let me walk around and blow off steam.'

'Dammit, Molotch–'

'Don't damn it at all. Enjoy it. What could I do, do you suppose? What could I do, just sitting here?'

'I don't know.'

Molotch removed a tiny phial from his sleeve and put it on the table top beside the *cauldro* of rice. 'Osicol Plague, in suspension. I took it from Orfeo's personal kit. If I release it here, I could decimate the entire city quarter.'

'For the love of– No!'

'I won't. There'd be no sense in that. But consider the options. The banker at the table to our left. He works at the city mint. He has a brooch on his waistcoat, before you ask. The sigil of the banking guild, and the office of coinage circulation. If I dropped the phial into his business case, he would find it and open it when he returned to his office. The mint would be contaminated, and would have to be sealed off for fifteen years. The local currency would crash, and bring the subsector economy down. Decades of damage. Or take that young man over there, the one in the private booth. He's the second son of a minor baron, slumming it, but I know he's in with the court crowd.'

Molotch produced a small medical injector from his pocket and put it down on the table beside the phial. It was full of clear fluid. 'Suspension liquid. Inert and viscous, metabolised in six hours. I could go into the washrooms, load the plague solution into it, and bump into that second son as I came back. In a day or two, the entire royal house of this planet would be dead from contact plague. An ideal moment to stage a coup.'

'But that's just... just...' she whispered.

'Now you're getting the idea,' he said. 'What about this? That drunk by the bar. I've been gently hypnotising him with finger movements since we came in. Allow me to prove it.'

Molotch moved his fingers. The drunken man lurched and tottered over to them.

'What's your name?' Molotch asked.

'Sire Garnis Govior, sir,' the man wobbled.

'And your job?'

'I am chief under translator to the House of the Governor, sir.'

Leyla stared at Molotch.

'And you thought I'd let you pick this bar,' he smiled. 'It's a famous haunt of the Administratum classes. I noticed Garnis here because of his signet ring.'

'This ring?' the man asked, displaying it so abruptly he swayed.

'The very same. You have face time with the governor, then?'

'I do, sir, I surely do,' the man said, wobbling.

'So, if I asked you to strangle him the next time you saw him, setting off a local sector war that would bring in Houses Gevaunt, Nightbray and Clovis, you'd have no problem?'

'None at all,' the man assured Molotch. 'Not a problem at all.'

'You'd strangle the Lord Governor?' Leyla asked.

'Like a bloody shot. Like he was a bloody whelp. Yes, mam.'

'But I won't,' said Molotch. 'You can go now, Garnis.'

'Thank you kindly,' the man said, and staggered off.

Molotch looked at the wide-eyed Leyla. 'Every opening. Every chance. Every chink. That's what the Cognitae are trained to do. To look, to see, to find, to use. In the course of this delightful lunch, Leyla, I could have brought the subsector down three or four times over. Just like that.'

He flicked something away with his thumb. It landed on the floor of the bar and broke, oozing fluid.

'Oh holy–!' Leyla began.

'Relax. It's just the suspension fluid. The plague's in my pocket. So, let's consider the Inquisition.'

'The Inquisition?'

'Most particularly, the office of the ordos on this world.'

'You can't see that from here.'

'Oh, I can. In the over-bar mirror. See?'

'Terra, I hadn't noticed that.'

He sipped his wine. 'I can see the fortress of the Inquisition from my seat. Such a big fortress. Towering over the city. It was built by the Black Templars, you know? Long since vacated, but one day they might be back. Until then, the Inquisition uses the keep. It's going to be a bloody fight the day the Templars return. Anyway, they're flying flags. Several dark flags. What does that mean?'

'Does it mean anything? They're flying flags.'

'The Inquisition doesn't suppose anyone understands their protocols and heraldry. Black flags above their fortress. Just for show. Just for threat. But I have made it

my business to understand and monitor the way they signal to one another.'

'So? I can barely see the mirror from where I'm sitting.'

'I'll tell you what it means. The flags are the black crests
of Siquo, Bilocke and Quist, symbols the Inquisition
identify with respect and honour. They are flying cere-
monially. There are envoys in residence. Several
high-ranking envoys. Actually, you can tell that simply by
the number of weapon ports they've uncovered. Someone important is here.'

'Meaning?'

'Meaning, Ravenor's here, as we feared, and they've
decided to rein him in. Which is good news for us.'

There was a sudden, brutal crash. Voices around the
eating house rose in alarm. Garnis had slipped over in
the pool of suspension fluid and brained himself on the
edge of the bar rail.

He was dead.

'Let's go,' said Molotch.

They rose and picked their way out of the eating house,
moving around the crowd that had gathered around Garnis's misfortune.

'That's nine, ' Leyla whispered. 'I thought you only
wanted eight?'

'I did, but I'm not stupid. This one isn't ritual. This is a
ninth to ruin the pattern. The ordos are sharp and clever.
They would have seen a pattern of eight except for this.'

He bent down in the edge of the crowd and picked up
a small piece of the broken glass phial Garnis had
slipped on.

'A present,' he said. 'A deodand for your master.'

'I'm sure he'll love it,' said Leyla Slade. 'Wait,' she
added.

He paused. She licked her right index finger, reached
out, and wiped away one last lone speck of blood from
his face that she'd missed earlier.

'Thank you,' he said.

They stepped out into the bright day and the bustling crowd swallowed them up.

TWO

AT HER MASTER'S mind-whispered instruction, Patience Kys opened the courtyard gates to let them in.

She didn't move from her seat on the stone bench. One nod of her head, one blink of her green eyes, and invisible hawsers of telekinetic power drew the heavy timber doors open. The lower edges of the doors scraped slightly on the ground, and lifted a small cloud of dust from the dry cobbles. The doors made a juddering, rumbling sound as they swung in. Fierce patches of yellow sunlight invaded the quiet shade of the courtyard through the opening gates.

Nayl, Thonius and Plyton came out of the house to watch the arrival.

Nayl's expression was unreadable. The skin of his shaved scalp had caught a touch of sun. He wore a tight grey bodyglove reinforced with articulated ceramite plates around the shoulders, neck and torso. He stood at the top of the house steps, in the shadow of the entrance archway, adjusting his gloves. He made no attempt to conceal the Hecuter Arms Midgard holstered on his left hip.

Maud Plyton emerged to stand next to him. She had taken to wearing Navy surplus fatigues since quitting the Magistratum. Today, she had chosen a one piece, zip-front flight suit of shabby khaki, heavy-laced combat boots, and a white undervest. The unflattering fit of the unisex clothing accentuated her large, slightly thickset frame, a build that contrasted sharply with the very delicate pinch of her features. She wore her dark hair cropped short, a Magistratum regulation she had found it hard to abandon.

Carl Thonius, slender and trim, wore the bottom half of a black bodyglove and the high, patent leather boots of a ceremonial cavalry officer, complete with rowel spurs that clinked when he walked. On his upper half he wore a purple tail coat with gold trim. Open, the coat framed a rectangle of scrawny white chest and washboard stomach above the glove's waistband. His long fingers were covered in rings, and his hair was dyed black and roughly chopped into a mane. He was a long way from the fey, fussy, impeccably dressed dandy who had first joined the inquisitor's company a decade before.

'Do we know who it is?' Nayl asked him.

Carl shook his head. 'Not a clue.'

Across the yard, Kara and Belknap emerged from another doorway. Kara was short, voluptuous, her bright red hair stridently clashing with her lime green vest and white pantaloons. Belknap, dressed in simple black combat trousers, was a slim man of average build, his hair short and unremarkably brown, his face unexceptionally ordinary except for a sleepy glitter of intense wisdom and reassurance in his eyes. Those eyes had seen a lot, as a battlefield medicae. They would see a whole lot more as the private physician to an inquisitor's warband.

Patience Kys, tall and feline, rose from the bench at last and joined Kara and Belknap. In her dark brown bodyglove, she seemed all legs. Her black hair was hanging loose, but as she walked, she reached up with her hands, gathered it, and twisted it into a neat tail that she secured with a silver pin.

'Brace yourselves,' she said. 'I smell trouble.'

The envoys entered the courtyard. First, an outrider on a long, low, powerful warbike, its engine issuing an indignant splutter that resonated around the courtyard walls. Then, one after another, three Chimera carriers, like monolithic stone blocks, their track sections clattering and squealing. The carriers were finished in a matt grey, as if they were supposed to be incognito. As if a trio of thirty-eight tonne armoured vehicles could be incognito. Their turbines grumbling, they drew up on the lower part of the courtyard, side-by-side. Six psyberskulls droned in with them, and took up hovering stations, like dragonflies.

A second outrider, low on his machine like the first, brought up the rear. This second bike raced around the parked carriers, and halted, revving. The rider put one foot down and sat up.

In a line: bike, carrier, carrier, carrier, bike.

+Close the gates.+

Kys nodded, and obliged. The gates rumbled shut.

The carriers shut down their engines. Exhaust fumes drifted away, up and out of the yard.

'Leave this to me,' said Nayl.

'Why?' asked Carl.

'Look at my face. Am I about to take any shit?'

Carl smiled and nodded. 'No. And I like that about you.'

Nayl looked at Maud. 'Got a piece?'

'I thought they were friends?'

'No such thing, girl. Go get a piece and stay inside behind the door.'

Maud looked back at Nayl, waiting for the punchline. Then she realised he was serious and disappeared back into the house.

Harlon Nayl left Thonius on the steps and stomped down into the sunlight. He walked towards the line of vehicles. The hovering psyberskulls whirred and buzzed, bobbing slightly, as he came into range.

The two outriders had killed the engines of their warbikes and rocked them over onto their stands. Both dismounted. They were clad in matching scale-armoured bodygloves, smeared in dust, which made them look like extensions of their matt-black and bare-metal bikes. They removed their helmets, yanking free the skeins of wires and plugs that linked them to the weapon-systems of the bikes.

The rider on the left was a young male, tall and slightly built, with long white hair that shook free and loose the moment his helmet was off. He looked at Nayl. He had the most distressingly blue eyes.

'We greet the master of the house, and humbly thank him for this audience,' he said. His voice was soft and clear, like rainwater.

'The greeting is returned,' said Nayl. He flicked his eyes up at the hovering psyberskulls. 'A little too many guns around for this to be cordial.'

The young man smiled broadly. 'I apologise,' he said. He took a control wand from his hip pocket and waved it. With a low murmur, the skulls deactivated and sank to the courtyard floor. 'That was rude. Just a precaution, you realise.'

He pocketed the wand, hung his helmet on the antlers of his bike and walked towards Nayl.

'Interrogator Gall Ballack,' he said, extending a hand the moment he'd peeled the glove off.

'Nayl,' said Nayl, shaking the hand.

'I know,' said Ballack. 'I have studied the records. I'm an admirer of your work. Where's Ravenor?'

'By that, I suppose you mean Inquisitor Ravenor?' Nayl replied.

Ballack pursed his lips and nodded. 'Presumptuous of me, and lacking respect. Of course, I meant Inquisitor Ravenor.'

'He's inside.'

'My senior has come to speak with him.'

'Perhaps your senior would like to get out of his tank and come in, then,' said Nayl.

Ballack snorted a laugh. 'You know, Harlon, I think she might just do that.'

There was a series of pneumatic clanks, and the boarding hatches of the Chimeras began to open. Over in the shadows, Kys jerked her head at Kara, and the pair of them slipped away into the house. Belknap, slightly at a loss, stayed put.

The second outrider had taken off his helmet. He was a she. A very tall she with long braided, beaded hair.

'Shit,' whispered Harlon Nayl.

+Great Throne of Terra.+

'You're seeing this?' Nayl murmured.

+Of course.+

'She's the dead spit,' Nayl said.

+It's uncanny.+

'This will be weird for you, then, I guess.'

+I can do weird, Harlon. I'm a professional.+

'Even so.'

+Bring them in. Let's get this done.+

PEOPLE DISMOUNTED FROM the carriers: two dozen troopers with mixed weapons, all of them wearing the rosette of the ordos: an old man with a cane; a tiny, child-framed woman in selpic blue leading a pair of servitor gunhounds; an ogryn slaved to a massive plasma cannon; a woman and a man in long leather coats; a quartet of rubricators with their writing machines; a man in shiny jet body armour; and another woman, ash-blonde, slender, dressed in a long gown of ochre Hydraphur silk. She was impressive. The sight of her made Nayl suck in his breath.

Then the chief envoy. Her body was armoured in red plate and she walked with a limp. Every centimetre of her armour was engraved and covered with seals. The parchment scrolls hung off her like feathers, as if she was fledged like a bird.

+Well, I should be flattered, I suppose.+

'Yeah,' whispered Nayl. 'Why?'

+That's Inquisitor Myzard. Senior secretary to the Ordos Helican, and Lord Rorken's immediate subordinate.+

'Throne, they're not playing around then, are they?'

Myzard limped across the yard to Nayl. She looked up into his face. She had once, Nayl could tell, been a beautiful woman: strong, articulate, animated. Her face was lined now, contoured by extreme age. Her hair was straw gold.

'Are you the interrogator?' she asked in a brittle, tired voice. 'Are you Thonius?'

'This is Nayl, ma'am,' Ballack said gently. 'The, ah–'

'Thug,' Nayl suggested with a rogue's smile, extending his hand.

Myzard grinned and shook his hand. 'I like you already,' she warned. 'Where's that bastard Ravenor? I need to have words.'

'As I just said, he's inside. And I'm sure he's got some of his own.'

Myzard laughed again. 'I do like you. Spunky. Let's go and talk to Gideon, shall we?'

'Allow me to lead you in, ma'am,' Thonius said, hurrying down the steps with a hand extended. 'I'm Interrogator Thonius. My master is awaiting your pleasure.'

Myzard sniffed. 'I've been awaiting my pleasure for sixty-eight years.' She glanced at Nayl. 'Possibly I've found it now, though.'

Nayl looked at Carl and mouthed, 'Help me'. Carl smiled. 'This way, ma'am.'

They filed in past Nayl, up into the house. The gunhounds barked at him as they were led by. The woman in ochre, the ash-blonde, turned Nayl's head as she passed. She didn't look at him.

They had gone in towards the house and only the female outrider remained, standing by the parked vehicles.

Nayl walked over to her.

'We had better go in,' he said.

She nodded. She was taller than he was.

'I have to ask,' he said. 'Esw Sweydyr?'

'You know the Carthaen clans?'

'I knew one of their number once. A long time ago. Ari-anhrod.'

'My mother's sister. I am Angharad.'

He made the sign of the aquila. 'Harlon Nayl. You should know, my master was deeply in love with your aunt, a long time ago.'

'I know this too. I know she died by his side. She was the reason I joined the Inquisition's service.' Angharad returned his respectful aquila with the fist-punch to sternum salute of Carthe.

He waited while she untied her long, sheathed sabre from the warbike's frame.

'Let's go in,' he said.

'Let's.'

'If you don't mind me asking... what's its name?'

She cinched the sword harness tighter around her shoulder.

'Evisorex,' she replied.

THREE

I SIT WAITING for them, in a pool of sunlight in the drawing room. I have banished my party to the far corners of the house, just in case. The only ones I allow to be present are Carl Thonius, leading the visitors in, and Harlon Nayl, bringing up the rear.

Nayl is walking with the woman Angharad. I find I am insanely jealous. Arianhrod was the only woman I ever loved, in my physical life. She died just a few short months before I was maimed and reduced to this state, and somehow, tragically, that had made it better. If Ari-anhrod had still been there, I would have...

Killed myself. Killed myself, without a doubt.

But she had died first. I had coped with all of my loss.

And now... her doppelganger appears. A Carthaen swordswoman so physically reminiscent of my long lost love it is painful.

I turn my chair to face Myzard,

'Gideon,' she announces. 'Good to see you.'

+And you, Ermina. Do you have any objections to thought conference? I can kick in my voxponder.+

'Mind's fine,' she says, and sits down on a tub chair that groans.

'Meet the others,' she says. 'D'mal Singh.'

The tiny woman with the gun hounds nods. The hounds snuffle and whine.

'Tarkos Mentator.'

The old savant, bent on his cane, also nods.

'Shugurth.'

The ogryn bows.

'Interrogator Claudel and Interrogator Gonzale. Interrogator Ballack.'

The man and the woman in the long coats snap to attention. Ballack inclines his head with a smile, his face framed by his long white hair.

'Angharad Esw Sweydyr.'

The towering swordswoman beside Nayl makes no movement whatsoever.

'Inquisitor Fenx.'

The man in the black body armour makes the sign of the aquila.

'And this is Inquisitor Lilith.'

The woman in the ochre gown with the ash-blonde hair offers me a respectful nod.

+Lilith. I've read your work and admired it. You have, I understand, a particular interest in the eldar xenotype.+

'I have, sir. And I have read your work too, and adored it,' she answered.

+Thank you.+

'Well, now every one loves every one else,' says Myzard, 'let's get to business. Gideon, you have to stop. You are this close to being branded a rogue.' She holds up her left hand and pinches the forefinger towards the thumb to indicate the distance.

I open the slot on the fore casing of my chair and display my blue rosette. +I am operating under Special Condition, and my Lord Rorken knows this.+

Myzard folds her hands. 'Such an understanding goes only so far. It's time to stop.'

'Molotch is still out there,' Thonius says.

+My own interrogator, Carl Thonius,+ I send.

'We've met,' says Myzard. 'Yes, Molotch is out there. But he's a loose end that others can deal with. You are requested to stop.'

+Requested?+

Myzard sniffs. 'Ordered. Requested is so much more mealy-mouthed. We've been requesting you for months and you've been avoiding us. Now it's an order.'

+From my lord?+

The senior envoy nods her head. Fenx steps forward and draws a sealed data-slate from his belt pouch. He holds it awkwardly for a moment and stares at my chair.

'Is there somewhere... somewhere I can insert this?'

'I've an idea,' mutters Nayl from the back of the room.

Myzard sniggers. 'Play nice, Gideon. Dataport?'

I open a dataport on the side of my chair unit and Fenx loads the slate. I open it, spin it out, and extend the hololithic display around me in my dark cocoon of virtual light. The missive has been recorded by my Lord Rorken personally. It is as if I was standing next to him. He looks tired, frustrated. He says my name. I kill the rest of the sequence. I don't need to see any more. Rorken is the only man I answer to, and he has spoken.

+All right. I'll come back in. There, it wasn't so painful, was it, Ermina?+

'Thankfully no, Gideon. Look, you have to understand you're not about to be censured. Rorken is pleased with your work. So am I, dammit. On Eustis, you did an extraordinary thing. You stopped something that could have destroyed everything. All of us.'

+Oh, so you have read my report?+

'Cover to cover,' says Lilith. 'But it is the very magnitude of the event that forces your recall, sir. Enuncia alone, and the collective knowledge of it gathered by your team, must be examined in forensic detail. A – forgive me – curt report is not enough.'

'And there is the matter of Eustis Majoris itself,' says the savant Mentator. His voice is as involved and thready as old, fused wiring.

'What matter might that be?' Thonius asks.

'The damage,' says Mentator. 'The destruction. The deaths.'

+Am I to be held responsible?+

'Oh, for goodness sake, Gideon,' Myzard says, getting to her feet and looking around the room. 'It's going to take years to rebuild the subsector capital. This whole region is in crisis, you understand? Crisis?'

+I know what crisis means.+

'Eighteen planetary governments about to fall. There are currency issues. Faith issues.' Interrogator Ballack was speaking fast, quietly. 'A loss of belief in Imperial rule. General unrest. Strikes and civil disobedience on nine major planets. A mutiny at the Navy yards on Lenk. The list is extensive. I won't bother you with every detail, but you need to understand... if Molotch had succeeded, he would have busted this subsector, this sector even, apart at the seams. You stopped him. But the price of you stopping him was still extensive. Scarus sector is damaged and fragile. Repairing the infrastructure will take generations. We need your help.'

+My help?+

'It is essential that you and every member of your team is extensively debriefed,' says Interrogator Gonzale. 'That process might take months. We can learn from you, inquisitor. And what we learn from you may save us years in the rebuilding process.'

'Put simply,' says Myzard, 'you can't just make a big old mess and leave others to clean it up.'

I know this. I have been avoiding it. It is a necessary part of any inquisitor's work. After the Gomek Violation, I spent three years in restorative, cooperative study with the planetary government. After the Nassar case, my old master Gregor Eisenhorn devoted the better part of a decade on Messina, tidying up behind himself. After the Necron Wars, Inquisitor Bilocke, blessed be his memory, set aside the remainder of his life to repairing the governments and substrate of the Tarquin Stars.

Myzard is still looking around.

+Carl, perhaps you could rustle up some wine and some food for our guests?+

Carl nods. 'No problem, sir.'

'That's very kind of you, Gideon,' Myzard says, sitting down again.

'What about Molotch?' Nayl asks. Everyone looks around at him.

'Did I say that out loud?' he adds. 'Good. What about Molotch?'

'What about him?' asks Fenx.

'He's loose. He's free. He's out there.'

'Out where?' asks Inquisitor Lilith.

Nayl shrugs a shoulder. 'Out there. In Basteen.'

'We've no reason to suppose he's here,' says Fenx.

'Haven't you?' Nayl asks. 'We have.'

'Evidence it,' demands Claudel.

Nayl pauses. I feel for him. He is so loyal. 'I can't just do that. It's–'

+It's a hunch.+

Myzard stares at my chair. 'A hunch?'

+Don't look at me like that, Ermina. A hunch. Yes, a hunch. I do that, and look what I do.+

'So noted. I trust you. But a hunch?'

+He's here.+

'A hunch is not enough.'

+I have... faith.+

Myzard and Fenx exchange looks.

+Molotch must be brought in. He's been at large for too many years. He's rabidly dangerous. That's why I've stayed out so long, ignoring your calls. I have to bring him in.+

'You're too close, Gideon.'

+That's why I'm the one to do it.+

'No, you're too close, Gideon,' Myzard repeats. Carl comes back in with a tray of drinks, and Myzard takes one. 'Molotch is your nemesis. You're twinned in destiny. Such a long, involved duel you've fought, down the years. You're too close. It's becoming a disadvantage.'

+I don't believe so.+

She sips her drink. 'That's your prerogative. But I'm telling you this, Gideon, in all frankness... the reason you've never brought Molotch down is that you're too close and therefore not the man to do it.'

+Rubbish.+

'How many times have you killed him now?' Lilith asks. 'Two? Three?'

+He's tenacious.+

'He's nigh-on bloody invulnerable to you,' Myzard smiles. 'Molotch isn't here, Gideon. He's fled. You're obsessed, and tired, and too long on the chase. You're needed elsewhere. Let other, fresher minds hunt Molotch down.'

+You might be right,+ I concede.

'I am right. Good wine, by the way.' Myzard puts her glass down.

+I'll take your word for it.+

'We are very able, inquisitor,' says Fenx.

+I'm sure you are, sir.+

'We will find Molotch and bring him to justice,' says Lilith.

+Am I allowed to ask how?+

Myzard nods. 'We have agents active all across the sub-sector. Some are uncovering strong leads. Fenx and his team leave Tancred tonight for Sancour. In two days, Lilith and her party head out for Ingeran. Six hours later, my interrogator here, Ballack, commands a party to the Halo Stars.'

+You say you have leads?+

'Currency accounts on Sancour have been traced to Molotch,' says Fenx. 'They've been accessed in the last month. That's a strong lead.'

'I have sourced Cognitae holdings on Ingeran to Molotch,' says Lilith. 'Orfeo Culzean has territory there. Someone is trying to dissolve those assets. That's also a strong lead.'

'Orfeo Culzean's collection of deodands was shipped out, via an unnamed cash wafer, to Encage, three weeks ago,' says Ballack. 'The collection had been held by the hotel at Petropolis. They were routed as cargo on a bulk trader.'

+I know. Don't waste your time. It's a double blind.+

Ballack shrugs. 'We'll see.'

'It's over, Gideon. You can stop now, and rest,' Myzard says.

+All right,+ I sent. +He's your problem now. Just don't come crying to me when–+

'Might I have some more wine?' Myzard asks, holding up her glass.

'YOU'RE JUST GOING to roll over on this?' Kara asks after Myzard has gone.

+I think so. Do you really want to spend the rest of your life hunting Molotch?+

She stands beside me in the courtyard of the house. Evening has stretched the shadows out into long, grey lines.

'No,' she answers. She looks at me. 'Because I don't believe it will take the rest of our lives.'

+Because we're close?+

'Because we're close. You believe so, so does Patience. You feel it.'

+It's still just a hunch. I have no solid proof. I felt quite embarrassed trying to explain it to Myzard and her people. Trying to justify...+

'What?'

+Gregor trained me to follow my instinct. But he also warned me against obsession.+

'He should talk,' she smiles.

+I've been sparring with Zygmunt Molotch for a lifetime, Kara. Myzard's right. It's become too personal. I can't see past it. So I have to let it go. The repair of Eustis Majoris is an obligation I cannot ignore. Every word they spoke was correct. In fact, I think they were quite diplomatic about it, all things considered. I have a duty to the rank I hold. I bested Molotch soundly and should content myself with that. For Throne's sake, let others waste their days hunting the mad bastard to his doom.+

Kara shakes her head and sits down on one of the stone benches. Over the years I have come to appreciate how gorgeous she is. Not beautiful like Kys, but warm and curved and appealing. I have known her physicality from inside, waring her on so many occasions. She is the closest thing to a lover I can claim any more, although only in the most tenuous, perverse sense. And now she has another in her life. A man who can provide her the simple, human consolations I will never manage. I know she feels this too. She has been far more unwilling to let me ware her lately. I chide myself that I am a fool for feeling cuckolded.

I am surprised and, I hate to admit it, delighted by her persistence.

'What about closure?' she asks.

+It's overrated.+

Kara snorts. 'Since when? Gregor always chased proper closure.'

+And look where he ended up. That's not for me. I have strayed as radically as I am comfortable with. I will not plunge on and become a rogue.+

I can taste the disappointment in her suddenly, even though I am not touching her mind. She cannot hide it. 'What about the rest of us, Gideon?' she asks.

+What about you?+

'Did you not consider that we might need closure too? For Majeskus? For Norah and Will and Eleena? For Zeph?'

+That's low.+

'But it's true.'

+Service is its own reward.+

'Not actually,' she says, getting to her feet. 'For you, maybe.'

+I thought you'd be pleased.+

'Pleased?'

+We'll be here another week while I get my affairs in order. Then we'll return to Eustis Majoris. Once there, it will be a long and forensic process of evaluation and report. The team will be non-active. It would be a good time for self-review and reorganisation. For changes. I thought you would be pleased at the opportunity.+

'Again, "pleased"?'

+I have sensed there is something on your mind, Kara. I think I know what it is.+

'There's nothing on my mind.'

+There is–+

'There's nothing! Get into my head if you want to! Take a look! But stop inferring from my surface moods! There's nothing!'

+Very well.+

'I mean it.'

+I can tell.+

She stares at me. She seems angry. Or is it guilty?

+I won't probe. I trust you.+

For a fleeting moment, Kara looks let down. She begins to walk away.

'We need closure,' she says.

+We got it. On Eustis Majoris, we got it. The rest is just housework.+

'But you had a hunch,' she says. 'Your instinct told you he was here.'

+Kara, I hate to diminish myself in your eyes, but it's quite possible I have been fooling myself. History makes me want to finish the business with Molotch and, moreover, I have little appetite for the arduous chores awaiting me on Eustis. This chase has become displacement activity, putting off the inevitable. Yes, I had a hunch. Just a hunch, and sometimes they don't pay out.+

'Yours always do,' she says. Throne, how those words will come to haunt me.

+Not this time. Molotch isn't here. My hunch is empty air. It's time we stopped this and got on with something useful.+

FOUR

NAKED, ORFEO CULZEAN lay face down on a suspensor couch, and allowed the inker to finish composing the final deed across the small of his back. Culzean found the tiny prickle and pinch of the inker's needles quite stimulating. The quiet gave him time to think, space to think. The tiny pain kept his thoughts sharp. His mind was a huge, purring engine, always active, and it benefited from reflection. Time to think, to consider, to pace around a problem and survey it, end to end.

'In my experience,' he said out loud, 'the Imperium is full of holes, and the trick is to identify those holes and exploit them.'

Working tightly with his steel needles, dabbing them occasionally into the ink pots spread out on the floor beside his knees, the inker grunted acknowledgement. He did not understand Culzean's words, because Culzean was speaking *idrish*, a Halo Star dialect he'd picked up in his formative years. The inker assumed his client was murmuring some pain-relieving mantra. People often found the needle work excruciating.

'I mean, billions and billions of lives, all herded and ordered by a vast bureaucracy. You find the spaces in that, you see. The gaps. You don't disrupt the system, for that makes you visible. You inhabit the voids within its structure and disappear.'

The inker grunted again.

Culzean shook his head. Fools, idiots. They were all fools and idiots. Except Molotch and Ravenor. And for the benefit of the former and the beguiling of the latter, he was engaged in this present business. It was a task few men could have risen to. But he was singular. And there would be rewards. My, what rewards there would be.

The exclave's perimeter alarm buzzed quietly. Lucius Worna got up to see to it. The huge, scar-faced bounty hunter, brought into Culzean's employ by fate and circumstances, had been sitting silently in a dark corner of the room like a stone idol. Culzean thought Worna an impressive specimen, though he preferred to work with more subtle, delicate tools. But there were times when the crude muscle and firepower of a beast like Worna were indispensable.

After a minute or so, Worna reappeared through the door at the end of the long room, followed by Leyla

Slade and Molotch himself. The candles flickered in the draft.

'Leyla! Zygmunk!' Culzean called, looking up.

'Busy?' she asked, grinning. 'Naked busy?'

'You are a tease, Leyla Slade,' Culzean chuckled. 'The nice man with the needles is almost done.'

The exchange had been made in Low Gothic, and the inker understood it. 'I am almost completed,' he said.

Leyla nodded. 'Making us legal?' she asked her master in *idrish*. Molotch looked on.

'Just so,' Culzean replied in the same dialect. 'The deeds to the exclave, transferred to my skin. All legal and above board. This work makes us invisible to the system.'

Tancred's property laws were obtuse and ancient. Ownership of land, dwellings, estates and slaves were considered binding only when they were tattooed onto flesh. A man had to have the deeds of his legacy pricked into his skin before the legislature would regard him with any genuine authority. The Guild of Inkers was an ancient and trusted office, and plied their trade in the merchant quarters. When deeds were transferred, existing tattoos were blacked out. To be blacked was to be disowned or disinherited. Certain ruthless and prosperous landowners entered the legislature wearing the dry, rustling skins of those they had inherited from, like capes.

The exclave was a little system of towers and habitats situated on the north end of the central city arm. Culzean had owned it for twenty years, since a certain deal he'd made, but he'd had the deeds held on the skin of a seneschal, a man in his pay. Now he had returned to claim the site, he'd paid the seneschal off, had the deeds blacked, and was having them rewritten on his own flesh. The seneschal had been remunerated well for his service. And then killed and disposed of by Lucius Worna. Culzean was not a man to take chances.

'We're almost done,' Culzean said in *idrish*.

'Well, hurry up. I have things I want to talk about,' Molotch replied. He had wandered around the couch and was examining the inker's needles. He had also spoken in *idrish*.

Culzean looked at him. 'My friend, I had no idea you were fluent.'

'I'm not. But it's easy enough to pick up.'

'From a few sentences?'

'Orfeo, I believe you still underestimate me.'

'He's a wonder,' Leyla said brightly. 'And he has a trick with a gun too that—'

'What?'

'Nothing.'

'It's done,' said the inker in Low Gothic, rising.

'Thank you,' said Culzean, gathering up his robes as he stood.

'There is the matter of payment, sir,' the inker mentioned, delicately.

'I'll cover it,' said Molotch in *idrish*. He weighed the needle he was holding and then, very simply, flicked it. It impaled the inker through the right tear duct, sticking out like an unnaturally long eyelash. The inker wavered. An ink-stained tear track ran down his right cheek. Then he fell, dropping onto his knees initially, then folding at the waist so his upper body crashed face first onto the tiled floor. Leyla Slade winced. The face-on impact had driven the needle in up to the stub.

'Coins would have sufficed,' Culzean said mildly. Lucius Worna chuckled a deep, dirty laugh.

'I would like to have a proper conversation with you, Orfeo,' Molotch said, taking a seat.

'That sounds ominous,' Orfeo replied. 'Drink?'

'Secum,' said Molotch. Orfeo nodded to Leyla. 'For all of us,' he said.

'What about–?' Leyla asked, glancing at the inker's corpse, kneeling as if in prayer.

'I don't think he needs anything.'

'I meant–'

'I know, Ley. We'll clean up later. Zygmunt here has things on his mind.'

Leyla brought the secum in heated drinking kettles. Culzean sipped, and arched his back a little to relieve the pressure on his raw tattoos. 'What's on your mind, Zygmunt Molotch?'

Molotch smiled. His smile, like his face, was woefully asymmetrical. 'Let me begin by saying I am in your debt. There's no question about that. You pulled me out of Petropolis when my plans came apart, and for six months you have protected me. I was telling Leyla this earlier. I owe you and I appreciate it. There's no guile here. When I can, I will reward you handsomely.'

Culzean nodded politely. 'And the "but" is?'

'I fear we are about to clash, you and I,' said Molotch. 'I broach this topic in the hope that we can avoid such an eventuality. But we will clash, sooner or later.'

'Your reasoning?'

'By any reasonable scale, I am an abnormal intellect. An alpha, a plus alpha. With due respect, judging from the time we have spent together, I see you are too.'

'Thank you.'

'You are a genius, Orfeo. The Cognitae would have been proud to own you.'

'Again, thank you. Are you trying to get me into bed, Zygmunt?'

Leyla chuckled.

Smiling again, Molotch shook his head. 'We are both manipulators, schemers, plotters. We both discern patterns where others see only nonsense. We can create and drive extravagantly complex ploys and see them to fruition. In short, we are, I fear, too much alike for it to be healthy.'

Culzean sipped from his kettle again, and then set it down. 'I agree with everything you've said so far. Go on.'

'If we work together, we could do unimaginable things. But we are not together in this. You call the shots. You do not confide in me. To begin with, this was expedient. Now, it has become a handicap. There is a real danger we will conflict, and tear each other apart. What I'm saying is, we need to be frank with one another.'

'Frank is good.'

Molotch rose to his feet. 'I'm not playing, Culzean. Since Petropolis, I have been your cargo, your trophy. I am valuable to you. I imagine you could earn a tidy sum by delivering me to all manner of interested parties. That is something I would not tolerate.'

'Really?' asked Culzean, sitting back, aware that, behind him, Leyla Slade had risen quietly and Lucius Worna had taken a step closer. 'You know, Zygmunt, that sounds ungrateful. I pulled you out of the furnace, but now I'm not useful any more?'

'That's not what I meant.'

'That's how it sounds.'

'It sounds like it sounds. I believe we could do great works together. But as partners. Not like this.'

Culzean got up and faced Molotch. Slade closed in beside him. 'You are alive because I made it so,' Culzean said. 'You have evaded capture and execution because I made sure of your safety. I have watched over you, schemed to protect you. Worked hard to–'

'I understand–'

'Ravenor would–'

'Ravenor has been behind us every step of the way!' Molotch snarled. 'Every step! He has followed us and hunted us and haunted us everywhere we've gone these last six months! He–'

'That's the point,' Culzean said, quietly.

'What?'

'That's the point!' It was one of the few times Leyla Slade had ever heard her master raise his voice.

'Where better to hide than in that bastard's shadow?' Culzean asked softly. 'You are the most wanted man in the sector, Zygmunt. Where do we go? In, towards the core? Not with your face on every tracking warrant and wanted list. What about out, into the Halo? No... because there's nothing out there! All we could do is hide! To work our magic, you and me, we have to stay inside the system. That's what I've been doing. Ghosting Ravenor's every move. Staying in his shade, in his blind spot. Your great enemy is hiding us by his very presence.'

Molotch paused, frowning.

'It wasn't easy to do,' said Culzean. 'So show me some damn respect.'

Molotch took a step backwards. It was rare for him to be blindsided. He groaned. 'Oh, Orfeo, this is precisely why we should be working together. Talking to each other. Your strategy with Ravenor is brilliant. I commend it. But you should have told me!'

'Calm down,' Leyla said. 'Just calm down. Don't make me draw on you twice in one day, Molotch.'

Molotch was too exasperated to be mollified. 'Draw away, Leyla. You know what happened last time.'

Annoyed, Slade pulled her pistol and aimed it at the side of Molotch's head.

'Again with this,' Molotch said, making that particular flicking gesture with his right arm. Slade's weapon tumbled up into the air. He caught it.

Her left hand was aiming a las-blunt body pistol at him.

'I learn,' she said. Behind her, Lucius Worna had quietly unshipped his bolt pistol.

'Oh, put them away, both of you,' Molotch said sourly. He looked at Culzean. 'We need to start sharing and cooperating right now.'

'Why?'

'Because I fear things have gone wrong.'

'Wrong?'

'Ignorant of your fine scheme and concerned with the situation, I have put plans of my own in motion. I fear they will now conflict with yours, and that conflict may harm us both.'

Culzean sighed. 'Throne, Zyg, what have you done?'

As if on cue, the exclave's outer gate bell chimed.

'Visitor,' said Leyla.

'See to it,' Culzean replied. Leyla holstered her las-blunt and caught her pistol as Molotch threw it. She locked it away and headed out of the room.

Culzean look at Molotch and repeated. 'What have you done?'

'I was looking after myself.'

'Leave that to me.'

'I will, if you keep me informed and remain open to my ideas. We have to work together or we'll destroy one another.'

'I heartily concur.'

Slade returned, trailed by a figure in a long grey storm cloak, the hood up.

'A visitor for our guest,' she said.

'Probably not a great idea to entertain with a corpse on the floor,' Worna rumbled, glaring at the dead inker.

'I won't stand on ceremony,' said the hooded figure. The newcomer turned and faced Molotch. 'This is a matter of the most pleasant fraternal confidence.'

Molotch smiled. The ancient Cognitae code greeting was like a lost, mournful echo to him. 'And I stand ready, in confidence, for a knowing brother,' he replied, as was the form.

'Ravenor is quitting this world. His hunt is over,' said the hooded figure.

'Good news,' Molotch replied.

'There is just the final business to conclude,' said the hooded figure.

'Oh, Zygmunt, tell me. What the hell have you gone and done?' Culzean whispered.

'I have made a commitment that must now be honoured,' Molotch said. 'We must make the best of it.' He stared at the hooded figure. 'What remains?'

The man drew his hood down and shook out his long, white hair.

'All that remains is the most dreadful amount of killing,' said Interrogator Ballack.

FIVE

THEY MET IN the pavilion of a salon in the depths of Basteen. It was a genteel place, the haunt of fashionable society. Dressed in robes, in jewelled gowns, in all their finery, the grandees of Basteen came to the salon and others like it, to see and to be seen. Carriages and ground cars queued to deposit their passengers under the tented awning where lasdancers and contortionists performed in the twitching brazier light.

Inside, the place was lit by glow-globes and hanging lanterns. Each booth and dining table was screened off in its own tent of white silk, which magnified the lamp light and created a creamy luminosity like vellum. Silhouettes moved across the silk screens. There were the sounds of laughter, of conversation, of clinking glasses, of soft chamber music. The smells were of perfume and obscura, secum and hot, intense chocolate. Servitors hurried to and fro, bearing laden trays.

He took a booth on the right-hand side of the salon, and had ordered amasec and a pot of mud-thick dark chocolate when she arrived.

'Drink?' asked Nayl.

She shook her head. She was wearing a black velvet overgown, as rich and black as the night outside, a matching hat with a lace veil, and a stole of jet-dyed fur. She looked regal, like an empress, like the dowager governor of an ancient core world.

'Sit, then.'

She sat on the satin upholstered couch across from him. Dainty laughter, prompted by some witty remark, peeled like bracelet bells through the white silk wall behind her. She reached her arms up, drew long silver pins out from behind her head, and removed her hat and veil. It was the most sexually charged disrobing he'd ever seen.

'Will your master miss you?' she asked.

'What?'

'Will your master miss you?'

'Oh. No, not tonight. Too much on his plate. You?'

'Fenx lets us out,' Angharad replied.

'Why did you want to meet with me?'

'You knew my aunt. I would hear you speak of her.'

Nayl sipped at his amasec. It tasted like molten gold. He couldn't take his eyes off her. 'If that's what you want,' he said. Nayl felt vulnerable, and it wasn't just the fact that he'd come unarmed because of the salon's potent weapon scanners. When she'd told him where she wanted to meet, he'd been obliged to dress up. A grey linen coat and trousers, a white shirt of sathoni cloth. He felt ridiculous. He felt under dressed. He felt... not at all like Harlon Nayl.

He also felt as if he was committing some kind of betrayal, like an illicit affair. He hadn't told anyone where he was going, especially not Ravenor, and he wasn't quite sure why.

'So, your aunt–' he began.

'Yes.'

'Your aunt. Well, I knew her, but my master knew her better.'

'Your master isn't going to talk to me. Not openly. I need to know about the blade.'

'The blade?'

'Yes, the blade.'

'Not your aunt?'

'She died. The clan has come to terms with that. But the blade, Barbarisater. It must be reclaimed.'

'Reclaimed?' Nayl asked.

'The steels belong to the clan. This is ancient law. Barbarisater must be reclaimed.'

'Well, that's tough. My master has it.'

'Your master? Ravenor?'

'No, uh... my previous master. Eisenhorn.' Nayl's voice faltered.

'Where is he?'

'Lost. Long lost. Sorry. But I know the blade. Know it well. It cut me.'

An expression that he couldn't read crossed Angharad's face. She rose, holding the train of her overgown, and moved around the low table where the drinks and silver chocolate pot had been placed. She sat down on the couch beside him. She gazed at him. The golden buttons on her high-throated black gown came right up under her chin.

'Where?' she asked.

'Where... sorry, what?' he asked back.

'Where did it cut you?'

'Through the body, years ago. Right through me.'

Angharad leaned forward and kissed him. Her lips were wet and slippery.

She took him by the hand and dragged him up from the couch.

'Going well so far,' he murmured.

She kissed him again. Lips locked, they rocked each other back and forth, knocking into the table with their legs, shivering the glasses. His amasec spilled. Her mouth was inhumanly hot, her tongue rapid like a wet snake.

'Here? Really?' he mumbled when their kiss finally parted.

A smile licked across her mouth like a flame across parchment. She gestured at the white silk walls around them and the flickering silhouettes cast upon them, with a casual flip of her black-gloved hand.

'The salon prides itself on privacy and discretion,' she said.

'But the walls are thin. Just silk–' he began.

'Are you afraid?'

He nodded. Then they both laughed. They kissed again, bumping into the couch and the table.

'Throne!' he gasped.

She pulled off his coat and yanked open his shirt, tearing the seams apart.

'Where?' she demanded.

'Gut level,' he replied, moving against her. She ripped his shirt down further to expose his torso, slick with sweat.

'Where?'

'There!' he whispered, pointing to the thumb-length, dark scar on his knotted lower abdomen, just above his hip.

She dropped to her knees in front of him.

'Oh, well now...' he sighed, blinking.

She kissed the scar. She lingered. Her tongue slid on his flesh. Then she stood again to face him.

'You're stopping there?' he gulped.

Something chimed. She took out her vox.

'My master summons me,' she said.

'Throne, really?'

'Really.'

She turned and picked up her hat. 'You shouldn't be alive,' she told him. 'Carthaen steel. You are one of a very select group, Harlon. What we call *Wyla Esw Fauhn*, which means "spared by the genius".'

'Will I see you again?' he asked, feeling foolish and fourteen the moment he said it.

Angharad smiled. The smile was predatory and thrilling to him.

'Always,' she said. Then she pulled back the silk drape and vanished.

Nayl sat down. A servitor peered in through the drape.

'What may I fetch for you, master?' it whirred.

'An amasec. A large one. And also a fresh shirt,' he replied.

SIX

'THE HOBBLED BASTARD was right, then,' muttered Inquisitor Fenx. 'You have to hand it to him.'

'You do, you really do,' replied Ballack.

'Here all the time,' Fenx continued. He slid down out of the halted carriage into the gloomy side street. 'And we laughed at his hunch.'

'Ravenor is old and experienced,' Ballack said, clambering out to join Fenx. 'What was it he said? He has *faith*.' Ballack spoke the word as if it was dirty. 'He knows his business.'

'I will have to make my apologies to him,' Fenx decided. 'Glory, Myzard will have to make her apologies too. Now I understand why he's so highly regarded.'

Fenx looked at Ballack.

'Provided, of course, that this is confirmed. This *is* confirmed, I take it?'

'The intelligence is immaculate,' said Ballack. 'Gathered from eight separate spy units, and corroborated by gene sensors. Molotch is here.'

'We have him cold?'

'We have him cold, sir.'

Fenx torched up the power to his black body armour. There was a whine, gathering in pitch. Green signal lights lit off around his high collar. He unshipped his bolter and racked it twice.

'Bring them up,' he ordered.

Interrogator Ballack nodded. The others dismounted from the waiting carriages. D'mal Singh and her gun-hounds, Shugurth, Claudel, Mentator.

'Where's Angharad?' Fenx asked.

'On her way. She's signalled.'

Fenx shook his head. 'We can't wait for her. Not with the target in sniffing range. We commence.'

'We commence!' Ballack called to the waiting figures.

'Not like that,' grumbled Tarkos Mentator, the old savant. He hobbled forward on his cane. 'Not with firearms.'

'What?' Fenx spat.

Mentator shrugged as if in the most humble of apologies. He aimed a palsied hand at the dark building before them. 'Your prey, sir, has made his nest in a house of generation. Public generation 987, to be accurate, serving the western district of Basteen. Quite apart from the power cells contained in this place, there are volatile chemicals held in suspension. Use of firearms would be a very bad idea.'

'Because?' Fenx asked. He caught himself. He was sounding stupid. 'Because we'll blow ourselves to hell, right. Thank you, savant.' He holstered his bolter. 'Muzzle your firearms!' he ordered, drawing a short, curved sword.

Claudel put away her plasma pistol and pulled out two bloodletting sickles, one in each hand. Cursing, Shugurth patiently detached his cannon from his shoulder socket, put it back in the carriage, and hefted up a war axe with a long, knurled grip.

'Guns, no!' D'mal Singh instructed her whining hounds. Their weapon systems deactivated and withdrew. 'Teeth, good!' she said. They chomped and clacked their razor edged jaws, growling.

Ballack had drawn a rapier and a matching poniard.

'Commence,' snapped Fenx, walking towards the building. 'Bonus pay to the one who brings me Molotch's head.'

THE CORPSE LAY face down in the dark on the cold steel decking.

'Where did you procure the cadaver?' Molotch asked.

'It's the inker you killed,' Worna said. 'We needed a body and we had one lying around. Not a great likeness, but then who knows what you look like any more?'

'Will it suffice?'

Lucius Worna, massive and massively scarred in his chipped power armour, nodded. 'I had it typed and matched to your gene, palm and retina. They won't know the difference.'

'End of story?' Molotch asked the giant bounty hunter.

Worna smiled. 'End of story.'

'That sort of typing and gene-scripting costs dearly,' Leyla Slade said.

'It costs what it costs,' Orfeo Culzean replied. 'Are we all ready? Zygmunt, you know how this has to work?'

'I know, Orfeo. I truly know. Consider this recompense for my mistake.'

'I will. I do. But Ballack–'

'Leave Ballack to me,' Molotch replied.

Warning runes lit up on Leyla Slade's auspex grid. 'Door four and door seven!' she hissed. 'Here they come.' She rose in one fluid movement from her cross-legged position on the deck and drew a stabbing sword. Lucius Worna moved forward beside her, a warhammer resting across his shoulder plate.

Molotch stepped in front of them. 'May I crave a favour? From you, Lucius, and you, Leyla? May I do this?'

'You'll need support,' growled Worna.

'No, I won't. But if I do, you won't be far away, will you?'

Worna shrugged, a tectonic gesture of his powered plate.

'Let me do this,' Molotch insisted. 'Let me enjoy this.'

'Let him,' said Culzean.

Leyla Slade grinned and offered the grip of her blade to Molotch.

'I won't need that,' he said. He turned, and vanished into the shadows.

THE HOUSE OF generation was very large, with a high roof and deep pockets of darkness. The main body of the hall was lined with generator hubs throbbing in the half-dark. The light was violet, dim. Fenx's team moved in, whisper quiet, spreading out between the aisles of humming hub units, slipping from shadow to shadow.

Bringing up the rear, Tarkos Mentator shuffled along on his cane. He let the others do the real work, the violence. He was only there to advise.

'Bad place for a fight,' a voice whispered in his ear.

'It is,' Mentator agreed lightly, then caught himself. He was suddenly terrified. Someone was walking along just behind him. Just a shadow, just a shape at his shoulder.

'I am reminded of *Purlingerius*, in the third act. The choral requiem,' the voice suggested. 'What is it again? "A man must choose his final resting place, as befits his soul." Quite magnificent.'

'Ah, I see you know your Stradhal,' Mentator answered timidly.

'Know it well,' the voice replied. 'You like opera, then?'

'I do.'

'So do I. Stradhal. Jevoith. Carnathi, apart from the awful final works.'

'Oh, they are awful, aren't they?' Mentator agreed. Fear was almost choking him.

'Are you afraid of me?' the voice beside him whispered.

'Yes, yes I am,' Mentator answered, 'very much.'

'You want to cry out to the others, don't you?'

'Y-yes.'

'But you dare not raise your voice, do you?'

'N-no.'

'You know who I am?'

'I... I can guess.'

'I think you guess right, my friend. If you did cry out, well then... things would become very painful and awkward for you. But I'd hate for that to happen to a fellow appreciator of the operatic art. Why don't we just walk for a while, side-by-side, you and me? We could discuss Stradhal some more.'

'Well...'

'That would be all right then, wouldn't it?'

'Yes.'

They walked on a little further.

'I'm about to be attacked,' said the voice calmly. 'Try to remember not to cry out.'

Mentator nodded.

A shadow moved suddenly. Interrogator Claudel pounced on them from behind a turbine hub. Her sickles were swinging, flashing like ice in the gloom.

They did not connect.

'Claudel,' Molotch said.

'What?' She faltered, robbed of action by the tone of command.

His fingers stabbed into her throat and she died. Molotch caught her falling body and carried it down to the ground gently. He picked up her sickles.

'Oh Throne, you have slain her!' Mentator stammered.

'Yes, I have.'

'Oh Throne! Oh Throne!' His voice started to rise.

'Remember what I said,' Molotch warned.

'Fenx! He's here!' Mentator yelled. 'He's here!'

'Oh dear me. I thought we had an understanding,' said Molotch. The sickles flashed.

INQUISITOR FENX HEARD the savant's urgent cry, cut off short. He ran back down the aisle of the turbine hall.

Claudel lay quiet and still on the decking, as if asleep. Behind her, Tarkos Mentator was curled in a foetal knot, his robes soaked black with blood.

'Throne!' Fenx growled. 'How did–'

'That happen?' Molotch finished for him.

Fenx swept around at the sound of the voice, but his sword sliced into empty shadows. Misdirection was Molotch's favourite game. He threw his voice well.

There was a blunt crack of bone. Fenx staggered backwards, bumping sidelong into the nearest hub. One of Claudel's sickles transfixed his skull, the handle jutting up from the crown of his head.

Fenx fell back against the hub and slid down until he was almost flat on the floor. He opened his mouth and blood trickled down his chin. The light in his eyes went out and his face went slack.

Molotch turned from Fenx's corpse as a wail of misery echoed down the aisle behind him. D'mal Singh stood twenty metres away, the gunhounds at her side. She gazed at Molotch in anguish and hatred.

'Murderer...' she gulped.

'Murderer...' he echoed quietly, not for sense, but to practise the timbre of her intonation.

'Kill, good!' she snarled.

The gunhounds took off towards Molotch. They were heavy and powerful, their scrambling paws slapping on the deck, their iron claws scraping. Their razor jaws opened.

'Kill, good...' Molotch murmured, getting a true measure of D'mal Singh's palate and tone. Gunhounds of this model were voice-controlled, specifically keyed to their owner's voice pattern.

A voice pattern he now used, perfectly. 'Down, good!'

Five metres short of him, the gunhounds skidded to a halt and lay supine, whimpering, resting their chins on their forepaws.

Molotch smiled. He saw the look of bafflement and horror cross the small woman's face. Confused, she was vulnerable to the tone of command.

'D'mal Singh,' he called. 'Mute.'

She opened her mouth to command her hounds again. No sound came out. She gaped, her jaw moving uselessly.

There was no time to enjoy her helpless state. Molotch felt a presence at his back, heard a heavy step. The ogryn. The ogryn was coming up behind him. He had a second or less to react.

Molotch threw himself forward between the gunhounds. The ogryn's axe crashed down into the deck where he had just been standing. As he dived, he hurled the remaining sickle. Spinning, chopping through the air like a fan, the sickle flew in a horizontal arc and smashed D'mal Singh clean off her feet.

Her body landed on its back with a thump and a violent, loose-limbed bounce.

Shugurth howled, yanked his axe-head up out of the punctured deck, and charged. Molotch leapt up, rotating to confront him.

'Kill, good!' he ordered in D'mal Singh's voice.

The gunhounds ploughed forward either side of him to meet the charging ogryn. They slammed into Shugurth with an impact that arrested his forward motion, and brought him down hard on his back. Then they were on top of him. To his credit, the ogryn didn't cry out much, even though his death was drawn out and messy.

Molotch turned and walked away from the sounds of slavering chops and cracking bone.

'You can come out now, Ballack,' he suggested casually.

Interrogator Ballack stepped into the open. His sword and dagger were both drawn.

'Well, aren't you quite the psycho bastard?' Ballack said, his longer blade rising to touch Molotch's throat.

'I am, I really am. You can put that away, Gall. We're done.'

Ballack sheathed his sword with a nod. 'Of course we are. That was just for show.' He flipped his dagger over in his other hand and tucked it into its scabbard.

'It's all just for show,' Molotch agreed. 'You are quite treacherous, Ballack.'

Ballack bowed and smiled. 'It is a matter of the most pleasant fraternal confidence.'

'How did an alumnus of the Cognitae end up in the ordos?' Molotch asked.

'Where else could I do most good?' Ballack asked.

'You efforts are noted,' said Molotch. 'Now all that's left is to make this look convincing.'

'I'll make the report, of course. The others died trying to bring you down.'

'Naturally.'

'You have a corpse prepared?'

Molotch nodded. 'I left it over there,' he said, pointing to their left.

'And it will convince the most scrupulous tests?'

'It will. Especially given the fact it will be extensively burned. A stray shot during the battle...'

Ballack smiled approvingly. 'That will conceal a multitude of sins.'

'Yours included,' said Molotch. He brushed against Ballack so fleetingly, the interrogator didn't understand what was happening until it had happened. There was a metallic clack as the handcuffs locked into place. Ballack suddenly found his left wrist cuffed tight against the casing of a turbine hub.

'Molotch? What... what is this?'

'This is goodbye, Ballack.'

'Molotch!' Ballack screamed. 'Molotch!'

SHE REACHED THE dark side street where Fenx's carriages were parked. There was no sign of anyone around. The last message she had received had informed her that the team was deploying into the house of generation across the street.

Something was wrong. Very wrong. She was getting only a dead response from her body-to-body comm. A trickle of dead air.

'Fenx? Sir?'

Vox static.

Angharad stripped off the rest of her formal black dress, tossed it aside, and cinched tight the straps and buckles of the form-fitting leather armour she was wearing underneath. Her clan armour. There was no time to find the cloak. She eased the Carthaen steel out of its long case.

She prowled across the empty street, the steel in her hands quivering like a diviner's rod. Overhead, the stars were cold smudges of light in a purple sky. Two of Tancred's moons were aloft, both claw shapes. Killing moons. A good omen, or a bad one, depending on who survived to see the following sunrise.

Under the eaves of the great building, it was as black as a cavern. She heard a distant sob from within, a stifled croak of pain. She pushed open the outer door and immediately smelled blood on the close air inside.

Evisorex smelled it too. Holding the long sword in a tight, raised grip, she stepped across the threshold and made her way into the turbine hall.

Dan Abnett

Silence. Darkness.

Ten seconds later, with a catastrophic roar, a tidal wave of boiling, golden flame blew out through all the windows and doors.

SEVEN

KARA HAD WALKED the long way around, through the recreational gardens where the gentlewomen of the city came in their long dresses and tall hats to sit under the trees and make civilised conversation, around the ornamental lake, and up through the patchwork of lesser shrines and chapel houses where the pilgrims queued. The temple of Saint Karyl sat on a shelf of dark volcanic rock at the western edge of Basteen, a white dome rising above the mosaic of red-brick buildings in the bright afternoon heat. Priests were calling the faithful to worship, and peddlers were hawking their votive trinkets from handcarts. Ritual banners hung limp against an indolent yellow sky.

She entered the temple through the western porch, and walked around the back of the vast church, relishing the stone cool. A small congregation was gathering at the altar rail, and their voices were muted echoes in the magnificent, spacious emptiness: motes of human life in a giant cave of stone.

She went through into the side chapel, a round chamber set off from the main body of the temple, where candles fluttered on a brass stand below high windows.

She knelt at the rail, and addressed a quiet prayer to the God-Emperor. It still seemed strange to her that she had found her faith again after so long. These days, she felt incomplete if she didn't go to temple or make some devotion regularly. Belknap had reawakened the need in her to begin with, but it was more than that now. She touched the silver aquila he had given her.

'Why here?' asked Carl Thonius.

She hadn't heard him enter. He didn't seem to have footsteps any more.

'Hello, Carl.'

'Why here, Kara?' He gazed up at the arched, painted roof of the ancient chapel.

'Privacy,' she said. It was a half-truth. Part of her had wanted to see if he could set foot in a place like this.

Carl smiled slightly. He looked directly at her with amused eyes. 'Privacy?'

'We need to talk,' Kara said, rising to her feet.

He feigned confusion. 'About what?'

'Don't, Carl,' she said. He frightened her, especially when they were alone together. And he knew it.

'About me, I suppose?' he mocked. 'It's all "me, me, me" with you, isn't it?'

'We're leaving Tancred,' Kara said.

'Yes, tomorrow. That's what he told me.'

'Our efforts here are done. We're returning to Eustis Majoris. A new start.'

'Of sorts. Why?'

Kara hesitated. 'Carl, I love you. Like a brother, I love you.'

'Only like a brother?' Carl asked playfully.

'You annoy me, and aggravate me, and most of the time I don't like you, but I would die for you. So, yes, like a brother.'

'Well, that's nice to know,' he said. 'I love you too.' He turned towards the doorway, as if to leave. 'Are we done?'

'I can't do this any more, Carl.'

'Can't do what?' he asked, halting, but not looking back.

'Lie for you. Lie about you. Cover for you.'

Carl Thonius turned, slowly. He stared at her. He looked as if he might be about to burst into tears.

'But you promised,' he said. There was such a plaintive tone in his voice.

'You made me promise. That's different.'

'There was no compulsion. I didn't pressure you.'

'You did. You have, and I can't do it any more.'

Thonius licked his lips and cleared his throat. 'Really?'

'Really.'

'What are you saying?' he asked.

'I can't lie to Gideon any more. I can't keep lying to him, to any of them. I owe them all too much to keep doing that. You asked for time, just a little time to beat this yourself, and I gave you that. I shouldn't have done, but I did. I can't give you any more. We have to tell Ravenor. *I* have to tell Ravenor.'

His voice diminished to a tiny whisper. 'Just a little longer. A tiny bit longer, I beg you. Please. I have been working, researching. I have found things, charms and incantations. I have found wards and bindings that–'

'No, Carl. It's not fair on me. Actually, it's not fair on you either. He can help you. If I tell him, he can help you.'

'He'll kill me, Kara,' Carl said softly.

'No.'

'He wouldn't have a choice.'

'I'm sorry.'

'He'd kill you too,' Carl said.

There was a long silence. Plainsong began in the main chapel outside.

'What did you say?' she asked.

'Don't be naive,' Carl said. 'You've known all this time and you've kept it a secret. You're tainted too. He'd kill you. He'd have to. He couldn't trust you, ever again.'

'You're wrong,' she said. 'Wrong on both counts. He'd help you, and he'd understand my position.'

'Would he?' asked Carl, sarcasm straining his voice. 'Let's review... Inquisitor Ravenor's own interrogator has become the vessel of a warp-thing, and not just any warp-thing, but an apocalyptic daemon of infamous prophecy.

But Ravenor doesn't know, even though the secret has been right there, for months, in front of his nose. And, wait for it, the only other person who knows is one of his most trusted and oldest friends. Unless that story ends with "...and the moment he found out, he executed them both" it's not going to sit well when Ravenor is brought before the High Elders of the Inquisition Helican. I mean, *is* it?'

She shook her head.

'Do you want to die, Kara?' he asked.

She took a step back.

'That wasn't a threat. I'm not threatening you. Throne! I just asked the question...'

'No, Carl, I don't, but I want to do what's right.'

'So do I,' he said. He was scratching at his right hand – *the* hand – as if it was starting to bother him. So many rings wound around those fingers. Kara watched him, her heart rate rising. *That hand...*

'It's hot in here,' he said.

'No, Carl, it's quite cool.'

'I'm hot.' He walked across to the chapel's stone basin and washed his face in the holy water. She was amazed the water didn't spit and boil on contact with his right hand.

'I'm tired,' he said, once he was done. 'I understand what you're saying, because I'm tired of it as well. The deceit. The fear. And, for me, the pain. It hurts, you know.'

'I'm sorry it does.'

'Every morning, waking and remembering, every night praying the dreams don't come. And they always do.'

'Carl–'

'Listen to me. If I am... cursed, Kara Swole, if I have evil ticking away inside me, then what kind of evil is it? It's been months, and I have controlled it. I have contained it. There has been no outburst. No one has died. And I beg you to remember, on Eustis Majoris, the thing inside me... it helped. It defeated Moloch. Kara, it took the sickness out of you. It saved you.'

'I know.'

'Then what?'

'I have to–'

'No! No, no! Listen to me! I've thought about this a lot. I think it's... a blessing.'

'Please, Carl, don't try to turn this–'

'Listen to me!' he hissed. She closed her mouth. 'Sorry,' he smiled. 'I didn't mean to snap, but I really have thought about this. To begin with, it was a problem. A dirty, nasty secret. I thought I would die. All I wanted to be was free of it. Free of... Slyte.'

'Don't say that word.'

He shrugged. 'Sorry. Again, sorry. Come closer.'

'No, Carl.'

'Come closer,' he insisted, gesturing with his left hand. 'I won't hurt you. I couldn't. That's the point. I'm not excusing my state, but what if it's more than just a curse?'

'I don't know what you mean, Carl,' she said, stepping slowly towards him and looking into his eyes. He was crying for real now. Tears ran down his pale cheeks.

He held out his left hand to her and she took it. He pulled her, very gently, close to him. 'What if this is a rare thing? Something we've never seen before? I have a daemon in me, but it is subdued. Imagine that! Subordinate to my will. I own its power, but I am not in its thrall. I can use its power.'

'You're fooling yourself,' Kara whispered.

'What if I'm not? What if I have the fury of a daemon at my disposal, the insight of the warp, but remain pure and true? What a transcendent asset would that be to mankind? What a miracle! Think of the secrets we could learn! I could be something our species has waited millennia for. A man with the mastery of daemons. A rational man with true insight into the warp. Kara, the Imperium would change. The warp would no longer threaten us as such an implacable–'

'Carl! Carl, please! How many other men have thought the self same thing? Slow or fast, the warp is always poison. This is basic to our understanding. I applaud the fact you've kept it contained for so long, but you can't keep it in forever.'

'I don't want to keep it in. Kara, I feel, I really feel, that this is a momentous thing. A daemon slaved to order. An ancient enemy, turned against the darkness. You must give me more time.'

'No, Carl–'

'More time! I can do this! I have mastered it and I can formulate that mastery so that others can do it too. We can change all creation, Kara. For the good of mankind, we can change thinking and change action, and banish forever our fear of the dark.'

'It's too late, Carl.'

He sighed. He bowed his head. 'Throne, you're right,' he said in a very quiet voice. 'Of course you're right. I'm a fool. Forgive me for all of this. Forgive me for putting you in this situation. You're right.'

'Carl–'

'I'll tell him. I'll tell him myself. Will you let me do that? Please?'

'Of course.'

'I'll come clean. Make him understand it was me all along. I'll protect you. Just let me be the one to tell him.'

'All right. Yes. When?'

'Tonight,' Carl said. He smiled sadly. 'Oh, Kara, the stuff you know.'

He pulled her close and they embraced in silence for a long time.

'So, tonight?' he asked.

'Tonight, what?'

'That's when I'll tell him.'

'Tell who what?' she asked.

'I'll tell Ravenor all about it.'

'About what?'

'Now, you see?' he grinned. 'Isn't that better?'

She laughed. She wasn't sure why. 'What were we talking about?'

'Faith,' he said.

'Oh, yes.'

'Faith gives us purpose, and a mind without purpose will walk in dark places.'

'That sounds familiar. Is it a quote?'

'I just made it up,' Carl said.

'We should go back. It's late,' Kara said.

'We should. I'm glad we had this talk, Kara. You were right to keep it private.'

He took her by the hand and led her towards the door.

Patience Kys was standing in the doorway. 'This is nice,' she remarked.

'What are you doing here?' Kara laughed.

'I was looking for you both. Your comms are off.'

'Sorry,' said Kara, adjusting her link.

'How long have you been there?' Carl asked.

'Long enough to wonder if Belknap should be worried,' Kys replied.

Kara laughed again. 'Carl just wanted me to show him where I made devotion. I think there are stirrings of faith in our friend here.'

'Fancy,' said Kys.

'It's true, it's true,' chuckled Carl. 'I've grown slack of late, and I'll never make inquisitor without a good record of temple attendance. Kara was just guiding me. I needed a little spiritual focus.'

Patience Kys nodded. 'Don't we all? There's been a development.'

'What kind of development?'

'The kind you wouldn't believe, but Ravenor has to tell you himself. He'd hate me if I ruined his thunder.'

They walked towards the doorway. 'What's that?' Kys asked.

Several curls of bent metal lay on the chapel floor, beside the basin. Tiny bent scraps, like the remains of rings that had been split apart.

'Just votive offerings,' Carl said. He took Kara's hand in his, her left in his right, and led the way out of the chapel.

There were no longer any rings on his right hand.

EIGHT

WHEN THEY ARRIVED back at the house, evening was falling and Envoy Myzard was just leaving. She stomped past them in the courtyard, flanked by two heavy weapons servitors, heading for her transport.

'A good man you have there,' she said to Thonius.

'Ma'am?'

'I've just been rendering my apologies to him. I won't underestimate him again. Get him back to Eustis, interrogator. Get him back on the job. His mind can be uncluttered now.'

As they walked up the steps into the house, they heard the engines of her transport growling as it trundled away.

Nayl, Plyton, Belknap, Unwerth and the manhound Fyflank were waiting in the inner hall.

Kara walked up to Belknap and kissed him.

'What's going on?'

'Where were you?'

'At temple. What's going on?'

'I'm not sure. But Molotch's dead.'

'What?'

Impelled by a powerful mind, the double doors at the end of the hall opened and Ravenor glided in to face them.

'Sir?' asked Thonius.

'It's done. We're done,' Ravenor said via his voxponder.

'We're still leaving?' asked Nayl.

'Yes, Harlon. We're still leaving, but we can leave happy that there are no more loose ends. Last night, three precincts away, Zygmunt Molotch was located, cornered and slain by Myzard's forces.'

There was a general commotion. Nayl smacked his raised palm against Kys's.

'So, you were right?' Kara grinned.

'I was right,' Ravenor replied. 'My hunch was correct. Molotch was here, just as I suspected. I'm only sorry it wasn't us who claimed him in the end.'

'The bastard's dead!' Nayl chuckled. He did a little dance that made Belknap and Plyton laugh.

'I can't believe it,' murmured Kys. 'All this time, all this time, and now it's done.'

'It's over,' said Ravenor. 'We have no excuses any more. Eustis Majoris awaits. I'd like us to leave tomorrow, as arranged.'

'Who got him?' asked Belknap. It was a good question, and Ravenor was surprised it was Belknap who asked it. The others fell silent.

Ravenor had swung his chair away. Now he slowly turned to face them. 'Ballack, it appears. It was bloody, at the end, so Myzard told me. There were losses.'

'Losses?' Nayl echoed. He suddenly had the most awful sense of premonition. He felt sick.

'Fenx tracked him to a house of generation,' said Ravenor slowly. His voxponder fumbled with the pace of his words. The monotone made it all the more horrible. 'There was a fight. Molotch did for most of Fenx's people, then a stray shot ignited the volatiles and the place went up. Molotch's corpse was identified by gene-fix.'

'Glory!' Thonius whistled.

'Who... who died?' Nayl asked.

'Fenx, Ballack, Claudel,' Ravenor replied, 'the ogryn, Mentator, the gunhound woman, and the Carthaen, Angharad.'

'Dead?'

'All of them.'

THEY WERE CLEARING out the house and making ready to head for the port on the transports. Ravenor had gone ahead, with Kys, Belknap and Kara. Sholto Unwerth and his manhound had left earlier that morning to light the ship's engines. Frauka was travelling with Zael in a secure buggy.

Porters were rolling the last of the luggage out to the carriages. Carl Thonius stood in the yard, finalising their dealings with the tattooed letting agent. Harlon Nayl did a last circuit, checking the empty rooms one by one.

'Harl?'

'Hello?' Nayl stuck his head out of the vacant room he had been inspecting. Maud Plyton was jogging up the staircase. She had a piece of paper in her hand.

'Message for you.'

'Message?'

'Came in by closed vox about ten minutes ago. Last thing Carl fielded before he shut the system down.'

Nayl took the slip from her and opened it.

'Problem?' Plyton asked.

'Why do you ask?'

'Uh, the look on your face?'

'No, no problem,' he said. 'Get going.'

Maud nodded and hurried away. He waited until she was gone, and then read the slip again.

It was from an unrecorded source, anonymous.

It read, 'Spared by the genius.'

Nayl stared at it for a long time. Then he took out his link.

PART TWO

The Wych House of Utochre

ONE

The door is half open. The door is old and made of wood. A very ordinary old door in a very ordinary frame. It swings back and forth slowly on its hinges, pushed and pulled by a wind that comes from neither side of the door, a wind that comes from somewhere else.

The door is waiting...

THE FACTOR'S NAME was Stine. This piece of information emerged early on in what turned out to be over twenty minutes of loquacious preamble. Stine liked to talk. It was part of his performance.

+Stick with it.+

Every factor they had made approaches to (every factor in every hall in Berynth, most likely) had his own version of the performance, some variation of the mercantile courtship dance, the wooing of the customer. It was all part of the purchasing experience. Customers expected it.

There would be a warm greeting, a guided stroll from
the reception chamber into the factor's display rooms, an
offer of refreshments and a steady, light flow of conversation leading to a more specific extolment of the merits
and traditions of the hall the customer had chosen to
patronise. Certain themes were developed by the factor,
with practiced verbal skill, designed to snag in the customer's thoughts and stay there: luxury, exclusivity,
quality. The customer was, after all, going to spend a
great deal of currency.

And the customer wasn't a customer. That was too
coarse a term. He or she was an emptor. Just as the factor
wasn't a salesman or a shopkeeper. There were standards
of decorum in Berynth.

+He's going on and on and on.+

+Stick with it.+

Stine had met her at reception. The hall stood at the
northern end of the Promenade St Jakob, an area of up-
hive Berynth densely and famously packed with noted
hall premises. The deep street-stacks outside were tiered
with ouslite walkways and black iron railings, and strung
with thimble lamps, a cavernously dark place of rising
black towers, some of which grew up through the hive's
great armoured roof like a sea urchin's thorns. He wore a
patterned coat and a practiced smile. Reception was a
wide, inviting vault panelled in varnished wood.

Stine had bowed and led her back through the show galleries into the main chamber of display. Pools of emerald
light contained glass showcases in the gloom. The floor
was panelled with bronze slabs, and centuries of footsteps
had worn a bright patina pathway across them. There was
a simple wooden desk, faced by some leather sofas, and he
invited her to sit down. Stine talked all the way. His performance, it seemed, would be all about words. Some of
the factors she had so far encountered favoured a discreet
approach, or a humble one, or allowed the emptor to lead

the conversation. He was prolix. He, said Stine, was the ninetieth Stine, uninterrupted, to serve in the post of factor for Stine and Stine's Hall. That was a legacy, a family business. Stines had been at Berynth for sixteen centuries. The hall was one of the oldest, their marks amongst the most noteworthy in the sector.

'Here,' said Stine, 'you may admire the hall's marks, on this trinket.' He held it up in front of a magnifying viewer for her to inspect. His hands were overly pale and well manicured, looming in the lens. The trinket had more pearls in it than some oceans. 'The Stine mark.'

'I see it repeated, in stylised form, upon your doublet coat,' the emptor remarked.

Stine simpered, delighted that she should notice. He complimented her, extensively, on her eye and her intelligence.

+I think he wants to marry me.+

+Shush. Stick with it+

Stine was very taken with this particular emptor: an elegant woman, well dressed, moneyed. Custom had been slack in the last few weeks, with few clients of note delivered by ferry ship to inspect the halls. This woman was something different. She had taste. She was beautiful, if you liked that kind of thing.

He was telling her a little more about the business, about the fact that he was not as accomplished in the lapidary work as his many brothers, which is why he was the factor. He left the skilled lapidary to his kin, who could 'assay and value', so he boasted, with their bare hands.

But he sensed she was becoming bored. That happened. She had stopped sipping the amasec he had fetched out on a lacquered tray, and she no longer picked at the candied ginger in the little finger bowl. A good factor noticed these details. A good factor knew when to up the tempo and move the courtship towards the consummation of purchase.

'Are you looking for a particular piece?' he asked, walking around the simple hardwood desk with its velvet panels. He took out his keys and opened the doors of the nearest plate glass displays. Recessed fans murmured in the invisible ceiling of the chamber of display. It was a comfortable twenty-two degrees, with the right amount of humidity and air-flow to keep emptors fresh and relaxed. Outside Berynth, it was a murderous sixty below.

'I am,' said the emptor, sitting back on one of the leather sofas and crossing her long legs. 'Or rather, a particular piece for a particular purpose. A society wedding on Gudrun. I won't use names–'

'Of course not!' the factor said with a bow.

The emptor smiled. 'But the match involves some people of influence. Of blood.'

'I understand.'

'The son of a governor subsector.'

'My word!'

+Oh, try to stay in the realms of reality, please!+

'Shut up.'

'Pardon?' asked the factor with a slightly bewitched blink.

'Nothing. I said, my niece... the bride... deserves something special.'

The factor bowed again. 'I do understand. And, if I may make so bold, financially...?'

He let the deadly word hang.

She shrugged. 'Nothing less than a quarter million,' she said mildly.

For the third time, he bowed. 'Oh, ma'am. I have a few trinkets that may well please your eye and your taste.'

+I think I just made him *very* happy.+

+Well, that's all he's getting. I'm not paying for a quarter million crowns' worth of anything.+

+Except information?+

+Except that.+

She kept her grin fixed. Oblivious, the factor began to lift red satin trays out of the display cases. Several servitors appeared from the shadows, took each tray as he lifted them out, and brought them over to her, holding them so as to display them. The servitors were old and worn, but of great mechanical quality. She realised that the hall cultivated a slightly worn, slightly Spartan feel, so that the pieces would glow by comparison. It was all very clever, very judged.

'A design for the throat is always appreciated. These on the first trays are allochromatic zalachite, with red gold. I have them in diamond too. Cabochon cut is usually preferred.'

'They're delicious.'

'Or a jewel setting for the brow? Sapphire, with opal and signet. Black silver or chased adamite are very sought after.'

'This one is nice,' the emptor said.

The factor came over, lifting the piece from its tray with a midwife's care. The jewels shone in the light. The lights above the desk were well placed to make jewels scintillate at that particular point in the chamber.

'The chrysoberyl? Yes, a favourite of mine. Note the glorious asterism. Would you like...?' he asked, holding it up.

'Please.'

'Glass!' the factor called, and other servitors hurried forward, holding up looking glasses all around the client. The factor placed the necklace around the emptor's throat and fastened it.

She admired herself.

'Has she your colouring?'

'I am somewhat paler than my niece,' the emptor said.

'Then something with cygate or quofire? Tourmaline, perhaps? I have a pendaloque-cut tourmaline with the most stunning dichroic properties.'

'You know your business, sir.'

She tried on three or four more pieces. The servitors held the looking glasses perfectly still.

'I worry,' she said, at length, 'this is a nuptial gift. It should be for the groom as much as the bride. He is my brother's son, after all.'

The factor paused. 'And the bride is your niece?'

'Did I say that?'

+You said that.+

'You said that, I'm sure.'

'By marriage, I mean. You know how it is, in the dynastic melee that is court life.'

'Court... life?'

'Yes,' she replied. +Did I get away with that?+

+He's too awestruck to notice. Play up the court thing. He thinks you're anonymous nobility.+

'I really don't like to talk about it,' the emptor said.

'Of course not. Well, perhaps I can show you some of our ornamental settings? Horologs, rosettes, Imperial aquilas. For aquilas, we favour gold and composites, and also organic gems. The oceans here on Utochre produce the most iridescent nacre effects.'

'You have a charter to produce authentic aquilas?'

'We are Imperial jewellers, of course. By appointment.'

'Show on,' she said.

He displayed several more complex objects to her. Some were so valuable he had to silently lock the suspension shields around the desk while she admired them.

'This is really stunning work,' she murmured, turning a piece over in her hands. She held it up to the light. 'What do you call this property?'

'Birefringence, or double refraction,' Stine replied.

'Oh, I can't decide.'

The factor smiled warmly.

'I just can't decide. I feel... incoherent.'

The factor's smile froze and became cold.

'What?'

'I feel incoherent. Can you help me with that?'

The factor took the piece out of her hands and put it back on its satin tray.

'Did I say something wrong?' the emptor asked, slightly taken aback.

+Yes, I think you did. He's not happy. Make your apologies and get out.+

'We don't cater for that sort of thing here,' Stine said sniffily. 'You've been wasting my time. Perhaps you'd like to leave.' The factor was angry with himself. It wasn't often he misread an emptor so completely.

'I'm sorry,' she said, rising. 'I didn't mean offence.'

'Please leave,' Stine spat. He took a control wand from his belt and waved it briskly. All the servitors retreated obediently back into the shadows.

+Get out.+

'I meant no offence,' she repeated. 'I'm sorry.'

'Your kind are always sorry,' said Stine. 'I should report you.'

'Report me to whom?' she asked.

+Get out, Patience. Now. We can't afford an incident.+

Stine turned to look at her. His face was hard, poisonous. 'You come in here, into this distinguished hall, looking for access to that ungodly place! Stine and Stine does not do that sort of thing!'

'I have apologised. I have apologised sincerely, sir.'

+Patience...+

'I should call the magistrates,' Stine blustered. He waved the control wand he had taken from his belt again, reaching into the air for a hive-hub connection. She heard the buzz of a handshake.

'Berynth Magistratum, I have you,' the speakers on the desk warbled.

'This is Stine at Stine and Stine. I have a–'

There was a click as the link disconnected.

'Hello? Hello?' Stine said.

+I've blocked his comm. Now, Patience, please walk out of there.+

Stine, of Stine and Stine, tried his wand again. When he looked around, the woman had gone.

SHE STORMED OUT of the hall's reception chamber onto the iron-railed promenade. The hanging thimble lamps shone overhead with a feeble, pearly light. Instinctively, she allowed the stream of pedestrian traffic to swallow her up and carry her along. All around her were the rich and privileged of a double-dozen worlds, strolling along, some body-guarded, some carried in ornate litters, some sporting parasols or long trains.

+Sorry,+ she sent. +I fumbled that.+

+It doesn't matter.+

+It does. It took me by surprise. His reaction. He was so... angry.+

+Proud, that's all. We aimed a little too high, trying an Imperial jeweller. We can learn from this.+

She threaded through the crowd and headed down a flight of iron steps onto a lower stack. It was quieter there. She stopped and leaned on the guard rail, gazing down into the deep interstack drop and the street levels below. She got her breath.

+I'm off my game, Gideon.+

+You're not. You're fine.+

+I can tell when you don't mean it. I'm off my game.+

+Maybe you are, Patience. Would you like to talk about why?+

+I'm off my game because I can't stand this. I hate what we're being forced to do.+

+That's only reasonable. So do I.+

She sighed, let go of the guard rail, and started walking again.

+How are the others getting on?+

+Much like you. They're not getting anywhere. Although they're not quite as combative as you.+

+I said I was sorry, Gideon. What happened back there? The last few places I tried just got a bit cagey when the subject came up, but that... he was so venomous. As if I was a criminal.+

+As I said, I think we aimed too high. Stine and Stine is about as illustrious a hall as there is on Utochre. The man felt insulted. His hall was insulted. The inference hurt him. Put it behind you.+

+I think you should switch me out for Kara. Kara would do this better.+

+Put it behind you.+

She had walked to the far end of the stack level, into the gloomy architectural cleft where the armoured curve of the roof dome met the stack ends. There was a small and dingy dining house there, built into the eaves of the giant outer roof. It clearly catered for under staff and the utility personnel who worked menial jobs in the halls. The staff frowned and whispered at the sight of her fine, expensive clothes. She ignored them and sat down at a vacant table. Around her, household staffers, gig drivers and stack-gutters hunched over and murmured to one another.

'Mamzel?' asked a maid in an apron, coming over. 'There is a good place a level up where you might be more comfortable.'

'I'm comfortable here, thanks,' said Kys. 'A caffeine. Black, sweet, and an amasec, if you have it. Cooking will do.'

'Yes, mamzel.'

Waiting for her order to arrive, she rose again and approached the heavy shield plate that formed the north wall of the dining house. She touched the control stud, and the shield slid up. She looked out on the world outside through the thick glass. The blackened, fat bellied

slopes of Berynth hive shelving away below, the ice
beyond, under a broiling sky. The savage gales beat at the
glass and bombarded it with ice crystals.

+We are criminals now, aren't we?'+

+Patience...+

+Oh, stop it. We are. I know it. Rogue.+

+It's the only way we have left.+

+I hate it, Gideon, and I hate the idea that he's still out
there. I hadn't realised before, but when you told me he
was dead, it felt like a weight lifting off me.+

+I'm sorry. It felt that way to me too, if that's any con-
solation.+

Kys put her hand against the glass and stared out at the
nocturnal blizzard.

+However... Patience, we need to retain control. We
can't afford to be seen, and I think you were about to pin
that Stine fellow to his chair by his scrotum+

She smiled. +At the very least. I am so sorry. I'm finding this hard. So... how are the others doing?+

+Maud and Carl have covered five halls between them.
Nothing. Harlon has managed to secure us an underboat.
Now Carl is off buying rings down in the brash quarters.+

+Doesn't he have enough rings?+

+I don't know. I don't pay attention to such things.
Can one have enough rings?+

+Not if you're Carl, apparently.'

The maid returned with the order. Kys went back to her
table, drank the amasec in one and sipped her caffeine. It
was too hot, and the amasec had been rough. Cooking,
definitely. She dropped a generous number of coins on
the table and stood up. +What's next?+

+Can you handle another?+

+Yes. Of course.+

+Only when you're ready. Exit and head up a stack. Then
along to your right. Corlos and Saquettar, Lapidary.+

Patience sighed. +How do I look?+

+Beautiful.+

+Then let's go.+

+Wait. Wait, Patience. Sit back down. Drink your caffeine. I believe Carl has found something.+

TWO

'INCOHERENT? WELL, THAT's a different thing altogether.'

'Oh? How so?' asked Carl Thonius sweetly.

Down in the brash quarters, in the low hive, things were more basic. The stack-depths were cluttered with dirty stalls and tented stands of soiled canvas, selling knock-off and bad-cut gems, trinkets, keepsakes, totems and charms. The air was smoggy from the oil drum fires and stank of liquor and refuse. Bagpipes keened and drums beat. There were fire dancers, shucksters, lhofers, and the constant, shabby bustle of the hab classes and the migrant workers, washing aimlessly back and forth in the low hive like rank water in a bilge.

The stall holder glanced around to see if anyone was listening. He had one sunken eye, from years of using a stubby jeweller's loupe.

'Seeing as how you've bought so many rings from me, my friend, let me tell you. Coherence comes at a price. You have to be introduced, for a start.'

'You do?'

'Have yourself an introduction. The halls expect that.'

'Can you provide such a service?'

The stall holder laughed a phlegmy laugh. 'Mercy, no!' He gestured around at his modest stall. 'I'm brash, born and bred. I don't move in those kind of circles.'

'But you know the system?'

He nodded.

'What's your name?' Thonius asked.

'I am Lenec Yanvil, sir,' the man replied. He was small and pot-bellied, with nimble hands. He smelled of pitch and polishing amalgams.

'Well, Lenec Yanvil, if I was to, say, purchase that gorgeous lapis signet I wavered over, would you confide in me?'

'I'd be delighted to,' said Yanvil.

Thonius produced some more large denomination coins and counted them out onto the stall's stained baize cover. Yanvil picked up the signet ring, and carefully wrapped it in a small piece of felt.

'It's all about reward, you see,' he said quietly. 'Palms greasing palms. The halls have an arrangement with the House. They have had for centuries. Some will admit it, quietly, others deny it, but they all benefit.'

'How so?'

'Every single hall in Berynth pays a retainer to the House in return for coherent information about new seams, stone beds and metal deposits. The jewellery business here is what Berynth is famous for, but it's just a by-product of Berynth's heavy industry. The first halls to set up here in the old days made their profits from the spoil of the intensive ore mining, but no one these days is going to sustain a business on accidental finds. Neither do the halls have the financial resources to maintain comprehensive mining operations of their own. So they pay to know where to look, and then hire out the mining complexes to do spot excavations. Everyone profits.'

'It sounds very companionable.'

Yanvil shrugged. 'The halls are very proprietorial about who gets access to the House. They vet. It's an exclusive service. But then, Throne knows, you have to be pretty exclusive to come all this way to go jewellery shopping.'

'How do they vet?'

'You need to find an agent. They're very exclusive too. They don't advertise. A client hooks up with an agent, the agent takes them to an appropriate hall and makes an introduction. Then the client has to make a purchase, something pricy. Horologs are good, I hear. The purchase price is the hall's fee. The client then gives the item to the agent as a gift. Later, the agent sells the item back to the hall for a cut of the fee. The item goes back in the hall's display, and the hall's made a tidy profit.'

'Very neat.'

'Palms are greased, backs are mutually scratched. Everyone smiles.'

'So, to find an agent…?'

'Well, I might know something.'

'Palms are greased and backs are mutually scratched, eh?' said Thonius. 'That gold thumb ring there…'

'So STINE KNEW all about it?' asked Patience.

'According to my source, they all do,' said Carl. 'They just don't like to talk about it.'

'That little shit. He made me feel this big, and–'

'Because you weren't introduced,' said Carl quietly. He was sitting on a couch in the bay window of the chamber, admiring the new rings on his hand. The winter night ticked and rattled at the window panes behind him.

'I've half a mind to go back there and shove a kineblade up his arse,' Kys growled.

'Half a mind is all you'll need for that,' said Ballack, overhearing her as he walked in from the adjoining room. 'We have to be careful.'

Kys turned slowly and glared at the interrogator. In the two months he'd been with them, he'd shown an unfailing ability to wind her up.

She felt sorry for him, of course. Ballack had been through an ordeal, and he'd lost the hand, after all. He'd also shown creditable initiative bringing the whole matter to Ravenor. Still, he was, as Kara might say, a smug little ninker when all was said and done, and far too pretty for his own good, with that long white hair and those ion-drive blue eyes.

For once, he seemed to notice her displeasure. 'Sorry, Kys,' he said. 'That was rude of me. It's just... sometimes I'm very aware that I'm risking my entire career doing this. No offence, sir.'

'None taken,' Ravenor replied, his voice issuing as an electronic monotone from his chair. 'We're all risking our careers.'

No one spoke for a moment. The fire crackled in the grate and warmed the room, part of a rented suite in Berynth high-hive. The floor was a checkerboard of brown and cream wooden tiles, the walls panelled in dark umwood. The fireplace was an extraordinary frame porcelain inlaid with silver and nacrous shell. The logs spat and coughed. Kys, Ballack and Thonius reflected quietly on their situation, each in their own way. Patience wondered what depth of worry knotted in Ravenor's mind.

+I realised why Stine's reaction upset me so,+ she sent.

+Go on.+

+It wasn't that he made me feel like a criminal. It was that I *am* a criminal and he forced me to realise what that means. Everything I've ever done in your service, Gideon, I've done in the knowledge that I'm serving the Emperor's ultimate will, but there's no legitimacy any more.'+

+There will be. I will make the ordos understand why I've had to take this course. We will have our sanction.+

+But there isn't any right now.+

The chair swung around from the fireplace and faced the three of them. They all looked up respectfully. 'I've said it before, but for the record, let me repeat... when we're done, I will bring us to Myzard. To Rorken, if necessary. I will make account, and I will take the reprimand.'

'I wonder who they'll send after us?' Carl mused, admiring his rings again. He looked up at Ravenor. 'I mean, they're bound to send someone, right?'

Ballack sat down on a tub chair. 'Lilith. Myzard will send Lilith and a team. Lilith Abfequarn is good. She already has a black notation rating. We can only hope she doesn't have the first clue where to start looking. That means, we can't make a scene.'

He looked pointedly at Kys.

'Fair point. It's been made already. No one needs to tell me again,' Patience replied. 'So, Carl? Where do we find this agent?'

Thonius was about to reply when the apartment's outer hatch slid open. Patience saw how quickly – how nervously – Ballack rose and placed his good hand on the grip of his pistol.

It was Maud Plyton. A version of Maud Plyton, at least. She looked strange, buttoned into a long gown of Parsiji lace and deep green silk. The material strained and bulged voluptuously. Her cropped hair and heavy make-up created the unfortunate suggestion of a man in drag. 'Nice to see you too,' she sneered at Ballack, seeing his hand on his gun.

'Not had a good day, Maud?' asked Kys.

Maud flopped down heavily on the nearest couch and yanked off her high, feminine shoes. She'd borrowed them from Kara and they didn't fit well. Her feet were sore. 'Bastard things!' she declared as she tossed them over the back of the couch. 'I'm sorry to say,' she said, 'I got nothing.'

'It's all right, Maud,' Ravenor replied, 'we have a lead now.'

'Oh, good,' Plyton replied, getting up. In one, ungainly upward drag, she wrenched her expensive dress off over her head. The dress was another lend from Kara, tight and too short for Maud Playton's frame. She wriggled the dress off her arms, and headed out of the room in her support hose and whalebone corsetry. There was a considerable sense of pneumatic tension. 'Thank Throne that's off! It was throttling me. I don't do posh.'

'You do it very well,' said Ravenor.

Plyton grunted dismissively from the next room and called out, 'I do undercover all right, but that was not a bit of me. I haven't had that many unfamiliar hands in my chest area since I was last assigned to vice.'

'Well, fancy,' said Carl.

Plyton stuck her head back around the door, and then lifted one arm and sniffed her armpit. 'And I stink. That's not high-class, is it?'

'I can't begin to tell you,' Carl said.

'Is there a drink going?' Maud asked.

'I'll get you one,' said Ballack.

'Help me unlace this bastard corsetry, someone. I beg you. Preferably you, Patience, seeing as it's yours. '

Smiling, Kys walked across the room and followed Plyton into the adjoining chamber. Plyton leaned forward and Kys started to untie the laces. It was a struggle.

'Emperor help me, I can't breathe. How do you wear this stuff, Kys?'

'Well,' said Patience smoothly.

'Here's that drink,' said Ballack, appearing in the doorway with a glass. He hovered.

'Here. In my hand!' Plyton said. 'I can't reach it when you're standing over there.'

'I was just... mindful of your...'

'I'm sure I haven't got anything you haven't seen before,' Plyton said.

'No, just a little more of it.'

'Oh, you wish!' mocked Plyton, taking the drink and sipping. 'Yum, lovely.'

'If anyone gets to go back to Stine and Stine,' Kys called out, tugging at the corset laces, 'it's going to be me. '

'I was hoping to participate myself,' said Ballack. He had returned to the fireside in the neighbouring room, and was trying to secure his long white hair into a pony tail. It was a hard feat to accomplish with just one hand. Evisorex had severed his left hand cleanly, and his wrist stump was sealed in a black leather nub packed with micro healing systems. It would be another month at least before it was ready for an augmetic graft. 'I really would like to serve, sir,' he said. 'I want to be useful.'

'The pair of you, then,' said Ravenor. 'If that's all right with you, Carl?'

Thonius shrugged. 'I'm happy.' He rose to his feet. 'Can I help you with that, Gall?'

'Thank you,' Ballack replied. Carl began to comb Ballack's mane with his fingers to tie it up.

'We'll wait for the others to return,' said Ravenor. 'You can get started in the morning.'

'So what's keeping Nayl?' grimaced Plyton as Kys slowly released her torso from its confinement.

SLEET WHIPPED AGAINST the windowpanes of the ground level hangar. The work crews had gone for the day, and the underboats sat in their ice pool like grey sea beasts, sleeping. Only a few spotlights shone down from the iron gantries.

Angharad made a soft noise like a sigh and rolled off him. They lay together in the dark for a while listening to the patter of sleet.

'I'm glad you lived,' Nayl said.

'That's a funny thing to say,' she replied, turning her shoulder against his chest.

'Is it?'

'Obvious then. You didn't need to say it. I felt how glad you were. Right then.'

'We should get back,' said Nayl.

'Is that thing really necessary?' she asked, nodding to the little psyk-block unit beside them.

'Yes.'

'Why?'

'It's hard to explain. Ravenor... I don't want to hurt him.'

'Hurt him?'

'You're so like Arianhrod.'

'I don't understand.'

'Forget it. Trust me. I've come to know how hard it must be for Gideon to be the way he is. He's human, after all.'

'He has his mind.'

'Yes, but he has his memories. It's just a feeling I get.'

'That he wouldn't approve?'

'Maybe. It'd be like rubbing his face in it. If he had a face.'

It was warm and dark under the vent panels. They'd made a bed of cold weather furs from a locker.

'We should go,' she said. She rose in one fluid motion, and began to look for her clothes. She was silhouetted against the bay's lamplight for a moment.

He looked at her. 'Maybe another five minutes won't hurt,' he said.

FOUR

WAITING MADE KARA Swole tense, and tension gave her a headache. At least, she hoped it was the tension. She didn't want to think about the other possibility.

She was alone on the *Arethusa's* main bridge, nominally on watch, although there was little to watch for. Most of the ship's systems were shut down and depowered: just enough juice running through the conduits to maintain basics. As soon as they had arrived at high anchor above Utochre, Unwerth had turned off the commercial transponder and deactivated the ship's carrier number and beacon. They had no wish to advertise their location, let alone their identity. Every three hours, automated systems lit up the *Arethusa's* vox-grid and allowed her to check in with the surface team. The silences in between were numbing. Naturally, if any problems developed, Ravenor could always summon them without waiting for the routine vox-check. Kara had made sure a lander was ready in the belly hold.

She checked her chron. Another forty-five minutes before the next check in. She was fidgety. She'd tried a workout to shake it off, a little blade practice, but it hadn't done the trick. She'd felt rusty, slow, her heart not in it. It had been a long time since they'd seen any combat. She had no lust for combat, but the discipline kept her sharp.

The worst of it was, her mind was cloudy. She felt befuddled, and she wasn't sure why. She remembered Ravenor remarking on it back on Tancred, just before they'd left, some comment about him sensing something on her mind. She could remember getting a little steamed about that, but couldn't recall why. Guilt, probably. She'd never told Ravenor about her illness, nor of its miraculous remission. She hated keeping secrets, especially from him.

The cloudiness had been on her since then. Maybe that's what he had detected. Maybe that's why he'd asked her to lead the second team and stay aboard the ship as back-up. Perhaps he didn't feel she could cut it as a principal agent any more. Perhaps he was right, but she hated the feeling that she was being sidelined.

She hated it almost as much as she hated the cloudiness. It was a nagging sensation, like the haunting awareness of a memory that temporarily refused to form. There was something on the tip of her tongue that just wouldn't realise itself.

Of course, forgetfulness was one of the primary symptoms to watch for.

She realised she was rubbing her temple with her fingers. She pulled her hand away.

She got up quickly and walked off the bridge, down the echoing spinal corridor of the ship. Most of the *Arethusa's* twenty-strong crew were sleeping, apart from a few running spot repairs in the enginarium. The old, wretched hulk creaked and groaned around her. The walls were scabby and decayed. Unwerth's vessel was neither a beautiful nor a reliable machine.

She heard Belknap's voice, picked up her pace, and then slowed again, realising he was in conversation. Through an open hatch, she spied him, sitting in the forward communal on the other side of a table from Sholto Unwerth. They were chatting and drinking glasses of dry Thracian muskell. Belknap got on with Unwerth better than most of them, with the exception of Kys, who had bonded with the little shipmaster during the perilous hours in Petropolis, and now deflected the worst of the teasing the likes of Carl and Nayl dished out at Unwerth's expense.

Belknap got on with everybody, of course, because medics usually possessed that reassuring knack. But Belknap and Unwerth were both outsiders, part of Ravenor's team only because of the support services of conveyance and healing they provided. Though both had faced serious danger on Eustis Majoris, neither was employed as a fighter or principal agent.

Unwerth had suffered badly. He had been tortured and mutilated at the whim of the infamous bounty hunter, Lucius Worna, before Kys had rescued him, but he had held out, loyal to them all. One look at his hands showed the pain he had endured for them, and yet the likes of Carl still delighted in teasing and mocking–

Carl. His name stung in her head as she thought of him. She frowned at the inexplicable strength of her own reaction. What had Carl ever done to her, except be an odious twit?

She backed away. Unwerth was telling Belknap some long and involved story about his own family history.

'...it is much derailed, in places high and low,' she heard the shipmaster saying, 'that there ever was a race of beings of the name the squats, and many scholams and those of the high mindful claim it's just a myth, a thing that never was, but my direst old grand avuncular sweared to me that the Unwerth lineament has some timbre of that blood in it, right back in all perspective, I mean...'

Kara had no wish to intrude. More properly, she wanted to speak to Belknap alone. She backed silently away.

'Kara?' Belknap called, looking around from the table. Eyes in the back of his head, that one. The old vigilance of an Imperial Guardsman on sentry duty.

'Just walking around,' she shrugged.

'Join us,' Belknap said.

'Have a sniff of this here numbskull,' Unwerth smiled, jiggling the bottle. 'We are just of mindless confabuling.'

'In a while, maybe. I've got to be on hand when the grid wakes up.'

She walked away, following a side corridor down to the ship's infirmary. She turned on the lamps and began to search the scrubbed steel cupboards for a pain killer. Her head was really thumping.

It couldn't be back. It couldn't be back, could it? Please, Throne–

She stopped searching, aware that she was starting to hyperventilate. Panic, that wasn't like her. She leaned on the side counter, breathing deep and slow. Nearby, packed into its carrying modules, was the expensive medical equipment Ravenor had purchased on Eustis Majoris. Belknap had used it to diagnose her condition and monitor it. He still checked her once every fortnight or so. She remembered the last occasion, en route from Tancred. She remembered his delight at the improbability of her health. The same every time. His joy.

How could she tell him? How could she ask?

'Are you all right?'

Kara switched around Wystan Frauka stood in the doorway.

'Sorry. You startled me,' she said.

Frauka shrugged. 'I saw the light on in here. Are you all right?'

'Bit of a headache,' she admitted.

Frauka dropped his half-smoked lho-stick onto the corridor deck, ground it out with his heel, and entered the infirmary. He opened a glass fronted cabinet and fished out a vial of capsules. 'I find these work pretty nicely,' he said.

'They're pain killers?'

He frowned, as if the question had never occurred to him. 'I suppose. The blue ones there are a lot stronger, but they give you funny dreams and a dry thirst. These are what you might call headache strength.'

'I didn't know you suffered from headaches,' she said, taking the vial from his hand.

'Well,' he began.

'Suffering from headaches is something I would be sympathetic to,' she said. 'As opposed to, say, random, secret experimentation with the infirmary's pharm supply.'

Frauka nodded sagely. 'Then we'll call it headaches,' he said, 'and say no more about it. I was just trying to help.' He stepped towards the door.

'Sorry,' she called. 'Sorry. Forgive me. I've got a real tension headache. Your life is quite boring, isn't it, Wystan?'

The blunter shrugged. 'It has its moments. They're usually brief and quite violent. The rest of the time... well, thanks for noticing.'

Kara poured a glass of water from the scrub sink and rolled some of the capsules into her palm. 'Two?'

'I usually take three or four,' he said. He patted his thick chest sadly. 'But then again, I've got more body mass than you, and usually very little to get up for in the morning.'

She laughed, and knocked down two of the pills.

'How's the boy?' she asked.

'Why don't you come and see?'

He led her down the short linking companionway to the small wardroom adjoining the infirmary and surgical chambers. Only one of the six cots was occupied. Zael lay, pale and thin, in his endless sleep, attached to a feeder and bio-monitor. Beside his cot, there was a single chair, and a cabinet on which sat a lamp, a data-slate, and a bowl full of lho-stick butts.

'Any change?' she whispered.

'Yeah. He woke up and started dancing. I forgot to tell you.'

'Shut up,' she scolded with a grin.

'I won't half miss him when he wakes up,' Frauka said with a sadness that surprised her. 'Who's going to listen to my stories then?'

'Can I get you anything?' she asked. Frauka shook his head.

'Well, good night, and thanks.'

She left. Frauka wandered over to the chair and sat down. He lit a lho-stick and picked up the data-slate, thumbing it live.

The glow of the screen reflected on his face.

'Where was I?' he said. 'Ah, yes... "Her nipples were hard and pink with excitement. She squealed in delight as his loincloth dropped to the deck. Very slowly, he–"'

Your nose is bleeding.

'What?'

Your nose is bleeding.

'Dammit!' Frauka said, moustaching his left index finger across his upper lip to staunch the flow. He put down the data-slate, slid the burning lho-stick into the dish, and pulled out a handkerchief. He swabbed his nose,

and peered at the smeared linen. It wasn't the first time it
had been spotted with blood. The old spots looked like
rust.

'Not much. It's stopped.'

But your nose was bleeding.

'Yes. So what?' He tucked the handkerchief away again,
sniffing.

Why?

'Why?' Frauka drew on his lho stick. 'Why? You ask
why?'

I'm waiting for the answer.

'Because it was. Shut up.'

Noses bleed for a reason.

'I'm sure they do. In my case, sonny, it's because I
picked it.'

Both nostrils?

'Do me a favour. Shut up. I was reading.'

I'm bored with the endless dirty stories.

'Well, hey, I'm not,' Frauka snapped. He raised the slate
again. '"Her full breasts were as white and round as–"'

He lowered the slate and gazed at the boy.

'You know what I have to do if you wake up?'

*Yeah. I can feel the weight of the gun in your pocket and the
weight of the promise you made to the Chair in your head.*

'Well, then.'

There was a long pause.

Then Wystan said. 'I'm an untouchable. There should-
n't be any way you can feel anything in my head.'

And yet?

'Shut up. Where was I?'

Something about breasts?

'Right. Yes.'

*You can't trust any of them any more. You know that? So
many dirty stories. So many secrets. Kara, Thonius, Ballack,
Nayl...*

'So I won't tell anyone. Will you?'

The boy on the cot lay as still as death.

'Right, where was I?'

SHE WAS MAKING her way up the spinal corridor to the bridge when Belknap appeared.

'Hi,' she said.

'Still just walking around?' he asked.

She nodded.

'Sholto's asleep. Too much numbskull. He's got some great stories. You know, he believes his family is descended from–'

'I'm scared,' she said abruptly.

He looked at her. He didn't need her to tell him why.

'Come with me to the infirmary.'

'I can't. I have to get to the bridge. The grid's going to wake in five minutes.'

'All right. Be calm. Check the grid. I'll go and set up, and then come and get you.'

She nodded again.

'Everything will be fine,' he said. He took hold of her hands and folded them into the sign of the aquila across her breasts. 'Have faith.'

He kissed her. She wrapped her arms around his neck as if she was going to break it.

'Ten minutes,' he said, pulling away.

She walked in the opposite direction.

Fyflank was on the bridge, running some impenetrable system checks on the main helm. The manhound looked up and grunted when she appeared, and then carried on with its work.

Kara sat down at the vox station. She rubbed her eyes with both palms and drew a deep breath.

The board lit up. Systems woke on automatic. Runes glowed, and then scrolled across the main comm screen. She waited for the graphics to settle down, and then keyed in the carrier signal.

Nest wishes Talon, she typed. *Above and starward, the voices of friends*.

A pause. Then letters typed out across the screen.

Too tired for Glossia, Kara. Everything's all right here. We have a lead, a possible in. How are things up there?

Everything's fine, she typed.

Good. Talk to you again in three hours. Goodnight, Kara. Goodnight, Gideon.

FIVE

BERYNTH IS A dark, dirty, ugly hive clamped to the south-western tip of Utochre's second main landmass, ringed by fifty smoke-belching mine stations. This mass of industry and habitation, over ten thousand kilometres in area, cannot be seen from orbit. It cannot be seen by the *Arethusa*. This is due to Utochre's miasmal cloud cover. Most of the moon, land and oceans both, is ice-clad, and the atmosphere a dense, opaque cloud mass, thanks to an impact winter that has lasted thirty thousand years. Astronomers blame the foul climactic circumstances on a past collision with a lesser moon.

I sift and consider such facts, to keep my mind turning.

A moon itself, the eighth moon of twenty-eight, Utochre circles the well populated Imperial world of Cyto at a great distance. Notably a claw-shaped new moon in Cyto's winter skies, Utochre has a reputation as a dark place. The early settlers on Cyto had invested Utochre with myths, suggesting it was a repository of evil, a place to which bad or twisted souls migrated after death.

Perhaps it is a repository of evil. Certainly, it has become a famous place. Nobility, and the wealthy, make pilgrimage to Utochre, usually on charter passage from the main planet. The ferries are regular. Fecund with minerals, metals and precious stones, thanks to its complex and active structure, Utochre has become, over the years, a place of intensive ore mining and, secondarily, a centre for lapidary craft. The rock seams under the moon's ice regularly yield the best uncut gems in the sector. All the key Imperial jewellers, and many hundreds of lesser halls, have set up premises at Berynth, exploiting this resource. The sector's nobility come here to indulge themselves, partly because of Utochre's resources, and partly because it is exclusive. Only the very rich and the most nobly born can afford the prices, and the effort, of the ferry connection.

But there is another service that Cyto's twenty-eighth moon offers, for those who are very wealthy, or very superstitious.

Or very desperate.

I have a bad feeling that I fall into the last category.

IT IS A risk. The Wych House was always going to be a risk. There have been so many attempts to find it and close it down over the years. It is elusive. It is well protected.

It is dangerous.

It is never wrong.

Going to the Wych House had been Carl's idea. I had blocked the notion to begin with, until Ballack weighed in with his support for it. I like Ballack, I admire him. Perhaps that's why I finally demurred and brought us to Utochre.

From the moment we left Tancred high anchor, we were rogue. Not Special Condition, *rogue*. The word has a specific definition in the Inquisition's rubric. It denotes an agent or agents who are deemed negligent, insubordinate and criminal. I have broken direct orders from my superiors. I have turned my back on an assigned duty. I have taken a mission upon myself without leave or permission. I have hidden myself so that I cannot be rebuked or stopped.

Rogue.

I never thought, never imagined myself in commission of such a sin, but this was my deliberate choice.

On Tancred, on the very hour of our departure, Ballack and Angharad had come to find us in secret. This was in the immediate aftermath of Molotch's bloody trap. Ballack had come forward and offered his intelligence to me. He had not dared to go to Myzard.

I had scanned the interrogator carefully, several times, with and without Ballack's consent. The story was consistent every time: closing on Molotch with Fenx, being trapped and picked off, one by one. Molotch jeering as he left Ballack to his doom, cuffed to a turbine hub. Angharad arriving just in time to cut Ballack free with her steel and haul him to safety.

'Molotch is alive,' Ballack had told me plainly. 'He staged it all so he could disappear behind a faked corpse. You were right, sir, Molotch was here on Tancred, and now he's alive and free. The Inquisition believes he's dead. We were betrayed. Someone in the ordos betrayed us. That's the only way Molotch could have known.'

'And you come to me because?'

'Because, sir, you were right, and you're the only one I trust.'

Molotch had escaped me too many times. Molotch had cost me too many times. Majeskus. Oh Throne, dear Will and Norah and Eleena.

The memory of their screams wakes me still.

Too many times, Zygmunt Molotch, but not any more. Even if it costs me my reputation and my career.

Someone inside the ordos betrayed Fenx to Molotch. Thus, the simple equation: the ordos cannot be trusted. To finish Molotch, I have to operate without their support or knowledge. I have to move in secret, and find Molotch before I am found.

It was always going to come down to this. Molotch is my nemesis. He was always going to be the one to destroy me.

Kara has just signed off. The vox-grid is dead again. She says everything is all right aboard the *Arethusa*, and I trust her, although I am still bothered by the mysterious secret she keeps. I stay awake and I think. I listen to the constant ticking of my obsession. Am I breaking all the rules I swore I'd never break, in order to do mankind a great service, a great service that only I am in a position to accomplish? Or am I just breaking all the rules? Either way, I fear I have led my friends into hell. I have doomed them all.

The Inquisition is not forgiving.

Kys, Maud and Carl are asleep. They are tired. I let them rest. Nayl is somewhere, screwing the Carthaen. He thinks I don't know. I'm happy for him and for her, and I want to kill them both. Throne, I haven't felt this way for a long time.

Not since the day I ended up in this box. It's quite enervating.

Bastard. That you're screwing her I don't mind. That you're hiding it from me, that I most certainly do. Did you think you were sparing my feelings? Did you? *Did you?*

SIX

THE SPOIL WELLS lay deep under the hive, deep in the subterranean foundations below the permafrost. They were dank, badly lit rockcrete vaults dozens of kilometres long where the slurry from the mining operations was dumped on a regular basis. The air smelled of stone dust and moisture and raw minerals. A bitingly cold wind seeped in from the surface, invading through loading slips and drop shafts, and gusted around the numbered silos raising a grey dust.

'Hiram Lucic?' Ballack called out.

The man halfway up the spoil slope rose and looked down at them. He was skinny, but bulked up by furs and thermal body lagging, topped off by parts of an old hostile environment suit. He was holding a hand scanner unit. Five rusty old prospector-servitors sorted and scrabbled around him on the heap, tossing lumps of black rock into their battered panniers with corroded skeletal forelimbs.

'Who wants to know?'

'We do.'

A male and a female stood at the base of the heap. They stared up at him.

'Yes, I'm Lucic. But I'm also busy. I've paid through the nose for two hours' free sweep of this mass, and I won't waste a minute of that. "We" can go away and come back later. Or just go away.'

'I think you'll want to speak with us,' the woman said. 'We were told to ask for you. We need an introduction.'

Lucic paused, and glanced at the scanner in his hands. Pretty much nothing was showing. The spoil coming out of Deep Nineteen was poor these days. That probably explained why he'd got the free sweep at a knock down.

He sighed and slithered down the loose rock waste towards them. He moved with the expert tread of someone used to moving about on broken spill.

'Go on, then,' he said. Close up, they didn't give much away, except that they were clean and well dressed, which suggested money.

'An introduction at Stine and Stine,' Kys said. Lucic was an odd fish, thin and lean, just sinew and bone under his cold gear. His face was all cheekbones and jaw corners and a long blade nose. He had large eyes, which seemed to bulge from meagre sockets.

'An introduction? That's an expensive undertaking.'

'We understand that,' Ballack said.

'I know Stine and Stine,' Lucic said, 'in my capacity as a prospector. They buy my stuff sometimes. Let's see, an introduction.' He did a little maths in his head, gauging them by their manner and their clothes. Too little and he diddled himself. Too much, and he'd lose the job. He assayed the circumstances. He was good at assaying things.

'Gonna be two or three, minimum,' he said.

'Hundred?' asked Kys.

'Hundred thousand,' Ballack corrected. 'I am right?' Ballack asked.

Lucic nodded. 'What you want is costly.'

'What we want is an introduction,' said Kys.

'Let me get cleaned up,' he said.

HE RE-JOINED THEM in a dirty public canteen where the spoil well workers and prospectors met and rested. He had changed into a grey bodyglove and a fur-lined coat. There was still dirt on his hands. Ballack bought three hot drinks and some wizened pastries from the stall. There was steam in the air, and the rank scent of over-worked heating units.

Lucic sat down with them at a battered metal table, lit a lho-stick in his nimble fingers, and put an old data-slate on the table top. Miners in bulky work suits shuffled past.

'I'll need names, details,' Lucic said. 'This isn't some-thing you can just walk into.'

'So we've found,' said Kys.

'You don't look like the normal sort,' Lucic said.

'And what's that?'

'Nobility. The kind with nothing better to do.'

'What do we look like?'

Lucic stuck his tongue in his lean cheek so it bulged. He thought about it. 'Trouble?' he suggested. 'Look, the halls don't like to be mucked about. They have real pull here. Magistratum, Arbites... hell, even the Inquisition. That's a no-no. Especially the Inquisition.'

'I understand,' said Ballack.

'What would happen if that was the case?' Kys asked.

'You'd get dead, and me along with you.'

'Wouldn't that cause a problem? I mean,' said Ballack, 'if we were Inquisition, let's say?'

'Here? No, not really. Easy to hide a corpse or three here. The spoil smelters. The pack ice. The undersea. Easy to get lost.'

'Well, we're not Inquisition,' said Ballack, 'or Magistratum or anything like that. But you've spotted we're not your regular type of clients, so we'd better come clean.'

'Go on.'

'We're operatives working for a certain important individual. He has business interests in this sub, and he wants an inside track to guide his investments. There's a lot at stake.'

'And he trusts the House to provide that guidance?'

'Shouldn't he?'

'Oh, the House is good. Investments, eh?'

Ballack handed Lucic a data crystal. The prospector loaded it into his slate.

'My name is Gaul,' said Ballack. 'My associate here is called Kine.'

There was a pause while the slate hummed. 'Linking to the hive substrate,' said Lucic. 'Just be a second. Gaul, Kine. There we go. From Eustis. Your biowork checks out.'

It ought to, thought Kys, the work Carl put in.

'I think we can do business,' said the prospector.

'WELL?' KARA ASKED slowly.

'Everything's good. There's no sign of any regrowth.' Belknap began to pack the medical kit away, carefully folding up the more delicate parts of the scanner.

He looked at her. She smiled. They embraced.

'I was so scared!' she sighed.

'So was I. When you came to me like that. Kara, my love, I don't want to scare you or jinx this, but you know you should–'

'What? Be dead?'

'You should be dead. The woman I met and fell in love with on Eustis Majoris had barely six months. Then, overnight, just like that, the cancer went. I kept thinking I'd made a mistake, that I'd missed something or it would come back. And when you came to me tonight... But, unless I'm very bad at my job, it hasn't. It isn't there. No sign. You're clear.'

She got up. They were alone in the ship's infirmary, apart from Frauka and the comatose boy in the ward nearby. Unwerth and Fyflank were up on the bridge

'Are you?' Kara asked.

'Am I what?'

'Very bad at your job?'

He laughed. 'No.'

She kissed his neck. Then she sat back.

'What's that look?' he asked, reclasping his kit and carrying it to a wall locker.

'I never told Ravenor. I kept it a secret. Now it's gone, but that secret inside me still remains.'

'What do you mean?'

Kara shrugged. 'I hated keeping it from him. I trained myself to cover the truth. Now there's no truth to cover, it still feels like I'm covering for something.'

'You've lost me,' he said.

She steepled her hands in front of her mouth thoughtfully and breathed out. 'It's hard to explain. I feel like I'm keeping a terrible secret, but there's no secret left to keep.'

'The mind becomes conditioned,' Belknap said. 'It gets used to what it gets used to. It'll pass.'

'I hope so. I wake up sometimes and feel I can almost catch what it is.'

'The secret?'

'Yes, the secret. It has something to do with Carl.'

'Carl?'

Kara sniggered. 'I know. It's stupid, but why do I feel like I'm lying on Carl's behalf all the time?'

'Guilt,' he said. 'Just your sense of guilt towards Ravenor. Throne knows why that has attached itself to Carl. Do you know something about him that I don't?'

'He's a pompous arse, he wears too many rings, and he's very good at his job.'

'So, no then?'

She shrugged. 'So why am I so muzzy? So clouded? Why have I got, doctor, this pressing sense of unease. This forgetfulness?'

'Lack of exercise,' he replied.

'Right.'

He paused, and looked around at her. She knew that look. 'We're alone, you know?'

'Frauka's in the next room.'

'Oh, what does porn-boy care?'

He kissed her, dragged off her vest, and cupped her breasts with his hands. She pulled him down onto the infirmary couch.

'Exercise, you reckon?' she murmured.

'HAVE YOU EVER wondered just how much you can get away with before someone notices?' Thonius asked.

'That's a curious question to ask,' Ravenor replied.

They had gone up onto observation bay high in Berynth Hive to pass the time while they waited for Ballack and Kys. With the dome shutters up, there was a considerable view of the icebound landscape and the belting, eternal storm.

There was no one else around apart from a courting couple, low habbers, at the far end of the rail. The place was like a temple to the elements.

Thonius sat down on a metal bench beside Ravenor's chair.

'Have you, though?' Carl asked.

'Have you what?' Maud Plyton asked as she joined them, carrying two metal cups of hot secum she'd bought at a stall in the hallway outside the bay. She handed one to Carl and then sat down on the other end of the bench.

'Thanks,' Carl said.

'I'm intrigued,' said Maud, sipping her drink.

'Carl just asked me if I'd ever wondered just how much I could get away with before someone noticed,' Ravenor said.

'That's a curious question to ask,' Plyton said.

'That was my response,' Ravenor agreed.

'No, look,' said Carl. 'We've gone rogue. I understand why we had to, and I support the decision. That's well and good. I just wondered how much you would risk? I mean, how much you would do in plain sight of others before you thought they would notice?'

'Myzard's people will be looking for any hint of our activity. So, very little is my answer.'

'It fascinates me,' Carl said, getting up. 'Subterfuge fascinates me. What a person can get away with, I mean.'

'You'd be surprised what a person can get away with,' Maud Plyton said, 'in my professional experience.' Ravenor's voxponder made a sound that indicated he was chuckling.

'Oh, I think I wouldn't,' said Carl. He put his cup down. 'Our work, sir, it's all about secrets, isn't it? Keeping secrets, opening secrets up. Molotch, forgive me for mentioning his name, is so damn dangerous because of his ability to keep secrets.'

'Does a point come with that, Thonius?' asked Plyton.

'I think so, Maud,' Carl replied. He looked out at the storm. 'It's not just keeping a secret, is it? It's about how you use it. What latitude you have.'

'"Latitude"?' asked Ravenor.

'Yes, sir. What you say and what you don't say. It's not just about keeping the secret locked in. It's about having the strength and confidence to reveal your secret when you know it won't matter.'

'That's an interesting notion,' Ravenor said. 'Develop it, Carl.'

Carl laughed. 'We're in class now, are we?'

'We're in class till I say we're not, Carl Thonius,' Ravenor replied.

'Fair point,' said Carl, although his face darkened. 'For a start, they say that liars have the best memories.'

'Old school lore,' said Plyton. 'First day on the job at interrogation, I learned that. Fakers need good memories to remember what they've faked. You need a first-class memory to hold a false story together under inspection.'

'Sound Magistratum advice,' Ravenor remarked.

'Yes, yes,' said Carl, 'but a liar... a real liar... needs to vent himself sometimes. Just to stay sane. He needs to confide, or act openly when he's sure no one will notice. He needs to be able to get away with telling the truth once in a while. Just to test the integrity of his deception.'

'You think Molotch might be so driven?' asked Ravenor.

'He might. It's worth considering.'

'So noted,' Ravenor said. 'That's good, clean thinking, Carl.'

Carl smiled. 'Thank you, sir. I mean to say, what if a person did this, right in front of you?'

He waved his right hand. Plyton set her cup down and drew her sidearm out of her jacket. She cocked it and set the muzzle against the side of her head.

'I think you're fretting, Carl,' Ravenor said. 'The tension's getting to you.'

'Or this?' Carl said, grinning, He waved his hand again. His hand was beginning to glow with a dull, red light.

At the far end of the platform, the courting couple was kissing. The man suddenly jerked away from his girl and floated backwards in the air towards the dome windows. She yelped, disbelieving, and stared at him. He was trying to cry out. His arms were flailing. He floated backwards, and hit the glass gently, like a balloon.

Then he went through the glass, like a hand through water.

Outside, hanging there, he screamed. No one could hear him, although his lover squealed at the sight. The sleet storm shredded his clothes and slammed him against the glass.

The constant barrage of the ice particles, like blades, shredded the meat off him in about thirty seconds. His skeleton, with gory strands of flesh and clothing still attached, with wounded organs still throbbing inside his ribcage, slowly slid down the glass leaving a red smear, and dropped away onto the blackness.

'I mean,' said Carl. 'What about that?'

'The storm is quite magnificent, don't you think?' Ravenor said. 'The primal quality of it.'

'You didn't see, did you?' Carl murmured. 'I did that, and you didn't see. Well, that's something.'

He looked at Maud Plyton. 'Not today,' he said.

She made her weapon safe and put it away. Then she picked up her cup and sipped again.

Carl lowered his hand. It had stopped glowing.

'That's good. Very good.'

Plyton looked up. 'Sir? Why is that woman down there screaming?' she asked.

LUCIC WALKED INTO the hall, past the sensors and the waiting servitors. He tracked muddy footprints across the worn bronze flooring.

'Get out. We're closed,' said Stine from behind the desk.

'I've got an introduction to make,' Lucic said. He sat down on one of the leather couches.

'Really?' Stine sneered across the desk.

'Yes, really. You'd better stay sharp.'

'Is it remunerative? Or is it like the last few losers you've brought in, Lucic? Stine and Stine is getting tired of your time wasting.'

'Neither. The Inquisition is onto us. Get ready.'

Stine looked up sharply, suddenly interested. 'The Inquisition? How do you know?'

'I was paid to know,' said Hiram Lucic.

SEVEN

STINE WAITED BY his wooden desk in the hall's main chamber of display. He was nervous, his palms sweating. He began to pace.

He stopped suddenly at the chime of a vox-link in the shadows nearby. There was a brief crackle of muted transmission, and then a voice said, 'Understood.'

The red-haired man who had been standing in the shadows stepped into one of the pools of emerald light containing the chamber's showcases. He was slipping a link back into his pocket.

'That was Lucic,' the man said. 'They're on their way. Five minutes.'

'I don't like this at all,' said Stine.

'You'll like the alternative even less,' said the red-haired man. Stine didn't know the man's name. He'd only met him an hour ago. 'Are you ready?'

'This isn't the way it's done,' said Stine. 'The relationship between the halls and the House is very delicate. We don't abuse it. There's too much at stake. Our livelihoods–'

'Stine–'

'Listen to me! If these people are agents of the Inquisition, then they cannot be allowed access to the House. We are very strict about this.'

'What? You jewellers gonna club together and take out an Inquisition team? I don't think so.'

'It's been done before,' Stine said haughtily. 'I think you underestimate how zealously we protect our interests or how capable the halls of Berynth are. Usually it doesn't come to that. We detect Inquisitorial approaches and frustrate them with false leads or dead ends. Since the foundation of the hive, no ordo agent has got past us, or close to the House.'

The red-haired man shrugged. 'It'll have to work differently this time. This is an exceptional case, and the halls of Berynth are most definitely out of their depth this time. Now get ready. You have to play your part. We're paying you well enough. It's essential that these people believe they are gaining access to the House through the proper channels. If they suspect for a moment that there's been any funny business, well... then you'll have a problem.'

'With them?'

'With them, and with us, Stine.'

Stine opened a desk drawer, took out a clean polishing cloth, and wiped his damp hands. He tossed the cloth into the back of the drawer and closed it again. He looked up at the red-haired man.

'No,' he said.

'I beg your pardon?'

'No,' the factor repeated. 'I'm not doing this. Call it off.'

'It's way too late for that, Stine.'

'I don't care. I won't be party to this. The halls have far too much to lose to play this kind of game. You will not manipulate me.'

The red-haired man glanced towards the chamber entrance. Two minutes left, maximum. 'Dammit,' he said. He turned to face the factor and reached into his coat. 'I didn't want to have to do this, Stine, but you've backed me into a corner. '

Stine's eyes widened. He took a step backwards, banging his hip against the desk. The man's hand was coming back out of his coat.

Stine was expecting to see a weapon in it, a gun.

The red-haired man was holding something far worse.

It was an Inquisitorial rosette.

LUCIC LED Kys and Ballack along the Promenade St Jakob. Lucic had dressed smartly for the occasion in a dark suit and a brown leather coat, both a little old, but respectable. He'd lacquered his hair. Ballack and Kys wore rather finer clothes, the image of understated wealth. Ballack carried a small grey case.

Lucic stopped a few hundred metres from the hall's main entrance, and drew them over to the promenade railing. A steady flow of well-to-do and stately clients moved past them in both directions.

'Now,' said Lucic, 'follow my lead and do as I indicate. One wrong move, and you can forget everything. The hall will not tolerate games.'

'We understand,' said Kys.

'I hope you do, Mamzel Kine,' said Lucic. He nodded at the case Ballack was carrying. 'Currency bonds?' he asked.

'Notarised wafers,' Ballack replied. 'I trust that will be acceptable.'

+It damn well better had.+

Kys smiled to herself at the touch of Ravenor's mind in her head. It was reassuring to know he was with them, and she knew he was right. Now they were operating rogue, Ravenor's access to funds was limited. Any access to fiscal holdings or trusts would flag them to the ordos. They were living off Ravenor's fast eroding personal resources, the 'small change' he carried with him as an operating budget, and the three hundred and twenty thousand in Ballack's case made a big dent in that reserve.

'Wafers? That's fine,' said Lucic.

+You getting anything on him?+ Kys sent.

+He's wearing a blocker, so, no. I presume that's standard for a man in his position, although it concerns me. It's as if he was expecting a psyker. But we have to go through with it.+

+Good. Right. Of course.+

+Before you ask, I'm getting nothing off the hall either. I cast ahead. The whole place is psy-opaque. Fielding, I think. I'm not surprised by that, though. Standard security practice for a high-class jewellers to be psy-blunted.+

+But you won't be with us once we're inside?+

+No, Patience, I won't. That's regrettable. Remember though, the Emperor protects.+

'Well, if we're ready and we're all clear?' Lucic said.

'As crystal,' said Ballack.

'Let's do it,' Lucic said.

'YOU UNDERSTAND NOW?' the red-haired man asked.

Stine swallowed, and sat down hard. 'The Inquisition…?'

'Has enjoyed regular access to the House for decades, Stine, despite what the halls of Berynth believe. We just don't advertise the fact. The House can be very useful to us. So, forget about keeping the ordos out. We've been inside for years. Concentrate your mind on this particular deal.'

The man stepped closer. 'Stine?'

Stine started and looked up. He was still reeling from the revelation. 'Yes,' he murmured. 'Yes.'

'The people you're about to deal with are the principal agents of a rogue inquisitor. Do you understand? A rogue. A criminal. A mass murderer. He is very dangerous. They are very dangerous. Their actions have led to the slaughter of thousands.'

'Th-thousands?' Stine echoed.

'The disaster on Eustis Majoris eight months ago. That was their doing.'

Stine shuddered. His hall, Berynth, Cyto, the whole Helican subsector was still reeling from the great trauma that had afflicted the capital world of the neighbouring subsector. The economy was in spasm.

'We're close,' said the red-haired man quietly, 'but we need to get closer. We need them where we want them, so we can finish them. They're too dangerous to live. Do you understand?'

'I understand.'

'Good. I'm counting on you. Help us with this, and it will go well for Stine and Stine. I might even forget your recent suggestion that your hall and others may have eliminated ordo agents in the past to protect your own interests.'

'Throne, I didn't mean—'

'Shush, Stine. Clean slate. That's what I'm authorised to offer you in exchange for helping us today. Do your part, give them what they want, and then forget anybody was ever here. Then the Inquisition of Mankind might forget about you too.'

'Very well,' said Stine, rising to his feet. 'Very well. I'll do it.'

'Do what?' the red-haired man asked. 'Tell me again, clearly.'

'I will make them believe they are in and that they are gaining access to the House through the proper channels. You can trust me.'

'Trust you, Stine?' the red-haired man laughed. 'You deal in millions of crowns worth of precious metal and gems. The accumulation of wealth is all that concerns you. Men like you are cut throat and mendacious, hard as corundum. I don't trust you at all, but I'm prepared to count on you this time. Do this, and do it well.'

Stine nodded. 'You can't be here.'

'I'll be in the next room. Through there,' the red-haired man said. 'If anything untoward occurs, I'll be ready.'

'Untoward?'

'Nothing will happen if you do your job right. We don't want it to happen here. I'm just saying.'

A burnished servitor approached.

'They're here,' said the red-haired man. 'Get on with it.'

Stine cleared his throat and walked slowly towards the door.

'WHERE'S THE FACTOR?' Kys asked. They were standing in Stine and Stine's wood-panelled reception chamber.

Lucic looked around awkwardly. 'I'm sure he'll be along,' he began.

'We had an appointment,' said Ballack.

'The factor should be here to greet us,' said Kys.

Lucic was clearly uncomfortable. Kys noticed he was showing too much of the whites of his eyes.

'Lucic?'

The prospector shrugged an open-handed gesture. 'I'm sure there's no problem.'

Ballack looked at Kys. She nodded.

'We're leaving,' she said.

'No!' Lucic cried. 'No, no, just give him a moment, please.'

'This stinks,' said Kys. 'Thanks but no thanks.'

'Throne's sake,' Lucic hissed, 'this is my reputation on the line. My career. Agenting is where the real money is. I can't get by on prospecting alone, and if I blow this, Stine and Stine won't ever touch me again, and they'll spread the word to the other halls. I've put a lot into this.'

'So have we,' said Ballack.

'Please...' Lucic sighed.

'My utmost apologies!' Stine cried, hurrying into the chamber towards them. 'I am so sorry to have kept you waiting, even for a moment. A servitor was meant to summon me, and he was waylaid. A thousand pardons!'

Lucic looked sidelong at his clients. 'We're all right,' he whispered.

'Are we?' Kys mouthed at Ballack. Ballack nodded.

Lucic turned to the beaming factor. 'Dear Factor Stine,' he said with a forced grin, 'not quite the seamless greeting I had led my friends here to expect.'

Stine bowed. 'Oh, of course not, my dear old good friend Hiram. I will have the entire servitor complex rebooted. The lapse in decorum is unforgivable. I hope I can make amends? Refreshments, perhaps?'

'Always welcome,' said Lucic, regaining his composure. 'May I present Master Gaul and Mamzel Kine?'

The factor came forward, and bowed to each of them in turn. 'A genuine pleasure. My dear old good friend Hiram has always brought the most distinguished emptors to Stine and Stine.'

He looked directly at Kys. 'My lady,' he said, 'I fear I was most awfully impolite to you on the occasion of our last meeting. I hope you will forgive my rudeness. We have to be so careful these days, and I quite misjudged you.'

Kys bowed back. 'Factor, I apologised then, and I apologise now. I should never have come to you so bluntly, without proper introduction.'

'Least said, soonest mended,' Stine replied with a cheery gesture. 'Let's begin again fresh. Now... a little amasec, perhaps. We have a last few casks of the Fibula '56, which I would keep to myself, truth be told, but I positively can't offer you anything less magnificent. And some birri truffles wrapped in nap leaves, and some local shellfish, I think. The scallops are prepared fresh by the hall's chefs, hoisted from the sub-ice ocean farms just three hours ago.'

'The scallops or the chefs?' asked Kys.

Stine brayed out a laugh. 'The scallops, naturally! My lady has a fine sense of humour!'

He clapped his hands and directed orders to the waiting servitors.

'Shall we go in?' he ventured. 'I have objects to show you.'

They followed him back into the show galleries. His performance had begun.

Kys had heard it all before. To Stine's credit, it wasn't the same. She had to admit the factor was good at what he did.

He stopped in front of a glass display of exquisite peridot and moonstone settings, in full flow, fluently describing every facet and cut.

Stine stopped suddenly, and turned to them with a smile. 'Forgive me for babbling. I get quite carried away. I ought to be telling you about the history of Stine and Stine. Sometimes, I forget myself. I am so enamoured of my hall's work, I get quite incoherent.'

'Does that interest you at all?' he asked.

'I think I speak for both of us,' said Ballack, 'when I say that coherence interests us a great deal.'

+PATIENCE?+

+Hello. We've got it. We're just leaving.+

Lucic led them out onto the promenade. With a final bow, the factor bade them adieu. 'An excellent choice,' he said, kissing Kys's hand.

'I hope so,' said Kys.

'It's been a genuine pleasure spending this time with you,' Stine said, his performance drawing towards its curtain call.

'You've been most obliging, sir,' Ballack said to the factor with a bow.

'If I can be of any further service,' Stine gushed.

'My thanks again, as ever,' said Lucic. Stine bowed for the thousandth time, and backed away into the hall.

Kys looked at Ballack. 'We're clear?'

'We're clear.'

'Thank Throne that's over,' Kys muttered.

'Let's keep walking,' Lucic advised. 'Come on now, briskly. I'm uncomfortable with you carrying that around in a public place. Even on the Promenade St Jakob, there are unscrupulous elements.'

That was the three hundred and ten thousand crown horolog piece that now occupied Ballack's case. Kys and Ballack trailed Lucic down the promenade.

'What happens now?' Kys asked.

'Depends. How quickly do you want it to happen?' Lucic asked.

'Quickly, the next few hours.'

Lucic nodded. 'Good. It's better that way. The cue Stine sold me for the House has an expiry date. The House moves.'

'We understand that.'

'Fine. So long as you do. Two hours then, in underboat pen seventy-two. We can make the exchange there. How many people will be in your party?'

'No,' said Kys. 'We have our own transport arranged. You meet us.'

'That's not how it works,' said Lucic.

'It is now,' said Ballack.

'No, no,' said Lucic. 'You'll screw this up!'

'It's how we want it,' said Ballack. 'Adjust. I'm sure you're capable. Boat pen sixty-one, two hours from now.'

'Then I'm coming with you,' said Lucic.

'No, you're not,' Ballack smiled.

'You want to use your own damn transport, fine!' Lucic snapped. 'But I'm coming with you. You'll need me. Cue or no cue, the House will blank you if you arrive in an unauthorised transport. You need me still.'

'You can get us in?'

'All part of the price. You have to take me along.'

Ballack nodded. 'Pen sixty-one. Two hours.'

'I'll be there,' said Lucic, and strode away into the crowds.

'What do you think?' Kys asked.

'I think he's rotten to the core,' Ballack replied, 'but he's all we've got. We have to run with this.'

Patience Kys sighed. 'Like we had to run with Stine of Stine and Stine. I know. I still wish I could have killed the obsequious bastard, though.'

STINE OF STINE and Stine walked slowly back into the hall's main chamber of display and sat down heavily in the chair behind the simple wooden desk.

'You did good,' said the red-haired man, emerging from the shadows.

'That's all very well,' Stine grumbled.

'Here's your reward,' the red-haired man said.

A man much larger than the red-haired man plodded out of the shadows. He was wearing heavy power armour, but he made very little sound. He handed a weapon to the red-haired man. The red-haired man activated the blade. It made a shrill, grating whine.

'Chainsword,' said the red-haired man lightly.

He raised the whirring weapon, and swung it at Stine. Stine was too astonished to attempt any evasion. The chainsword struck him on the left arm just below the shoulder, and carried on through, slicing him laterally across the upper chest. Stine's head and shoulders, like a statuary bust, flopped backwards over the chair back, and his arms, severed at the top of the biceps, dropped leadenly onto the ground. The top half of the chair's back rest, severed along with the upper part of Factor Stine, hit the floor too. Upholstery padding fluffed into the air like thistledown. Pressurised arterial blood squirted from the factor's anatomically cross-sectioned body in shuddering jets and spattered noisily across the top of the wooden desk.

The red-haired man stepped back sharply in order to avoid getting splashed. He deactivated the chainsword and handed it back to the larger, armoured man beside him.

'No one leaves Stine and Stine alive,' he said. 'Make sure of it.'

'No one?'

'End of story.'

'No problem,' said the armoured man. He reactivated the chainsword so it was buzzing in his fist and clicked his link as he walked away across the chamber. 'All teams, attention. Deploy, and execute everyone in the building.'

EIGHT

THE UNDERBOAT NAYL had leased left pen sixty-one three hours later. It was a chisel-nosed grey tube of steel and ceramite twenty-four metres long, with a quiet cavitation drive along the centreline and two heavy-bladed propulsion fans fixed ventrally in cage nacelles.

It descended into the oily murk of the pen, lit up stablights on its prow frame, and purred out through the pen mouth.

The pen's sea doors opened into a long, square-cut channel of blue ice and then out into the open water beyond the subframe of the giant hive. They passed gigantic foundation struts and derricks, brown with tar and mineral deposits that jutted down through the ice pack and disappeared far below into the black deeps. A few bulk capacity underboats went by along the same channel, inbound to the hive, laden with ore. Their stablight rigs were lit up like the lures of abyssal fish.

There were nine people on board the craft: Ravenor, Thonius, Ballack, Kys, Plyton, Nayl and the Carthaen, along with Lucic and the pilot servitor Nayl had leased along with the boat.

'Quite a crowd you travel with,' Lucic commented to Kys when he joined them at the pen quay.

'Names don't matter,' Kys replied.

'I wasn't asking for any,' Lucic told her, though his gaze lingered on Ravenor's support chair. Lucic had come dressed in dirty work clothes: a faded, patched body-glove, furs and a quilted coat. He also carried a grubby shoulder pack.

'Weapons?' Ballack asked him.

'Just tools of the trade,' Lucic replied, offering up the pack so Ballack could wand it.

Lucic chose to ride up front with Nayl and the pilot. From the main passenger trunk, a Spartan space with drop down seats, they could see forward into the pilot house through the open hatch. Instrumentation glowed below the gloomy forward ports. Lucic was sensible enough not to attempt conversation with Nayl. Once they had reached open water, Nayl handed him the grey case containing the very expensive timepiece. Lucic looked inside briefly, put the case with his pack, and accessed the navigation punch-box on the instrument panel. He entered a nineteen digit code. The cue. Screens blinked and rolled as graphics redrew and remapped. Then a spidery red chart came up, with route and way-marker graphics overlaid in white.

'That's some distance,' Nayl said.

'Eight hours minimum,' said Lucic, 'provided we don't encounter any holdups.'

'Holdups?' Nayl asked.

'Ice-falls. Sub-currents. That's probably the worst we might get, this season of the year.'

'There's worse?'

'There's maelstroms. Believe me, if there was any chance we'd run into one of those, we wouldn't have left the pen.'

Nayl pointed to the nav display. 'Is that the House?'

Lucic shook his head. 'The House is currently sitting 'neath side about forty kilometres south south-west of that. The chart resolution's too large to show it. That's Berynth Eighty-Eight, one of the deep water mining rigs, sitting in a two-kilometre hole it's made for itself in the pack ice. That's our excuse for heading out that way. We'll divert when we reach Eighty-Eight.'

The others made themselves comfortable in the passenger trunk. Plyton leaned by one of the small armoured port lights, craning her neck to see up and out. They were three hundred metres down, and the water was black and clear like glass, but above them, it graduated into a green twilight.

'Creepy,' she murmured.

Angharad glanced at her.

'All this water on top of us. The pressure. The cold. Even if you could reach the surface, there is no surface. Just a roof of ice.'

Angharad shrugged and looked away. Little seemed to impress her.

'The whole ocean's covered in pack ice, right?' Plyton asked.

'The whole thing,' Ravenor replied, 'apart from a few anomalous breaks. In most places, the pack is five or six hundred metres thick. Quite a roof.'

Plyton grimaced. 'A fine time to discover I'm claustrophobic,' she said.

'You've travelled in the void,' Angharad said. 'Compared to that, this is nothing.'

'It'll kill you just as fast,' said Plyton. 'Besides, we can all have our own private fears, can't we?'

'I do not have private fears,' said Anagharad. That made Plyton laugh.

'Any life out there?' Plyton asked.

'Algae. Aggregated bacteria. Phytoplankton. There may be no sunlight, but the moon's excessively active. A lot of thermal venting.'

'Anything bigger than that?'

'No. There are rumours, but no.'

'Cold,' said Plyton, glancing back out.

'It's deep, too,' Ravenor said. 'The ocean floor depth varies, but in some places it's technically immeasurable.'

'Immeasurable?' asked Plyton.

'Abyssal.'

'What do you mean, immeasurable?'

'I mean it's so deep, any instrument sent down to sound it is crushed by the extremity of pressure.'

'What about auspex? Modar?'

'That deep, that cold, that pressurised, the water starts to behave in very strange ways. It doesn't give up its secrets. You were right, Maud. In some ways it is much, much more dangerous than the void. The deep ocean of Utochre may be one of the strangest places in the Imperium. Which is probably why the House is here.'

'Are you telling me this to reassure me?' Plyton asked, slightly pale.

'One can face one's private fears better if one understands their limits, I always think. I was giving you the best information I could.'

'That below us is a freaky abyss that we don't understand and could never escape from?' Plyton asked.

Ravenor was silent for a moment. 'I probably shouldn't have opened my mouth,' he said.

He moved across the cabin to where Kys was sitting.

+Just so you know, we're out of contact. The vox isn't making it through the water and the ice, not even via a relay at the hive. Something – the ice I think, but I don't know why – is bouncing psychic transmission. We can't talk to Kara.+

'You spoke to her before we left?'

+Just before. She knows what we're doing. I told her not to start fretting unless a week went by.+

Ravenor saw that Kys was still silently staring forward, keeping an eye on Lucic through the pilot house hatch.

+Can we trust him?+

'No,' she said, 'not at all. He's in it for the money, I think. Besides, it's too late now.'

+And if he proves untrustworthy?+

'We're all armed. That kind of cancels everything out.'

LUCIC'S ESTIMATE TURNS out to be conservative. It takes the best part of eleven hours just to reach the vicinity of the Berynth Eighty-Eight deep water rig. He blames contra-currents, and an undertow effect called the Neath Stream, which cannot be predicted. Strange, on a moon where prediction is the most exclusive commodity.

The journey becomes laborious. There's nothing but the sluggish purr of the cavitation system. The under-boat's enviro-systems are not the best, and it grows colder and the air stales. I sense the discomfort of the others, the body stink of anxiety and confinement. Maud is the worst. Her unexpected claustrophobia becomes physi-cally oppressive to her. I do not 'ware Maud, nor would I attempt to without her consent, except in the most criti-cal of situations, but I extend psy-feelers gently into the periphery of her mindscape and work to reduce her clog-ging panic by influencing her respiratory rate and slowing her pulse. I adjust her metabolism into an instru-ment to fight her fears.

Her mind, as I nestle against it, is in retreat, like a sick animal. I swim in her surface thoughts, her petty tensions and spectral fears. That's when I see the footprint.

It's been carefully disguised, like a track in snow scuffed over to conceal it. It's been so carefully disguised, I cannot be sure it's what I think it is without a more invasive probe, and this isn't the time or the place for that.

But I know what I think it is. I know what my years of experience scream to me it is.

Sometime in the last two or three days, another mind has been in her. Another presence has taken a much firmer hold of Maud Plyton than I am doing with my light psy-caresses. She has been, briefly, under considerable mental duress.

From who? And how? I haven't read another psyker, and she's hardly been out of my company. Kys couldn't do this, and why would she? Now I feel a creeping dread upon me. What have I missed? What's been in amongst my people without my permission, or even my knowledge? Lucic wears a blocker. Is there more to that casual insurance? Is he blocking the outside, or is he hiding something? Or is it...

I try to reassure myself. The footprint could be false, a side-effect of Maud's troubled state that I am misreading. Then again, her troubled state, her sudden claustrophobia, could have been triggered by aggressive manipulation.

I broaden my mind for a moment, and cast around. I feel the other heartbeats and minds around me, together with the hard negative of Lucic. Everyone's on edge, except Angharad, who is still and cold and silent like a pool. Nayl is restless, Ballack and Carl are both closed off and busy with thoughts of their own. Kys feels me stir and looks up, a question on her face.

+It's nothing, Patience. Relax.+

It's not nothing. What has done this?

I reach outside the underboat, but the sea is too cold and too blank for me to extend far.

'EIGHTY-EIGHT,' LUCIC announced. The sound of the underboat's drive systems altered slightly as the pilot brought the craft around and slowed it. The sea ahead was lighter, more radiant.

Nayl studied the console displays, and saw the vast hole, an artificial polynya, in the roof of ice above. Berynth Eighty-Eight was a filthy, gargantuan engine sticking up out of the hole like a dagger in a wound. The lower limbs of the mining rig, its huge drilling members, extended down into the lightless depths below, churning up cloud banks of heated silt.

'Vox links are live,' Nayl said.

'The rig will have a fleet of boats down on operation, guiding the drilling,' Lucic replied.

'Lots of backwash litter too,' Nayl added, adjusting the listening scopes and the detectors to wash out the noise and minimise interference.

'The rig's drill engines, circulator pumps and hydraulics,' Lucic replied, 'not to mention signals chopped and bounced by rising silt, and the suck-rattle of the excavation tubes, and the low-level vibration of the icebreaker systems keeping the hole open. The sea's a funny place. 'Neath side, you have to get used to a lot of data clutter, and learn not to trust the sensors all the time.'

He made a course adjustment with the pilot servitor's approval. The underboat nosed slowly around, and slugged away on a fresh track, skirting the industrial site and its cloud of noise.

They were running under the ice again in five minutes, heading south south-west into clearer, colder water. The rig noise gradually receded behind them.

'This water is colder,' said Nayl, reading off the instruments. 'Six or seven points and falling.'

'That's because the sea bed just dropped away under us,' said Lucic. He glanced at the pilot, who nodded confirmation. 'We just went off over the Berynth Shelf. Eighty-Eight mines out about as far as there is ocean floor to reach. We just crossed from deep water to what we call Wholly Water.'

'Holy water?'

'Wholly,' Lucic repeated with a lean grin, 'as in there's wholly nothing below us any more. We're out over the abyssal zone.'

Nayl woofed out a breath. 'Don't tell Maud,' he said.

'Which one is Maud?' asked Lucic, looking back into the passenger trunk.

Nayl didn't tell him.

Lucic grinned wider and shook his head. 'Deep ocean, my friend. We're in deep ocean now.'

'I'm not your friend,' Nayl said sullenly.

Lucic shrugged. 'You might want to reconsider that. Out here, all alone, a man needs all the friends he can get.'

'SHOLTO?'

The little shipmaster didn't look up immediately. He was sitting at the master control of the *Arethusa's* bridge, with Fyflank and two of his most senior crewmen huddled around his shoulders.

Kara approached. She'd slept, but not well. That surprised her, given that she was buoyant with relief. She'd had another dream in which Carl had come to her in some wild, desert place, and done nothing but laugh. She'd asked him questions, asked him why he was acting so strangely, and he'd just laughed at her. She'd woken in a cold sweat, sharply and suddenly, the headache pounding her temples. Belknap had been deep asleep in the bed beside her, his limbs twisted in the curious, boneless attitude of intense exhaustion slumber. She'd lain awake beside him for five minutes and then jumped when the vox intercom beeped. Leaping up gingerly, naked, she'd hit the stud before the second beep, hoping it wouldn't rouse Belknap.

'Kara,' she had whispered.

'Might it be permeable for you to come to the bridge, with all effluviancy?'

'Problem?'

'A very curiousnessity.'

'I'll be there in five.'

She had dressed in silence. Belknap hadn't stirred.

'Master Sholto?' she said again.

Fyflank and the crew mates looked around at her, and backed away to make space for her. She stepped in closer and crouched down beside the shipmaster's raised seat.

'Mistress Kara,' Sholto said, glancing around with a thin smile. He looked awful: pale, jowly, drawn.

'Sholto, are you all right?'

He shook his head. 'Forgive my unsanguine bearing. I fancy I took a little too much numbskull last night with your gentleman, the good doctor. He is a drinker of thirst, and I was thirsty, but not, in point all goodly made, a drinker.'

'You have a hangover?' she smiled, relaxing slightly.

'A terrible head, as you ask, all of throbbing and whimsy. Never again, as I have told myself before. And such dreams, as I had. Quite a colostomy of nightmares.'

'Why did you send for me, Sholto? Is it Ravenor? Has he signalled?'

Unwerth shook his head. 'The grid has lit twice, with no reponderance from our friends below. They remonstrate themselves beyond our call. I sent for you because I was sent for in turn, so as it–'

'Sholto?' Kara said firmly.

He nodded. 'I will cut to the cheese. Master Boguin was sitting night watch–'

One of the crewmen behind her, a portly fellow from Ur-Haven with less than adequate hygiene or dental maintenance, nodded expressively.

'Master Boguin was on night watch,' Unwerth continued, 'here at this veritable station, and he detected a noise.'

'A noise?'

'A noise, in all certainty.'

Kara frowned. 'A noise?' she repeated.

Unwerth fiddled with the vox dials. 'I'm trying to locale it again.'

'What sort of noise?' Kara asked.

Unwerth shrugged.

'Well, internal or external source?'

To her dismay, Unwerth shrugged again.

Kara breathed carefully. Her head was killing her. 'Sholto, I'm trying to be patient. What are you talking about?'

'There's something here,' Master Boguin said. Fyflank growled in support.

'Get up,' said Kara. She was in no mood for this. Unwerth hopped down from the master's seat and let her take his place. He stood on the deck beside her.

Kara settled down. She started to adjust the console controls. 'You're getting a vox signal? Another ship? Or just back-chatter traffic from Utochre's vox-space?'

Sholto Unwerth simply shrugged again.

Kara gently turned the dials. A ghost frequency fluttered across the scope.

'There!' Unwerth said.

'I saw it. Hang on.'

She made some alterations. The signal wave became cleaner. Kara peered at it. 'That could be another vessel, pinging us with its primary auspex.'

'In all assurity, there is no other vessel in range.'

'I think you're right,' said Kara. 'It's not external. This print is a signal coming from inside the ship. Let me just–'

She halted suddenly, froze.

'What is it?' Unwerth asked.

She didn't dare tell him. She was looking at her hands as they worked the instruments. Her right hand. There was a ring on the middle finger of her right hand, a ring that didn't belong to her, and that she had no memory of putting on.

In one awful, sweeping moment, she was sure it was one of Carl's.

'Shit!' she cried, pulling her hands back from the station as if stung. She tried to pull the ring off. It wouldn't budge.

Unwerth was still staring at the flickering signal, a yellow zigzag pulse that rippled like a cardiogram across the vox-screen.

He leant in and made a final, tiny adjustment, locking the signal down. The noise came over the speakers.

It made all of them shiver.

It was the sound of a grown man, sobbing. It went on and on, shuddering tinnily from the console speakers, sob after sob, a wracking pain.

'What in hell's name is that?' Kara whispered. She tried to sound defiant, but her words wilted as they came out. Her guts were like ice. 'Where's that coming from?'

'I know not,' said Unwerth, 'except that I don't like it.'

He reached one of his mutilated hands over towards the vox-system's main switch and threw it, shutting the system down. The screen went blank and the chasing zigzag signal wave vanished.

But the sound of the sobbing man kept coming from the speakers.

NINE

'You HAD BETTER see this,' Nayl said.

They were thirteen hours into the trip. The pilot servitor was suddenly slowing the cavitation system and back-thrusting with the ventral fans. Kys came forward into the pilot house and let Ravenor use her eyes.

'There's your Wych House,' Nayl said.

The underboat's rigged stablights were illuminating something in the murk ahead, a structure suspended below the glowing roof of ice.

'Oh God-Emperor,' Kys muttered, craning forward between Nayl and Lucic.

'Quite a thing, isn't it?' the prospector said.

The Wych House was an armoured metallic orb three hundred metres in diameter. 'Neath side, everything was upside down. The orb was supported on five articulated mechanical legs, which gripped the canopy of ice above them. As they approached, the House scuttled back a few paces, its bladed claws scuffing the 'neath side of the ice cover. It was walking on the underside of the pack ice as if the pack ice was land.

'There's a legend on Loki,' Nayl began. 'The hut of a witch that runs through the forest on the legs of a game bird.'

'Baba Yagga's hut,' Kys murmured.

+Baba Yagga's hut.+

'Baba Yagga,' Nayl nodded. 'You've heard of it?'

+It's not an old Loki legend. It's an Old Earth legend.+

'That so?' asked Nayl.

+That is so. Bring us in.+

Nayl glanced at the pilot. 'Bring us in.'

Lucic shook his head. 'Wait. I need to broadcast the proper greetings. If we just close in, it'll run.'

'Run?'

'I've seen it run, if it's scared, or feels threatened. It can out run this boat.'

+Send the greetings.+

'My boss says send the greetings, Lucic,' Kys relayed.

'He's a psyker, then?' Lucic asked. 'I thought as much.'

Kys and Nayl exchanged looks. 'At this stage,' Nayl said, 'we really don't care what you think, Lucic. Send the greeting. Do what we paid you to do or you'll be leaving this underboat through the wet-lock with no breathing apparatus and a bullet up your arse.'

'I don't answer for him,' said Kys quietly, 'but he's more than capable of that, so don't piss him off.'

Lucic pursed his lips and entered a contact code into the underboat's transponder. He checked it for fidelity once, and then pressed 'broadcast'.

They heard and felt the pulse of the system through the hull.

They waited.

'Does it usually take this long?' asked Kys.

Lucic tapped a long, scrawny finger against his bony chin. 'No. The House is worried. Nervous. Probably because we're bringing a psyker aboard.'

'It can sense that?' Nayl wondered. He saw the look on Lucic's face and shrugged. 'Of course it can.'

Kys leaned forward suddenly. 'It's sending something. Throne, missiles?'

Nayl leaned on the controls. Two darting shapes had burst from the Wych House and were racing towards them, leaving bubble tracks in the semi-glazed water behind them.

'Relax,' said Lucic, 'pilot fish.'

The missiles slowed as they neared the underboat, and turned, flashing and pulsing. The pilot servitor underwent some form of seizure, and began to act mechanically. His mind and systems were locked to the navigation systems of the Wych House. He steered them in, following the blinking pilot fish skimming just ahead of them.

The bulk of the Wych House loomed over the little underboat. They were being drawn up into a lighted cavity on the underside of the armoured orb.

The pilot fish zipped in ahead of them and vanished.

'We're going in,' said Nayl.

'Lock and load,' Ravenor ordered from the passenger trunk. Angharad rose and clutched her sheathed steel. Maud Plyton got up and racked her combat shotgun. Ballack drew his laspistol and checked its heat. Carl rose to his feet and double-clicked the slide on his autopistol.

Nayl flipped his handgun out of its rig, banged back the slide, and put it away again. He glanced at Kys.

'You ready?'

Kys had slid out two kineblades, one in each hand. She nodded.

'We're ready,' Nayl announced.

The underboat slowly entered the House's docking pool.

HUGE HYDRAULIC CLAMPS had once lifted underboats in and out of the docking pool and secured them to the wharf, but rust and neglect had long since rendered them useless. They protruded like the rotting claws of behemoth crabs from the gantry, trailing streamers of calcite and algae into the soupy dock basin. As the underboat surfaced, its fans blowing and sputtering the grease ice coating the pool's surface, Lucic opened the upper hatch, and climbed out to make them steady, using dirty old chains and hooks that dangled from the gantry piers.

The docking pool was dim, illuminated only by the underboat's light rig and a few faded lumin strips high up in the arched roof. The skeletal bulk of the gantry wharf and the perished docking clamps made distressing silhouettes above them, and the light cast wan, foggy reflections off the slowly wallowing, viscous surface of the pool. A pair of corroded metal ladders allowed them to clamber up onto the wharf platform. Nayl opened the larger side hatch so that Ravenor could move out and rise to the walkway.

'Bad air,' muttered Carl. The House's atmosphere held the sickly tang of an air supply recirculated and poorly scrubbed too many times, like a starship that had been sealed in transit for too long. There was no sound, except for the slap of the grease ice, the dying thump of the underboat's fans, and the brittle clump of their footsteps. Nayl, Lucic and Plyton switched on lamp packs.

'Cold,' Plyton shivered, buttoning her coat. Her mood seemed to have lifted, however, now she was out of the underboat's drab metal confines.

'This way,' said Lucic, and set off down the walkway.

'Why don't they keep this place in good order?' Carl wondered aloud.

'It's not a way station or a depot,' Lucic replied, gesturing with one gangly arm. 'The residents of the House expect those who come here to be perfectly capable of leaving again without supply or repair.'

'Residents?' Ravenor asked. 'How many?'

Lucic shrugged. 'They don't tell me things like that. Come on.'

Ballack and Nayl pushed past him to lead the way. The metal surfaces of the decks, walls and machinery around them were caked in rust, or limed with verdigris and blooms of algae. There was an open, unlit hatchway at the back of the wharf platform, a hatchway that had clearly been open for so long, corrosion would not allow it to be sealed again.

The deck beneath them shuddered. All the loose chains and hanging filaments in the dock swayed and clanked. Every weapon in the party rose ready.

'Don't panic,' said Lucic, 'the House just took a step to steady itself. Get used to the sensation.'

The hatch led through into a service tunnel where the lights had long since burned dead, or had been robbed out for spares. Their weaving lamp beams caught strange surface mottling on the walls, but it wasn't rust.

'Look at this,' said Carl, training his lamp. The area of wall he was illuminating was entirely covered in a curious, tight patterning that appeared to have been etched. As he moved the beam around slowly, they could see that the pattern covered everything.

'What is that?' Kys asked, leaning close.

'Fingerprints,' said Angharad.

'No, it can't–'

'Fingerprints,' the Carthaen repeated.

'She's right,' Ravenor said, his transponder a dry rattle in the darkness beside them. 'Human fingerprints.'

The prints were life size, packed in so close to each other that barely a scrap of wall remained unmarked. They looked as if they had been left by thousands upon thousands of finger touches, but the touch of a fingertip did not excise its shape perfectly into bare metal in miniature bas-relief.

'They must have been engraved,' said Carl, 'but the workmanship is astonishing. Who has the time to engrave so many individual, perfect marks?'

'This is the House,' Lucic replied, in an annoyingly off-hand way.

'What's really astonishing,' said Ravenor, 'is that every single print is different.'

A ripple of deep unease ran through them. For the first time, Ravenor felt the inscrutable Angharad register a scintilla of fear.

THE SERVICE TUNNEL continued on for thirty metres and opened into a wide, drum-shaped chamber. This was also unlit. Their lamp beams revealed a rickety metal spiral staircase against one wall, leading up into the shadows to a roof hatch. The centre of the chamber was occupied by a cargo hoist, a cage of machinery surrounding a low, rectangular plinth crusted in filth and oil residue. Above it in the ceiling, the dim space of a riser shaft yawned like a throat. The rest of the chamber was cluttered with metal litter and rusting machine junk. There were two other doors, both of them sealed forever by rust and decay.

Like the service tunnel, every part of the chamber's walls was covered with fingerprints.

'Do we go up?' asked Nayl.

'We wait,' said Lucic.

'For what?'

'Just wait. We can't rush them. This is their party now.'

They waited in edgy silence. The House rocked gently again, as it took another adjusting step.

'This–' said Plyton.

'Shhhhhh!' said Nayl. He was gazing up into the open darkness of the riser shaft above them.

A light came on far above them. It was thin and washy, a dirty fuzz of yellow radiance that penetrated only very faintly to their level. There was a distant, muffled thump of heavy gear, then a grinding noise. The hoist was descending.

It came down the shaft slowly, bringing the wash of light with it. The hoist was an open-sided, rectangular platform that matched exactly the dimensions of the plinth at the foot of the shaft. It lowered into view and settled with a resounding metal clang. Half a dozen mismatched oil lamps and bottle tapers stood on the platform, higgeldy-piggeldy, shedding their dirty, smoky glow. A figure stood in their midst, short, slender, like a youth or a child. The figure was shrouded in a hooded, floor-length cloak, and no face could be detected under the cowl. Ravenor hesitated from scanning. He did not want to provoke the residents of the House.

The figure wore an old, large, rusty key on a ribbon around its neck. It looked like the sort of antique key that might have once opened the gatehouse of a pre-Heresy bastion.

The figure gazed at them.

'These people come seeking coherence,' Lucic called out, taking a step forward. There was a nervous tremor in his voice. 'I am their guide.'

For a brief moment, there was a murmur of voices in the air around them, an unintelligible flutter of whispering, hissing voices, overlapped and urgent.

Then it died away. The figure raised its left hand and beckoned them onto the hoist platform with a single, slow gesture.

As Ravenor steered his chair onto the platform, he knew he'd just tasted the first, undeniable trace of the Wych House's psykcraft.

TEN

THE HOIST CARRIED them slowly up eighty metres of rusty riser shaft into a vast circular theatre that was lit around its edges by thousands of candles and lamps. The floor was formed of metal grille plates, and arranged on a split level, with a raised ring walkway around the outside of the chamber divided by an iron handrail from a circular central floor space. There were several heavy duty hatches at intervals around the chamber walls.

The hoist platform brought them up on the edge of the inner floor space. Above them, at the limits of the candlelight, the theatre chamber's domed roof was a mass of support girders and heavy black frames in shadow.

They looked around, assessing their circumstances. Their weapons were sheathed and holstered, so as not to cause problems, but they were ready.

Angharad glanced at Nayl and nodded across the chamber. On the far side from the hoist, the room's raised ring walkway had a broad set of seven metal steps set into its lip, virtually identical to the set that rose from the centre floor space to the ring walkway itself. This upper set interrupted the encircling handrail and jutted out into the chamber over the inner floor space, leading to nothing.

They'd all seen it. Nayl glanced up into the roof's shadows. Was there something concealed up there that required step access when it descended?

The robed figure walked off the platform onto the lower level. They followed, halting as the figure stopped and turned to face them again.

'Hell's teeth!' Nayl growled.

A dozen more hooded figures, identical to the first, were suddenly standing on the raised walkway above them, staring down. They'd heard no hatch open. There had been no flicker of the candles. Each of the newcomers had a key around its neck, but no two keys were identical.

'Someone say something,' Plyton whispered. 'The tension is killing me.'

Another flutter of sighing, hissing voices breathed around them. Ravenor tentatively reached out with his mind. The situation was precarious, but he dared not wait any longer. Immediately, he encountered a strong background aura of psychic activity. The place was alive with it, as if it saturated the walls and the deck. It was resonating in a slow, gentle pulse, like breathing, but it wasn't coming from the hooded figures. They were utterly blank and inert to his inspection. The aura was around them all, as if they stood within a vast, psy-active mind.

Or as if the ocean outside was alive.

'I have come seeking coherence,' Ravenor said. Lucic made no objection. He stood back.

'I have come seeking coherence,' Ravenor repeated.

The figure that had brought them up on the hoist had walked slowly up the steps to join the others of its kind on the raised walkway.

'Do you have names? Voices?' Ravenor asked.

'We have both,' said one of the figures. Its speech was audible and precise, though little more than a murmur in volume. The voice seemed young too, although it was impossible to tell whether it was male or female.

'Will you tell me your names?' Ravenor asked.

'Will you tell us yours?'

'Is that essential for our transaction?'

'No,' said another of the figures, 'though to receive accurate coherence, you must be truly known. This is not our function. It is up to the House to know you.'

'What is your function?'

'We are merely housekeepers.'

'I see, and how will the House know me?'

'It is learning already. You may speed the process by explaining your incoherence.'

Ravenor swung his chair around and faced Plyton. 'Maud?'

'Sir?'

'I'd like you to escort Mr Lucic back down the hoist to our craft and watch over him there.'

'Wait–' Lucic began.

'Does our guide need to be here any longer?' Ravenor asked the hooded figures.

'His function is complete.'

'The housekeepers have spoken, Lucic,' Ravenor told the prospector. 'I thank you for your services of guidance and introduction, but I don't want you around while this is happening. Remove yourself, stay with the underboat, and we can remain friends.'

Lucic glanced around, agitated and clearly unhappy. He knew he wasn't in a situation where he could put up an effective argument or fight. He forced a beaming grin onto his slender face, and bowed. 'Of course,' he said, 'I have no wish to fall out with you. Out here, a man needs all the friends he can get.'

Plyton gestured with the muzzle of the shotgun slung over her shoulder. 'Let's go,' she said.

+Watch him, Maud.+

Plyton nodded. She was still not used to directly sent thoughts. She followed Lucic onto the hoist platform, pulled the lever, and they slowly dropped below the floor.

Ravenor turned back to face the housekeepers.

'Explain what I can do in more detail.'

'Describe the parameters of your incoherence, in plain terms,' one of the housekeepers replied. 'Allow the House to know you.'

'And how is coherence communicated?'

'The right key opens the right door,' said a housekeeper.

Ravenor's companions exchanged troubled looks.

Ravenor rolled his chair forward until he was directly beneath the watching housekeepers on the raised walkway. 'I seek coherence,' he announced, as if speaking not to them but to the chamber as a whole. 'My name is Gideon Ravenor. There's no point hiding that. I am searching for someone... a great enemy of mine, there's no point hiding that fact either. He has eluded me for a long time, and driven me into a state of near ruin in my efforts to find him. The stars are a vast place, and he could be anywhere. I decided it would be better to search for something or someone that could tell me where and how to find him, than to spend lifetimes searching for him fruitlessly. The Wych House of Utochre has a great and ancient reputation for prediction. It is said the House's accuracy in such matters is extraordinary. In my past life, I was an Imperial inquisitor and a loyal servant of the Ordos Helican. To seek out the guidance and psykcraft of a place such as this would have been deemed the act of a radical or a heretic. It would not have been remotely condoned by the men I called my masters. But I am rogue now, and desperate, and I am acting outside the scope, knowledge and permission of the Holy Inquisition. I am no longer an inquisitor. Perhaps I am damned, but I'll surely be damned if I don't know.'

The whispering voices of the House billowed around them. They reminded Kys uncomfortably of the rushing wings of the sheen birds at Petropolis. She was fighting the desire to weep. Ravenor's spoken admission, even if it had been uttered with unnecessary emphasis to convince the Wych House, had been painful to hear. *I am no longer an inquisitor. Perhaps I am damned.*

Perhaps they were all damned.

'The one I seek goes by the name of Zygmunt Molotch,' Ravenor said.

The voices swirled, their whispers becoming more sibilant and sharp. They streamed around Ravenor like an eddying wind, like the frail sighs of phantoms.

Now they could all hear what the voices were saying.

Molotch, Molotch, Molotch...

AT THE BASE of the riser shaft, down in the gloom, Plyton led Lucic off the platform. She turned, dragged back the lever, and allowed the empty platform to trundle back up the shaft.

'How do we get back up?' Lucic asked.

'Please Throne we don't have to,' Plyton replied. They both carried oil lamps taken from the platform. By the light of hers, Plyton indicated the spiral staircase. 'That's got to lead up somewhere,' she said, 'if needs be, but they need to hoist more than we do. Come on.'

They walked back along the service tunnel towards the docking pool.

'So, you're Maud,' said Lucic lightly.

'Don't talk to me,' she replied.

They stepped back out into the gloomy wharf area, amongst the hanging, rusty chainwork and rotting machinery. The underboat sat quietly below them, moored against the wharf's fenders by the heavy sea chains Lucic had fixed. The underboat's top and side hatches were still open, and pale electric light shone out.

'Checking in,' Plyton said into her link.

The pilot servitor's voice crackled back an acknowledgement.

'Well, we could be in for a long wait,' Lucic said, sitting down on the pier's edge so his feet dangled over the drop into the pool. He set the lamp down beside him. 'How will we pass the time if not in friendly conversation, Maud?'

'Don't talk to me,' she replied.

ELEVEN

'I HAVE A theory,' Carl said.

'About?' Ravenor asked.

'About how this place might work,' Carl said. They were still waiting down on the theatre's lower space. The housekeepers had not moved or spoken, not even when the empty hoist returned. The flutter of whispers came and went like a breeze.

'Go on,' Ravenor prompted.

'I don't think it's the House itself. There might be some active material or device here that acts as a focus, but I think what really matters is where the House is.'

'Interesting. Go on.'

'I think it's the ocean. I think it's the ocean itself. Somehow, that responds and resonates to...' he faltered. 'Actually, my theory is rather weak and open-ended.'

'I think you're halfway there,' said Ravenor. 'That's good reasoning, but you're not taking it far enough. I agree the ocean is part of it, functioning as a resonating medium, but I think the real secret is the moon itself.'

'Utochre?'

'Yes. How often do we find crystals or crystalline materials employed in divination and prediction? Sensing crystals, scrying crystals, crystals used to refract and focus psy-impulses?'

'Crystal balls?'

'Exactly. The technique and belief is as old as man, and we're not the only species to appreciate the method.'

'The eldar?'

'Precisely – the eldar. Mineral resonance. Let's face it, it wouldn't be wildly incorrect to define wraithbone as an organic gemstone. This moon is infamously rich in a

myriad different forms of crystal deposit. The Wych
House–'

'–uses Utochre as a gigantic crystal ball,' Carl said with
a grin. 'Am I close?'

'I don't know. If you are, it's a crude analogy, but those
are the lines I was thinking along.'

Carl looked pleased with himself.

'You were almost there ahead of me that time, interrogator. I soon won't be able to teach you anything.'

'The stuff I know,' Carl chuckled.

The fluttering whispers suddenly stopped. The abrupt
silence was a little unnerving. With a shudder, the Wych
House adjusted its footing.

'The House is ready,' said one of the hooded figures.

'Step up onto this level,' instructed another. Ravenor
guided his chair up over the lower steps onto the raised
walkway, and his companions followed obediently until
they all stood, waiting, beside the housekeepers.

They heard a rapid series of metal clanks and the
whine of hydraulics. Slowly, ponderously, a broad, circular platform descended from the domed roof space on
heavy telescopic stanchions. The platform fitted concen-
trically over the lower floor space but was several metres
smaller in diameter. It lowered until it was precisely as far
above the level of the raised walkway as the walkway was
above the lower floor, creating a third tier to the chamber.
The edge of the circular platform met the top of the steps
jutting up and out from the raised circuit, and locked in
place with a thump of mag-bolts. There was enough
headroom beneath it for a man to descend to the lower
floor space and walk around without ducking.

The circular platform was a thick and pitted disc of
iron or steel with the six elevator stanchions, each one
currently at full extension, rising like columns at regular
intervals around its rim. Above it, black girders and the
beams of the dome space slowly became illuminated by

the gradually intensifying ghost glare of a dozen photo-lumin lamps.

The open space of the platform was empty apart from a single object: a half-open door, held upright in the centre of the platform by its frame. The door was old and made of wood, a very ordinary old door in a very ordinary frame.

They all stared at it for a moment. Above them, the House altered its foothold once again, and the motion caused the old door to swing back and forth in its frame slightly, as if blown by a breeze. It thumped to, and then swung open a hand's breadth ajar.

'I give in, what is it?' asked Nayl.

'A door,' replied Angharad, who, Ravenor had found, could always be relied upon for a prosaic answer.

'A door,' Carl echoed. 'Could it be what I think it is?'

'It rather depends on what you think it is, Carl,' Ravenor replied.

The housekeepers moved past them in procession, carrying lamps up the steps onto the door platform and arranging them around the edges of the disc. Ravenor lifted up onto the platform too and approached the door. The others slowly followed him.

'A propylaeum tripartite?' Thonius ventured, speaking in hushed tones. 'A... tri-portal?'

'That was my thought,' Ravenor said. 'Again, your deduction is excellent. As is your knowledge of abstruse lore and esoterica. Where have you come across the concept?'

Carl shrugged. 'I remember finding references to the idea in study, years ago. I can't... I can't remember the reference.'

'Sarnique's *Codex Atrox*,' Ballack said quietly, 'and also *The Ochre Book*.' He looked around at Ravenor and Thonius. 'Access to such works is restricted but, like Carl, I have made use of my interrogator status for the purpose of study. Three years ago, working with Inquisitor Fenx on Mirepoix, we were called to investigate a cult, which, it was claimed, operated a functional propylaeum tripartite. It proved to be a hoax, but I did my research. This design matches the woodcuts in Sarnique's work.'

'Sarnique,' Thonius nodded, 'that's the fellow.'

'Are we supposed to believe this is a genuine tri-portal?' Ballack asked, walking around to the far side of the door frame so they could see him through the half-open door.

'Anyone fancy, I dunno,' Nayl murmured, 'telling me what you're talking about?'

'Carl? Ballack?' Ravenor asked.

Thonius took a step forward until he was on the opposite side of the door to Ballack. He approached it gingerly. The door thumped slightly and loosely in its frame, as if caught by a persistent breeze.

'A propylaeum tripartite,' Carl said.

'You keep saying that,' Nayl chided.

'A three-way door,' Carl Thonius corrected with a disdainful look at the heavy bounty-man. 'A mythical device of augury and divination. Its manner of function has never been explained, not even in psionic terms, though it may simply be a totem for psychic focus. An elaborate fetish.'

'How does it work?' asked Kys. 'I mean... in what way does it work?'

'It has one side here,' said Thonius.

'And a second here,' said Ballack, from the other side of the door. 'But if one passes through the door...' Ballack hesitated. Neither he nor Thonius showed any willingness to perform that act. 'Well, Kys, it is said that one finds a third side. A third way. The door transports the subject to another location in space-time entirely, a site where the answer to a specific question of augury may be learned.'

'A portal?' asked Kys.

Ballack shrugged.

'Yes, a portal,' said Ravenor. 'The door is said to be able to convey a subject elsewhere. In fact, to more than one place, depending on the sequence of use and the complexity of the answer sought after.'

He swung his chair away from the door. The others grouped around him. 'I wasn't expecting this,' Ravenor said, 'which was foolish of me. Unless it proved to be fraudulent, the Wych House was always going to contain a truly dark secret. This is what we came all this way to find. I just don't like the idea of using it.'

'Me neither,' said Thonius.

'I'm still struggling with the basic concept,' Nayl admitted.

'It's just an old wooden door,' Angharad repeated, leadenly.

'We have to use it.'

They all turned to regard Kys. She was watching the housekeepers set out the fluttering lamps and tapers around the rim of the platform. 'We've come all this way, like you said. We've broken every rule we care about. We knew we would be tampering with the dark, the heretical. I don't like this one bit, but we're in it now. We're committed.'

'What are you suggesting?' Thonius asked her.

'What are you suggesting?' Kys snapped back. 'Do we turn away? Go home? Give up? If we were going to do that, Throne help me, we should have done it months ago. We've come too far to get squeamish now.'

+You're right, Patience. Thank you for being the voice of reason.+

+I don't feel very reasonable.+

'We're doing this,' Ravenor said. 'Well, some of us are. I won't risk the entire group. I need to leave someone here to cover our backs.'

'That's assuming,' said Angharad archly, 'that this isn't just an old wooden door flapping in the breeze.'

'Assuming that it isn't,' said Ravenor. 'Perhaps you'd like to come with me and find out? Ballack, Carl you too, please. Harlon, you and Patience stay put and keep watch over this flapping door.'

A dark look crossed Nayl's face. He glanced at the swordswoman. 'No, I–' he began. He stopped short.

+She'll be fine with me, Harlon, I promise. I'll take care of her. Besides, she can take care of herself. And her mind is wonderfully strong, marvellously resilient. There is a great deal of unworldliness she can withstand.+

Nayl glowered. 'But–'

+I need your strength here. I need Kys here too, as a psychic link. Don't argue, Nayl.+

'I'd never argue with you.'

+Harlon, I know how much you care about the Carthaen. I know everything. I will protect her.+

Nayl nodded, grudgingly. He caught Angharad's eye and made the fist-to-sternum punch salute of the clans. She returned it.

Ravenor caught Kys's mind intimately. +I'll try casting to you.+

+I'll be listening for you.+

+Keep us grounded, Patience.+

+I will.+

THE ENTIRE RIM of the platform was by then flickering with candles and lamps. More lamps had been brought out onto the raised walkway too. The theatre chamber's overhead lights dimmed to a slight glimmer.

The flutter of whispering voices swirled around them once more, for the first time in half an hour. The moment they ceased, the door slammed shut tight with a loud bang, and they heard the ancient lock turn.

'The House is ready for you,' said one of the house-keepers.

'The door is ready to be unlocked,' said another. They stood in a ragged circle around Ravenor's team on the disc.

'Who has the right key?' asked Ravenor.

Another chilling murmur of whispers.

One of the housekeepers stepped forward, taking hold of the key it wore around its neck.

'I do,' the housekeeper said. The other housekeepers muttered softly, as if congratulating the chosen one.

'Who goes and who stays?' asked another of the hooded figures.

'I'm staying,' replied Kys.

'Me too,' Nayl grunted. The housekeeper motioned for them to follow. All but the chosen housekeeper processed slowly off the upper platform onto the walkway below. Kys walked after them. She paused and looked back.

'The Emperor protects,' she called out.

+Not this time, I'm afraid.'+

'Then you protect, Gideon,' she said. She turned and walked down the steps.

Nayl moved to go after her. He stopped, and then strode deliberately back to Angharad and kissed her roughly on the lips. 'Damn it,' he growled. 'I want to see you all again alive. Even you, Thonius.'

'I'll be counting the minutes, dear heart,' Carl grinned back.

Nayl turned and plodded across the platform towards the steps.

He thumped down them and stood beside Kys, amongst the silent housekeepers, gazing up onto the door platform.

'So, you and the warrior woman,' Kys whispered.

'Shut it.'

'How long has that been going on?'

'Two words, Kys. Shut the frig up.'

'My lips are sealed,' she smirked. 'Unlike yours. Or hers.'

He glared at her. She pointed up at the platform. 'You're missing the show,' she told him.

She turned to watch. Despite her smile, she had started to pray.

'ARE YOU CONTENT to begin?' asked the housekeeper beside the door.

'Oh, I can't wait,' said Thonius. Angharad looked bored. Ballack rested his good hand on the grip of his holstered weapon.

'We are content,' Ravenor replied.

The housekeeper removed the key from around its neck and slid it into the door's ancient lock. The key turned with a loud, unlubricated clack.

The door opened.

Thonius snorted. Through the open frame, they could see the other side of the platform disc, the uninterrupted ring of the flickering lamps and tapers.

'I'm really impressed so far,' Thonius remarked.

+Quiet!+

'This way,' the housekeeper instructed, ushering them through the open doorway.

They stepped forward.

The door slammed behind them and locked itself.

NAYL TURNED TO stare at Kys. She was wide-eyed, startled, terrified.

'Holy living shit,' Nayl said. 'Did you see?'

'I saw,' said Kys.

They'd watched their comrades and the chosen house-keeper step through the door, watched the door slam.

Now there was nothing at all on the platform except the closed and locked door.

* * *

TWELVE

'WHAT WAS THAT?' Plyton asked, getting up suddenly.

'What was what?' asked Lucic. He had been playing jacks on his coat spread out across the grille deck of the dock.

'Like a door,' Plyton replied, raising her shotgun. 'Like a door slamming somewhere.'

'The House is old, and full of noises,' the scrawny prospector remarked. 'Get used to it.'

She ignored him, walked the length of the dock to the hatchway and shone her lamp pack up the service tunnel. Nothing stirred. She opened her link.

'Checking in,' she called.

'Nothing to report,' the pilot servitor crackled back from the docked underboat. She retraced her steps through the spooky shadows of the corroded machinery. The dock lights flickered slightly as the House took another step. Chains rocked and swung.

Lucic was sitting where she'd left him.

'What are you doing?' she asked sharply.

'Playing jacks,' he replied.

'You were doing something with your coat!' she snapped, aiming the shotgun.

'Yes, Maud. I was playing jacks on my coat!' He gazed at her with his bulging, thyroid eyes, his skinny face comically honest.

'All right then,' she said, lowering her weapon and sitting back down on a rusting coil winder.

'You're awful jumpy, Maud,' Lucic observed.

'Don't talk to me.'

I AM STRUCK by the distinct impression that Carl is about to say, 'I told you this was a waste of time.'

'I told you this–' he begins. His voice fails him. Like all of us, he is looking around, dumbstruck, astonished.

I cannot believe it either. I reach out, with almost instinctive alarm, and sweep with my mind.

This is no lie. Or, if it is a lie, it is a lie impervious to the scrutiny of even a mind like mine.

We are no longer aboard the Wych House. We are no longer on Utochre or, I'll wager, in the Cyto system, or even in the Helican subsector. My chair's internal horolog has just failed, erased, and restarted. A condition of portal transit, perhaps, or an indication we are no longer even in the same year as the one we left.

It is stunning and awful and fundamentally disconcerting. I look at Ballack, open-mouthed, gazing into the distance; at Carl, bending down to touch the hot, dry dust; at Angharad, narrowing her eyes and slowly drawing her Carthaen steel. Only the housekeeper, holding onto its wretched key, seems unperturbed. The hot wind flaps the housekeeper's dark robes.

'Everybody all right?' I ask.

We are standing in a sweltering dust bowl of gritty red dunes, surrounded by an ominous ring of jagged, black volcanic outcrops. A strong desert wind drives the dust up at us, and I hear it pattering off the shell of my chair. The sky is a red haze of sickly light and whorled cloud banks. There is a star, flaring and wounded, blood-red like a gunshot wound to the sky.

I have no idea where we are.

I rotate my chair slowly, pict recording every millimetre of our surroundings on my chair's internal recorders. I use the chair's systems to sample the dust, the regolith and the air, and ping out with my internal auspex. This is a dead place. The air temperature is soaring and the rocks around us radiate hellish heat.

This is real. This isn't a dream, or a vision, or an autoseance trance. This is real, and I have to get used to that fact fast or lose my sanity.

The door is behind me, standing anachronistically in the middle of nowhere, tall and firm and closed tight. I watch Ballack move around it in a circle. He tries the handle, and finds it locked.

'Master–' he says to me. He has seldom called me that. He must be very afraid.

I circle the door myself, my chair's impellers gusting up eddies of dust. I go right around it. It is as solid and real as the new world around us. Shut tight, one side baking in the alien sun's glare, the other dark in shadow. The door itself casts a long, oblong shadow across the red dust.

'Oh, Throne,' Carl whines.

'I would like to know where...' Angharad says, her sword in her hand. 'I would like to know exactly... I mean... where…?'

+Be calm.+

'I want to know where we are!' Angharad snarls, glancing at the housekeeper.

+Calm!+

I send a wave of reassurance into her, and stop her in her tracks before she has the housekeeper by the throat.

'Is this the place?' I ask. 'Is this the place where I find my answer?'

'Well, I don't see Molotch anywhere around, so I'm guessing no,' Carl whines.

'It won't be that simple,' I tell him. 'Will it, housekeeper?'

'This is just the first step,' the housekeeper replies in that oh-so androgynous way they have. 'The first step. Your question was convoluted. The door will have to open several times, I believe.'

'Then why are we here?' Carl demands.

+Calm!+ I send again, to Carl this time.

'This is a place the House wanted to show you. I don't know why,' the housekeeper says. 'I am not told such things. It is not my function.'

'What happens now?' Ballack asks. Of all of them, he has kept his head the best.

'We wait,' says our hooded guide.

'I don't want to wait,' Angharad says quickly. 'I don't want to stay here. Something's coming.'

'I sense nothing,' I say, checking.

'I see nothing,' adds Ballack.

'Something's coming,' Angharad insists, 'something bad. Evisorex can taste it.' The long steel is twitching in her hands. It is taking her trained double grip to contain it.

'Over that ridge,' she says. I regard the ridge she has indicated, a long, low line of black basalt rising from the dunes like rotted teeth from a gum. I sense nothing, but there seems to be a gathering pall of dust closing in behind the wild outcrop.

'For Throne's sake!' Carl snaps. 'I want to get out of here! Can we get out of here? Please?'

'Calm down and–'

Then I feel it. I feel what they're all feeling: doom, a creeping, penetrating sense of doom and fear, as intolerable as the pervasive red light. It pulls at my mind, dark, like a shadow in the warp.

'I don't like this,' says Ballack.

'Housekeeper?'

'We must wait for the door,' the housekeeper replies.

'Damn the door! Damn the frigging door!' Carl cries. He throws himself at it, banging his hands against the wood and rattling the handle with futile effort. 'Oh, Throne, master!'

He races around to the other side and tries again. 'Let us back! Let us through!'

'Stop it, Carl. Stop it now.'

But Carl Thonius won't stop it. The fear has gripped him. He hammers and hammer and hammers–

IN THE THEATRE chamber, still and quiet, Kys glanced at Nayl. 'Did you hear that?' she asked.

They both looked at the door.

'Nothing. Just the House settling again.'

'No,' she said. 'Didn't you hear the banging? Like someone thumping on the other side of the door?'

'No,' he replied, without confidence. As they watched, the door's handle rotated to and fro, as if someone, somewhere, was trying to open it.

'Shit!' said Nayl, stepping forward. Kys stopped him.

'There's nothing we can do except wait,' she told him.

+CARL!+

Ravenor's command pulled him back from the door. He was sweating profusely from the overwhelming heat and the fear. 'Sorry,' he said. 'Sorry.'

'Housekeeper?' Ravenor asked.

The housekeeper waited a moment or two longer, and then stepped forward and fitted the key back into the lock.

It turned, and the door reopened.

'This way,' the housekeeper said.

They hurried through the doorway and let it slam shut behind them. Ravenor heard it lock again.

Their body sweat turned clammy on their backs in an instant. Even more than before, they were overwhelmed by the sensation of being somewhere utterly and completely else. Not just because of the light and temperature conditions, but because of the infinitesimally altered pull of gravity, the imperceptible change of air pressure, the smell, the pheromone of the place.

Ballack drew his weapon. He glanced around. They were inside a stone cloister of Imperial Gothic construction. It was old, and eroded by time and weather. They could all hear the bash of ocean breakers striking an invisible shore nearby. It was dark, night. Stars were out in the clear black sky.

'Master?' Thonius whispered.

Ravenor was trying to reset his chair's internal horolog. Its jumping readings were nonsense.

'Master!'

Ravenor turned his perception outwards and scanned the location. 'I know this,' he said.

'The door is locked,' announced Angharad. The door stood behind them in the dim cloister, strange and out of place. 'It's locked from either side,' she added, having tried both.

'Those stars,' Ravenor said.

Carl looked up. 'I... I don't know them.'

'But we should,' said Ravenor. 'I'm checking them against my data coils, trying to find a match. 'Wait, wait...'

'We're in the Ordo Malleus chapter house on Gudrun,' said Ballack. He turned to look at them. 'I wish I could claim some clever insight, sir, but it's written here on the wall.'

Ballack showed them the ancient, faded plaque.

'But this is a ruin,' said Thonius.

They moved out along the cloister and into the crumbling, stunted wreckage of the chapter house that spread out across an overgrown headland. The place had been reduced to this state many years before. Weeds and climbing plants festooned the tumbled stones, twitching fretfully in the night wind off the sea.

'I was here a year ago!' Ballack cried. 'It was intact, I swear, it was intact and–'

'This isn't a year ago, or a year hence,' Ravenor said. 'I don't know when we are. I think the door is showing us some important consequence of fate. I believe we are in our own future.'

'Look–' said Angharad. Across the bay, where the night sea crashed relentlessly against a broken shore, they could see the desolate, empty silhouette of a great city.

It had been dead for many years.

'Great Throne of Terra,' Ravenor murmured. 'That's
Dorsay.'

He rotated his chair to face the housekeeper. 'Take us
back through the door,' he said.

'The door is not ready.'

'Take us back through the door! Now!'

THE DOOR OPENED and closed behind them again, thanks
to the housekeeper's key.

A summer evening waited on the other side. The
long, low rake of a recently harvested field stretched
down in the easy light towards a bank of hedges, with
trees beyond. A slowly fading sky above was ribboned
with white clouds that were just taking on the colours
of dusk.

A hundred metres away down the field, a plain wooden
chair sat forlorn amongst the hewn, dry strands of the
crop.

Birds sang, twittering overhead in the twilight and
chasing in the hedgerows. A few early stars had come out
on the depth of the sky.

A lone figure was toiling up the field towards the chair.

Ravenor turned his own chair and regarded his companions. They stood in front of the locked door, which
rose improbably from the field crest behind them.

'Stay here,' Ravenor instructed.

'But–' Ballack began.

'Stay here and do nothing unless I signal.'

He coasted away across the dead stubble and followed
the slope of the field down towards the lonely wooden
seat. The figure was approaching, walking up into the
twilight air with confidence and effort.

Ravenor approached the waiting chair. He stopped
short ten metres away. The residue of the harvested crop,
the remaining stalks, had been carefully raked and
twisted into a circle around the wooden chair. The circle

was five metres in diameter, with the wooden seat at its dead centre. Ravenor recognised the complex weaving and design of the circle's rim.

He hovered outside it, waiting, as the figure approached up the slope.

The figure arrived, stepped into the corn circle, and sat down on the chair. He was breathing hard. The legs of the old wooden chair rested unevenly in the loose soil, and set him at an angle.

'Well, hello,' the man on the chair said at last, dabbing at his brow with a handkerchief. He was a portly man in late middle age, dressed in a high-buttoned, green silk suit. His thick dark hair and beard were perfectly groomed. 'I was wondering when you'd get here. You are Gideon Ravenor, aren't you? Of course you are. So we meet, finally, face to face.'

He leaned forward. 'Uh, you do know who I am?'

'Yes,' said Ravenor.

'Excellent!' replied Orfeo Culzean. 'So, let's talk.'

THIRTEEN

MAUD PLYTON WAS pacing. Her footsteps rang up and down the docking pool's deck. Lucic watched her with some amusement.

She looked at her link wistfully, but for the umpteenth time decided she shouldn't disturb whatever was taking place in the upper chambers of the House.

She was slipping the link back in her coat pocket when she heard a muffled sound.

'What was that?' she demanded, turning to look at Lucic.

'What was what?' he grinned at her.

'I heard a noise.'

'This again? Maud, come on! You're so jumpy. You're getting quite paranoid.'

Plyton stepped towards him and brought the heavy combat shotgun up. 'I heard a noise,' she hissed, 'the trill-tone of a link.'

'You're imagining it.'

'Get up and back away,' she told him. Lucic rose, and took a few steps backwards down the dock. He left his coat spread out on the decking, the loose jack pieces scattered across it.

Keeping her eyes on Lucic, her gun raised in her right hand, she stooped and lifted the coat by the collar and threw it over on the decking.

'Hey!' Lucic cried. The jack pieces tumbled away across the deck, and most fell through the grille into the water below.

Kneeling, Plyton patted down the empty coat with her left hand, feeling into the pockets, her eyes never leaving the prospector.

'Stuff your "hey",' she said. Her left hand emerged from a deep pocket holding a worn, old link device. 'You lying bastard.'

'Oh, come on,' Lucic said. 'Since when was it against the rules to own a link?'

'Who were you talking to? Who were you signalling?'

Lucic didn't reply. His meagre mouth became tight and pinched below his blade of a nose. 'I don't know what you're talking about, Maud.' He looked down at the deck.

'Who was it, Lucic?'

He looked up at her again, a broad smile slowly extending across his face.

Without turning, she knew why. She went cold. She felt the muzzle of a weapon press against the back of her head.

'Like I keep saying,' said Lucic, stepping forward and taking the shotgun from her, 'out here, a man needs all the friends he can get.'

* * *

NAYL TOOK A strip of dry jerky from his pocket and tore off a chunk with his teeth. He offered the fistful of food to Kys. She shook her head.

'Waiting makes me hungry,' he said.

The door had been silent for over an hour. Nayl and Kys idled on the raised walkway, sometimes walking up onto the top platform to take a closer look at the door. The housekeepers had all remained as still as statues.

'So, you and Angharad?' Kys asked.

'It's a private thing.'

'A private thing for how long?'

'Does it matter?'

'Will it matter to Gideon?'

Nayl scowled. 'I don't want to hurt him, but it's none of his business.'

'You must have known it would matter to him, or you wouldn't have hidden it.'

'Shut up, Kys. You don't know anything.'

'You know I do.' She paused suddenly and looked away. 'Nayl–'

He was already reaching for his sidearm, but it was too late.

The heavy hatches around the theatre chamber's walls slammed open and figures surged in onto the raised walkway: a dozen grizzled, hard-bodied men in grubby combat armour and fur-trimmed hostile environment suits. They aimed their lascarbines and shotguns with a professional confidence that matched their stony expressions.

Nayl and Kys froze and slowly raised their hands. There was no cover, no room to resist. One of the men pushed the barrel of his carbine into Nayl's face while he reached over and confiscated the bounty hunter's sidearm.

'Who are you?' asked Nayl. None of them answered. Two of them were herding the housekeepers into a tight huddle. Meek, the housekeepers made no sound or any gesture of resistance.

'Watch the woman,' a voice echoed out across the chamber. Nayl and Kys turned. A large figure was walking around the circuit towards them, accompanied by two more hired guns. His carapace armour gleamed like mother of pearl in the lamp light. His head was a mass of livid scar tissue, with a bleached stripe of hair across his scalp. He held a psy-scanner in one gauntleted hand.

'She's telekinetic,' he said. He glared at Kys, and waved the scanner at her. 'One hint of psy, I'll know it, and you'll be dead.'

'Lucius frigging Worna,' Nayl growled.

The massive bounty hunter regarded Nayl. 'Long time, Nayl,' he said. 'I see you've fallen on hard times, scrabbling for dung work like this. Working for the Throne, brother. Shit, I'm disappointed in you. Gives our kind a bad name.'

'You do that all by yourself,' Nayl replied.

Kys stared at Lucius Worna. This was the callous monster who had tortured and mutilated Sholto Unwerth. The last they'd heard of him, he'd been working for the opposition. She had no doubt he still was, and that meant—

'What happens?' Nayl asked.

'Oh, it's happened already,' Worna replied. 'You tried a little gambit, but we outplayed you. We've won. You've lost. End of story.'

FOURTEEN

'So, this is a trap.'

Orfeo Culzean gestured around himself with both hands, indicating both the harvested field and the twilight sky. 'This? No, this is not a trap. This is a conversation.'

'But the Wych House, the three-way door... that was a trap,' Ravenor said.

Culzean chuckled. 'Trap this, trap that, trap, trap, trap! I suppose it must be the inquisitor in you that makes you so very suspicious all the time, Gideon. May I call you Gideon, incidentally?'

'You may not. I watch for traps all the time because Zygmunt Molotch is supremely gifted at setting them, and he's caught me more than once before.'

Culzean thought about that. 'Well,' he said gently, 'if it is a trap, it would be safe to conclude you're not getting any better at spotting them, are you?'

'I've never underestimated Molotch's guile,' Ravenor replied. 'The only thing I seem to keep underestimating is his talent for coming back from the dead.' He scanned around gently. On his seat in the warded ring of corn, Culzean was a blank. There were human life signs in the woods behind him, support, no doubt, but too far away to be an immediate threat. Thonius, Ballack and Angharad remained at the top of the hilly field, watching from beside the door.

'Where is Molotch?' Ravenor asked. 'Is he too afraid to face me himself?'

'Where is Molotch? That's the question, isn't it. The big question, the one you came to Utochre to answer. I think the door's done a splendid job of answering you. It's brought you here. Molotch is close by, but I am much better at this kind of negotiation. I don't know how much you know about me?'

'Enough not to underestimate you either. But you're not like Molotch. You're a different breed of evil altogether. A facilitator. A mercenary. A prostitute–'

'Well, let's not bandy semantics, shall we?' Culzean frowned. 'This should be amicable. A conversation between peers.'

Birds sang high in the darkening sky above them. Their songs seemed painfully innocent to Ravenor.

'You have arranged all this so we can talk?' Ravenor asked.

'No, actually,' replied Culzean. He settled back. 'It's quite the most curious thing. It arranged itself. Oh, I had to make a few judicious improvements and alterations so it would all run smoothly, but generally, this just happened.' His eyes sparkled with enthusiastic cunning. 'That's just amazing, isn't it? That's why I decided we had to talk.'

'So talk.'

Culzean nodded and brushed corn chaff off the hem of his jacket. 'To business then. I'll keep it simple. You have been chasing Zygmunt Molotch for a long time, and with due cause, I will admit. If I was an Imperial inquisitor – perish the thought! – I would have made it my life's work to hunt him down too. The pair of you dance and dance around each other, jabbing and sparring, daring and thwarting. You've done it for years. You'll be doing it forever, I believe, unless someone intervenes and brings matters to a head.'

'Is that someone you?'

'In part. Working on Zygmunt's behalf, I have discovered some strange facts, Gideon. I found out things I don't think either of you are aware of.'

'Such as?'

'The pair of you are bound by destiny. Bound by a single, shared destiny.'

'That's merely a fanciful and melodramatic way of describing my ongoing prosecution of the heretic Zygmunt Molotch. If that's the best you can–'

'Whoa, whoa!' Culzean said, raising a hand. 'Settle down. I mean it literally, as it happens. Right at the start, the first time you met, something happened that spliced you together in a grand, cosmic design.'

'And what is that design?'

'Ah, that's why I wanted to talk to you.'

'This is just nonsense. Make your play if you're going to. My people are ready.' Ravenor cast out a simple command and, on the crest of the hill behind him, his three companions drew their weapons.

'I don't want to fight you,' said Culzean. 'That's the point. All the time we're fighting each other we're missing what's really important. And what's really important is Slyte.'

Ravenor paused. 'You have two minutes, Culzean.'

Culzean licked his lips and smiled. 'You came all the way to Utochre because you believed it was the only way you'd find out where Zygmunt was hiding. A good plan. A very good plan, in fact, because Zygmunt had the very same idea. When we made our exit from Tancred, Zygmunt decided that the only way he could ever be safe from you, truly safe, was to consult the future and find out your part in it. He wanted coherence too. Isn't that funny? Both of you deciding to take precisely the same course of action?'

He leaned forward and tapped an index finger against his temple. 'It's because you think the same way. Bound in destiny, remember?'

Ravenor didn't reply.

'We arrived at Utochre about three weeks ahead of you. I made the appropriate arrangements, and secured us a consultation at the Wych House. And what was the first thing we found out when the door opened? That you were coming to the Wych House too, hell-bent on the same scheme. That took me aback, I can tell you. Zygmunt, for his part, was delighted. He was all for setting a final and very nasty trap for you. And we've established his penchant for traps already. But I talked him out of it. The whole thing fascinated me, piqued my facilitator's mind. I think along different lines to Zygmunt, you see. We perceive different patterns, which is why we complement each other. Zygmunt saw it all as moves in a great game, you and he as pieces on a regicide board, one stratagem out stepping the next, blah bla-blah. But I was scared.'

'Scared?'

'Of the implications. There are coincidences and there are coincidences. A great deal can be dismissed on the basis of your shared history and experiences. You have similar knowledge, similar talents and, although it's a blood rivalry, you walk in similarly dark places. Both of you simultaneously decide to come to the Wych House? I can accept that. Coincidence. But what brought you both to Eustis Majoris? What brought you to the other worlds where you've clashed?'

'We're antagonists, Culzean. I'm hunting him. It's not hard to grasp.'

'What about Tancred? Of all the places in the sector, you tracked him to Tancred. We left no trail that you could have followed. What brought you there? A hunch?'

Again, Ravenor didn't answer.

'I'm right, aren't I?' smiled Culzean. He stroked his beard. 'A hunch. A hunch here, a little intuition there, a handful of happenstance and accident. Doesn't it scare you too, just a little bit?'

'What's your explanation? And don't say shared destiny.'

'This is what I decided to find out. I sat down with Zygmunt and interviewed him over a period of days. He'd told me of your past encounters already, but I wanted to hear them from him again, every last detail. He kindly and patiently told me everything, and that's when I saw it. Clear as day. The way the two of you had been bound.'

He rose to his feet and walked around the wooden chair, staying within the corn ring. 'You have been bound by the forces of the warp, Gideon, bound together to accomplish a great task. Neither of you realises you're being used. Left to your own devices, I doubt either of you would have ever realised it. Apart, perhaps, for one brief, gurgling moment of insight as death claimed you. The warp has chosen you, selected you both carefully, and set you about its work. Without realising it, as you wage your sporadic bloody squabble down the years, you are acting as facilitators. As midwives.'

'For Slyte,' Ravenor said.

Culzean clapped his hands. 'Sharp as a new crown! I knew I wouldn't be disappointed in you, Gideon. Yes, for Slyte. The Ruinous Powers want Slyte to be born. Don't ask me why, because they don't copy me on their meetings–' Culzean snorted at his own words. 'But you can bet it's going to be bloody horrible.'

'The birth of Slyte was predicted,' said Ravenor uneasily. 'The Fratery predicted it. You were there, Culzean. The hour has passed. The prophesy was unfulfilled.'

'Was it? Was it really?' Culzean looked at Ravenor as if he knew something. 'Or has it already happened? Or... look at it this way, Gideon. The birthing of a daemon in our reality is likely to be a long and protracted labour. There will be complications. If, let's agree for a moment, you and Zygmunt have been obliviously working towards this end since the first day you met, then the birth pangs have lasted, what, sixty years already?'

'Sixty-six, if you're right.'

'Not an easy birth,' Culzean mused, 'not an easy birth at all.'

'How are you suggesting the Ruinous Powers bound us, Culzean? Explain how I could have been used by the Archenemy for so long without realising it? I am no one's pawn.'

'Please, no pawn ever realises he or she is a pawn,' said Culzean. 'And look at you. You've broken from the ordos, gone rogue, and come to Utochre hunting heretical divination. You're not exactly pure.'

'How did the warp bind us?' Ravenor repeated.

Culzean waved his hands in frustration. 'At your first meeting, Sleef Outworld. I haven't got time to fill in all the blanks for you, Gideon. You're smart. You figure it out. We've got more important things to consider right here.'

'Like?'

'Like the very purpose of this meeting.' He paused. 'I'm proposing a truce. A pooling of resources towards a common goal.'

'A truce? That's a spectacularly unlikely notion, Culzean. In fact, it sounds to me very much like the groundwork of one of Molotch's elaborate traps.'

'If we wanted you dead,' said Culzean, 'you'd have been dead by now. We've kept you alive because there's a good chance you and Zygmunt need each other. You need to come together to defy the Ruinous Powers and stop Slyte.'

Ravenor rolled his chair back a little way. 'Tell me, Culzean, why would a fiend like Molotch even want to stop Slyte? It sounds like the sort of thing he would ordinarily be working his fingers to the bone to accomplish.'

Culzean sat down again. 'You don't really understand us, do you, Gideon? You don't really understand our beliefs and our ambitions. We're just evil, an evil to be stopped. And all evil is the same to you. It carries the same weight... me, Zygmunt, Slyte. You're so blinkered.' He stared at Ravenor intently. 'You've been through the door, Gideon. I'll wager it showed you a future or two. Pleasant?'

'Inconclusive. But no, not pleasant.'

'I know what Zygmunt and I saw when we went through the door. A galaxy in flames. An age of apocalypse. Daemon time. No Imperium except a burning shell populated by the last dying dregs of mankind. You don't want that, I know you don't. You've spent your life defending society against just such a doom. We don't want it either. Our ambitions are wildly different to yours, Gideon, and in definite conflict. But Zygmunt and I can only flourish, prosper and achieve our own goals so long as the Imperium persists. The Imperium is our playground, mankind our instrument. We weave our schemes through the complex fabric of Imperial life, to benefit ourselves. I'm not pretending you'd like what we want from our lives, but it would be nothing compared to Daemon time. Slyte must be stopped. The alternative is too awful for any of us to contemplate.'

'A truce,' Ravenor said. 'Molotch and I, working together, to defy the bond and destroy Slyte? This is what you're proposing?'

Culzean nodded. 'If you agree, Gideon, I'll send you back through the door to Utochre. I'll arrange for a message to be sent to you at Berynth, giving you this location. This world where we're sitting now. You bring your people here, and we start to plan in earnest.'

'If I refuse?'

'Then you'll never know where here is, and we'll have to manage on our own. The Imperium may suffer. If you refuse, go back through the door and we'll say goodbye.'

There was a long pause, stirred only by the evening breeze and the twitter of hedgerow birds.

'Goodbye,' said Ravenor. He turned his chair around and began to glide back up the hill.

'I'm disappointed!' Culzean called after him. 'Truly, I am! You're making a mistake!'

Ravenor ignored him. He re-joined his companions at the top of the slope.

'What's going on?' asked Thonius.

'Who was that man?' asked Angharad.

'We're leaving,' Ravenor said. 'Open the door, housekeeper.'

The housekeeper placed the key in the door's old lock.

They looked back down the field for a moment. In the dusk, Orfeo Culzean was still sitting on his chair in the corn ring, watching them. He raised his right hand to his lips and blew them a kiss.

'I don't like this,' Thonius said.

'You haven't liked much of anything so far,' Ballack snapped.

'Open the door,' Ravenor repeated.

The door creaked open. They saw the evening fields beyond the door frame, the first stars now bright in the violet sky.

They stepped through.

FIFTEEN

THE DRIPPING, STINKING bowels of an underhive surrounded them.

It was gloomy and oppressively muggy. Water – probably not rainwater – pattered down on them from high above, down the sheer ravine depths of the stack foundations. High above, a thousand metres up, tiny moving dots showed the criss-cross of upper level air traffic buzzing between the hive towers.

They heard running footsteps approaching down a nearby alley, a caterwauling laugh that sounded slightly insane.

'This isn't right,' Thonius said, 'not right at all.' He looked at the housekeeper. 'Why aren't we in the right place?'

'The route back is often not the same as the route there,' the housekeeper said blandly. 'The door chooses.'

'How many steps until we're back at the Wych House?' asked Ballack firmly.

'The door chooses. It's not my function,' the housekeeper replied.

'Open the door again,' said Ravenor.

The footsteps and laughter were getting closer.

'Whoever is approaching,' said Angharad, 'they're out of their minds on some substance. I can smell it on their sweat.'

'You can smell anything above this general stink?' asked Thonius.

Angharad ignored him and looked at Ravenor. 'They will be violent. There will be violence.'

'Open the door,' Ravenor repeated.

The housekeeper tried the key. It refused to turn. 'The door is not ready to be opened again.'

'Open the door.'

'We must wait until it is ready,' the housekeeper said.

Thonius flinched as shots banged off loudly in a stack-sink nearby. They heard the distinct whine of a hard round spanking off stone. More laughter, shouts. A scream.

'Gangs,' said Ballack. He raised his laspistol and took a careful aim at the alleyway end, 'pharmed up and juicing for an argument. First head around that wall gets a new nostril.'

There were more shots, closer now, and more screaming laughter.

Angharad took up a place beside Ballack. 'Don't shoot them all,' she told him, 'Evisorex thirsts.'

'You realise I wouldn't be here to have all this fun if it wasn't for you,' Ballack said sarcastically.

'You can thank me later,' she replied.

'Come on,' said Thonius. 'The door?'

The housekeeper tried the key. It turned.

RED LIGHT, HOT wind, red dust.

'Damn,' said Ballack, raising his arm to shield his eyes from the gritty wind.

'Not this again,' said Thonius.

The black volcanic rocks loomed in the distance above the sculpted red dunes. The heat from the gunshot star burned their skins.

'Not here again,' he murmured.

For all her bravado in the underhive, Angharad was immediately spooked. 'This is a bad place and we have to leave it now,' she declared. 'Something is coming.'

She was right. Even Ravenor could feel it in the back of his mind: a crawling itch, the same sense of impending doom that had surrounded them the last, brief time they had passed through the red desert.

The housekeeper was clearly affected too. Without having to be asked or ordered, the housekeeper put the key in the lock and attempted to turn it. The door remained defiantly locked.

'Come on, come on...' Thonius sobbed.

The wind picked up, scooping sand from the ground and winnowing it around them. The housekeeper tried the door again.

'Come on!' screamed Thonius.

The housekeeper began rattling the key furiously, and then started banging at the door.

'It won't open,' the housekeeper cried. It was the first emotional expression any of the housekeepers had made. 'It won't open! My key doesn't work!'

'No!' cried Thonius.

'Keep trying,' Ravenor said.

'Oh look, by the blood of my clan, look!' Angharad called.

Something had appeared, cresting the line of black rocks. It looked like a wave at first, like fast-flowing liquid spilling over the rocks in a flood and rushing on across the duned regolith towards them.

But it wasn't liquid.

'Open the door,' said Ravenor firmly.

'It won't open!' the housekeeper screamed back.

The wave was made of organisms, a swarm of fast-moving black and white creatures. They came on in a rippling, scurrying tide, chittering and yapping. Organic armour glinted like lacquered steel in the sunlight. The organisms were man-sized bipeds with torsos and heads hunched low and forward like sprinters, and rigid, spike tails held out high to counterbalance them. Their limbs and bellies gleamed off-white, like dirty ice, but their backs and long heads were a polished onyx black where the armour was thickest. Dead black eyes, mere slits, gazed out from behind heavy nasal horns. The snapping, chittering mouths were full of needle teeth. Four sickle-hook arms were neatly folded under their upper bodies. There was a smell coming off them that was even more distressing than the clicking, chattering cries they were making. The smell was worse because it was not like anything any of them had ever smelled before. It was dry, and musky, and caustic, like wood polish, like fermented fruit-mash, like the funerary spices of a mummified corpse. It was all of those things and none of them.

It was alien in the most extreme sense.

'Please, please open the door!' Thonius begged.

Bounding, sprinting, clicking, the wave bore down on the figures at the lonely door, gleaming, jostling black and white bodies and bouncing counterbalance tails. They were so fast, so agile, so many. Regolith dust rose in a shimmering cloud above them, lifted by their scurrying feet.

'Holy Throne,' Ballack managed to stammer.

The front of the wave was on them. Long-hooked limbs flicked up to strike.

'Open the door!' wailed Thonius.

'It's too late,' said Ravenor.

PART THREE

The long way round

ONE

SHE WAS FREEZING cold. Lucic had taken her environment coat off her in an act of petty spite. 'That's for losing my jacks,' he had said sullenly, tossing her garment off the dock into the pool.

Lucic's friend was evidently a bounty hunter or hired gun. Tall and coarse, with a well-conditioned body of sinewy muscle, and a face that had been decorated with puckered burn tissue down one side, he wore a body-glove armoured with reinforcing plates, and a quilted, fur-trimmed jacket. His weapon of choice was a cut-down lascarbine, ex-Guard issue. The man himself was probably ex-Guard issue too.

He'd searched Plyton unsympathetically for concealed weapons, tugging out the little Tronsvasse insurance she kept stowed in her waistband. His grubby hands had gone everywhere, and he'd been smiling while he worked.

'Pig,' Plyton had called him when he was done. Without hesitation, he had smacked her hard across the face with the back of his hand, and knocked her onto the deck.

'Hey, don't!' Lucic had cried out.

'What's she to you?' burn-face had asked. The look in burn-face's eyes had forced Lucic to shrug and back down. Not so much a 'friend' after all. Down on the deck, her face stinging and her eyes hot, Plyton had noticed this detail.

Burn-face had dragged her up roughly and forced her to sit on an empty lube drum.

'Don't move,' he had instructed.

It was hard to track the time, but she figured an hour must have passed. Lucic put on his coat and started to pace, Plyton's combat shotgun slung over his lanky shoulder. Burn-face had briefly dropped down into the underboat, and then returned, chewing on a ration bar from the boat's supply. He had several other bars stuffed into his coat pocket.

'So, what's the play?' Lucic had asked the hired gun lightly.

'We stay planted here and wait for the word,' burn-face had replied, munching. He ate fast and messily, like a wild animal. He sat down on a coil winder, and chewed some more. After a while, he rested his carbine against his leg, and took out Plyton's Tronsvasse. He started to play with it, stripping it out, popping the clip, and flicking the safety on and off. He aimed it at several imaginary targets around the docking pool to gauge its qualities.

'Nice piece,' he remarked. He looked at Plyton. She avoided his gaze. The cold was getting to her bones. She was shivering, and sat with her arms wrapped around her body.

Burn-face ate another ration bar and threw the waxed paper wrapper into the pool. Through the grille decking,

Plyton could see it floating beneath her in the grease ice beside her slowly sinking coat.

The hired gun patted his pockets. 'Got a smoke? Lho or anything?' he asked Lucic.

'I'm out,' said Lucic distractedly, taking out his link and staring at it as if willing it to chime.

Burn-face looked at Plyton. 'You?'

She shook her head. Then, on inspiration, added, 'They were in my coat.'

Burn-face glared at Lucic. 'You daft bastard,' he growled.

Out here, a man needs all the friends he can get, eh? Well, Lucic, you're losing your only one fast.

'Best find something else to do to pass the time,' burn-face mused. He looked at Plyton again. 'You cold?'

She nodded.

'Maybe we get you a little colder still, then warm you up some.'

'Hey!' Lucic said. 'Don't be getting nasty with her.'

The bounty hunter got to his feet. 'Don't be getting nasty?' he replied, mimicking Lucic's prissy outrage. 'Frig you, nasty is what we do.'

'Even so–'

'I was told you were in on this. I was told you could be counted on.'

'I can, I can,' said Lucic, hastily. 'I did what you people wanted, didn't I? I did it right.'

The bounty hunter shrugged. He was chasing a lodged scrap of ration bar out of his teeth with his tongue. He found the scrap and spat it out.

'Big boys' games now,' he told Lucic. 'Big boys' rules. You better keep up.'

'I can keep up.'

'So why you so protective of this bitch?'

'I...' Lucic began. 'I didn't know we'd have to kill all of them.'

'Maybe we won't. Maybe we can all be very good friends. We'll see. They'll call and tell us how it pans out.'

'If it's a no?'

'Don't worry,' burn-face said, sitting back down and taking out Plyton's Tronsvasse again. 'That time comes, I'll do her. If you know what I mean.'

Lucic scowled and resumed pacing the deck.

The bounty hunter eased back on his seat and stared at the lapping water below.

Another ten minutes crawled by. Plyton was getting so bone cold she was afraid she might shut down. Hypothermia. If she passed out, Throne help her.

There was a rumble and a shudder. The hanging chains in the wharf area, some of them massive, trembled and swung. The House was adjusting its stance again. Chunks of grubby ice that had formed around the chain links were dislodged by the movement, and splashed down into the pool.

'It's taking too long,' Lucic said.

'It takes as long as it takes.'

'I'm going to call up,' Lucic said, taking out his link again.

Burn-face shrugged. 'Knock yourself out.'

Lucic keyed his link. 'Hello? Copy back. This is Lucic in the dock. What's taking so long up there?'

'I DON'T NEED your frigging agitation in my ear, Lucic,' Worna snarled into his wrist-mounted link. 'We're sitting tight, so sit tight with us. I'll tell you whoa or go as soon as there's a whoa or go to tell you.'

The Wych House's theatre chamber was painfully silent. Worna's paid guns had spread out around the room in a securing spread. The housekeepers had been forced down in a little huddle of seated figures, with two men watching them. The candles and lamps flickered.

Kys and Nayl sat side-by-side on the raised walkway with their backs against the outer wall. Two men had been posted to watch them too. One of them had been given the psy-scanner, and was studying it closely, as if his life depended on it.

Which it does, Nayl thought, in a small, savoured moment of optimism.

Worna was standing on the upper platform, staring at the closed, silent door. They'd heard his side of the vox-link exchange. At the mention of Lucic's name, Nayl had risked a look at Kys.

She met the look. *Lucic. Betrayed.*

Worna clumped down the steps to rejoin them. He towered over their seated figures, then squatted down. Kys could smell his breath. Gutter meat. Bad rations.

'Taking a long time,' he offered, almost comradely.

'I don't know what's taking a long time, because I don't know what's going on,' Kys replied.

'Not so much talk from you, witch,' Worna grumbled in his penetratingly low voice. He looked at Nayl.

'What the hell happened to you?' he asked.

'Life happened,' Nayl replied coldly.

Worna frowned. 'We saw some fine times in the old days. You and me, and the others. Scored plenty. Now look at you, taking the Throne's coin. What drives a man to do that, I wonder?'

'I got a good offer.'

'From the ordos?' Worna laughed. 'This Ravenor cripple?'

'Originally, no. His master, Eisenhorn,' Nayl replied.

'Oh, yeah. I heard of him. Eisenhorn. Tough old bird. But he's dead, right? That's what I was told.'

'I think he's dead.'

'And now you throw your lot in with this crippled scumbag?'

'You wouldn't understand.'

'No?' Lucius Worna shrugged. 'Maybe not. This isn't some frigging loyalty thing, is it? Please, please, powers that be, don't tell me Harlon frigging Nayl went and got himself a conscience.'

Nayl laughed despite himself, and shook his head.

'Walk with me,' Worna said, rising, and beckoning Nayl to follow him. Nayl got up and joined Worna in a long, slow circuit of the railed deck.

'You wanna smoke?' Worna asked.

'A smoke'd be good.'

Worna flicked his fingers and one of his men proffered a pack of lho-sticks. They took one each, and the man lit them obediently.

Kys watched. The Harlon Nayl she knew never smoked these days.

Lucius Worna took a deep draw and exhaled. Nayl toyed with his lho-stick rather more circumspectly.

'Wanted to get you away from that witch,' Worna confided. 'She's bad news.'

'If you say so.'

'If I say so? What is this, be nice to Lucius week?'

'You got the guns, you got the manpower, hell, you got the drop, Lu. What the frig else am I gonna do except be nice to you?'

Worna chuckled. 'In your place, I'd do the same. But then, you always knew how to play a scene, didn't you, Nayl?'

'I've had my moments.'

'Hell, yeah. Good work. We did good work. You remember what's his name?'

'Probably. What was his name?'

'Shinto... Shinko... Shimko... some frig like that.'

'Alek Shinato?'

'That's the frigger!' Worna exclaimed. 'Throne, that was a good day. Sarum, on the look out. You got a tip on the down low and we were in. But how many frigging gun-happy trogs did that guy have waiting for us?'

'Almost too many,' Nayl admitted.

'Almost too many, that's a fact. Las like confetti. Bracer bought it right off.'

'Bracer was a stump,' said Nayl. 'He was asking to be wiped the day he applied for his licence.'

'Yeah, that's true.'

They walked on a little way.

'I was in the chasm that day, Nayl,' said Worna. 'Pinned. Took one in the leg, still pains me. But you came through. Cleanest kill shots I ever saw, no lie. The two stiffs with the cannon, then Shinto himself. End of story.'

'Shinato.'

Worna grunted. 'He's dead. What does it matter?'

'I'm the one pinned now, Lu.'

'Yes, yes, you are.'

'Never seems fair to me,' Nayl remarked, knocking the ash off his lho-stick. 'We work for coin, always have. It's never about ties or bonds or loyalties. I saved your life that day, but it doesn't count now.'

'Maybe so, maybe no,' Worna replied. 'This is why I wanted to talk to you, in private, so to speak. I don't like to see you go swirling down the head with these other mongrels. There'd be a place for you, just say the word.'

'A place?'

Worna gestured around them. 'I got a new crew together, with a good source of retainer fees, all the perks. These bastards are the best, but I could always use another good gun. Say the word, and you're working for me.'

'You're joking? I've been serving the Inquisition for decades.'

'I know. But, like you said, we work for coin. No ties, no bonds, no loyalties. You've been working for pay, and pay is what I'm offering. Since when did you or me care who was servicing our bill?'

'This is because you owe me?' asked Nayl.

'This is precisely because I owe you. My life, I owe you.
I'm offering you your life in payment of that debt. Join
my crew. I can square it with Culzean. Pay's sweet, did I
mention that? I don't like the thought of you skull-shot
with the others, and I have a strong feeling that's how it's
going to end. Come and play with the winning team,
now, before it's too late.'

Nayl drew on his lho-stick. 'Nice offer. Tempting. But
how the frig would you ever trust me? Hello? Ordo work,
for decades, remember?'

'Well,' murmured Worna, 'you'd have to prove yourself,
to me and the crew.'

'How?'

Lucius Worna looked back around the chamber to
where Kys was sitting under guard. He slid a vicious combat dagger out of his hip rig. 'Gut the frigging telekine
witch for me, would you?'

Nayl blinked. Then he smiled and took hold of the
blade.

'Make it last,' Lucius Worna advised.

TWO

LEAPING, BOUNDING, SKIPPING, they pour down over us
under the red heat of the gunshot sun. Their chitter hits
us first, then their stink, and then the impressing weight
of their torrent.

Carl is screaming. The housekeeper is screaming. Both
are hammering at the unyielding door.

I know the door is sealed and will not open because I
know this is a trap. Zygmunt Molotch's last, best and
most horrific trap.

The first of them land on me, scraping their hook
blades off my chair's hull. The weight of them pushes my
chair down into the dust and threatens to topple me.
There is a sour stink of the adrenal hormone driving their
aggression.

What are these chattering creatures, these monsters? They are unknown to me, unknown to Imperial lore. What does it matter anyway? They are death. They are my death.

Ballack is firing his weapon, yelling out. The wave rolling in on him falters, punctured. Vile, purplish ichor explodes from shot-blasted bodies and clumps the dry sand where it splashes. How long can he hold them back?

Angharad. No wonder Harlon is so enamoured of her. She's like a fury, standing her ground, her long steel swinging. Limbs fly off, hooked members flipping and spinning away through the air. Snouts are truncated. Horns are turned aside, hooks deflected. Ichor sprays. Evisorex bites. The Ewl Wyla Scryi. The genius of sharpness. I doubt any Carthaen in clan history has ever faced down such a foe single-handed. She is magnificent. She turns and spins, kicks and slices, driving the organisms back, damaged and slain.

I estimate she will last another minute and a half.

Carl turns from the door, firing his autopistol wildly. He scores hits. It's difficult not to, given the sheer wall of squirming menace driving into us. Leaping forms burst in mid-air and tumble, twitching.

These are impossible odds. We are going to die. Hook blades squeal and scrape against my chair's surface. We are going to die. How quickly is up to me.

I fling the increasing layers of gouging, yapping bodies off me with a mind-flick. Some of the creatures sail back a long way into the ranks behind them. Righting my chair, I send out another telekinetic burst that pulps the front rank in a blizzard of purple-black jelly and shattering chitin.

I am an Imperial inquisitor. I will not go down without a fight.

I pop my weapon modules out of my chair's chassis. Paired psy-cannons. I open fire and blitz the black and white organisms bounding towards me. Ballack has drawn his back-up weapon, an auto-snub. He fires into the oncoming swarm. There's been no time to reload his las.

Evisorex rips and shreds. Bodies are opened, bisected. Hind limbs still attached to violently lashing tails fly past, gushing noxious liquid from their severed waists. I sustain my fire, as long as my hopper loads last. Leaping horrors pop, burst, fracture, explode in showers of viscous matter.

'Open the door! Open the door!' Carl is screaming.

The housekeeper has sunk to the ground in shock, the key falling from limp hands.

I can just hear the housekeeper murmuring. What is that?

The Great Devourer. The Great Devourer...

The action is savage, unstinting. The more I hit and burst, the more of them there are, capering and bounding in. Their chattering mouths seem to be laughing at us.

'I'm out!' Ballack shrieks. Angharad leaps to defend him, decapitating two of the creatures and kicking another aside. The bodies are piling up. Ballack cowers behind her, trying to slam home a fresh clip.

He's too slow. A scything limb catches Angharad across the forehead and knocks her down. A glancing blow, not enough to kill.

But she's dead anyway.

Unless–

I keep the chair's cannons firing. I reach out, and 'ware Angharad, snatching her up before she hits the ground. Evisorex is a purring monster in my hands. It knows what it has to do. I let it drive into the enemy, remembering my blade schooling – from dear, lost Arianhrod long ago – and allowing Angharad's training to leak from her unconscious mind to inform my movements. I cut them apart, monster after monster after leaping, pouncing monster.

Ballack has reloaded. He stands up, blasting into the endless wave. He kills every single thing charging at him except one. A gouging hook tears into his thigh. He falls, passing out in pain-shock.

I 'ware him too, dragging him back into the fight, making him shoot again. His gun roars.

+Carl! I need you!+

Thonius has also reloaded. He fires his pistol point-blank into the wall of jabbing, black, chitinous snouts and sees braincases burst with each pump of his trigger.

He has only a few shots left.

+Carl!+

Carl Thonius goes down. I see it happen. I see his frail body, limbs cartwheeling, carried over by the pouring wave of creatures. I try to reach out, but I can't 'ware him too. I'm stretched too far with Ballack, Angharad, and my own chair. The chair is still valiantly pumping cannon shots into the endless legion of monsters.

They land on me, clawing and clacking. They push me back, despite the holes I blast in them. The chittering monsters explode and topple away, but there are always more pouring in behind.

They weigh me down. They overturn me. This is the end. Their abominable hooks screech and tear at my chair. Internal system alarms sound as they puncture my armour. Too many, way too many.

This is the end. *Gregor, I'm so sorry. I–*

The world, red already, goes blood-red.

I am blinded by blood. I feel their blades dig into me. I try one last time to–

RED, RED, RED, *a flare of insulted rage–*

LUCIUS WORNA LOOKED up at the door sharply.

'What the hell?' he muttered.

The door was rocking in its frame, pounding. Red light, like the issue of a dying sun, seeped through the gaps between the door and its frame, and shafted into the Wych House.

'Something's coming back,' Nayl said. As Worna looked back around at him, Nayl flicked the smouldering butt of his lho-stick into Worna's left eye. Worna snarled in pain and recoiled, clutching his face. Nayl lunged forward with the blade Worna had given him, but there was suddenly no time to finish the job. No time at all.

Up on the highest platform, the door shuddered. It flexed in its frame, the wood bulging, and blew open on its hinges. A huge, pressurised gout of scouring fire and boiling red energy vomited out of the doorway.

The fire-cloud was filthy and red. It seared out through the door's frame in a great, concussive belch that shook the platform and the room itself. Everyone in the theatre chamber was knocked to the floor. All the candles and lamps around the edge of the platform flew off and smashed in the lower floor space. Spilled lamp oil ignited. The expanding fireball from the doorway rolled up into the dome overhead. Several electrical systems, overcooked, exploded in showers of sparks.

Another belch of flame gusted out of the open door, as fierce as the first. The chamber shook again. Fires caught and began to blaze in the girdered vault of the theatre's dome. Something, a photo-lumin lamp perhaps, exploded with a volatile report and spat debris across the chamber.

The Wych House lurched, as if wounded or stung. It staggered. Those who had managed to get on their feet fell back down again. The chamber was lit amber by the spreading, cracking fires and the eerie red glow pouring through the open door.

Nayl struggled to rise, but Worna was already standing. He grabbed Nayl by the throat, lifted him off the walkway with one hand, and threw him like a doll. Nayl hit the rail, tumbled over it, and disappeared down onto the lower deck where the lamp oil fires were raging. Worna turned, gazing at the wide open door and the red sunlight streaming through it.

More flames, weaker now, billowed out of the open doorway, followed by a shimmer of alien dust. Then silence.

'On your frigging feet!' Worna yelled at his men. He drew his chainsword, moving towards the steps that led up to the top platform. Dazed and bewildered, his men hurried to follow him, all except the two watching Kys. The hooded housekeepers remained in a cowering huddle.

Something quick and jerky moved, fleetingly, inside the red glare of the doorway. Two gleaming silhouettes leapt forwards together, and hung for a moment, perching on the sides of the door frame with their nimble, clawed feet, like birds. Then they bounced down onto the platform into view. Tails high and straight, they stepped forward slowly, their hook claws scraping the deck.

The organisms chattered back and forth, snouts clacking, stabbing tongues flicking out between needle teeth, as they advanced carefully into this new, unknown location. The smell of them was rank and sickening. Crouching against the wall on the walkway ring behind the men guarding her, Kys stared up at the prowling creatures in disgust and involuntary fear. Some of the bounty hunters around Worna began backing away. Even Worna had come to a halt, halfway up the steps.

'Doren, Kixo,' Worna hissed. 'Get up there and take those ugly sons of bitches down.'

The two men chosen advanced nervously up the steps onto the upper platform, carbines raised. The creatures stopped in their tracks and seemed to observe the slowly approaching men with curiosity.

'Got a clean kill shot on the first,' one of the cautious bounty hunters muttered, aiming his carbine from the shoulder. 'Get ready to take the oth–'

The nearest of the monsters turned, regarded him with a tilt of its head, and pounced with an abrupt, effortless spring of its hind legs. The bounty hunter was brought down under its weight, his carbine firing uselessly into the roof. It had him pinned for an instant, face up, on the deck. He began to scream. Its four hook limbs flicked out and snapped down like shears, quartering him like a portioned game bird.

The entire kill had taken barely a second. With an anguished howl, the other man opened fire, blasting the predator off his colleague's messy corpse. The shots blew its torso open in a spatter of purple, sticky sap, and knocked it clean off the platform. The second monster yapped like a feral dog and sprang at the shooter.

All of the other bounty hunters opened fire instinctively, shooting from their positions on the raised walkway and the upper steps. The broadside of frantic shots shredded the thing in mid-air. They also slew its intended prey. The bounty hunter toppled forward in a mist of blood.

'Cease fire!' Worna yelled. 'Cease fire, you dumb friggers! You just wasted Kixo!' His spooked men were no longer listening to him. A few were backing towards the exits. The rest were training their weapons at the open door.

Horned black snouts came snuffling out of the red light. Drooling teeth chittered. A dozen more of the black and white things sprang through the doorway into the chamber, then a dozen more, bouncing and jumping.

All hell broke loose.

Worna's men began blasting indiscriminately. The red glow of the burning chamber lit up with a shower of bright white las-bolts. Gleaming alien bodies ruptured and fell, thrashing in death agonies, but there were too many of them. The chittering predators, agile and shockingly fast, ploughed forwards into the men, cutting them apart. The shooting turned to screaming. Those of Worna's men that could, broke and ran.

'Stand your frigging ground!' Worna bellowed from the upper steps. He turned in time to see one of the black and white horrors launching itself at him. Lucius Worna didn't flinch. He met its attack with his chainsword and cut it in half. It was not a clean kill. The creature's limbs were still flailing and stabbing wildly and it crashed into him, throwing him backwards down the steps.

The men guarding Kys had fled. She rose, fighting the urge to follow them. She had to find Nayl. She had to see if Ravenor would return, although if these things were gathered on the far side of the door, she didn't hold out much hope of that happening.

She ran towards the huddled, moaning housekeepers. Behind her, Worna's men were blasting and dying.

'Move!' she yelled at the housekeepers. 'Get out of here!'

None of them stirred. They rocked and mumbled.

'You idiots!' she cried. Something slammed her into the wall. One of Worna's bruisers had shoved her aside in his effort to escape.

A black and white shape landed directly on his back. He grunted as he was flattened, face down, beneath it. It quickly snipped off his arms and head.

Kys heard and smelled the torrent of human blood emptying down through the grilled walkway decking from the butchered corpse. She rose slowly into a crouch, edging her kineblades out. The long metal blades came free from her bodice and floated up on either side of her face, pointing forward, suspended by her telekinetic impulse.

The monster calmly bent down and nipped meat from the corpse with a delicate snap of its teeth. She saw the glossy blackness of its upper armour, scribbled with lines of old scars, the waxy whiteness of its lower body, where patches of thread-worm parasites clustered. She could smell the metallic hormone stench of it, and feel its presence scratching against her mind. It raised its head slowly and turned its horned snout towards Kys. Its eyes were awful, lifeless slits above a rictus grin. Rivulets of bright human blood dribbled down its gleaming, bone-white chin and dripped onto the walkway.

It chittered, its mouth snapping and chattering, tongue stabbing. Tasting, sensing, smelling, all at once. Throat sacs under its chin pulsed and swelled.

Its powerful legs tensed, and it sprang towards her.

Kys rolled furiously. Her paired kineblades met the pouncing thing in mid-air, punching clean through it like high velocity rounds. She'd aimed for the throat sacs, the softest, least armoured part of it. The sacs burst as the blades punctured them, and yellow fluid sprayed out. Chitinous dorsal plates cracked a nanosecond later, as the exiting blades blew out of the monster's back in foggy sprays. The kinetic shock stopped it short, mid-pounce, and dropped it onto the walkway beside her. It writhed, snapping at her, tail curling and flopping, its hook limbs thrashing. Then the entire walkway section it lay on fell away, eaten to pulp by the bio-acid that had poured out of its throat sacs. It crashed down onto the theatre floor space below.

Kys leapt to her feet, summoning her kineblades back. There was nothing left of them. They had been reduced to spurs of dissolving metal by the corrosive contents of the throat sacs.

Kys let them fall. The hairs on her neck rose. She turned, very, very slowly.

Head down, yapping softly, another of the things stepped towards her along the walkway.

THREE

THE HOUSE SHOOK and staggered. There was an echoing boom from above them, and then another. Plyton was thrown off her perch. She landed hard on the dock's decking and rolled several times. She almost pitched off into the water.

'What the hell was that?' Lucic was demanding, ripping out his link. Burn-face had been thrown onto the deck too. He got up, angry.

'Give me that!' he snarled.

Her arms shaking, Plyton pulled herself up. Down in the dock pool, the water was slopping feverishly. The underboat was straining at its chains, bucking in the icy froth. The chains creaked and pulled. The House shook again – a deep, ugly lurch – and the boat bucked more furiously. The hanging chains swished and shook. Ice crackled down into the washing swell.

'Worna? Worna!' burn-face yelled into the link.

There was no response.

'Worna?'

Plyton ploughed into them both from behind. Lucic fell and hit his head against a fuel drum. Burn-face tried to turn, but she slammed her fist into the side of his head repeatedly.

They landed hard. The bounty hunter's carbine hit the decking and slithered out of reach. He rolled, tucked his legs up and savagely kicked her in the torso with both feet.

Winded, gasping, Plyton flew backwards through the air. She smashed into some of the dangling chains and managed to grab one.

She was still travelling. Momentum turned her into a pendulum. Hanging from the chain, she soared out over the pool. Thrashing ice water sloshed ten metres below her.

Plyton clung on. The chain swung her back over the dock. Burn-face had rolled onto his knees, and she kicked out at him, but missed, as she swung past. He was reaching for the fallen carbine.

She swung back, missing him again, dangling out above the churning pool at the extremity of her back-swing. Her hands had locked up, turned to aching numbness by the touch of the chain loops.

She swung in for a second time. Burn-face had risen, dodging her sweeping form as it came in. He rolled hard and came up with her Tronsvasse in his hands as she swept back again.

He grinned as he fired it at her. The weapon dry clicked. He hadn't reloaded it since stripping it down.

She swung past him, her momentum diminishing. Then the House staggered again and wrenched her around furiously, jerking her up over the pool with such violence her chain became slack for a second.

Burn-face rolled again, diving for the fallen carbine. She sailed down at him and struck him hard. Plyton viced her dangling legs around him and carried him on with her.

Burn-face smashed head-first into an oil drum.

He fell away from her, his neck snapped, and slammed onto the dock.

Plyton let go of the chain and fell hard.

Dazed, she rose and glanced around. Burn-face's corpse lay face down on the grilled deck. Lucic had vanished. She stumbled forward and picked up the bounty hunter's lascarbine.

The House shook again. It listed badly to one side and she fell onto the sloping deck. With a gunshot bang, one of the chains mooring the underboat broke. Its prow swung around in the frothing pool.

'Lucic?' she yelled.

LUCIC HAD RUN down the service tunnel into the drum chamber. The cargo hoist was still up. He gathered Plyton's shotgun to his chest. Weird echoes rang down the riser shaft. Was that gunfire? Shouting?

Lucic strode towards the spiral staircase, coping with the relentless, sickening roll and shift of the deck.

He started up the stairs and reached the roof hatch.

He pulled the inset handle and it swung down. He looked up into the dark shaft above.

THE CREATURE LUNGED at Kys. She met it with her kineforce, and hurled it away from her along the walkway.

That took effort. The creature was strong, vital, bristling with energy, and its chitinous structure was as hard as steel. It landed in an ungainly sprawl, powerful hind limbs skidding and scrabbling for purchase. It sprang up again, undeterred, and charged back towards her. Kys turned and leapt across the gaping walkway section that the acid had removed. She landed beside the dead bounty hunter, held out her hand, and his fallen carbine flew from the deck into her grasp. She turned back and blew the bounding creature in half.

The whole chamber was on fire. The House shuddered and realigned, wounded and dying. Predatory shapes, tails-high, leapt through the smoke and flames, dismembering the last of Worna's troop.

'Harlon?' she yelled. 'Harlon?'

'He ain't here,' Lucius Worna said. He stood in front of her, aiming a bolt pistol at her heart. Part of his face was eaten away to the bone by acid, and his carapace armour was covered in fresh, deep gouges. 'He ain't here, you witch. Toss the carbine.'

She obeyed. Covering her, he raised his link. Kys glanced up, and saw a pair of predators on the platform rail above, rocking as they prepared to pounce on him.

'Siskind!' Worna yelled into his link. 'Teleport me! Now!'

Lucius Worna smiled at her, fired his pistol, and vanished. A cyclonic blur of pink light sucked him away.

With a pop of decompression, the teleport cone removed Worna, his weapon and his smile.

All it left behind as it faded was the bolt round, ripping towards her.

Kys caught it. It took all of her telekinetic strength. She stopped the blistering round in mid-air a metre from her body and held it dead, at bay. She fought, her mind bending with the effort. The bolt round, stationary, began to deform and melt against the mind-wall her kine force had thrown up. It thrust against her will, half a metre away, gouging through her telekinetic defence.

She could see it clearly, spinning in space, metal sweating off it in slow, blobby droplets as it superheated.

With a gasp, Kys threw herself down. Released, the bolt round tore over her head and hit the wall behind her with an explosive crump.

Kys rose, the smoke making her choke. The two creatures perched on the rail bounced down onto the walkway ahead of her and began to advance.

They yapped and chattered.

She had no mind-strength left any more, nothing to keep them at bay.

They leapt.

They burst in splashes of ichor.

Gun pods blazing, Ravenor's chair swept out of the doorway. It was horribly gouged and dented. Suspension fluid trickled out of deep cut scars.

Ravenor turned slowly, raking the walkway with sustained pod fire. Skipping, jinking predators exploded and died.

+Patience!+

+Throne, you're alive!+

+Help me!+

He was in pain. He was hurt. Kys scrambled up the steps onto the upper platform.

'The Wych House is finished,' she yelled over the roar of the flames. 'We have to leave.'

+Help me, Patience.+

Bleeding from an awful leg wound, Ballack stumbled out of the doorway behind Ravenor. He was carrying Thonius, who was limp and lifeless.

'What happened?' Kys yelled.

+No time to explain. Get them clear, Patience. That's all I ask.+

Kys ran to Ballack and grabbed hold of him. His eyes were blank. He was being puppetted by Ravenor.

'I've got him!' she cried.

Ravenor let Ballack go, and he slumped. Thonius looked dead. He was covered with blood. The House shuddered again, and slipped. The deck pitched wildly.

+Gideon!+

Something detonated above them. The House rocked.

+Get them clear, Patience! Get them to the underboat while there's still a chance!+

Kys sucked in her breath and took hold of Ballack and Thonius. She carried them, more with her tired mind than with her arms, down the steps onto the walkway, and then down again into the burning hell of the chamber's floor space.

+Please come with me!+ she sent back.

+I'll follow. Angharad is still through there. I'm 'waring her. I can get her out.+

Up on the top platform, Ravenor swung around to face the doorway.

+Come on. Come *on*.+

A black and white form pounced at his chair. He blew it apart with his cannons.

Kys reached the hoist and dropped Ballack and Thonius onto its platform. She reached for the lever.

+Gideon!+

+Go, Patience! I'll be right after you!+

Kys threw the lever. The hoist began to descend.

Kys heard a scuttering, scrabbling sound. She looked up.

Five of the glossy, black and white monsters were racing down the sheer walls of the riser shaft after her, limbs rippling as they tore down the soot-black sides of the drop.

SHOTGUN RAISED, LUCIC took another step up the spiral staircase. The House shook again, violently. That was bad, and he knew it. The House was reaching the end of its existence.

Lucic aimed his shotgun up into the darkness of the stair shaft. He was sure he'd heard something above him, something descending.

He couldn't see anything. He lowered his gun. Reaching into his back pocket, he took out his stablight and flicked it on. He shone the narrow beam up into the gloom.

Nothing. Except... teeth.

Something above him yapped.

Hiram Lucic made a frantic grab for his shotgun.

KYS GRABBED BALLACK'S laspistol and fired it up at the monsters scurrying down the shaft after them.

It snapped dead. It was spent. She reached frantically into his pockets for a fresh clip.

The hoist was descending too slowly, far slower than the scurrying monsters.

CARBINE RAISED IN one hand, lamp in the other, Plyton stepped into the drum chamber. She could hear the hoist trundling down.

A loud, rattling crash came from the direction of the spiral staircase. She stepped closer to investigate. It was her shotgun. Her shotgun had just fallen down the spiral staircase onto the deck. The last time she'd seen, it had been in Lucic's possession.

With slow, nauseating horror, Plyton realised that an astonishingly copious amount of blood was streaming down out of the roof hatch.

Swallowing hard, Plyton cinched the carbine over her shoulder and picked up her shotgun. She backed away from the staircase towards the base plate of the hoist, keeping her shotgun steady. She tried to watch both: the staircase and the hoist, as soon as it appeared.

The hoist dropped into view. Kys was crouching at the centre of the platform, with Ballack and Thonius sprawled on either side of her.

'Maud! Maud! Shoot!' Kys screamed, pointing up the shaft. Plyton leapt up onto the hoist platform between Kys and the unconscious men. She fired upwards, blindly pumping shot after shot up into the dark. Kys dragged Ballack and Thonius off the hoist behind her.

Kys looked back. She had a prickling feeling that Plyton had hit something. Kys reached out and jerked Plyton backwards off the hoist with her telekinesis the instant before three ruptured, flopping bodies crashed down onto it out of the shaft.

Plyton got up, staring at the dead things. 'What the hell are those?' she asked in total revulsion.

'We've got to get back to the boat,' Kys barked, ignoring the question.

'Where's Ravenor?'

'He's coming.' Kys hurried forward to throw the lever and send the hoist back up, but it was dead. Noxious bio-acid leaking from the burst throat sacs of one of the dead things had reduced the motor to metal goo.

'How is he coming?' asked Plyton. 'What about Nayl and swordgirl?'

'He'll use his psi,' Kys replied. +Gideon, the hoist is out of action. Gideon?+

There was no answer. Kys dragged Ballack to his feet. He was coming around, groggy. She threw Thonius's limp body over her shoulder.

'Come on!' She started off towards the service tunnel, dragging Ballack after her, stumbling and confused. Plyton fell in behind her, moving backwards, shotgun raised. Something black and white scuttled down the spiral staircase, and smiled. She blasted it apart.

The deck had twisted to a sharper angle, and the House was rattling with a constant shudder. Metal groaned and protested. In the docking pool, the water was boiling up through the wharf decking, a mass of froth and pressure. The underboat, still anchored by one sea chain, was bucking and thumping violently against the dockside fenders in the immense swell.

Using telekinesis, Kys shoved Thonius's body unceremoniously across and in through the side hatch. Then she jumped across with Ballack. They nearly slipped off into the surging water, but she braced them with her mind and they scrambled in through the hatch.

The pilot servitor had already closed the top hatch.

'We have to leave. Right now,' he told Kys.

'We're not all here,' she replied, moving back to the side hatch.

'If the House goes,' the servitor replied, 'it'll take us with it. We won't have clearance to exit the dock pool. Cut the chain loose.'

'We're not all here yet!' Kys yelled at him. 'Get to the helm and get ready!'

The pilot servitor scurried forward. She heard the fans start up and test-rev. She got to the hatch and looked out. Plyton had remained on the dock side, and was standing with her back to the pool, watching the approach from the service tunnel.

'Maud?'

'No sign!' Plyton yelled back over the roaring water and squealing metal.

+Gideon?+

Nothing.

Plyton was suddenly shooting. The gritty boom of her shotgun rang out again and again. Over a dozen of the creatures were scurrying out of the service tunnel towards her. She killed two of them.

'Maud!'

There was a sudden, stomach-flipping lurch and the House tilted even more sharply, throwing Plyton down. A curious, deep moaning sound began. It was coming from the pool. It was the sound of water, stirring in vast quantities. The house had dipped so steeply, the air bell of the docking pool had lost its integrity, and oceanic water was surging up into the pool bay with shocking speed and fury. The docking pool was flooding.

'Maud!'

Plyton rose on the sharply inclined decking and leapt. She hit the side of the see-sawing underboat and Kys dragged her in through the hatch. Scrambling, slipping, half-falling, the chattering things came after her.

Kys slammed the hatch shut and heard hooks clang and scrape against the outer hull.

'The sea chain!' the pilot servitor shouted at her. 'What about the sea chain?'

The colossal power of the ocean answered him. The force of the flood lifted the underboat, slammed it against the metal dock, and then yanked it away. Black and white bodies tumbled away into the boiling water. The remaining sea chain caught, strained, and parted with an explosive crack.

Released, the underboat rolled, righted, and fought the rising, crushing energy of the sea. The pilot blew air ballast and gunned his cavitation drive and attitude fans.

'What are you doing?' Kys screamed.

'We have to get out!' the pilot servitor yelled back.

She lunged forward, but stopped herself. What could she do? Force him to stay? Kill him?

Even if they stayed, what could they accomplish? The House was flooding, and was minutes, maybe seconds, from losing its foothold forever.

Patience Kys was a supremely capable, confident woman. She could do many things, against almost any odds.

But she couldn't beat this. She was helpless. They were helpless. The ones they'd left behind, if they weren't dead already, were doomed.

+Gideon!+ She sent with such anguished force Plyton and Ballack winced.

There was no answer. There would never be again.

FOUR

NAYL WOKE TO find himself in hell.

He was sprawled in the bottom floor space of the theatre chamber. The deck was at an almost forty degree slope. His head pounded and his throat hurt. He remembered Worna grabbing him.

He rose, swaying. The area around him was alive with leaping flames. His coat was on fire. He took it off and threw it aside.

He made his way over to the hoist, but it was gone, and the black riser shaft stared up at him.

There were bodies on the ground, two of Worna's hired guns. They looked as if they had been snipped clumsily into pieces by giant scissors. He helped himself to the shotgun one of them had dropped.

Something moved in the flames nearby. A dead-eyed horror with a rictus smile leapt out of the dancing fire to kill him.

No hesitation. His newly acquired shotgun barked, and punched it back where it had come from in a drizzle of purple fluid.

Fighting the sloping deck, he reached the lower steps and got onto the walkway. There was no one around, no one alive, anyway. He saw four more dead from Worna's band, the corpses of two housekeepers rent limb from limb, and the crumpled forms of three more things like the one he had just wasted.

'What in Throne's name are these things?' he muttered.

Nayl clambered around the walkway, leaping over a missing section of deck that looked as if it had been burned away by acid. He made it to the upper steps. Serious-sounding explosions thumped somewhere outside the ruined chamber. The whole place was on fire.

He crawled up onto the sloping upper platform. The roof dome above was a riotous inferno, and flames from below were searing up around the metal disk of the platform. The doorframe was still standing, the door open and swinging, the red light of somewhere else shining through it.

Ravenor's chair sat facing the door. It was scratched and battered, punctured in places. Clear fluid was dripping out of it.

'Ravenor?'

'Is that you, Harlon?'

Nayl staggered over to reach him.

'What the hell is going on?'

'I'm sorry,' Ravenor replied, his voxponded voice frail and thready, as if the system were damaged. Or as if *he* were damaged. 'I'm very sorry. We're not getting out of here.'

'Where are the others?'

'Kys has made her way out. She took Carl and Ballack with her. I hope they made it to the underboat. I pray they did. I keep calling, but I'm very tired. My mind is weak. I can't reach Kys.'

'What about Plyton?' Nayl asked.

Ravenor sighed.

Dan Abnett

'What about Angharad?' Nayl said more firmly.

'I'm still trying. She's there, I can feel her. But...'

'Gideon? For Throne's sake, is she still in there?'

'I'm waring her. She... she kept them at bay. She's still fighting them. I don't know how much longer she can last. She's an amazing woman, that Arianhrod.'

'You mean Angharad.'

'What?'

'You mean Angharad.'

'Yes, of course.'

Another explosion rocked the chamber. Nayl stepped towards the door. 'Angharad!' he yelled into the red light. 'Angharad!'

'Wait, Harlon,' Ravenor whispered. 'Wait, she's...'

Something moved on the other side of the door. Backlit by the red glow, a figure limped into view.

Angharad. She was covered in blood and smears of purple ichor. Her leather armour was torn, and hanging off her in places. Her long steel smoked. She walked slowly out of the doorway onto the platform, leading the housekeeper guide behind her by the hand, like a child.

'Oh Throne!' Nayl cried, running to them. The door slammed shut in its frame behind them.

With a sob of pain and exhaustion, Ravenor let Angharad go. She swayed, but she was conscious. Blood dripped from her mouth. Nayl tried to hold her, but she pushed him off. She took two long steps towards Ravenor's dented chair and rested the tip of Evisorex on its front cowling.

'You bastard,' she rasped. 'Without my permission. Without my permission! You were inside me. You *were* me.'

'I apologise,' said Ravenor.

'You have violated my honour and the honour of my clan. You were inside me! I alone choose who gets to be inside me! That was mind-rape! I should gut you for this offence and–'

'I apologise,' Ravenor repeated. 'I did what I had to do. Ballack and Thonius may be alive, alive right now, because of what I did.'

Angharad sank to her knees and let Evisorex slip to the deck. She shook with wracking sobs. Nayl crouched beside her and held her.

'But as a consequence, we are doomed,' said Ravenor. 'I am so very sorry I have brought you to this end with me. The House is flooding and dying. There is no escape.'

'There's got to be,' said Nayl, looking up. He suddenly pushed Angharad away and leapt upright with his shotgun raised. A black and white shape, tail high, had just crept onto the upper platform behind Ravenor. It stole forwards, claws scratching off the deck plates. It raised its head, sniffing and yapping, its tongue stabbing out between its teeth.

'Same to you,' said Nayl, and killed it with a single shot. Its thrashing body flew backwards off the platform. Nayl looked around at Ravenor. 'There's got to be a way out.'

'I can't find one,' Ravenor replied. 'I have been searching. I'm right, aren't I, housekeeper?'

The housekeeper looked up sharply. Its cowled head had been bowed. It was toying with the key in its hands with grazed, bleeding fingers.

'Yes,' the housekeeper replied. 'We have no boats, no escape pods. When the House dies, we die too.'

'That's a load of–' Nayl began.

'Harlon,' said Ravenor calmly. His fatigue was so great, he could barely summon the effort. 'When the House dies, it will let go of the ice above. It will fall, and when it falls, it will fall into the abyss. What was it Lucic called it? Wholly Water, Harlon. Without a measurable bottom. In a minute or two, the water pressure will crush the

House like an egg. Even at my best, I couldn't protect us, certainly not long enough to get us back to the surface. Even then, the ice... and, as you may have noticed, I'm not at my best.'

'The Plyton woman was right,' said Angharad softly. 'This place will kill us more surely than the void itself.'

'No,' murmured Nayl. 'Screw this, no. We don't just give up and wait to die.'

'Sometimes, that's a warrior's fate,' said Angharad. She picked up her steel and wiped the blade before sheathing it. The blade was stained and bruised with acid.

'Balls to that,' Nayl snapped. 'That's fancy warrior talk. I'm a paid gun. We think percentages. I don't worship any frigging honour code. Lu was right about that. About me. I worship chances, edges, survival. We have a way out.'

'No, Harlon,' Ravenor sighed. 'We're done.'

Nayl glared at Ravenor. 'We have a frigging way out!' he insisted. 'We still have one way out left to us.' He nodded towards the door.

'Absolutely not,' said Angharad with a shudder. 'You haven't seen what's through there.'

'You have.'

'That's why I won't go. It's death.'

'You survived it, lady.'

'Barely.'

'We can survive it together.'

'It's death, Harlon Nayl,' she said flatly.

'So is this,' he said. 'I'd rather die fighting for a chance than roll over and wait for death to get me.'

The Wych House shuddered again, and tilted more steeply. They had to hold on. Nayl looked down. Through the mesh of the platform he could see black water pouring up through the riser shaft to flood the floor space below them. Fires, caught by the swirling water, guttered and went out.

'Last call,' he said. 'Who's with me.'

Angharad raised her head and wiped the blood from her mouth. She drew her sword. 'I am, I suppose,' she said.

There was a long pause, broken only by the death throe explosions of the House.

'So am I,' said Ravenor. He turned his chair to face the housekeeper. 'Come with us,' he said.

The housekeeper nodded.

'We need your key.'

The housekeeper nodded again.

'What's your name?' Ravenor asked.

The housekeeper slowly lowered the hood of its gown. It was a she, a young girl barely into adolescence. Her face was thin, pale, and fringed by cropped, blonde hair. 'I am Iosob,' she said.

'I am glad to know you, Iosob,' Ravenor said. 'Open the door for us.'

The girl raised her ancient key and fitted it into the lock. It turned, and the door opened. Nayl and Angharad stood beside her, weapons raised and ready.

The door opened. Gunshot red sunlight glowed out. They all recoiled at the alien smell.

'Let's go, if we're going,' said Harlon Nayl, racking the slide of his shotgun.

They stepped through the door, and it slammed shut behind them.

A second later, the Wych House died.

THEY WERE BEING shaken around like beads in a drum. Thunderous water had entirely flooded the docking pool, but the upthrust of current was such that the underboat couldn't right itself or dive. Twice, the boat slammed into the dock roof. Water seethed around them, aspirated, shimmering with bubbles. Kys, Plyton and Ballack had all been cut or bruised by impacts sustained from the underboat's violent capture. Thonius, dead, as far as Kys was concerned, had fallen off his bench seat. He rolled, leaden, across the trunk flooring.

Only the pilot servitor, strapped into his chair, was intact.

'Get us out!' Kys yelled at him, holding on tight. 'You wanted to get us out, so get us out!'

'I can't!' the servitor wailed back, fighting with the helm controls. 'The pressure wave coming in is too great! It's forcing us up into the dock roof!'

The underboat heaved and slammed again. Warning lights lit up. Plyton was thrown the length of the trunk. Ballack, clinging grimly to handholds, blood pouring down his leg, stared at Kys.

'Blow all the ballast,' he suggested.

'Would that work?' Kys asked the pilot frantically.

'Do I ask you how to do your job?' the pilot snapped back. 'No, it wouldn't work!'

'Ask him why,' Ballack yelled.

'Why?' Kys relayed.

'Because I've already blown the ballast,' the pilot replied. 'What am I, an amateur? I'm hardwired to drive underboats and I'm telling you, miss, that we're–'

An upswell of water hit them and punched them into the dock roof so hard the hull buckled. Klaxons sang out, but they were all too busy falling and rolling. Kys landed on Ballack, who screamed in pain.

'Oh good Throne–' the pilot began. He had seen how fast and violently the needle of the depthmeter was spinning.

'What?' Kys demanded.

'We're dropping!'

With one last, aching shudder, the Wych House lost its grip on the ceiling of ice. It fell away in a huge, expanding cloud of ice particles and streaming, exhaling air. Legs flailing, it sank like a stone into the dark expanse of Wholly Water yawning below.

The darkness embraced it. Its superstructure began to crimp and crush with the pressure. Fluttering, winking trails of silver bubbles streamed up from its vents like contrails.

The falling House rotated, rolled, and inverted.

Upside down, the docking pool flushed out violently. The stricken underboat flew up out of the entry hatch like a cork.

'Steady it, steady it!' Kys yelled, holding tight to the seat back.

'I'm trying!' the pilot servitor cried. His augmented hands pulled at the steering controls. The ventral fans spun, floundering, drowning in the under-rip of the falling House. The pilot hit the cavitation drive.

The underboat struggled, dragged down, then turned its nose upwards. They shot up, like a released buoy, hull plates groaning and bending.

'Where's the House?' Plyton asked, struggling into the pilot house. Kys shook her head. Far below, in the blackness, they glimpsed a falling structure that swiftly dropped out of sight into the abyss.

'Auspex?' Kys asked the pilot servitor.

He hit several switches.

The scanner system painted the descending House as a small yellow blip.

'Great Throne,' Ballack whispered. He had climbed in beside them, staring at the console.

The blip dropped away into the lower depths. It fizzled once, twice, and then vanished forever.

'Crushed by the pressure,' the pilot servitor said. 'It's gone.'

Kys sat back and began to cry.

No one said anything for a very long time.

FIVE

'TELL ME AGAIN, slowly,' said Kara Swole, 'what happened when you went through this door.'

'We were in the hellish red place at first,' Ballack said.
'It just had a feeling to it, a terrible feeling of menace.
Then the housekeeper opened the door again, and we
went through to a place that was near Dorsay, on
Gudrun. But it wasn't now, it was... the future. Many
years in the future.'

'This portal took you to different places and times?'
Kara asked cautiously, like a scholam tutor examining a
pupil's elaborate excuse for inconsistencies.

'Yes,' said Ballack. 'It was a distressing and disorientat-
ing experience. The door was in control all the time. It
made us wait while it opened, as if it was choosing what
to show us next. That is how I understood it to work. You
asked it a question, and it took you to places from which
some answer or answers might be discerned. What those
answers are, I believe, is very much a matter of interpre-
tation.'

'And then?'

'And then it took us to another place. A rural field. I
don't know the time or the place. A man was waiting
there for us. Ravenor went down and spoke with him,
then he returned and told us we were going back.'

'Who was the man?' asked Kara.

'It was the facilitator, Orfeo Culzean,' said Ballack.

'How do you know?' asked Kara.

'Ravenor told us.'

'I don't remember him saying anything of the sort,' said
Carl Thonius.

They looked around at him. Carl was sitting in the window seat of the Berynth's apartment main room,
huddled in blankets. His haggard face was especially thin
and pale, and discoloured by bruises and dozens of lin-
ear scabs. His voice was an unhealthy whisper.

'My dear Carl,' said Ballack gently, 'you were quite agitated at the time. I doubt you remember much of
anything.'

Thonius shrugged and looked away, out through the window. Once they'd got clear of the House, and there had been time to attend to him, Kys and Plyton had found Carl to be only superficially hurt, his face and body battered and scratched. His death-like state, from which he had gradually recovered, had been put down to severe shock.

'Culzean,' said Kara rising to her feet. 'So he and Molotch were three steps ahead of us the whole while. It was all a trap, in other words, down to Worna being on hand to close the House down once you were in.'

'It worked well, didn't it?' said Kys bitterly.

Kara took a deep breath. She had come down to the surface the moment Kys had restored contact. She could still not believe the news they had broken to her. Ravenor and Nayl, dead. Angharad too. Dead and gone. Everyone was numb. Grief would follow, later.

She looked around the room: Carl, the most physically hurt of them all, huddled in the window seat; Ballack by the fire, his ugly leg wound bound and strapped, a walking cane to hand; Maud Plyton in the corner, lost in her own thoughts, staring at the floor; Kys, standing by the door, head bowed, suffering the most intensely.

Kara stepped towards her and, not for the first time since their reunion, embraced her. They held onto each other for a moment. The two of them had lost the most. Gideon Ravenor and Harlon Nayl had been their true friends and comrades for a long time. Kara fought the urge to cry. She could feel the heat of sorrow rising. She held it back. They all seemed to be looking to her now, the heart of the shattered group or, at least, what remained of it. Kys was too wrapped up in anguish and self-loathing to be a leader. More than once, as she had haltingly told Kara of Ravenor's death, she had said, 'I should have stayed with him. I left him behind.'

Kara let Kys go, and made her sit. She looked back at Ballack. 'The rest now. Let me hear it. I want to hear it.'

'We went back through the door. It took us to a hive somewhere, as if it was playing with us, refusing Ravenor's request to take us home. Then back to the red hell again. Once it had us there, it refused to open any more. That was Molotch's trap for us. I believe he may have commanded the door somehow to take us to that place and maroon us there where those things could find us and kill us. I would not put such a feat past Zygmunt Molotch.'

'Nor I,' said Carl. 'Except...'

'Except, Carl?' Kara asked.

'Why so elaborate? I know Molotch has a penchant for the baroque and theatrical, but why all that? Why take us to Culzean? Why arrange a meeting where they conversed for some minutes? Why not just kill us?'

'He wanted something from us,' said Kys, looking up. 'He wanted something from Ravenor. A deal, I think. Worna could have just killed us, but he was waiting for something. Waiting for... orders to kill us or spare us.'

'That's right,' said Plyton, speaking for the first time in hours. 'Lucic and the gunman holding me had a conversation to that effect. They were waiting for word to come. They were holding us until they knew if we could be friends or not.'

'Friends?' Kara echoed.

'I heard them say it,' said Plyton. 'That very word. The bounty hunter seemed to doubt it. I think he was pretty certain they'd just end up executing us. But from what's been said, I think it depended on Ravenor's answer to whatever this Culzean was offering.'

Kys shook her head. 'What in the name of Terra could Molotch and Culzean have been proffering that could have made us friends? I mean, what? What were they thinking? Ravenor would never side with Molotch, for any reason.'

'Well, he clearly said no,' said Thonius.

'But there must have been a chance he'd say yes,' said Kara, 'or they wouldn't have gone to all that effort.'

'Whatever, he said no,' Thonius snapped. 'Which is why we were sent back into Molotch's trap. That was his insurance, to wipe us out if Ravenor refused him.'

'That's when the door wouldn't open?' Kara asked Ballack. The interrogator smoothed back his long white hair and nodded. 'And then the creatures came for us. I don't know what they were. I have never even heard of their like. They were–'

'Awful,' said Thonius quietly. 'Beautiful.'

'That's a strange choice of words,' said Kys. 'I saw them too, remember?'

'So did I,' shuddered Plyton. 'They weren't beautiful, they–'

'Anything that is so immaculately designed to do what it does is beautiful,' Thonius cut in. 'They were the most terrifying things I have ever seen, but they were perfect too. Perfect killing machines, so driven and single-minded and pure.'

'Pure evil,' said Ballack.

'Not even that,' said Thonius. 'Just pure. Just themselves. Hungry and alien, implacable. Utterly lacking in any emotional or intellectual quality we might recognise except ruthless, relentless hunger. I'd rather have tried to reason with an ork, or a scion of the Archenemy. At least they have needs and urges and ambitions, diction and intellect. At least there could be, however unlikely, a basis for dialogue. But those things... Molotch chose his assassins well.'

'So the door was locked,' Kara said to Ballack. 'These things were upon you. I have to ask... how did you get out?'

Kys rose and walked into the adjacent room to pour herself a drink from the stand. Her nerves were shot but, more particularly, she didn't want any of the others to see how incapable she was of controlling her tears. They streamed down her cheeks. Her body ached, and her hands shook as she selected a clean glass and filled it with amasec.

Gideon, I'm so sorry. I should not have left you.

Through the open door behind her, she heard Ballack's voice.

'We were overrun. It was a nightmare. We were seconds away from being torn to ribbons. Ravenor was waring me and Angharad. It was relentless, just a blur of instinct and frenzy. Then Carl fell to them. I thought he was dead for sure. I thought I was next.'

Kys sipped her drink, listening.

Ballack's voice had dropped low, and had become strained with emotion. 'There was... there was a sudden flash. Red light, red energy. I remembered thinking it was all red, but everything was already red in that place. This was intense and sudden, like a bomb going off. The energy flared like–'

'Like what?' Kys heard Kara ask.

'Like pain. Like rage. It tasted of rage and fury. I swear, it was a psychic event.'

'Ravenor.'

'No,' Ballack whispered. 'I don't think so. It didn't come from him. It was just there, a daemonic spasm from the depths of the immaterium. It lashed out, and burned the creatures off us. It threw them back, melted and twisted and broken. It saved us. It blew the door open, against the door's will.'

'Then what?'

'I don't remember. Just scraps, really. I remember staggering back through the door, still under Ravenor's control. I'd found Carl on the ground, surrounded by the slaughtered ruins of a dozen creatures. Ravenor willed me to pick him up, and of course I did.'

Kys walked back into the doorway. 'It *was* psychic,' she said. Kara looked around at her. 'I was in the theatre chamber when the door blew. Ballack is absolutely right. It was a psychic event. I felt it. I smelled it. It was raw and uncontrolled. It was feral. I assumed it was Ravenor's doing. I assumed it was his desperation.'

Kara nodded, adding as she did so, 'And then?'

'Ravenor was wounded, dreadfully wounded,' Kys said. 'Ballack was out of it, conquered by pain. Carl was unconscious too. Ravenor told me to get them clear, to get them back to the underboat. He told me he would follow as soon as he had Angharad. And like a fool, I obeyed him. I took them, and I made my escape and I left Gideon there to die.'

She looked down at the drink in her hand and set it down. 'Excuse me,' she said, and walked towards to the apartment's exit.

'Patience,' Kara called after her.

'Not now, Kar,' Kys replied, and slammed the hatch behind her.

There was a long silence. The fire guttered in the grate.

'Kys will move past this in time,' Ballack said. 'She will accommodate this, and–'

'Shut up, you ninker,' Kara snapped. 'You don't know the first thing about what we–'

'Kara,' said Carl quietly.

Kara breathed in and out hard. 'Forgive me, Ballack. This is a difficult time for us, and I shouldn't have said that to you. I know you were only trying to help.'

'It's all right,' said Ballack. 'I'm aware I am an outsider here, new to this company. I should remember that.'

'What happens now?' asked Plyton. 'I mean, apart from the fact that it's over and everything?'

'There may be some traces left here on Utochre of Molotch or Worna,' said Ballack. 'Some leads, some signs of their handiwork. They went to a lot of trouble setting this up.'

'And if we find them?' Kara asked.

'Molotch is still out there,' said Ballack. 'Our mission is still not completed. If we can find a single lead, I say we use it. In Ravenor's name, we use it. We track Molotch to ground and make him pay for what he has done.'

'Closure?' asked Kara.

'Closure,' Ballack agreed. 'It's all we have left. And it's what Ravenor would have wanted.'

Kara nodded. Plyton shrugged, tears in her eyes, then nodded too.

'It's not at all what he'd have wanted,' said Thonius, rising to his feet and dropping his blankets.

'What?'

'Come on,' said Thonius, looking at Kara. 'This is stupid. This is becoming mindless. We've torn ourselves apart hunting for this heretic, and still he eludes us. Maybe it's time we recognised that he's always going to beat us.'

'No.'

'Well, Kara Swole, I say yes,' said Thonius. 'And, funnily enough, I think I'm in charge here now. I am Ravenor's interrogator. That gives me acting command in his... his absence. There is only one course of action left open to us now.'

'And what might that be?' asked Kara.

Thonius shrugged. 'We should go directly to Thracian Primaris and present ourselves to the High Conclave of the Ordos Helican. We should make full account of our misadventure, in all detail, and throw ourselves upon the mercy of Lord Rorken.'

'No,' said Kara.

'Again, yes, Kara,' Thonius said, clearly and precisely. 'We broke all the rules, and we still failed. I doubt very much I've got a career left, but I know what's right. Ravenor should have done this months ago. It behoves us to make amends and start repairing the damage we have done. Even if it means we offer ourselves up to the most stringent discipline of the Inquisition.'

He limped across the room, picked up Kys's abandoned drink, and knocked it back. 'Let's pack up and make our way as penitents. Let's try to make good the wrong we have wrought. It's too late to even think otherwise.'

GIDEON, I'M SO *sorry. I should not have left you.*

Two floors down from the apartment, Kys sat alone in the dim stairwell of the ancient building and wept. Two floors down was as far as she'd got after storming out. She'd been intending to find a saloon or a bar, to purchase a drink, and maybe get into a pointless argument or a fight. But her legs had failed, and she'd sat down on the worn wooden steps.

Ravenor was gone. Ravenor was dead. Harlon was dead. Nothing would ever be the same again. Ever.

She heard footsteps coming up the stairwell below her. A resident of the block, perhaps. She ignored the approach, hoping whoever it was would step by her and leave her be, perhaps mistaking her for some stack wretch who'd come into the building to attempt begging.

The footsteps came closer. Someone sat down on the stairs beside her.

'I... I am abjectly aloof for any words to make fulsome expression,' said Sholto Unwerth.

Kys laughed despite herself. 'Where did you come from?'

'I was, foremost, checking of the lander, so that with all convenientness, it might be ready to take us aloft.'

'Is it ready?'

'It is, Patience.'

He reached into his pocket and offered her a handkerchief. 'Avoid that part,' he said, indicating, 'for I may have subsequently blown on it. The rest is quite fresh.'

'Don't look at me,' she said, her eyes streaming. 'I have snot coming out of my nose.'

'It is quite dark,' he said, looking around. 'I can define little of your mucus, so modestly is assured.'

She laughed again.

'Is it true?' he asked.

She nodded and blew her nose.

'Well, I am five saken,' he said.

'Five?'

'It is one more than four saken,' he replied. 'It is a level of grief behind which there is no furthestmost.'

'Except six?'

'Pray no one ever experiences six saken,' Unwerth said. She could see he had small tears in his eyes.

'I am pre-empt,' he said quietly. 'I am stricken. I am beside yourself.'

'I'm glad of that,' she said.

'He was a good man, as floating chairs go,' said Unwerth.

'He was.'

'I think he likened of me, to the end, and made his trust upon me, in some measuring. I hope so.'

'I believe he did, Sholto. Gideon would not have kept in your company if he didn't trust you.'

'Well, I had a ship, and I was excrescently pliantable,' Unwerth countered.

'There is that.'

Unwerth frowned thoughtfully. 'Are you all right?' he asked.

'I will be.'

Unbidden, he curled his short arms up around her shoulders and pulled her tight.

'You will, indeed, be,' he said.

'Sholto,' Kys said, sniffing, comforted by his little embrace. 'He was there. I saw him.'

'Who?'

She nodded. 'The man who hurt you. Lucius Worna. He nearly killed me. I nearly killed him. I wish I had, for your sake. I would have done it, but he had the drop on me and teleported away. He–'

She paused.

'What?' Unwerth asked.

'He teleported away,' Kys whispered with growing realisation. 'He called to Siskind and teleported away.'

She broke the embrace. 'Siskind. Siskind! It's got to be the same Siskind, hasn't it? The *Allure's* here. Throne, why didn't I connect this before? The *Allure's* here!'

She got up, and turned back up the stairs.

'Can you scan for it?' she asked as she ran.

'It will be of significated disguise,' he said, scrambling after her. 'But I know its particulates. Its draft and measure, its signature. The *Arethusa* can match its pattern.'

'Come on! Can't you run any faster?'

'There is a bigness to these stairs that I am not as copius with as your long leggage!'

'Do you want me to carry you?' she snapped.

He stopped. She stopped too, and looked back at him.

'That would just be undignified, wouldn't it?' she said.

'Incandescently,' he replied.

SIX

RED HEAT. AGAIN, the gunshot sun.

The area around the lonely door is heaped with the mangled corpses of the black and white organisms.

I feel some pride that we managed to slay so many. Most of this was Angharad's work.

There is no sign of life, but there is still the sense of dread, the shadow in the warp. I am trusting that the door will allow us to step away from this place. We cannot stay here long.

Angharad feels it. She watches the horizon, Evisorex angled in her grip. She is exhausted. She will not withstand another clash like the one we have just been through.

Nayl feels it too, coming new to this experience of stepping into another time-place. He raises his weapon, tense suddenly.

He was right. This is the only option. Staying in the House to die along with it would have been the decision of one foolish and weak.

I am weary and I am wounded, but I am not foolish and I am not weak. Not yet. Soon, perhaps. The damage I have sustained to my support systems, the leakage of fluid, may be critical. I believe I am already dying. Worse, my mind is frail and utterly incapable of defending us. Every movement is an effort to me.

'What happens now?' Nayl asks me, nervously.

'We wait,' I tell him, trying to hide from him how useless I am.

'For how long?'

'For however long it takes.'

'They're coming,' says Angharad, the Carthaen steel bristling in her fists. 'Evisorex thirsts.'

'I'm sure it does,' I reply. I look at Iosob, the child, the housekeeper. She is afraid. Things have never gone this way for her before.

'Iosob?'

She fumbles with the key. 'We wait.'

'And then?'

'Then the key may turn. But the door locked us here before. Your enemy... what was his name?'

'Molotch?'

'Molotch. He made adjustments to the door. He prepared it. It may not open again. He was very knowledgeable.'

I look out at the black headland of volcanic rock Angharad is watching.

'What else do you know about him?' I ask.

'Nothing,' Iosob says. 'He came, he contained us. He killed some of the housekeepers to make his point. He was very skilled in his work.'

'I have some skills of my own,' I say.

'But you no longer have the daemon.'

'What?'

'The daemon. The daemon that saved us, when the hooked things came the first time. It drove them back, and threw the door wide open. I assumed it was your daemon.'

'You are mistaken. I don't own a daemon,' I reply. 'What are you talking about?'

'The House knows,' she says. 'You brought a daemon in here with you, last time. A howling fury of the warp. It is the only reason you survived.'

'What the hell is she talking about?' Nayl asks.

'Iosob, what do you mean?' I feel she is terribly confused, her memory of the traumatic incident patchy. Perhaps she mistook my mental powers for something darker.

Iosob looks away at the black outcrop, scared. 'They're coming again, Gideon who is Ravenor.'

'Last time, you called them *the Great Devourer*, Iosob. I heard you. What are they?'

'They are the future. Passing through the three-way door, we have seen them several times. Three hundred years from our now, they will come. Behemoth.'

'What is Behemoth?'

'Behemoth, Kraken, Leviathan.'

'Iosob?'

She whimpers and drops the key. She bends down and searches for it in the dust.

'The Imperium will shake. They will be the worst enemies mankind has ever faced.'

'What are they called?' I ask.

'They don't have a name yet,' she replies, 'not yet.' She finds the key and rises again.

'This is the future, then?' I ask.

'This is what the door shows. Three, four hundred years gone by from our now. This is what we have seen, sometimes.'

She glances around. 'Oh, they're coming back.'

'The child is right,' grunts Angharad.

'I've got eighteen shells in this pump-shot,' says Nayl. 'What happens when they're spent?'

'Try the door, please, Iosob,' I instruct. I look back at Nayl. 'I have a feeling, Harlon, that just after you expend your seventeenth round, you're going to wish you had stayed aboard the Wych House and died.'

'Charming,' he replies. 'I can always count on you for a positive spin.'

Iosob tries the key in the lock. It refuses to turn.

'The door is not ready,' she tells me. 'Or, well, it may not ever be ready.'

'Keep trying the key, please.'

I wait. Nayl strides around me. 'Gideon,' he asks, 'if the Wych House dies, how long will this damn door last?'

'I don't know. If it was anchored to the House, not long. I'm hoping, praying, it exists beyond the House's dimensions.'

'Well, that's a relief,' he mocks.

'Ravenor!' Angharad is alert suddenly. I turn and see what she has seen: a dust cloud rising above the black volcanic outcrop. It drifts slowly, a yellow oblong smudge.

'More of them!'

'Please, Iosob try the key again.'

This time, miraculously, it turns. The door opens.

THE DOOR OPENS three times, in fact. To an empty, wind-blown steppe; to a hazed plain of duricrust under a night sky where what can only be the Eye of Terror swirls and crackles like a diseased sun; and then to a forest of white, glassy trees beside a green-black lake.

There is no immediate threat here, no sense of doom, no trace of life apart from the curious trees and small, pale wasps.

We rest there, just for an hour or two. We have to keep going, for I cannot tell how long we will have use of the door, or how many times we will have to walk through it before we find a time and place remotely connected to our origin.

But we can only go on if we rest first. We have no food, and cannot trust the lake's water. I test it with my systems, and find it is unpotable. It isn't even water.

Angharad lies down and sleeps. So does the housekeeper, her small head resting against the trunk of a glassy tree. Nayl paces up and down.

It is cold. Up through the white branches of the trees, the sky is a silky grey, and sprinkled with star systems I don't know. How far away are we, I wonder? How many parsecs, how many years? Is this even our galaxy?

I try to rest my mind, and soothe it with psykana rituals, probing it for damage, cleansing it of fatigue. Meditation may restore some of my strength.

But I am aware of my body, I am aware of physicality, my shrunken form, cold and helpless and dense inside the chair. These are sensations the chair usually spares me.

I consider again what Iosob said. What daemon did she think she saw? If there is any truth to her words, I have one suspicion, one I cannot do anything about.

In extremis, when I had to ware him, there was something artificial in Ballack's head that previous scans had not shown to me. To ware someone, though, gives a different, deeper insight. At the time, I had been far too busy – far too frantic – to pay it much heed, but now in quiet reflection, I remember it.

It was a block. A baffle, artificially imposed, almost undetectable, a very sophisticated piece of psychic architecture. It was designed to keep a part of Ballack's mind invisible to me. I have seen the type of thing before in my life, most particularly in a technique honed by the Cognitae, which they called the Black Dam.

What was he hiding behind it? What was his connection to the noetic school? Did he install the dam himself, or was it placed there without his knowledge by someone else?

Was it Ballack who left a footprint on Maud Plyton's psyche?

Has Ballack been hiding a daemon in his mind all along?

'GIDEON?' NAYL TOOK a step closer to the silent chair. The surface of it was scratched and battered, with a patina that looked as if it had been sandblasted. Congealed fluid clogged some of the deeper gouges.

'Gideon?'

'Harlon?' Ravenor's voxponder wheezed and replied.

'Were you asleep?'

'I think so. I think I must have been.'

'Ah, sorry. It's hard to tell.' Nayl looked around. Angharad was curled up and slumbering like a cat. The housekeeper looked like a lost child, huddled in a storybook woodland. 'It's been about three hours. Actually, that's a guess, because my chron is acting really funny, but my gut says three hours.' He glanced at the sky. 'And it's getting darker and colder.'

'We should use the door again,' said Ravenor.

'Do you think it really will take us home?' he asked.

'I doubt we'll get anything as precise as that,' said Ravenor. 'I'm hoping for a recognisable Imperial location, even a remote one or a ship, within five years either way of our exit point.'

'Five years?' Nayl asked, doubtfully. 'As much as that?'

'If we get as close as that, I'll be content,' Ravenor replied. 'I'm rather afraid the door's operating system is impaired. It's no longer opening in response to a question of coherence. I think we're travelling at random. I'm not even sure that the locations it's opening for us are going to be compatible with human forms.'

Nayl raised his eyebrows. 'That's a nice thought I hadn't yet considered. So the next time we open the door, it could lead to... what? An airless world? A toxic atmosphere?'

'The open void. The warp. The heart of a star. Or back to the Wych House. This escape route comes with no guarantee it is an escape route at all. We may have simply postponed our fate. In the light of that, I'm sure you'll agree, five years and a few light years out would be something of a miracle.'

Nayl nodded thoughtfully. 'You never did tell me if you got an answer,' he said.

'I got part of one. The door took me to Molotch, or to the world where he was hiding, at least.'

'Where was that?'

'There was no way to tell. Orfeo Culzean was waiting for me there.'

'To kill you?'

'To talk to me.'

'You're joking!' Nayl laughed.

'He had a proposition. He wanted to make a pact with me. It seems he and Molotch are deeply concerned about Slyte.'

Nayl rubbed the bruises Worna's hand had left on his throat. 'Slyte?'

'Culzean was suggesting that Molotch and I worked together to combat Slyte. He wanted us to put an end to our fight and work in unison against a mutual enemy. I said no.'

Ravenor fell silent. He had no intention of telling Nayl the details of the conversation.

'If you'd said yes?' Nayl asked.

'Culzean would have sent us back through the door, and Worna would have conveyed us off Utochre to whereever Molotch was waiting. Because I said no, he used the door as a murder weapon.'

'I thought the Slyte business was over. I thought we'd gone past the critical point. What does Molotch know that we don't?'

'Perhaps nothing. We may know more about it than him. He may not be aware that the critical point, as you put it, has passed.'

'I doubt that,' said Nayl. 'Since when has he ever known less than us?'

'Wake the others,' Ravenor said.

THE NEXT TURN of the key brought them out onto a ragged plateau of ancient, crumbling granite. Extreme age had caused the rock to rot and lose its constitution. Beyond the plateau, a ragged world stretched away under a sky threaded by blinking whiskers of lightning.

The next opened the door to a fogbound marsh. It was humid, and the air was bad. So was the standing water. Thread-thin worms writhed in the mire, pulsing their wretched mouths and firing millivolt electrical impulses that prickled at the travellers' legs as they waded around.

The door opened and closed behind them again. A vast rift valley of yellow rock, gouged out under a selpic blue sky, spread out in front of them. The valley was ten kilometres wide, and four or five deep. It was achingly hot, and the heat was dry. The air smelled like metal.

'Leave this place quickly,' Ravenor said. His chair systems were reading a blaze of solar radiation.

Next, a small coral atoll in the middle of a choppy ocean washed violet by small, wobbling jellyfish in vast profusion. There was no other land in sight. The sky was a pink haze. A booming sound kept echoing out across the distance. Very far away, indistinct in the haze, some great, basking shape rose from the sea and rolled slowly back in.

'Next,' said Nayl.

Next was a dark, black forest, bitter and damp. The air hinted at advanced decay, and the merest pricks of white sky penetrated the thick, black fronds of the trees. They moved a little way from the door, hoping to see signs of habitation or perhaps a trail. Odd sounds knocked and chirruped in the darkness. Tiny black flies began to buzz around them. Angharad brushed them away from her face. They were very small, like fleas.

In a few seconds, the clouds of them had become unbearably thick, blackening exposed skin and swirling into nostrils, ears and eyes.

'Exit!' Ravenor ordered. Iosob struggled with the key, moaning through tightly pursed lips as she tried to shake off the flies.

Ravenor summoned a little of what was left of his will and let it wash out, sweeping the flies away for a second.

The door opened.

Here, a bone yard, a windy, cold desert of blue-grey dust. The chasing wind fanned horsetails of loose dust off the tops of dunes. The vast, dry bones of long dead animals covered the landscape as far as they could see, tumbled in disarticulated heaps, half submerged in the dust. These animals had been giants. The sky was a mottled brown, and the las-fire streaks of shooting stars, all descending at the same forty-five degree angle, flickered across it like sparks off a grinding wheel. Ravenor's three companions crunched out amongst the bone waste, spitting phlegm black with dead flies out of their mouths.

'Open the door again,' said Angharad, humourlessly.

Iosob obeyed, and they came into a city. It was a frigid, bare place of cyclopean blocks under a yellow sky dominated by a ringed gas giant. There was little doubt at all that the city was not of human construction.

'Have you seen anything like this before?' Nayl asked. Sound had a strange, hollow echo to it. The cold air held a sweet tang, like sugar.

'No,' said Ravenor. They wandered the area around the door for five minutes.

'It's been dead a long time, hasn't it?' asked Angharad.

'No,' said Ravenor. 'I can feel something here, a presence.' Nayl raised his gun.

'It's far away,' said Ravenor, 'but I can feel it. It's not human.' He turned his chair. 'Open the door again, please, Iosob. I don't think we're safe here.'

As they went through the door, Nayl wondered quite what Ravenor had felt to make him so sure of that.

The next place was an arid plain, cracked and shrunken like sun-damaged skin. Weird succulent plant growth, like sprouts of brain tissue, formed forests on either side of the parched plain. A few kilometres away, the rusted, buckled shell of some colossal machine lay derelict on the ground. It looked like part of a starship, but what kind they couldn't tell. There was no time to debate or investigate. The atmosphere was barely breathable. Nausea enveloped them, and they started to gasp and choke.

It seemed to take forever for the key to turn.

'Throne!' Nayl exclaimed as they made their next exit. 'Be careful! Watch your step!'

The door had opened onto a narrow platform of rough-hewn, untreated wood. It was part of a massive, and not altogether reliable-looking, matrix of scaffolding erected around a huge, decaying ouslite tower. They were close to the top, in bright midday sunlight and fresh wind, and the platform was a thousand metres above the hazy sprawl of a huge city. Hundreds of dirty smoke trails rose from the city roofscape.

The platform swayed as they moved gingerly out across it. Iosob held onto a scaffold cross-member and refused to look down. She shut her eyes.

'I don't like this,' she said.

'Do we climb down?' asked Angharad, blithely standing on the edge and staring down, her hands on her hips. 'There is life here. I can hear it. Bustle. There is movement in the streets. Teeming life. It looks like an Imperial city.'

'I think we would regret doing that,' said Ravenor. 'It's teeming with life, all right, but I'm not reading human minds anywhere. I think this *was* an Imperial city once.'

'So who's down there now?' asked Nayl. 'And might they not at least have things like water and food?'

The towers and buildings nearest to them, none as tall as their vantage place, were also in bad repair and strung with complex networks of primitive scaffolding. It was hard to tell if the city was being repaired or dismantled by its new owners.

Angharad's keen eyes picked out figures moving on the scaffolding on a neighbouring tower, four hundred metres below them: labourers, at work.

'Ravenor is right. There's no point climbing down.'

'What can you see?' Nayl asked.

'Orks,' she replied mildly.

When the door opened next, it was into a black space. There was no light whatsoever, just cold, musty air.

'Gideon?' Nayl called out.

Ravenor ignited his chair's lamp systems. His power was alarmingly low, because the lamps did not blaze with their usual white intensity. The yellow glow revealed their surroundings: a stone chamber, rectangular, about the size of the *Arethusa's* secondary hold. Walls, floor and ceiling were made of the same, flush-fitting stone blocks, expertly built and, though there were no signs of wear or decay or even dust, very old.

'There's no door,' said Angharad.

'Ah, you noticed that,' said Nayl.

'I mean, no other door,' she said. 'Unless it is concealed.'

'It isn't,' Ravenor said. 'I have scanned. The chamber is sealed and solid.'

'Why would someone build it, then? For what purpose, if you can't get in and out of it?'

'Maybe *they* can,' said Ravenor. 'Maybe they have a teleport. Maybe they don't want to come in here. Maybe it's sealed to keep something in.'

'But there's nothing in here except us,' said Nayl. He looked at Ravenor sharply. 'Is there?'

'I don't think so.'

'Door!' Angharad declared.

'We could at least rest here for a few minutes,' said Ravenor. 'It has the merit of being free from the sort of health hazards we've found elsewhere.'

They sat down beside his chair and stared at the door.

'Iosob,' said Ravenor, after a while, 'I've been thinking about the door. It's operating randomly, isn't it?'

She shrugged. 'I do not know. That is not my function. But I think that's very likely.'

'Without the House to anchor it, the door is cut loose, directionless?'

She shrugged again. 'That is not–'

'–your function, I know. How old are you, Iosob?'

'Fourteen years.'

'You were raised in the House?'

'I was raised by the family of housekeepers to be a housekeeper, as my mothers before me.'

'And you're not psychically active in any way?'

'I don't believe I am. How would I know?'

Ravenor was already pretty certain. He had gently scanned her several times, and found no trace. Her mind, indeed, seemed a strangely lonely, unhappy place, empty of the usual buzz of thoughts. 'None of the housekeepers were psykers, were they?' he asked.

She shook her head.

'Is that important?' Nayl asked.

'However the door operates,' Ravenor said, 'it involves a strong psychic process. I don't know if the House was doing that, or someone we never met. The housekeepers are not active, because active psykers would have interfered with the door's operation. In fact, I think they were brought up under very particular circumstances, extensive ritual conditioning to keep their minds very... calm.' He had been going to say 'vacant', but didn't want to in front of Iosob.

'With the House gone,' Ravenor said, 'I was wondering if I could start to influence it. I was wondering if my mind could engage with it enough to guide us.'

They got back on their feet.

Ravenor reached out and probed the door the way he would a living mind. He felt foolish doing it, for although the door had an undeniable background vibration of power, it was just a wooden door.

'Our most immediate concern is thirst,' said Ravenor. 'Open the door.'

SEVEN

THEY STEPPED THROUGH into a blustery, fresh, cold wind. They were in a rocky foreshore, a strand of limestone with a crashing grey sea on one side and a range of low cliffs on the other. A low sky full of murky clouds was racing past at what seemed an abnormally fast rate. There was moisture in the wind, and the bluster was raising eddies of chasing spray off the wet rock.

'You found water,' said Nayl. He nodded towards the breaking sea fifty metres away, 'but unless that's freshwater...'

'It isn't,' said Angharad. 'You can taste the brine in the air.' She paused. 'Step towards me slowly, Nayl.'

'What?'

+Do as she says.+

Ten metres behind Nayl, what they had taken to be a slab of wet rock had stirred. It was an immense, pallid crocodilian creature with a long, slender snout. It had been basking on the foreshore in the ocean spray. It raised its broad body on four large flipper limbs, and slithered lazily down towards the water.

They looked around and saw there were a great number of the things, camouflaged into the grey limestone, basking in colonies all along the chilly shore. Some lay with their mouths wide open. They seemed languid, and not the least interested in the visitors.

'Think there's more than eighteen of them?' Nayl asked.

'W-why?' asked Iosob, gazing in some trepidation at the landscape of monsters.

Nayl patted his shotgun. He looked at Ravenor. 'What do you think? Is this a near miss? Or did you get the door to find us water?'

'It's probably a coincidence.' Ravenor replied. 'Let's try again.'

There was a soft, crumping boom of thunder, and it began to rain, a few large drops at first, and then a sustained, torrential downpour of monsoon proportions. They were all drenched in an instant.

'That's fresh!' Nayl shouted. He tilted his head back and opened his mouth. 'Throne be, that's fresh!' Angharad and Iosob were already drinking in the rain. Iosob cupped her hands and lapped from them as they rapidly filled. With head tilted back, it was impossible not to drink down whole mouthfuls.

Ravenor opened the catchment vents on his chair and collected what water he could from the gulleys of the hull. Even a little would help restore the fluid balance of his support systems.

The rain stopped as quickly as it had begun. Nayl wiped his hand across his wet face and laughed out loud. 'It was worth coming here after all,' he said.

* * *

I SETTLE MY mind for another attempt. I am becoming increasingly fatigued. My concerns about my own deterioration are grave. I believe the support chair's damaged systems are shutting down, and without them, my life will become untenable. I have hidden this from the others, although I suspect Harlon has some idea.

I focus on the door, and on the key in Iosob's hand. I wish I understood the arcane mechanisms of the three-way door better, for blind meddling with such powerful artefacts is usually extremely inadvisable.

I try to connect anyway. I try to make the door, or some sentience beyond its physical substance, understand what I need from it. This time I concentrate my thoughts on memories on the *Arethusa*. If there is a place I could wish us to be, it is there.

I think of the *Arethusa*. I think of the year 404. Will it comprehend me? Will it be able to act upon that comprehension? I told it *thirst*, and it brought us to water, if only in the most tenuous sense.

'Open the door.'

A WARM, DUSTY wind blew into their faces. A hard sun beat down from a cloudless sky. The door stood in a thicket of odd, twisted thorn brush, hard as bone and twice as tall as a fully grown man. The brush was gnarled and wrinkled, powder grey on its bark, and its thorns were long and sharp.

'Is this what you were trying for?' Nayl asked.

'No,' said Ravenor, gliding out of the doorway behind him. 'Not at all.'

'We take a look around?' asked Nayl. 'Seeing as we're here?'

They moved away from the door, following the dusty slope up through the tangled brush. The wind was only light, but the brush seemed to move and creak around them.

'Not liking the plant life much,' muttered Nayl.

'It's only plants,' said Angharad. 'Plants cannot kill you.'

'Well, let me put the lie to that,' Nayl began. 'I was in this place once–'

'Shut up,' said Ravenor. He was so weary, it was an effort even to be polite. Disappointment was suffocating him.

'What's that?' asked Angharad, pointing ahead of them. They could glimpse some structure, like a derrick or mast, rising from above the brush cover at the top of the slope.

'Let's find out,' said Nayl. 'Look, ahead of us, the thorn scrub thins out.'

They advanced, toiling up the slope, ducking under the spiked boughs. The thorn thicket came to an abrupt halt in a ragged line. Beyond it, the rising land had been cleared for several hundred metres. The earth looked scorched, as if flamers had been used to burn back the resilient brush.

'Look at that,' said Nayl.

Clear of the scrub, they had a good view up the slope to the crown of the hill, where a drab, uninviting compound had been constructed. The compound was surrounded by a high security fence, and the summit of the hill had been entirely denuded of thorn brush within three hundred metres of the fence line. Inside the fence lay a complex of modular buildings surrounding several tall masts.

The masts were high gain vox antennae. The modular buildings were of a recognisably Imperial template.

'It's not home, but it's the best break we've had so far,' Nayl murmured.

'We will approach?' asked Angharad.

'Yes,' said Ravenor. 'I'm reading human mind patterns, but they're oddly dulled. I can't fix numbers or much thought detail.'

'Why?' asked Nayl.

'I'm... I'm having trouble concentrating,' said Ravenor. 'I'm sorry.'

'Are you in pain, Gideon?' Nayl asked.

'Let that be my problem, Harlon.' The chair moved forwards. They began to follow it up the cleared slope. A voice suddenly rang out, distorted by vox speakers, and stopped them in their tracks.

Three humans were trudging up the slope behind them from the brush. They were male, clad in dusty Guard-issue uniforms that had been heavily reinforced with chainmail and shielding plates. They wore heavy, full-visored helmets like pit fighters. The visor plates, like the shielding they wore, were scratched and shabby. All three of them were aiming heavy, dirty flamers.

'Stay where you are,' ordered one of them. His voice crackled out of his helmet relay. He gestured with his flamer. 'Where the hell did you come from?'

Nayl gestured honestly at the brush cover behind them.

'Some kind of joker?' asked another of the men.

'Where's your ship?' demanded the leader. 'We didn't see any ship come in. Where did you set down?'

'We didn't come in a ship,' said Ravenor through his voxponder. He was alarmed that he hadn't been fore-warned of their approach, but much more alarmed that, now they were visible, he couldn't read their minds at all.

The men stared at Ravenor's chair.

'What is that?' asked the leader.

'A support chair,' said Nayl.

'For a cripple?'

'Yes,' said Ravenor.

The trio circled around them. 'Let's lose the shotgun,' one told Nayl. Nayl tossed it into the dust obligingly.

'And the sword, you,' another said to Angharad. The three men seemed particularly fascinated by the towering woman in her torn leather armour.

'I will not draw it, for I have no intention of harming you,' Angharad replied clearly. 'But I will not be divorced from Evisorex.'

Iosob jumped and squealed as the leader of the trio fired his flamer at the ground in a roaring gale of heat. Burned dust billowed up from the vitrified scorch mark.

'Drop the bloody sword,' the leader said.

'Do it,' Nayl hissed sidelong at Angharad. 'I understand your code, woman, but we've come too far – and I mean too very far – for you to screw this up.'

With an expression on her face like she was sawing off her own arm, Angharad unbuckled the steel's long case and lowered it respectfully into the dust.

'Burn gang two chief to base,' they heard the leader vox.

'Come back, BG3,' the link crackled.

'Turn out a security squad to the main gates and meet us there. We're coming in. Tell the boss she won't believe what we've just found out here.'

THE ROOM IN the modular shelter was cool and quiet, air circulating through well-maintained vent systems. There was a steel table, and half a dozen folding chairs. Nayl sat down on one, and sighed, bone-tired. Iosob sat on the floor at his feet, and curled up.

Angharad paced. She was visibly agitated at having her steel taken from her against her will.

Ravenor lowered his chair onto the deck to conserve power, and rested. Watching him, Nayl was concerned for his master's wellbeing. Fluid had begun to leak from the gouges in the chair again, and this time it was running dark and unclear, as if dirt or biological waste was mixing with the chair's circulation system.

The trio of chainmailed troopers had led them up to the compound gates, one of them lugging the shotgun and the sword. A squad of regular Imperial Guard had assembled to meet them. They carried bull pup-format lasguns, and wore more standard combat fatigues, lacking the mail and plate armour of the flamer team. Nayl hadn't been able to recognise the regimental insignia.

The men wore helmets, but their faces were bare except for dust goggles. They had stared in complete incomprehension at the prisoners being brought in. Nayl had wondered if it was because of the odd mix of them – a towering Amazon with sullen eyes and leather bodywear ripped in places to reveal toned skin scabbed with scratches, a barely pubescent girl in a robe, a crippled freak in a floating chair, and a bald bruiser in bodygloving that had seen better days. He had a nasty feeling they were simply baffled at seeing any visitors at all.

+I can't read any of them at all,+ Ravenor had sent. +Cough if you hear this, Nayl.+

Nayl had coughed.

+Then my mind's not totally useless. They must be blocked.+

The squad had brought them into the module chamber, and locked the hatch. Ten minutes passed.

Nayl got up off his chair and moved to peer out of one of the small, recessed windows.

'Listening station, you think?' he asked.

'Yes,' said Ravenor, his voice just a dry wheeze, like an asthmatic whisper.

'I thought so. From those masts. High security in places like this. No wonder they weren't too happy to see us strolling around. You know the regiment flashes, by the way?'

'No,' said Ravenor.

Nayl shrugged. 'Me neither. Are you sure you're coping, Gideon?'

'I have had better days. Listen to me... we may have walked into trouble here. A high security zone, as you said. I will try to talk us out of this, because it is our best chance of salvation. It is the only hope of escape the door has offered us so far. Imperial contact. Please follow my lead. Do not do anything... provocative.'

'Hey,' said Nayl, with an open handed shrug.

'I meant Angharad specifically.'

'I understand,' the Carthaen snapped. 'But Evisorex needs me and–'

'Evisorex can sit and wait, Angharad. For Throne's sake–' Ravenor's voxponder suddenly cut off, and the monotone voice pattern was lost in a series of strangulated gulps and rattles.

Nayl hurried to the chair. He realised the sounds were coughing, or even choking.

'Gideon?'

'What's wrong with him?' asked Angharad, with a tone that suggested she didn't really care how much Ravenor suffered.

'Frig, I don't know. I know he was hurt bad. Oh, Throne–'

Nayl took a hand away from the chair's side. It was smeared with blood. Blood was weeping out of the puncture marks the hook-limbed monsters had punched into its casing.

'I think he's dying in there.'

+You are quite probably correct.+

'Gideon?'

+I think we've known each other long enough for me to be honest with you, Harlon.+

'I would hope that to be true.'

+I could put up a brave front, and try to keep being the strong leader, but I am not feeling so very strong any more. My support systems are close to shut down. When they are gone, my body will start to die. Furthermore, I believe I may have sustained physical injury. A wound, maybe more than one. I cannot tell, because my chair's medical supervision system has cut out. My voxponder also just malfunctioned. I am attempting system repairs to it.+

'So I have to do the talking?'

+For now. These people seem blocked to my mind. That may be because of my reduced performance, but I think they're properly blocked. I need you to–+

'Shhhhh!' said Nayl.

The chamber door had just opened. Two troopers entered, and were followed by a small, brunette woman in the uniform of a Guard colonel. She was strong-featured, and almost attractive, although her face was lined and worn by years of care and sunlight. She gave a nod, and one of the troopers closed the door.

The woman walked around and sat down behind the table. She regarded her four detainees.

+I can't read her either, Harlon. She's blocked too.+

Nayl rose from beside the chair and faced the seated woman.

'I'm sorry for this trouble, ma'am,' he said. 'My name is Harlon Nayl. I am an accredited bounty hunter, carrying license to hunt in the Scarus, Electif and Borodance sectors.'

'That's an interesting series of lies,' the woman replied with a husky voice, 'or at least unlikely, considering how far away those sectors lie.'

'May I ask, ma'am, where we are?'

She hesitated, with a confused smirk. 'Are you telling me you don't know?'

'Would I ask such a stupid question if I did?'

'I suppose not. This is Rahjez.'

'I don't know it.'

+Please, Harlon, be careful what you say.+

'I'm interested... how could you be on a world,' asked the woman, 'without the slightest knowledge of where it is?'

'I could tell you a story about how I was kidnapped by slavers, and made my escape along with these three companions, landing on a world I had no way of identifying.'

'Would that story be true?' she asked mildly.

'Look at me. Look at the three people I'm travelling with. Are we remotely... likely? Don't we look like escapees from a slaver ship?'

'That makes more immediate sense than the suspicions I have.'

'What might they be?'

'That you're spies. Good spies disguise themselves in the most unlikely ways, in my experience.'

Nayl nodded towards Angharad, aloof at the back of the room. 'Look at her. Built for fighting. That's why the slavers chose her. Good breeding stock for the arenas.'

'I am not good breeding stock for–'

'+Shut. Up. Angharad.+'

'But the slavers, they obviously saw that in me,' Angharad added.

'Slavers?' asked the woman. 'We haven't had slaver activity since... when did we last have slaver activity in this sub, Kerter?'

'Never,' answered one of the troopers.

'Do spies just walk out into the open to get captured?' asked Nayl.

'They might,' the woman said. 'It rather depends on their agenda.'

Nayl shrugged and risked a smile at the woman. 'This isn't going well, is it?'

'I'd say not.' the woman rose. 'I am obliged to tell you that I am Colonel Asa Lang, in operational command of this station, and that's all I am obliged to tell you. You are prisoners of war.'

'There's a war?'

'Oh, please,' Lang replied.

'Are you obliged to offer us aid?' Nayl asked.

'What kind of aid?'

'Water would be nice. We haven't had liquid in a while, or food. The kid there is suffering. Medicae aid would be nice too. My... acquaintance Gideon there, he's been hurt.'

Lang looked at the support chair. 'He is a disabled person? In a support unit?'

'He's been stabbed.'

'By what?'

'Long story,' Nayl began.

+Harlon. Just cut to the chase.+

Nayl nodded at Ravenor. 'May I show you something, Colonel Lang?' he asked.

'Go on.'

He moved to the chair. 'Don't get jumpy or trigger happy now,' he added to the two troopers. 'Hand it to me, Gideon.'

The chair opened a mechanical slot on its nose and displayed Ravenor's Inquisitorial rosette, the badge of Special Condition. Nayl took it out and handed it to Lang.

'This is Inquisitor Gideon Ravenor, of the Ordos Helican. The rest of us are part of his chosen company. We have been through a terrible experience that has deposited us here on your world. We request, by the authority of the Inquisition, your immediate help.'

Lang handed the rosette to one of the troopers. 'Get this checked,' she said. The man hurried out of the chamber.

'If that claim is true, I apologise for your treatment.' She took out a link. 'I need Medicae Bashesvili standing ready in the infirmary quickly, and get someone to bring water and food.'

'Thank you, colonel, ' said Nayl. 'We–'

'How did you get here?' asked Lang.

'Via a portal.'

'A what?'

'A portal.'

'I don't understand.'

'Neither do I, really. It's been rough, but that's why I want to know where we are.'

'This is Rahjez, in the Fantomine subsector.'

'Fantomine? Throne, that's... that's right out on the edge of the Ultima Segmentum.'

'If your story is more than a story, you're a long way from home,' Lang replied. 'This is Listening Station Arethusa on–'

'What did you say?' Nayl cut in, sharply.

'That this is Listening Station Arethusa.'

Nayl looked at the chair. 'You were aiming for the *Arethusa*, weren't you?'

+Yes, Harlon.+

'Shit,' Nayl moaned. 'That frigging door...'

'Who are you talking to?' asked Lang nervously. 'Are you talking to the cripple? Is he speaking?'

'My master Ravenor is a psyker,' said Nayl. 'For some reason, he can't read you.'

Lang nodded. 'It's because we're implanted with blockers when we do a tour here on Rahjez. The ku'kud screams when we burn it.'

'The what?'

'The thorn weed. It grows very rapidly, and would choke the station if we didn't use the burn gangs to crop it back on a daily basis, but it is psy-active. At night, it whispers. When we kill it, it screams. The cumulative effect of either can be lethal. When we are sent here for a duty rotation, we are psychically blocked to preserve our sanity.' She leaned forwards, and pulled back her hair to reveal the implant lodged in the base of her skull. 'Unblocked, you will quickly start to suffer.'

'May I ask you another question?' asked Nayl.

'I suppose so,' Lang replied.

'What year is this?'

'What *what*?'

'What year is this, the calendar date?' Nayl asked, looking her in the eyes.

'It is 404, of course,' she said. '404.M40.'

EIGHT

THE ARETHUSA WAS cold and forbidding when they came back from the surface. It had never been the most comfortable ship, nor the most welcoming, but as they stepped in through the air-gate, it felt especially dank and stale.

Unwerth scampered ahead of them, excited. 'Fyflank has fixated something!' he exclaimed.

'It had better be something good,' Thonius said to the others. 'My mind is made up. It would take a lot to change it.'

'Wait to see what Unwerth has found,' said Kys. 'If it's Siskind's ship–'

'If, if, if...' echoed Thonius. 'I want a course set for Thracian by tonight.'

Kys and Kara waited while the others wandered despondently out of the dock bay.

'Is Thracian such a good idea, Patience?' Kara asked once the others were out of earshot. 'The mercy of Lord Rorken?'

Kys shrugged. 'It's Carl's call, Kar, and maybe he's right. We should try to make amends now he's gone.'

'Has he, though?'

Kys looked at her. 'What do you mean?'

Kara tilted her head. 'Since when did Gideon ever not beat the odds?'

'Nice try, Kara Swole,' Kys replied. 'I'm afraid I just can't buy in to that sort of optimism. I saw the Wych House perish and I saw how damaged he was. He's gone from us.'

Kara sighed. Kys felt how close to tears the smaller woman was.

'It's been hard, up here,' Kara said.

'What do you mean?'

'The ship's been misbehaving. On again, off again, while we were waiting for you. I didn't want to bother you with it, so I never sent.'

'How is the ship misbehaving?' asked Kys quietly.

Kara laughed humourlessly. 'Oh, like it's haunted. The whole crew is spooked. No one can sleep, and we keep hearing sobbing.'

'I thought you looked tired.'

'Tired?'

'Drained. Strung out.'

'Well, I am. Everyone aboard is. Even before we heard what... what had happened. '

'So, sobbing?'

'Yes, and manic laughter, through the vox, even when it's shut down.'

'I don't sense anything,' said Kys, uncertainly, tentatively allowing her mind to reach out.

'You will. You won't sleep, or if you do, it won't be calm. That's why I said what I said about Gideon.'

'Explain?'

Kara shrugged. 'I thought it might be him, somewhere, trying to get through.'

'Let me look into it,' said Kys. She had a distinct notion of what might be wrong, and there was no way she was going to scare Kara Swole with the idea yet.

'Look,' she said brightly, 'there's someone who loves you.'

Kara turned around. Belknap was waiting for her in the arch of the main docking clamp.

She crossed to him and they hugged.

'Is it true?' Belknap asked Kys as she approached.

'Is what true, Patric?'

He cleared his throat. 'Is Ravenor dead, Kys?'

'Yes, I'm afraid he is,' she replied.

* * *

KYS STRODE INTO the infirmary ward. There was no sign of Frauka, except a dish full of lho-stick butts and a forsaken data-slate. Zael lay on the cot, thin and cold as ice.

+Zael?+

No response.

+Zael?+

She turned as Wystan Frauka re-entered the room behind her. He was dabbing his nose with a paper swab from the surgery.

'Oh, you're back then?' he asked.

'Where were you?'

'Out there,' Frauka gestured, meaning the surgery chamber. 'Don't often see you down here.'

'I didn't realise I needed an appointment,' she snapped.

'Steady,' he soothed. 'Listen, I heard what happened. I'm sorry, truly.'

She stared at him. She was aware that a rising tide of grief was making her irritable and short-fused. 'Has he woken?'

'Zael? No.'

'And you'd tell me if he had?'

'No, I'd keep it a secret,' Frauka retorted, sitting down on his chair. 'What is this?'

'Kara told me the ship has been troubled while we were away.'

Frauka blew up his cheeks and exhaled a sort of resigned sigh. 'So I've heard.'

'Not felt anything yourself?'

'I'm an untouchable, baby.'

'I'd appreciate it if you kept the pet-names to yourself. Have you experienced any of the phenomena the others have reported?'

'No,' he said. He sat down and reached for a lho-stick but didn't light it. Untouchable though he was, he was aware of the tension in the room.

'They've told me things. Sobbing on the vox. Boguin was in the galley last night, and he heard laughter coming out of plumbing. Fyflank says he hears footsteps following him every time he takes a stroll along the holds. Other stuff. I dunno, Kys, show me a ship that isn't full of noises. The crew's agitated, especially now they know he's not coming back. Imagination does stuff to you.'

'But you've heard nothing?'

'No.'

'And Zael hasn't woken, even for a moment?'

Frauka met her eyes. 'I know what's at stake, Kys, and you know the damned responsibility Ravenor handed me. You think I like that? You think I'd lie to you?'

'I don't know. Truth is, Frauka, none of us know you very well at all. We can't read you.'

'Story of my life. You have no idea whatsoever how hard it is to be an untouchable. Everyone feels the absence, and it makes them uncomfortable. You get treated like shit. Working for Ravenor's the only decent job I've ever had, the only time I've felt worth anything. I guess that's over now, isn't it? Get off my back. I've covered yours long enough, and I deserve more respect, even if I make you uncomfortable.'

They stared at each other. On a different day, under different circumstances, she might have been more sympathetic. In his own, alien fashion, Wystan Frauka had saved them more times than she could count. He certainly deserved their respect, but just then, she felt unable to give it. She was too scared.

'Where were you?' she asked.

'When?'

'When I came in here?'

'Back there,' said Frauka defensively. 'Like I said–'

'Why?'

'I was looking for a swab. I had a nosebleed.'

'A nosebleed?'

'Yes, I had a nosebleed.'

'Only one?' Kys asked, glancing down at several blood-soaked swabs littering the floor under Zael's cot. She looked up again slowly and stared at Frauka. 'Nose-bleeds: secondary indicative symptom of proximal psychic activity.'

'Or of picking your nose,' Frauka snapped. 'I'm an untouchable, remember?'

'He's awake, though, isn't he?' Kys asked, looking back at Zael.

'I'd have sensed it.'

'Sensed it?'

'Blocked it, I mean.'

'You know what he is? What he could be?'

'I'm very aware of what he *might* be, Mamzel Kys.'

Kys lunged at Frauka and dragged him out of his chair. The bedside cabinet crashed over, spilling Frauka's dish of lho-stick butts and his data-slate onto the deck. He cried out in surprise, and tried to fight her off. He was strong, and large, but she was determined and she was a trained, principal agent of the Inquisition. She outclassed him many times over. She slammed Frauka back into the wall, and pinned him, her forearm across his throat.

'Why? Why are you doing this?' he gasped.

'You tell me why,' she hissed. She reached out with her telekinesis, still pinning him physically, and pulled the autopistol out of his pocket. It floated up beside their faces.

'I know why you have this. You know why you have this. Ravenor trusted you.'

'Kys!'

'He woke up, didn't he? He's awake. That's why the ship is sobbing out of its decks. What's the matter, Frauka, too pussy to do it?'

'No,' Frauka yelled. Kys stepped away and shoved Frauka away onto the deck. He fell awkwardly. She turned and grabbed hold of the floating pistol, racking the slide with her mind.

Kys stepped forwards. She aimed the pistol at Zael's head with a steady, two-handed grip.

'I'm sorry,' she said.

Frauka crashed into her and brought her down hard. They wrestled on the floor. The weapon went off, and the slug tore into the ceiling.

Belknap burst into the infirmary. Without hesitation, he dived at the pair of them. Guard training took over and he managed to pull them apart.

'Get off!' Belknap shouted, pushing Frauka away. Frauka bashed into the wall, and sat down heavily. He blinked, dazed, at Belknap fighting brutally to contain Kys. Kys had caught the doctor in a telekinetic hold and was lifting him away from her. Frauka reached up and turned off his limiter.

Belknap crashed down onto Kys. They rolled, slamming into the legs of Zael's cot. Belknap headbutted Kys in the nose and, as she floundered, pincered her in a secure restraint hold.

'Get off me!' Kys howled, blood dribbling from her nostrils. 'Get off me, you bastard, or so help me–'

'Drop it!' Belknap ordered, tightening his hold. He pinched at the soft pressure points, and then yanked Kys's hand back and squeezed until she let go of the gun. It clattered onto the decking.

'Not in my damn infirmary,' he snarled. 'Never in my place of care! You don't do this!'

'He's Slyte!' Kys screamed, struggling back. 'We have to kill him before–'

'Not in here, ever,' said Belknap firmly. He forced one of his knees forwards to pin her right forearm and then, reluctantly, chopped a punch into Kys's spinal nerve cluster. Kys backed out and went limp.

'Get Kara down here,' he told Frauka.

* * *

'WHAT THE FRIG were you thinking of, you daft ninker?' Kara asked. She came into the little holding tank in the *Arethusa's* brig block where Kys was sprawled. Wystan Frauka, diligently smoking a lho-stick, hovered in the doorway behind her.

'I was thinking about keeping all of us alive, Kar,' Kys replied, rolling over and sitting up. 'Let me out of here.'

'I can't.'

'Why?'

'You tried to murder Zael.'

'He's not Zael, he's Slyte.'

Kara shook her head.

'Your boyfriend's a tough bastard,' Kys said, rubbing her neck. 'He doesn't mess around.'

'He's not my boyfriend,' said Kara.

'What is he, then?'

'My... lover. Boyfriend is a stupid word.'

'Whatever he is, he smacked me up. Very gentlemanly. I would have been impressed if I wasn't spark out. Fancy moves, if you're easily impressed by a man beating a woman. He ever do that to you, Kar?'

'Stop it.'

'Thing is,' Kys said quietly, 'he should have let me do it.'

'Murder Zael? A helpless kid?'

'Not so helpless. He's a daemon, and he's waking up.'

'Why are you saying this, Patience?'

'You know why, Kar. Gideon told us. Slyte could be sleeping in that boy's body.'

'*Could* being the operative word. You went crazy.'

'Come on. That's why Gideon set Frauka to watch him and told him to shoot the boy if he ever woke up.'

'What?' asked Kara, recoiling.

'It's true, ask the frigging blunter yourself!'

'Hello? Standing in the room? In earshot?' Frauka remarked.

'Is this true?' Kara asked him.

'Oh, of course not,' said Frauka.

'Liar!' Kys telled. 'Gideon told me–'

'Patience–' Kara shushed.

'It's not a lie,' said Frauka.

'Kara, he's tainted. He's no longer secure,' Kys cried desperately. 'Frauka is suffering nosebleeds.'

'It's congenital,' said Frauka.

'Screw congenital,' said Kys. 'He's impaired. Zael's psychic force has penetrated him. Wake up, Kara! The blunter safeguard is compromised, the boy is stirring, the frigging ship is haunted! Gideon told me to watch for this!'

'And execute a teenage boy?' Kara turned away. 'Sholto has a fix on what he believes is the *Allure*. We are trying to talk Carl into pursuing it. I wish I had your backing on that, Patience, but you're... messed up. I'm sorry.'

She left the tank. The door slammed shut and the lock turned.

'Kara!' Kys screamed.

'WELL, THAT WAS unpleasant,' Frauka said as he walked down the brig block hallway with Kara.

She paused, and looked around at him. 'If it turns out there's any truth in what she said, Wystan, I will gut you myself. That's a promise.'

'Fair play,' he replied, 'but I'm telling the truth.'

Kara nodded. 'I've got to get upstairs.'

'Are we going after this *Allure* then?' Frauka asked.

'I hope so.'

There was a long, awkward pause as they faced one another. 'Well, it's been pleasant chatting,' Frauka said, and turned. She watched him walk away down the companionway.

Kara headed for the bridge.

* * *

MOST OF THE crew had assembled on the bridge deck. A few looked up as Kara walked in.

Sholto Unwerth was in his command seat, studying several consoles of flickering data.

Belknap was waiting by the main entry hatch. He stopped Kara and held her for a moment.

'I didn't enjoy that,' he said quietly. 'Kys is your friend, mine too, I thought, but she was just crazy. I had to stop her. I've never seen–'

'It's all right,' Kara replied. 'Kys has been through a lot. You did what you had to do.'

'What's the matter?'

'With me? Nothing. Something at the back of my mind.'

'Still?'

'I'll get over it.'

She broke from him and walked down onto the main bridge deck of the *Arethusa*.

'Sholto?'

Unwerth looked up from his consoles. 'Is Patience all right?' he asked.

'She's fine. What have you got?'

'A strengthy lead,' Unwerth replied. 'We have been able to fixate a vehicle pattern on that yonder. I'm plucking it up for you now.'

Graphic display detail lit up on the main viewer: the digitally enhanced plot of one of the sixty starships at high anchor over Utochre.

'That's the *Allure*?' she asked.

'It took a good deal of fidgetation to locate,' Unwerth replied.

'But it's the *Allure*?'

'I would staple my life on it,' said Unwerth. 'It's displaying alternating running codes and signals, but its inheritable pattern is that of the *Allure*.'

'Current situation?'

'It's taking on supplies from service boats prior to disembarkation,' said Plyton.

'How long before it breaks anchor?'

'Six hours, eight maybe,' Plyton said.

Kara nodded. She turned and looked at the pale man standing by the main viewer, a galeweave throw draped around his hunched shoulders.

'Carl?'

Thonius turned to look at them. 'What do you want me to say, Kara? We don't have the manpower or the firepower to board or seize them. They're three times our displacement.'

'We're just going to let them go?' she asked.

Thonius shrugged. 'I'd love to bring them down, but I don't see how.'

'A stealth boarding raid,' suggested Ballack. 'Two or three gigs with muzzled drives.'

'A loveable conception,' said Unwerth, 'accept for the veritable factor that the *Arethusa* doesn't have two or three gigs. It doesn't even have one. We have two cargo landers, and that's the summation. Neither are muzzleable.'

Fyflank nodded.

'See?' said Thonius. 'There's nothing we can do.'

'Except watch them translate away?' said Ballack. 'Throne, Carl, that ship is our last lead to Molotch.'

Thonius sighed. 'I'm tired of hunting Molotch. I say we lay course for Thracian Primaris now and get the unpleasantness over with.'

'We could, in all benediction, follow them,' said Unwerth quietly.

'Follow a ship through the warp?' Thonius scoffed. 'I knew you were short, Unwerth, I didn't realise you were also short on brains. We could translate after them, but after that, in the Immaterium...'

'That was not my meaning,' said Unwerth. 'We could follow them, if we knew where they were going.'

'There's a sort of brilliant, simple logic to that,' said Kara.

'Oh, yes, let's give the shipmaster a big round of applause,' said Thonius.

'Don't mock, Carl,' said Kara.

'Please,' Thonius retorted. 'Do I actually have to remind you that we *don't* know where they are going? Which largely clobbers the brilliant, simple logic out of Unwerth's idea.'

'*They* know where they're going,' said Plyton, nodding at the screen plot.

'Well, of course *they* do,' replied Thonius.

'Right now,' Plyton pressed, quietly, 'they'll have chosen a heading, begun stellar translation computations, started the disembarkation rituals. The Navigator will already be focusing and preparing, readying himself for the trials of the Empyrean...'

'So if somebody got aboard,' said Kara, 'say via a service boat...'

'Oh, no,' said Thonius. 'No, no, no.'

'Carl,' Kara began.

'Please, Carl,' said Ballack. 'I think it's worth a try.'

'It would be suicide,' said Thonius. 'Even if a person could get aboard, and stay out of sight and harm's way, even if that person could identify the destination, and signal the information, they would never get out again.'

'If I got in,' said Kara, 'I'd get out.'

'If it was you,' said Ballack. 'However, I'm volunteering.'

'Wait a minute,' objected Plyton. 'I called it–'

'No one called it,' Thonius snapped. 'No one's going!'

'One last try, Carl,' Kara said. 'For Gideon's sake. One last try to find Molotch and finish him.'

Thonius didn't reply. He stared at the deck and shrugged. 'You're mad,' he said.

'I'm not mad,' said Kara, 'but I am going.' She looked at Plyton and Ballack. 'Sorry, no arguments. Only one of us three has been on that vessel before. Someone get a lander prepped for me, quickly.'

Kara walked back to the hatchway where Belknap was standing.

'I'm not very happy about this,' he said quietly. 'Thonius is right, this is suicide. There are too many risks and too many variables.'

'I'm sorry,' she said. 'I knew you wouldn't like it, but this is what I do.'

'Kara, the risks–'

She smiled at him, and made the sign of the aquila. 'Have faith,' she said.

FRAUKA WALKED BACK into the infirmary and righted his chair. He sat down.

Thank you.

'For what?'

Protecting me.

'I don't know why I did. I don't know anything any more.'

But you can hear me?

'Yes. That still bothers me. I shouldn't be able to.'

No, you shouldn't. I think the time's coming when you won't be an untouchable any more. I've burnt you out. I've made you touchable. I'm sorry about that.

'I know this is all wrong. I know you've screwed up my head. You made me lie.'

Not really.

'I should tell someone.'

No.

Frauka blinked, and seemed to find focus for a second. Fear crossed his face. 'Throne, I know what you're doing to me! Stop it! For Throne's sake! You made me lie, you made me lie to them! To Kys, and Swole, and–'

Quiet, Wystan.

'I will not be quiet!' he rose to his feet, and scrabbled for the wall link. 'I need t–'

Sit down. You need to sit down and be quiet. We're not there yet.

Frauka lowered his hand and sat down, obediently. His eyes were blank.

'Mmm, yes,' he said. 'Sit down. That's a good idea.' He picked up his data-slate.

'Where were we?'

'She was gasping in gleeful pleasure as he took her'. Uh, Wystan?

'Yes?'

Your nose is bleeding.

Frauka looked down at the spots of blood plipping onto his shirt front.

'Damn, my nose is bleeding.'

Get a swab.

'I'll get a swab,' he said, rising up out of the chair.

KYS CROUCHED AGAINST the door of the brig tank, her ear to the lock. Once again, she tried to kine her way through the tumblers and align them so that the bolt would slide. Ravenor himself had inscribed the tumblers with wards to make it hard for a psyker to manipulate them the day he had taken over the *Arethusa*.

There was a clunk. The door remained in place. She cursed aloud and placed her ear back against the key hole.

+Kys.+

Patience lurched back.

+Hello?+

There was silence. Her imagination.

She leaned back to try again.

+Kysssss.+

'Throne!' she pulled back and scrambled away from the door on her backside.

+Who is that? Who is that?+

+It's me, Kys. It's me.+

She swallowed. +Gideon?+

+It's me, Kys. I'm just here, on the other side of the door.+

+The door?+ Kys hurried back to the lock and examined it. +Gideon?+

+Still here, Kys, but so far away. It feels like a thousand years. I am so trapped, so lost. I want to be there.+

+Gideon, great Throne, you're alive!+

There was a long silence.

+Gideon?+

+Kys? I lost you there. I'm weak. So very weak. I lost you there for a moment. Are you still there?+

+Yes, I am!+

She pressed her cheek harder to the cold steel door, listening at the keyhole.

+Gideon? Gideon?+

+I'm here, but I'm so far away. I want to be there. I'm hurt. I'm locked in. The door won't open.+

+I'm trying to open it!+ Kys fell back, panting with the effort.

+I want to be with you, Kys. I can feel it coming. I'm weak. I don't know what to do.+

+What's coming?+

+Death. I can feel it. It's coming. I can taste it. It wants me. It wants to take me. I've been keeping it at bay, fending it off, but I can't much longer.+

+How can I help you?+ she sent, frantically.

+Open the door. Open the door. Open the door.+

+I'm trying! I'm trying, Gideon!+ she sent back, fumbling with her mind into the delicate cylinders of the door's lock. +I think I can open it!+

The lock squeezed tighter. With a gasp of fatigue, Kys fell back.

+Kys, can I ask you a question?+

+Of course!+

+Who's Gideon?+

Kys scrambled back from the hatch into the far corner of the tank. +What do you mean? What the hell do you mean "Who's Gideon?" Who am I talking to?+

+Don't be like that, Kys.+

+Who am I talking to?+

The handle of the tank door began to move by itself, jerking impotently up and down. A sheen of ice suddenly crackled across the face of the door, forming slow, lazy crusts across the metal. Laughter, manic and wild, began to echo out of the keyhole.

+You know who I am,+ the voice said.

NINE

MEDICAE LUDMILLA BASHESVILI was a tall, scrawny woman in her late fifties. She had spent too much of her career treating dog troop Guardsmen for clap, ear infections and sprains. She entered the infirmary and her gaze fell on the battered chair, her hands tucked into the front pocket of her smock.

'What the hell is this?' she asked. 'I'm a doctor, not a tech adept.'

'It's a life-support system,' said Nayl, standing nearby under the careful watch of two armed troopers. Angharad and Iosob had already been taken away into detention. Lang had allowed Nayl to stay with Ravenor.

'And who might you be?' Bashesvili asked.

'My name is Harlon Nayl,' Nayl replied.

'Oh, fancy,' said Bashesvili. 'Tough guy, I suppose?'

'You mean me or the chair?' asked Nayl.

Bashesvili bent down and examined the chair. She peered at it, and ran her hands over the chair's surface, touching the dent-wounds and scratches. She wiped an index finger into some of the discharged fluid, sniffed it, and made a face. 'Does he speak?'

'Ordinarily, but his voxponder is broken. He sends to me.'

'He's a psyker?'

Nayl nodded.

Bashesvili exhaled and stood upright, putting her hands on her hips. 'He's dying. That much is clear. Critical impairment to the support system and the device's integument.'

She gently steered the chair into the diagnosis bay, pushing aside the gurney where her more regular patients usually reclined. Nayl watched her. Bashesvili turned on a number of the devices, including an array of raised scanner pads held upright on a chrome frame. She bent a few of them over to better address the chair. Monitor screens lit up on the display consoles, and she studied them. Then she took out a paddle sensor and ran it over the casing.

'This is thick armour,' she said. 'I dread to think what might have punched holes in plating this tough. Trouble is, it's so thick, I'm not getting any kind of useful imaging through it.'

'What can you do?' asked Nayl.

'I could attempt to link up an external life support system to stabilise him, but...' She bent down to examine the recessed ports and ducts in the chair's back.

'But?'

'But... looks like the connectors and feeds are non standard fitting. This chair is a custom build. So that's no good. It'd be a stop-gap anyway. To attempt to save him, I'll have to get in there.'

'No,' said Nayl firmly. 'He doesn't allow that.' The armed guards either side of him tensed, ready to restrain him.

'Does he allow himself to die?' Bashesvili asked Nayl.

'What?'

'I simply can't help him if I can't get in there. Will he allow that, if his life is in the balance?'

Nayl shrugged. 'He is an Imperial inquisitor. His name is Gideon Ravenor. As far as I know, he hasn't been out of that chair since he was placed in it.'

'How long ago?'

'Decades. He is a private person.'

'I'm a medicae,' said Bashesvili. 'We reach our own understandings.'

She ran her hands over the cowling of Ravenor's chair again.

The hatch banged open. It was Lang and two more troopers.

'Colonel!' said Bashesvili, straightening up and saluting.

'Doctor,' Lang nodded. She looked at Nayl. 'We have consulted with the local ordos. They're searching their records. So far, they cannot find any trace of your credentials. Nice try. The badge had me fooled.'

'Colonel–' Nayl began.

'They're still checking,' Lang said, 'and signals have been sent astropathically to nearby sector conclaves. I have been promised an answer with all due haste, but realistically, this could take days, even weeks. In the meantime, sir, I have to presume the worst and deprive you of your liberty.'

'Please,' said Nayl.

'This is wartime,' said Lang, 'and wartime rules apply. I cannot take post security anything less than seriously. The rebels have attacked this station before and may do it again, at any moment.' She stared at Nayl. 'They may already be here.'

'Take him to the cell block,' Lang told the guards. They marched Nayl out of the room.

'This one needs attention, colonel,' Bashesvili said. 'He's in a poor state.'

'Do what you can to make him fit for interrogation,' said Lang.

The colonel and her escort left. The hatch closed. Alone, Bashesvili looked down at the battered chair.

'Where possible,' she said, 'I like to establish a dialogue with my patients.'

A tiny rasp of response came from the machine.

'You know,' said Bashesvili, 'a does it hurt? Doesn't it hurt? Say "ahhh" type of thing.'

There was another tiny gasp.

'I shouldn't do this,' said Bashesvili, 'but I'm wilful, and menopausal, and at the bad end of a long drudge tour out here on Rahjez.' She reached up into her hairline and slowly unscrewed her blocker implant. She set it down on the polished table beside her.

'Is that better? Hello in there?'

+It is better. Can you hear me?+

'Extraordinary! Yes, I can. You're strong. Like a song in my head. You have a nice voice. Mellow. You were a handsome devil, weren't you?'

+I don't know.+

'Yes, you were, once. I can tell. Now, what's your name?'

+Gideon.+

'Hello, I'm Ludmilla. Don't you dare think of messing with my head now, you understand? I have a responsibility here.'

+I won't. I promise. Believe me, Ludmilla. All I want is for this pain to stop.+

'Yeah, well, you're screwed. I can tell just by the whiff of you. You're rotting inside that box. I need to open you up. Your friend seemed to think that was a no-go. What do you say?'

+I say... I can't hold on much longer, Ludmilla.+

'That's a start,' she said. She reached over and swung in a hinged table of sterile tools. 'What happens? Do you open your case, or do I have to crack it with a cutter?'

+Wait.+

'What for?' she asked. She wiped at her face suddenly, as if cobwebs had brushed against it. 'What are you doing? I can feel that! What are you doing?'

+Forgive me. I was looking into your mind.+

'Oh. Kindly don't do it again.' She paused, and then asked, 'What did you see?'

+I saw enough to know I can trust you. I have to trust you. I will open the casing. Please don't be distressed by what you see inside.+

'Bloody hell, Gideon,' she snorted. 'You haven't got anything I haven't seen before. How does the casing open?'

Ravenor didn't reply. There was a slow hiss of releasing catches, and the upper part of his chair slowly lifted away. Vapour oozed out. A dull, blue light shone from the open cavity.

'Oh, Gideon,' she said, peering inside. 'Oh, you poor man.'

She turned, pulled on surgical gloves and looked back into the cavity. 'I think I'm going to have to call for interns to help me so I can–'

+No interns. No one else. Just you.+

'Ow!' she said. 'Not so fierce with the sending, please.'

+I'm sorry, but please– +

'All right. If that's what you want.' She bent down and reached into the cup of warm, stagnant fluid. She circled her arms underneath Ravenor's physical form.

'Have I got you? Are you supported?'

+Yes.+

Bashesvili lifted him out of the chair. Tiny ducting relays and drip feeds, clustered in their thousands, like fronds of hair, pulled away.

+Nhhhg!+

'It's all right, Gideon,' she soothed. 'Shush, shush. It's all right. I've got you. Gideon?'

The wet, blood-smeared, respiring sack of pale flesh she held in her arms had gone very quiet.

'Gideon?'

* * *

'THEY DON'T BELIEVE US?' snarled Angharad.

'No.'

'They don't believe us?' she repeated.

'No!' said Nayl. 'Now, hush. I'm thinking.'

'We're a thousand years out,' said Iosob from the corner of the cell. 'That's an awful long way.'

'I know it is,' said Nayl. 'That means a confirmation of our status is never going to come because we don't exist yet. I was just hoping we could delay them. It's ironic. The rosette is genuine, but to them it's a fake. Now shut up both of you and let me think.'

'Ow!' he said, almost immediately. Spiky pain had jabbed into his head.

'I feel that too,' said Angharad, massaging her temples.

'It's Gideon,' said Nayl, rising. 'It's Gideon. He's hurting.'

'Maybe,' said Angharad, 'but didn't they warn us? Something about the thorns after dark?'

Night had fallen outside. Through the small, barred slit of a window, they could hear the thorn brush – the ku'kud – around the compound whispering and rustling.

'Oh, great,' Nayl growled. 'All right, our choices have just been reduced to one.'

'Which is?'

'We bust out of here.'

Angharad gazed at him with steady, hooded eyes. 'Far be it for me to mention a few "if's", but–'

'But?'

'*If* we can open that cell hatch, *if* we can evade the guards without getting gunned down, *if* we can find a way out of the compound, and *if* Ravenor is fit enough to accompany us–'

'Reach a point, please, woman,' Nayl said.

'If your good friend Gideon is hurt and can't be moved, will you leave him here?'

'No,' said Nayl.

'Then there's no point breaking out. It would be signing our own death warrant. To escape, and then not flee?'

Nayl sighed and leaned his back against the cell wall. He slid down it until he was sitting on the floor. Angharad presumed he had given up.

'Are all Carthaen women so pessimistic?' he asked. 'I thought you were a warrior?'

'A good warrior knows when to fight,' said Angharad.

'And a better one knows when to improvise,' Nayl countered. He'd sat down to tug off one of his boots.

'What is he doing?' asked Iosob, sitting up to watch. Angharad shrugged.

Lang's guards had searched them all, and scanned them scrupulously for metallics and concealed weapons. They'd found Nayl's boot knife, the coil of multi-purpose wire he carried around his waist, and the small pebble charge he kept in a wrist pocket.

He levered open the heel of his boot, and carefully teased something out of the rubberised sole. It was a slim jemmy pick, made of inert plastek.

'This answers your first *if*,' he said, holding it up. 'This opens the hatch. The points you raised were good, and I can't argue with them, but we still have to do this.'

'And when the hatch opens?' she asked.

'Like I said, we improvise,' he grinned. 'I'm good at that.'

Angharad nodded. 'One of the few things I like about you.'

IF THIS IS how I am going to die, I am strangely happy about it. To be free, one last time. To be outside the chair. To feel the air on my skin.

I cannot say what fate I expected, but it was certainly some titanic doom, suffered in the service of the ordos.

I suppose this is exactly that in a way, but it's also a calm end, and a free one. The plight we are in seems so very far away. The impossible divorce from our own place-time. It fades, and seems insubstantial.

I fade too.

Stay awake, stay awake. All that seems important any more is lying here, in the cool air. I'm feeling the useless, dying body I own twitch and tremble as Ludmilla Bash-esvili works.

She is breathing hard. I can feel her tension. I can also feel her devotion. She has fixed various links to my circulatory systems and organs. I can hear machines beeping and chiming. I can feel a warm glow, which I presume is either anaesthetic or the in-feed of intravenous fluids and blood.

I can also feel a scratching around the edges of my mind. Ludmilla feels it too, and it bothers her. The ku'kud. Night has fallen, and the brush is active outside. It is not a sentience, just a dry, gristly hiss of residual psychic activity. It is not unpleasant, just irritating, like a chorus of insects. A vast body of psi-responsive matter, like a sponge.

'Gideon?' she asks, putting a bloody tool down in a steel dish with a clatter. 'With me, still?'

+Yes.+

'Good,' she says.

She's lying. I go free for a moment, and see the world through her eyes. I see the shrunken, twisted thing that is me lying on the surgery table. Bunches of squirting pipes and sucking tubes intrude into me through catheters. I have not seen myself in the flesh for a long time.

Poor, withered flesh. A wrinkled sack of organs and redundant bones, the vague, vestigial remains of a human face, sunk low like a tumour on the top of the sack. God-Emperor, how did I ever survive the

Thracian Atrocity? God-Emperor, why did you let me survive?

I see the discoloured flesh, the atrophied ends of truncated joints. I see the pallor of my burn-tissue skin, the cicatrice scars of my original surgery. I notice also the patches of black bruising and necrotisation, creeping across my form like the shadows of leaves on the ground. I see the wounds the hooked things made, pussy and raw, like gaping mouths. I was hurt even more than I thought. Ludmilla has just removed a hank of hook bone ten centimetres long from what I once called my belly. She drops it into a bowl in disgust. *The Great Devourer.*

My mind swims. There is pain, but beyond the pain, there is a solace, which I think might be death. Ludmilla threads a needle.

I have to stay awake. I know this. I know this.

I look into her. I slide through reefs of sadness and concern that part easily because she is concentrating elsewhere. The life of a field medicae is no life, I quickly realise. Hers has been long and unrewarding. Thought engrams dazzle and open. I see her siblings in the family home. Laughing children, a cherished nugget of memory. A blue dress. Her father's posting. Her father's death. I see a bad marriage, and a few disastrous love affairs. I see a child she lost.

I am a voyeur. I should care, and be ashamed of myself, but I'm not. The front of her mind is locked in effort. The back drifts, like a warm sea, forgotten.

I see the war. Thirty years long already. Rebels on Veda have risen in the cause of emancipation. Imperial secessionists. The Guard has locked the systems down. Protracted fighting on three worlds. Rumours of Guard-sanctioned massacres.

A dirty war. The Imperium fighting itself. No wonder Asa Lang was driven. The Archenemy, the greenskin, the eldar, all terrible foes. But I know, ultimately, there is no more bitter and distressing enemy than our own kind, when humans turn on humans. Ludmilla loathes it. Ah, I see... her family was from Veda. She hates this posting more. Rahjez. Right on the front, a listening watch. Front-line defenders, alert and wired all the time. She hates this.

She hates it most of all because of the ku'kud. The whispering thorn. Isolated out here, humans would be paranoid anyway. The brush makes it worse.

I wish I could soothe her. I–

+Gnnhhh!+

'Gideon? Are you still with me? I felt that?'

+I'm here.+

My voice is less than a whisper. She has just extracted another chip of broken hook bone. It clinks into a bowl.

'I'm worried about your vitals, Gideon. Please, try to stay here with me.'

+I will.+

The ku'kud is scratching at my mind. I wish I could blank it, but I can't. It's like a chorus, an insensate chorus. I–

It resonates. As I push up into it, it rustles back. Sentient or not, it amplifies my thoughts as echoes. Throne, I could–

+Annghhhhh!+

'Gideon? Gid–'

I THINK I blacked out for a moment. Yes, the table-mounted chron has skipped eight minutes.

Eight?

+Ludmilla?+

'Gideon? Oh, for Throne's sake! I thought I'd frigging lost you!'

+Language.+

She laughs. Ludmilla has a good laugh. The men she courted would have loved her for that. Why did she never find one good enough to keep?

I feel so distant now. I feel–

'GIDEON! COME BACK to me, you bastard!'

+I'm still here.+

'I'm going to have to go deeper in this wound. You're going to have to be strong. Can you stand this?'

+Yes.+

'Concentrate on something. Focus on it.'

+Yes.+

I focus on... I drift. I try to remember what I am supposed to be doing. Everything is so vapid and thin. I think of Nayl, of Kys, of Kara, I think of Will...

He's dead. I know he's dead. Molotch killed him.

I think of Molotch and some measure of focus returns. Zygmunt Molotch. But for him, I would not be here. But for him, my life would have been entirely different.

I feel a passionate hatred. The energy lifts me up.

'That's better. Good vitals. Now, this is going to really hurt.'

Molotch. Molotch. I want him. I want to finish him. A thousand years and half a galaxy away, I remember him and want to finish him. He did this to me. He put me here.

'Gideon, your pulse rate is all off. Gideon?'

The ku'kud. The door. I can see it now. Now I can see it and–

'Gideon?'

I can see it. Throne, I'm fading fast, I can tell. Each instrument Ludmilla pushes into me tastes different. The salt tang of the scalpel, the iron hit of the tweezers, the bleach sip of the retractors.

Oh, Throne. Oh, *Throne*, I am really dying.

But I can see it now. Oh, how I can see it. The door. The key. The ku'kud. I send it into Ludmilla's mind. If only I could... if only I could–

'Ow!' she cries, jolting up. 'Stop it with that!'

If only I could. If only I could. If only I could–

IF ONLY I could.

IF–

BASHESVILI JERKED BACK from the operating table.

'Gideon?' she asked.

Every single monitor device around her stopped pinging and wailed out a flat line drone.

'No!' she cried.

NINE

THERE WAS A bumping scrape of metal on metal, and the service boat locked into the docking clamps of the *Allure*. Servitors and deck wranglers began to move around, shouting back and forth as they started loading the modular crates of perishables and victuals onto the through-deck cargo hoists. Hydraulics sighed, bulk hatches opened, vapour drifted.

The cargo area was dark, and lit only by frosty amber overheads. Kara swung down from a crawlspace above a large duct circulator where she had hung, concealed, during the ride from the orbital station. Keeping low, she ran along the edge of the hold's raised loading pad, and then swung over onto one of the laden hoists as it started to rise.

The hoist rose into the bulk hold of the rogue trader *Allure*. The air smelled of spices and rotting fruit. Crewmen and servitors were busy onloading one of the crate stacks, moving some of the containers on trolleys through to adjacent secondary holds.

Kara slipped off the hoist into the shadows. She was wearing a black bodyglove, with a tight hood to conceal her red hair. Crewmen strolled past her, chatting. She could smell their sweat, the stale lho-scent clinging to their work clothes. She shifted to a second hiding place, and tucked in. From her position, she could see the main floor of the hold. There was Siskind himself, in his glass jacket, a cruelly handsome, red-haired man. He was talking to the master of the service boat and signing off a manifest.

Kara had been aboard the *Allure* once before, when the *Hinterlight* had seized her and inspected her en route to Lenk. That seemed like a lifetime ago, but she still had a pretty good memory of the layout. She waited for a suitable lull in the activity nearby, and then made another dash along the side access to a companionway hatch.

The hall beyond the hatch was quiet and empty. She darted through, and headed forwards.

It took her ten minutes to make her way up three decks. Five times, she had to find cover as crewmembers came by. By her estimation, the bridge was not far off.

She hurried forwards, then heard footsteps and voices approaching. She looked around.

There was nowhere to hide.

Lucius Worna clanged down the companionway at Siskind's side. He towered over the shipmaster. The ugly wounds he had taken at the Wych House had been left untreated, and had begun to scab in black, scaly patches.

'How long now?' he asked.

'Thirty minutes, and we'll be shot of the last supplier,' Siskind replied. 'Then another hour as we light the engines, disengage anchors and calculate the last of the mass-velocity transactions. I thought I'd take supper now. Will you join me?'

Worna grunted. They reached the far end of the companionway, and Siskind swung open the hatch. Worna stopped and looked back.

'What?' asked Siskind.

Worna stared back down the empty walkway. He shrugged. 'I thought I... smelt something.'

'Like what?' Siskind asked.

Worna shook his head. 'Doesn't matter,' he said. They passed through the hatch and out of sight.

Kara breathed out. She dropped down out of the ceiling space and landed on her feet. Too close.

Thirty minutes, she'd heard Siskind say. If she wanted to be on that service boat when it left, that's how long she had.

THE BRIDGE, WIDE and low-ceilinged, was almost empty. Systems were cycling on automatic standby. Kara waited in the shadows as the *Allure's* first officer – Ornales, she seemed to recall him being called – checked over some console displays with two of his men. Then all three disappeared towards the navigation chamber.

The data was there, on the main console that extended down from the ceiling over the master's seat, blocks of information glowing on the repeater screen. She scrolled down carefully, reading off, until she was sure she was sure.

Voices. She ducked down behind the master's seat. She heard Ornales return, and walk through the bridge with his two companions. They left through the hatch she had entered by.

Kara rose again, and crept across to the comm station. The high gain vox was of an unfamiliar design, but she made sense of it. She set the band, altered the directional array slightly, and selected signal/non-voice. Very carefully, she typed her message on the worn, yellowing keys.

Dancer wishes Nest. Gudrun.

She pressed transmit. The machine warbled to itself quietly, and the words she'd entered on the display disappeared, to be replaced by *signal sent.*

She turned, and headed for the exit. She had, by her own maths, less than ten minutes remaining. It had taken her longer than that to reach the bridge.

She ran down the bridge-link companionway, across a four-way junction, and turned left down an access walk. She heard voices a long way behind her, but nothing close. A ladder well took her down through the deck and onto a lateral access. The mess was nearby. She could smell boiled vegetables and grease.

She hurried on to the next hatchway.

She was just a few metres away from it when Lucius Worna stepped out into the light, blocking the hatch. He stared at her with malicious intent.

She backed away, fast, and turned.

Siskind was standing ten metres behind her. The red-haired man wore a strange, satisfied smile. He was aiming a laspistol at her, straight-armed.

'Hello,' he said. 'Or, as I should say, goodbye.'

'THAT'S NEVER GOING to open, is it?' asked Angharad, watching Nayl work.

Nayl sat back from the cell door and shook his head. He had been working so intently that his scalp was beaded with perspiration. The plastek jemmy was twisted out of shape and deformed. 'Let me give it one more–'

'You've been saying that for an hour,' Angharad said.

'He isn't ever going to open it,' said Iosob. 'Keys are funny things, and that's not a key.'

'Be quiet, child,' Angharad spat.

'She's right,' said Nayl, rising to his feet. He turned his back on the cell door and hurled the useless jemmy away with a grunt of frustration. It hit the far wall, and dropped onto the floor.

Outside, the ku'kud was hissing and scratching in the darkness.

There was a soft thump, a click of retracting bolts, and the cell door swung open.

'Very good!' cried Iosob, clapping her hands.

Nayl turned slowly around. 'That wasn't me,' he said.

Ludmilla Bashesvili peered in at them.

'There's very little time,' she whispered. 'Come on.'

The three of them stared at her.

'Are you... what are you doing? Are you springing us?' Nayl asked.

'Yes,' whispered Bashesvili impatiently. 'Come on!'

'What about Ravenor?' Nayl demanded.

Bashesvili looked at him. 'I'm sorry. I have just informed Colonel Lang. Your friend Gideon died fifteen minutes ago on the operating table.'

'IF YOU SAT down, perhaps?' Thonius suggested.

'No thanks,' replied Belknap, and continued pacing the bridge.

'I'm not thinking of you, so much,' said Thonius. 'You pacing up and down is starting to piss me off.'

Belknap glared at him.

'We should have heard something by now,' said Plyton. 'What's taking her so long?'

'Just... wait,' said Ballack. 'She'll be fine. She–'

Unwerth, hunched over the master console, made a small sound.

'What?' asked Belknap, switching around to face him. 'What?'

Unwerth pointed dismally at the display with a disfigured hand.

'The *Allure* just lit its drive,' said Plyton, staring.

'No,' said Belknap. 'Come on, Kara, come on. By the grace of the Throne and the blessing of the God-Emperor...'

'It's left grav anchorage,' Plyton whispered. She rose to her feet, staring at the plot display. 'Oh no.'

'She's running,' said Ballack, 'accelerating onto an out-system vector.'

'Kara!' Belknap howled, helplessly. The *Allure* was departing. There was nothing they could do.

The vox-bank behind Thonius chimed.

PART FOUR

End of Story

ONE

PATIENCE KYS REMAINED in the brig aboard the *Arethusa* for
thirteen days. In part, her stay was enforced, in part vol-
untary.

On the first day of her incarceration, less than an hour
after the terrifying voice had spoken to her from the keyhole, she felt the deck shiver. Various rumbles and
vibrations followed, and she knew they were casting off.
The main drives cycled up until the air filled with a long,
throbbing background hum. An hour after that, she felt
the brief, disconcerting shudder of translation.

Several hours later, the tank door swung open and
Thonius came in with a mess tray of food and a flask of
water. He set them down on the end of the tank's small
cot and looked at her.

'Do you need anything else?' he asked stiffly. 'A book,
perhaps?'

'I need to be let out of here,' she said.

He sighed. 'Kys, I can't do that. You know I can't.'

'Listen to me, Carl, please,' Kys said quickly, rising to her feet. 'Zael represents an absolute threat to us. Every second we waste brings us closer to disaster. You know what Gideon thought about the boy.'

'I know he didn't kill him immediately,' said Carl. 'I know he left the boy alive and gave him the benefit of the doubt.'

'That doubt is gone.'

'Ravenor left Frauka–'

'Frauka is compromised. Zael is awake. The daemon is here, waking, among us.'

Thonius smiled sadly. 'Patience, old thing, I feel for you, I really do. I know you think you're right, but I'll tell you what's really happening. Gideon is dead. You are undermined by grief and a mistaken feeling of responsibility. You are not thinking clearly. You're reacting too extremely. It's understandable. You think you let Ravenor down in life, and you're trying not to do the same now he's dead.'

'Do I pay extra for the cod psychoanalysis?' she asked.

He pouted. 'This has been a bad, bad time for all of us. Don't make it worse by lashing out at phantoms.'

'You won't let me out?'

'Can I trust you not to try and kill Zael again?'

She didn't answer.

'Well, at least you didn't try to lie to me,' he said. 'You have to stay in here for now, for your own safety as much as Zael's. Maybe in a day or two–'

'I'll have calmed down? Seen sense?'

'You need time to reflect.'

Kys stared at him. 'Just a few hours ago, it spoke to me. It spoke to me through the door.'

'What did?'

She swallowed. 'Slyte.'

Thonius shook his head.

'I experienced a major psychic event,' she insisted.

'One that nobody else felt? One that didn't set off any of the ship's detectors?'

'Please, Carl! Please! I'm begging you! Examine Zael yourself, examine Frauka too. He's lying. He's protecting the boy. Please tell me you'll check it yourself. We are all in danger and–'

'Eat some food. Get some rest,' he said, moving back towards the door.

She sat down heavily on the cot. 'Where are we going?' she asked.

'Gudrun.'

'Why?'

'It's where we believe Molotch is.'

'Why?' she repeated.

'Information received. Look, I've got things to do.'

'Let me talk to Kara, then.'

A strange expression crossed his face. 'I'll check back later,' he said.

SHE SLEPT FOR a while. As Kara had warned her, the quality of her sleep was not good. Flocks of whispers circled her dreams, like the eerie twittering of the Wych House.

Thonius returned six hours later with another tray, and removed the first. She'd picked at the meal.

'Will you let me out?' she asked.

'Will you try to kill Zael?'

She shrugged.

'I'll see you in the morning.'

'Where's Kara?' she asked.

With great reluctance, he told her how Kara had boarded the *Allure*, obtained the information they needed, and never returned. The news knifed shock into her. Coming so soon after the hammer blow of Ravenor's death, it seemed extravagantly cruel and unnecessary. She wept inconsolably, tormented by a feeling of helplessness. Thonius made some half-hearted soothing noises and then left her alone.

Kys continued to weep for hours. She was so wracked with sobs it seemed that she was crying out her own grief as well as the grief Ravenor would have expressed if he had lived to witness Kara's fate.

THE PATTERN WAS repeated for the next ten days. Carl Thonius visited her twice each day, bringing her food and water, and the occasional book or data-slate, none of which she read. She would ask to be released, and he would ask her if she still intended to hurt Zael. She would beg him to take her seriously, and he would tell her to rest and reflect.

It was always Thonius. He never made the mistake of sending Belknap or Frauka, either of whom she would have had no hesitation in trying to overpower. Carl Thonius was canny. He clearly understood this, and understood that she would not raise a hand against him. The things he knew.

Neither Plyton nor Unwerth were sent to look in on her with food. Kys suspected Thonius didn't trust either of them to be unsympathetic.

The rest of the time was largely silent, apart from the throb of the gunning drive. Several times, she thought about trying the door again, certain she had recouped enough strength to manipulate the lock. The memory of the whispering voice dissuaded her every time.

The voice, mercifully, never returned, although the whispers haunted her edgy dreams, and on more than one occasion, wide awake, she heard distant laughter coming from nowhere.

ON THE TWELFTH day, the ship shuddered, and the tone of the drive altered, and she knew they had returned to normal space. Carl came in two hours later, but he seemed preoccupied and his visit was brief. Pausing only long enough to comment that she wasn't eating enough as he picked up the last tray, he left and locked the door.

After that, no one came at all.

The drone of the drive cut out, and the *Arethusa* fell silent. Kys paced. She waited. The silence bore down on her, total silence, apart from the sporadic stress creaks and groans of the settling hull.

When the next visit was missed, Kys drank the rest of her water and ate what remained of the last meal. Anxiety had robbed her of her appetite for eleven days. Now the waiting made her ravenous.

When she was sure she was in the thirteenth day of imprisonment, she went to the tank door and banged her fist on it, calling out. She did this for some minutes.

No one answered.

Scared, she sat down in the corner of the cell furthest from the door and waited. The hours ticked slowly by.

SHE WOKE WITH a start, still sitting in the corner. Something had woken her, some noise.

She listened. She reached out cautiously with her mind.

The first howl came out of nowhere. It lasted ten seconds, and was essentially pure psychic noise. It was like some great beast bellowing in pain, or the throat-roar of an apex predator. The first touch of it was so loud, so fierce that her mind recoiled in shock.

The echo of the howl lingered in the ship's hull.

Eyes wide in fear, she made herself as small as possible, arms around her upthrust knees. Her body was bathed in cold sweat, fear sweat, and her mind was sore from just that brief touch. She could hear her heart pounding like a marching drum.

A second howl split the air. The deck vibrated with its intensity. Kys whimpered involuntarily, viced by an extreme terror she had never known before.

Ice rime formed around the edges of the tank door, and glistened at the key hole.

A third howl issued, longer and more anguished than either of the first two. She heard hatches bang and footsteps running past along the hallway outside. Someone was shouting, but she couldn't hear what. Someone else shouted back.

Silence.

More shouting. Distant footsteps, running along a deck above. Then, an odd, piping sound that she finally, fearfully, realised was a muffled, persistent screaming. She dared not reach out with her mind.

Everything went quiet for an agonising thirty or forty minutes. The ice around the door melted into glinting spots of dew. Just when she thought nothing more would come, there was a fourth, dreadful psychic roar, and then a fifth, the longest of all. It was followed by a long, painful bout of sobbing. A man was wailing somewhere, wailing with his mind. She grimaced and tried to shut it out. The sobs clawed at the edges of her thoughts until they became frayed.

The sobbing faded. More shouting began, real voices shouting. Kys jumped at the sudden boom of a gun, a shotgun or an autorifle. It fired four times in quick succession. Someone shouted, distantly, and then a barrage of angry voices started up, yelling over one another. The shotgun fired again. A lasgun wailed.

Then silence drifted back into place.

She could bear it no longer. Kys rose and slowly approached the door, swallowing her fear back. It was like a bolus of food stuck in her throat, choking her.

She was three metres from the tank door when the most terrifying event of her life took place.

The centre of the steel door, at a little above waist height, began to bulge, as if the metal was alive. The bulge pushed in towards her, and she backed away.

An impression formed: bared teeth. The frontal denti-
tion, upper and lower, of an adult male's skull, complete
with chin bone below and traces of nasal bone above.
There was no sign of eye sockets or forehead. It was as if
the door had become a taut, flexible skin of rubber, and
someone on the other side was pushing the lower part of
an incomplete skull into it.

Something hit Kys from behind. It was the rear wall of
the tank. She had backed away as far as it was physically
possible to go. The imprint of the skull smile bulged in
further, until it was a hand's breadth proud of the door's
surface. It became even more clearly defined. The metal
strained around it.

'The Emperor protects,' Kys stammered. 'The Emperor
protects.'

The skull smile slowly opened its jaws.

Then it pulled away sharply and vanished. The door
became flat again. Kys kept staring at the door.

After a second or two, the smile reappeared, bulging in
at a different, higher part of the door. It opened and
closed its jaws twice.

It withdrew as rapidly as before, and then reappeared lower down. This time, it writhed back and
forth as it opened and closed, turning to the left, to the
right, biting at the air. Kys could hear sobbing, loud
and close.

The smile withdrew again. Ice sweat tricked down the
door's surface, twinkling and glittering like frost. It
formed a crust, like on the inside of a refrigeration unit,
and then the caked bulk of it collapsed under its own
weight and shattered across the cell floor in a shower of
snowy debris.

Her back to the rear wall of the tank, Kys slid down and
began to shake.

* * *

THE ARETHUSA STAYED quiet for a long time after that. There was no more sobbing or shouting or gun-shots, no more howling. The door did not smile at her again.

Kys got up, walked towards the door, and listened.

Nothing.

She breathed in, exhaled, and quickly reached her mind into the lock. Fear and fury in equal measure fuelled her with a clinical precision. She seized the lock, scorching the tips of her mind's tendrils on the anti-psi wards, and rattled the tumblers into place.

The lock slumped open with a heavy clack and she mind-wrenched the bolt back.

Kys touched the edge of the door with the tip of one shoe and it swung open heavily.

Her thirteen-day stay in the *Arethusa's* brig had come to an end.

SHE WALKED ALONG the grim, poorly lit hallway of the brig block. Nothing howled, nothing sobbed, nothing smiled. The air was close and warm, as if the ship's air pumps had shut down.

She looked for a weapon, but the best she could find was a set of keys hanging on a peg. She took the old, heavy keys off their ring and put them in a pocket. In an emergency, she could kine them.

She stole through the brig's half open outer hatch onto the grille mesh of the lower third access. There was no sign of anything in either direction. The access was lit by wall globes, one or two of which were flickering on and off like candle flames guttering in a draught.

Her spike heels caught in the deck mesh, so she slipped her shoes off and carried them.

Padding forwards in stocking feet, she reached a junction. Ahead, the short, bulk-headed passage to the aft air gate. Left, a flicker-lit companionway turned back to the enginarium.

To the right, a corridor led forwards.

She turned right. Ten metres along, she found a spilled box of shotgun cartridges, a discarded boot and a damp towel.

The air was still very stale. More of the glow-globes and lumin panels were flickering on and off.

Kys bent down and pressed her hand against the cast iron wall, low down. There was no vibration at all. No throb of power plant, or of idling drive. Although the air was fuggy, it was getting colder.

The *Arethusa* was like a cooling corpse.

At the next junction, she reached a wall-mounted intercom, a recessed speaker cone with a brass switch. She put her shoes down and reached out for the switch.

It took her a long time to pluck up the courage to push it.

Click. A long, empty sigh of dead leaves and static breathed out of the speaker.

She took her finger off the switch and the sound went dead. She pressed the switch again, and said, into the rustling, 'Hello?'

The static shushed her.

'Hello? Anyone?'

Somewhere far away, behind the hiss of dry leaves, a man started sobbing.

Kys took her finger off the switch and killed the sound.

At the next junction, there was a fire control point riveted to the hull. She helped herself to the heavy, saw-toothed fire axe hanging over the sand box. Axe in one hand, shoes in the other, she continued on her way.

THE ARETHUSA'S SMALL excursion bay was empty. The docking clamps were vacant. Neither of the ship's two battered landers were present. Kys stood on the overlook platform for a while, staring down into the open vault. The heavy duty docking clamps, thick with black grease

and lubricant jelly, stared back at her. Some of the
fuelling hoses on the right-hand side of the bay had been
disconnected in a hurry. Pools of spilled fuel covered the
deck plates.

'Where did everyone go?' she asked out loud. She
didn't dare ask her real question.

Why did everyone go?

HALFWAY ALONG THE companionway leading to the forward junction, she found a place where the wall plates
had been dented and scorched by gunfire. The marks
were fresh, carbonised. A metre or two further along,
there was a smeared streak of blood on the wall, and a
track of drops leading away down the tunnel.

Wall lights blinked on and off, strobing manically.

She bent down. The blood was cold.

SHE ENTERED THE infirmary. She put her shoes on before
she did, because the floors in the upper decks were solid
plate.

She slithered in slowly, her axe raised.

The outer surgery was empty. Water drizzled out of a
half open tap into a scrub bowl. She turned the faucet
off. The doors to the pharm cupboards were open, and
the contents ransacked. Pill boxes littered the floor. She
was crunching over scattered capsules, grinding them to
powder.

She could hear a soft, panting, purring sound.

Kys nudged the adjoining door open with the head of
her axe. The panting grew louder. She reached out, but
her mind touched nothing at all.

She entered the ward room. The air stank of Frauka's
lho-sticks, a cold, distant, tarnished after-smell.

There was nobody in the ward room. Zael's cot was
empty. The plug feeds and drip tubes that had been keeping him alive were draped over the crumpled bed,

leaking fluids. The life support unit he had been attached to was grinding and rattling, its lung bellow rising and falling with a dry pant. Cardiac systems and brainwave monitors purred aimlessly.

Kys walked over to the cot. She scraped the sheets back with the blade of her fire axe, although she knew the cot was empty. She reached over and turned off the relentless life support unit.

The bellows ceased their panting and became still. The monitors buzzed. Viscous fluid squirted out of the lank tubes left on the bed. A flat line alarm began to ping.

She wrenched the unit away from the wall to make it shut up. The bellows flapped and sighed.

Silence returned.

She walked around the cot and sat down in Frauka's chair. His dish of lho-butts sat on the bedside cabinet. The last one had burned itself out in a long, perfect column of white ash. His data-slate was on the floor in front of the chair. It was still switched on, the *battery low* warning flashing.

She reached down and picked it up.

'He slowly, hungrily, licked the juice off her ample–' she read out. She switched the data-slate off and hurled it at the ward room wall. It broke and fell in pieces.

She rose and then sat down again. She'd seen something on the floor beside the bedside cabinet. She reached down with her mind and picked it up. It hovered in front of her face.

It was Frauka's autopistol.

Kys took hold of it with her hand and thumbed out the clip. Full.

She looked down at the floor again. It was littered with blood-soaked swabs.

'Oh, you stupid, stupid bastard,' she said.

* * *

THE ARETHUSA'S BRIDGE was as empty as everything else on the ship. She walked in, Frauka's pistol in one hand, the fire axe in the other.

The viewers and repeater screens flicked and scrolled mindlessly. Auto-systems chattered on and off like muffled gunfire.

'Hello?' she called out, hoping for an answer and no answer at the same time.

Kys sat down in the master's chair, put down her pistol and her axe, and began tapping the keys of the main station board.

Gudrun, the screen told her. They were at high anchor above Gudrun, in the Helican sub. The ship had been set to dormancy. She punched some keys and corrected that. Cool air began to hiss through the air-scrubbers. She heard the power plant wake up.

She heard distant sobbing too, but she ignored it.

Replay recent log, she typed.

The console blinked and replied *Void*.

She repeated her command.

Void.

She was about to type again when she heard a tiny sound. It came from behind her, in the companionway leading up into the bridge. Kys picked up the autopistol, and slid down behind the master's chair, aiming the weapon. She picked the axe up too, with her telekinesis, and lifted it into the ceiling above, just under the roof stanchions. It began to spin, chopping around like a murderous propeller.

She heard another sound, a footstep. Someone stepped onto the bridge.

Her index finger pulled at the trigger.

SHOLTO UNWERTH PEERED at her. 'Hello?' he said.

Kys rammed the pistol down, so that it fired into the thick deck.

'Sorry, sorry!' she exclaimed.

He blinked at her, baffled, flinching from the retort of the shot. She dropped the gun and ran to him, hugged him tightly, and kissed him.

'I'm very glad to see you,' she exclaimed.

He stared back at her, lips slightly parted in surprise as hers pulled away. She let him go. She coughed and brushed the front of his jacket as if to smooth it.

'Master Unwerth.'

'Patience.'

'It's really good to see you again. I thought I was alone up here.'

'You kissed me.' He frowned.

'Yes, I did. I did kiss you. Sorry.'

'Do not be apoplectic. It was... it was unexpectorant.'

'Well, forgive me. I'm just happy to see a friendly face.'

'Me also,' he said. He smiled, and then cringed as the fire axe fell out of the roof onto the deck. She'd forgotten it and let it go.

'What, maychance, was that?'

'Insurance,' she smiled. 'Are you alone?'

'Indeed, no,' Unwerth said. He gestured to the men behind him. Fyflank emerged into the light of the bridge, followed by Onofrio, the head cook, and Saintout, the tertiary helmsman.

'We four are all that's left,' said Unwerth. 'Following the mutiny all such.'

Fyflank grumbled his disgust.

'Mutiny?' Kys asked.

'Mutiny, indeed,' said Unwerth. 'My crew was stricken by a mutational urge. Just after we made arrival. Just after Master Thonius took them down.'

'Who?'

'Mam Plyton, Masters Ballack and Belknap, and himself.'

'Down?'

'In a lander, number one lander, to the surface.'

'What happened here, Sholto?' Kys asked.

He shrugged. 'Screaming and crying,' he said.

'And howling,' added Saintout behind him.

'Yes, and that. My poor ship went mad. Oh, the screaming and the howling! Oh, the upsetment! Boguin led the mutiny–'

'I never liked him much,' put in Onofrio.

'Me neither,' said Saintout.

'It was Boguin's doing,' said Unwerth. 'He was enspooked. When the howling started, he gripped the crew with all forcefulness. They had guns. They debarked on the second lander.'

'Thonius had already taken the first?' Kys nodded. 'Sholto, where did the howling come from?'

Unwerth shrugged.

'Where is Frauka? Where is Zael?'

'I have no idea,' he replied, timid and worried.

'Sholto, we're in trouble,' said Kys.

Fyflank nudged Unwerth. The little shipmaster ran to his command console and adjusted some dials. Several warning lights had started to flash.

'What?' asked Kys, coming over.

'Something is extruding,' Unwerth said.

'Extruding?' Kys replied.

'A ship,' said Unwerth. 'Bearing in towards us.'

Kys looked at the flaring screen. It was a mess of complex graphics, with little clarity.

'Are you certain?' Kys asked. 'It could just be an imaging artefact.'

Unwerth fine-tuned the scanners, and the display cleaned up. The track became very legible. Plotting data overwrote the curving trajectory marker, showing comparative speed, position and size. The approaching ship was decelerating from an immaterium exit point nine astronomical units out. It seemed twice the size of the *Arethusa*.

'Pict feed?' she asked. 'Can we get a visual with the stern array?'

He stabbed at some of the controls. On a secondary imaging plate, a ghost image appeared, a fog of green and amber pixilation. The screen image jumped and panned as the pict array grabbed focus and range.

They could see it. A long way off, and small but, to Patience Kys, unmistakable.

'Oh Throne,' Kys gasped. 'That's the *Hinterlight*.'

The vox bank lit up behind Unwerth. 'Hailing signal,' he said, 'pict and voice in simulation.'

'Take it,' said Kys.

Unwerth nodded to Saintout, who hurried to the comm station and woke the vox bank. The main screen blinked twice and then lit up.

The distorted, blinking view of a woman's face appeared, peering at them.

'Hello, *Arethusa*? Hello, *Arethusa*?' The words came through a yowl of white noise.

Kys lifted the vox mic on its heavy cable. 'Hello, *Hinterlight*, hello. Mistress Cynia, is that you?'

The fuzzy visual frowned at them. 'Confirmed. Who am I speaking to? Is that you, Kara?' More white noise squalled.

'No, it's me,' Kys called into the mic. 'It's Patience.'

'It's Patience,' the blur on the viewer said to someone off screen. There was yet more crackle and fuzz. 'Get me a clean link, Halstrom, for Throne's sake,' they heard her say.

The viewer image suddenly sharpened. Kys looked up at the unsmiling, troubled features of Cynia Preest, mistress of the *Hinterlight*.

'This is an unexpected pleasure,' said Kys, aware she had tears in her eyes.

'I imagine you're surprised to see me,' said Preest over the speakers. 'Believe me, you're not half as surprised as I was a week ago.'

'What?' asked Kys.

The image of Preest jumped and fluttered. She glanced sidelong at someone off view and stepped back. A figure moved into her place and looked into the picter with a half-smile.

It was Harlon Nayl.

TWO

THERE WAS A storm coming.

Leyla Slade could hear the brewing grumble of thunder rolling down from the hog's back of dark mountains above Elmingard. The fulminous sky, and the increase in negative ions, made her scratchy and irritable.

It was late afternoon. She stood on the dry, bare stone of the high terrace, and looked down the crag. Elmingard occupied the crown of a buttress of old, black rock, which dropped away, sheer in places, about a thousand metres to the valley below. Down there, only a few kilometres away, there was sunlight and arable land, low hills skirted by woodland, post-harvest fields full of dry straw, the rural belt of southern Sarre, where the headwaters of the Pellitor sprang, about as comfortable and pastoral a tract of land as you could find on any old Imperial world.

Things turned darker and wilder, however, when you reached the abrupt feet of the Kell Mountains. Smaller, surly, westerly cousins to the mighty Atenates that dominated the continental heartland, they rose like a mistake from the undulating countryside of Sarre. Storms fretted around them all year long, as if their thorny backs snagged the passing weather and detained it until it became annoyed. Mists filled the abyssal gorges and steep ravines like uncombed wool. Often, the cloud and haze descended so deeply that the entire range was lost from sight. One could stand in a cornfield ten kilometres away and not know there were mountains there at all.

It was not Leyla Slade's favourite place in the galaxy. Elmingard had been built as a monastic retreat seventeen hundred years earlier, during a period of plague and schismatic war that had marred Gudrun's history. Subsequently, it had been derelict, and then the home of a feral astronomer. For many years after that it had been the impractical country seat of wealthy Sarrean viticulturists who cultivated vast vineyards in the peaceful country below.

They had died out and departed, defeated by the lonely eminence, and Elmingard had fallen back into disuse, scavenged by the weather.

Orfeo Culzean had purchased it through a chain of faceless middlemen twenty years before. He'd had extensive work done to restore and develop the rambling property, but Leyla still had little love for the place. It had been too many things in its bleak lifetime, and the result was a schizophrenic knot of identities. It was too large, too jumbled, too muddled. The long, austere sections of monastic origin were cold and damp, sagging under patches of sloped grey tile roof that looked like snakeskin. The viticulturists' contributions consisted of dirty, white-stone halls grafted in between the monastic wings, halls that interlocked oddly and had too many storeys. There were stairs and abutting terraces everywhere. The astronomer, in a characteristic act of whimsy, had raised a crude tower of black stone at the north end of the crag, perhaps as an observatory platform. Its construction was not especially sound, and it had become a leaning ruin, but it had never been demolished. Culzean believed it lent Elmingard an 'alchemical charm'.

Slade walked back along the high terrace, under the shadow of the astronomer's tower. Roosting birds clacked and cawed like lost souls. Thick beards of ivy and asterolia covered the face of the grey walls below her.

Culzean and Molotch were arguing in the solar. She could hear their voices. Another storm brewing. They had been arguing for several weeks. Culzean described it to her as 'debate', but she'd seen the growing resentment in the eyes of both men. The essential nature of the 'debate', as far as she understood it, was to agree upon the scheme they would undertake together.

There was the recurring question of Slyte. Since Culzean had first posited the notion of Molotch's relationship with Slyte – and Ravenor – Molotch had become increasingly obsessed and distracted. He was starting to exhibit what Slade believed was paranoia, pure and simple. He had been gravely disappointed to learn that Ravenor had bluntly rejected Culzean's proposal, as if he had actually been expecting a positive response. He stayed up late into the night, in his room in the dormitory wing, filling up notebooks with rapid, almost feverish penmanship, consulting the library of books and manuscripts that Culzean had imported.

A vast number of books, manuscripts and other esoteric objects filled the rooms and corridors of Elmingard, many of them still in shipping cases, waiting to be unpacked. Culzean had sent for them when he had decided on the place as his latest bolthole, and they had arrived by freight shipment from storage deposits, bank vaults and discreet caches all over the sector. Culzean was a collector of many things, and he magpied away his lifetime's accumulation of arcane ephemera in a thousand separate hiding places for later retrieval.

Only the most valuable items came with him on his travels. Certain potent devices, his 'shining weapons of destiny', certain books of special provenance, certain charts and grimoires. He always carried his small but priceless library of anthropodermic bibliopegy – the life stories of significant saints, savants, murderers and heretics bound in the skins of the men themselves, and his collection of deodands. The desperate nature of their flight from Eustis Majoris had forced him to leave his precious deodands in Petropolis, a fact that he still complained about. He had arranged for their private recovery, again through an untraceable chain of anonymous intermediaries, but the caution he had to exercise to procure them meant he probably wouldn't be reunited with the collection for several years.

Slade walked to the solar and peered in through the half-open door. Molotch and Culzean were conversing with some vehemence. For the third day running, the talk had turned to the feasibility of constructing new gnosis engines for a return to Sleef. When Slade had first heard them mentioned, she had questioned Culzean about them privately.

'Sleef Outworld, Ley,' he had said. 'Dirty little mudball, far away from all things good, out in the skirts of Callixes sector.'

'Have you been there?'

'No,' he said, 'but I've studied various reports. Molotch has been there. It was where Ravenor killed him the first time.'

Leyla Slade had looked at Culzean, puzzled. Culzean had snorted, as if he'd made a fabulous joke. 'I don't understand. What's so wonderful about this place?'

'There are vents there, Leyla, volcanic vents. They have a special quality. The skin of reality is thin there, Leyla. One can hear the vibration of the Immaterium, just out of reach. The vents speak.'

'They speak, do they?'

'They do. Voices from the warp, mumbling fragments from the daemonverse. With the correct equipment – in this case a very curious and expensive device called a gnosis engine – the voices can be collected and stored.'

'For analysis?'

'Yes, and as a source of infernal power.'

Culzean had then rambled on at length, his terminology becoming more and more technical and arcane, until Leyla was lost. She knew he knew she hadn't the slightest hope of understanding the workings of the gnosis engine, but he insisted on explaining it. He had even drawn a little sketch for her.

Then he had told her about Ravenor. Molotch had been on Sleef Outworld with several gnosis engines built by the Cognitae, and the Inquisition had arrived to destroy the project. Molotch and Ravenor had battled – they hadn't even known who each other was – and Molotch had escaped with his life, just.

He had jumped, or fallen, into a vent. A teleport had saved him, but not before he had been caught in an upblast of venting fire. He had been scorched by daemonic energy, injuries that took him a long time to recover from.

Culzean told her he believed that was the moment when Ravenor and Molotch had their destinies linked and placed in the hands of the Ruinous Powers. Through the vents, the warp had scented them, tasted them, acquired them. The Ruinous Powers had enigmatic plans, plans too long, too involved, and too abstruse for any mortal mind to comprehend. But the powers could see that, before their brief lives ended, Ravenor and Molotch would perform a great service for them.

'And this service is Slyte?' she had asked.

'This service is Slyte, yes,' he had replied.

Leyla stepped back from the solar door. From what she could hear, Molotch and her master had managed to disagree on the precise configuration of a gnosis engine, and what alloy best served as an inner lining. There was talk of engaging private fabricators, possibly from Caxton or Sarum, at great expense, and a discussion of how the engine would be shipped.

The only thing they seemed to agree on was that the vents of Sleef Outworld might be a conduit through which they could learn pertinent and valuable information about the mysterious Slyte.

Her ear tag pinged, and she left the solar, coming out of the building across a small, walled courtyard, before running up the steps into the central block of the house sprawl.

Thunder grumbled in the sky behind her, and a breeze had picked up, nodding the tight buds of the arid roses that grew in the courtyard. The sky itself, bright yellow in the east, had bruised black with a thunderhead in the west, as if night and day were co-existing in the same sky.

She reached the security control centre. Like many rooms in Elmingard, its crumbling exterior of flaked plaster and patchy stone belied an extensive modern interior. The walls had been panelled with brushed steel plates, and a grilled deck allowed an under floor gap for power cables and data trunking. There were six cogitator desks arranged in a star pattern, all facing into the centre. The machines clacked and hummed, their valve tubes glowing, and their imaging plates rippling with green sine waves. In the centre of the circle, in the heart of the star, was a large, three-sixty degree hololithic display. Each cogitator desk had a vox assembly bolted on to it, linked under the floor to a bulky, high gain voxcaster in the corner of the room. Extractor fans in the ceiling kept the accumulation of machine heat in the room to a minimum.

Drouet and Tzabo, two members of Culzean's hired, immaculately vetted staff were on duty. They wore plain suits of navy blue wool with neat silver buttons.

'Yes?' she asked.

'Incoming transport, mam,' said Drouet.

'Origin?'

'The landing fields at Dorsay. It's broadcasting the correct code fields.'

'How far out is it?' Slade asked.

'Six minutes, mam,' said Tzabo.

'Ask for the final handshake code, and direct it to the landing. I'll be there to meet it.'

The two men nodded, and turned back to their cogitators.

Leyla Slade hurried out of the security room, back out across the courtyard, and began to descend through the rambling labyrinth of Elmingard via terraces, stone staircases, and twisting steps. As she strode along, she opened her link.

'This is Slade. I want three guns to meet me on the landing immediately.'

'Yes, mam.'

She adjusted her link setting and made another connection.

'Leyla?'

'Sorry to disturb you, sir. There's a transport approaching.'

'Any surprises?'

'I'm making sure there aren't.'

She had reached the southern end of the mountain fastness. Beyond the line of the old monastic wall, a large part of the cliff top had been cleared back to form a natural landing pad of granite. She stood facing the landing, looking out at the evening sunlight over Sarre. The monastic wall and the shadow of Elmingard rose behind her, and then the wilder shadows of the mountains. She felt the first few spots of rain in the air. Thunder growled.

Three men in light body armour appeared through the wall gate behind her. They carried lascarbines.

'Just a precaution,' she told them. She spoke into her link again. 'Security control? Arm the wall sentry guns, please. Voice command to me.'

'Yes, mam,' the link crackled back.

Slade heard the sentry pods go live over the gusting breeze, and arm with a clatter of autoloaders.

They could see the transport: a light lander, a gig, its running lights bright white like stars in the fading sky as it came head on towards them.

Slade slid out her autopistol, popped the standard clip and switched it for one she carried in her belt pouch, one of Culzean's special loads. She slammed it home, but she didn't rack it. You didn't walk around with something like that in the spout.

The lander swept in, big and dark in the threatening sky, its winglets hooked like the pinions of a stooping hawk. Its nose light was blinking. Its landing claws descended from their hatches with whines audible over the thruster downwash.

The wind picked up on the landing, and the down draught lashed grit up in a wide spiral.

The lander touched down with a final howl of thrusters, its claw struts bending to take its weight. The thruster wash immediately dropped, though the belly lights kept flashing, lighting the rock shelf amber. Slade could see the pilot servitor through the cockpit windows, shutting down systems in the green glow of his instrumentation.

The side hatch opened like petals. A tall, red-haired man in a glass jacket came down the ramp and walked briskly over to Leyla. He was followed more lethargically by the pearl-armoured bulk of Lucius Worna.

'Stand down, deactivate systems,' Leyla Slade said into her link.

'Yes, mam.'

'Master Siskind,' she said.

'My dear Leyla,' the red-haired man replied with a smile. He leaned in and kissed her on each cheek, 'You're looking as radiant as ever.'

Slade couldn't abide Siskind's familiarity, but she tolerated it. You didn't shoot the shipmaster your employer was retaining.

'A good trip?' she asked.

He nodded. 'A bumpy ride in places. Utochre turned into something of a fracas. But all's done. We made high anchor this morning.'

Worna joined them. 'Slade,' he growled.

'Lucius.' She changed out the special load from her weapon, replaced it with the standard clip, and put the gun away.

'Fracas is probably not a word you should use in your report to Orfeo,' she said to Siskind, 'not if you're trying to ingratiate yourself.'

'Oh, I don't know,' a voice said from behind them. 'I enjoy a good fracas once in a while.'

Culzean had joined them on the landing. He was wearing a richly embroidered gown of Hesperan silk over a simple black bodyglove. He looked like the hereditary ruler of some ancient mountain satrapy.

'Sir,' said Siskind with a smile, shaking his hand. Worna nodded respectfully.

'So?' Culzean asked with a cunning smirk. 'Fracas, wasn't it?'

'It all went to hell,' Worna told him in his deep, bass voice, like a testament of doom. 'I lost some men. The Wych House got scragged.'

'You didn't come out unscathed yourself, I see,' said Culzean, nodding at the raw, healing weals on Worna's moonscape face.

'It'll heal,' the bounty hunter replied.

'But the trap worked?' Culzean asked. 'Tell me it worked, after all the trouble we went to.'

'It worked,' said Siskind. 'Ravenor is very, very dead.'

'End of story,' said Worna.

A smile spread across Culzean's face. He checked it. 'We're sure about that?'

'Oh, yes,' said Siskind. He gestured back at the lander. 'We had it confirmed by a very reliable source.'

Siskind's first officer Ornales appeared from the lander. He was escorting someone at gunpoint.

Her hands were bound, and she had obviously suffered extensively. She was limping and her face was bruised.

'Her name is Kara Swole,' said Siskind. 'Until we got our hands on her, she was one of Ravenor's principal agents.'

'Really?' asked Culzean. His eyes brightened. 'Of course. Molotch has mentioned her name. How did you come by her?'

'She penetrated the *Allure* while we were still at anchor over Utochre,' said Siskind. 'She was attempting to discover where we were bound, so that the remnants of Ravenor's team could pursue us in some pathetic attempt at vengeance. However, Lucius and I apprehended her before she could gain access to anything valuable.'

'This is what she claims?'

'This is the truth of it,' said Siskind. 'I have been... how can I put this delicately? I have been questioning her for several days. My methods are reliable. This is the truth. Ravenor died in the Wych House and the remains of his band are leaderless, divided and lost. I was going to kill her, but I had a feeling both you and Molotch would chastise me for robbing you of a diversion.'

'You thought wisely, Master Siskind,' said Culzean. 'There'll be a bonus in this for you. Ley, let's get the cook to produce something special tonight. A welcoming feast, and a celebratory one. Have the lovely Mam Swole secured in the Alcove.'

Slade nodded. 'This way,' she said. Dead-eyed, the prisoner limped in the direction indicated.

Leyla Slade almost felt sorry for her. No one deserved to be left in Siskind's care for days on end.

* * *

THREE

'COME WITH ME,' said Harlon Nayl the moment Patience stepped through the *Hinterlight's* airgate. He hugged her tight. 'Come with me.'

'There's too much to–'

'Just come with me.'

Nayl nodded to Unwerth and the other three crewmen who had come across from the *Arethusa* in the *Hinterlight's* launch. At Kys's insistence, no one remained behind on the haunted derelict. Elman Halstrom, Preest's solid, dependable first officer, a Navy vet, had come to meet them at the airgate with Nayl.

'Gentlemen,' he said, 'Master Unwerth, allow me to welcome you to the *Hinterlight*. Perhaps you'd care for some refreshment?'

Nayl led Kys away down the *Hinterlight's* long access tunnels. The smell, the quality of the lamp light, the stylistic details: it felt almost unbearably familiar to Kys.

'I thought you were dead,' she whispered.

'I thought I was dead,' he agreed.

'Why aren't you dead? Where did you go?'

'Those are two questions I find it almost impossible to answer, Patience,' he replied, hustling her along. 'We went through the door. It was the only escape.'

'To where?'

'Places you wouldn't believe.'

'Why not?'

'Because I was there, and I don't frigging believe them,' he replied.

'But–' she began.

'We'll get to the but and the why and the what later,' he said. He led her into the *Hinterlight's* well-equipped infirmary. The ship's medicae, Zarjaran, nodded to her. Kys came to a slow halt. She stared.

A vague shape, amorphous, hung suspended in a stasis tube, veiled in a sheen of blue light. The tube apparatus was connected to a wealth of humming, pinging, gurgling mechanical equipment. It looked as if most of the infirmary's battery of devices had been hooked up to it.

'Oh, Throne,' she whispered.

'He's resting,' said Nayl. 'He's going to need a long, slow recovery time.'

'He was in a very poor state when I got to him,' said the medicae softly, inspecting a few console read-outs. 'Massive stab trauma, organ failure, necrotisation, exhaustion, secondary and tertiary infections. He'd been out of support for some time while he received emergency surgery. Very rudimentary surgery, in my opinion.'

'She did her best,' Nayl said.

Zarjaran shrugged. 'He arrested all vitals at least three times under her knife but, yes, I think she did.'

Kys stepped forward. She felt numb. She couldn't really see what was in the tube. It was just a dark blur, but she could feel what was in it.

She reached out her hand and touched the glass.

'Gideon?'

+Patience.+

The send was distant, like a whisper. Tears sprang up in her eyes.

+I'm so sorry, Gideon, I'm so sorry! I should not have left you. I should never have–+

+Shhhhh,+ the whisper sent back.

ZARJARAN INSISTED THEY leave Ravenor to rest. Nayl took Kys up to the *Hinterlight's* ready room. It was a sumptuous private lounge, as befitted the mistress's character. Shipmistress Cynia Preest was already there, with Halstrom, entertaining Unwerth and his three crewmen. Cynia Preest was more than two hundred and eighty years old, although she always claimed, not unconvincingly, a much lower figure. She had a womanly, matronly frame, cropped blonde hair, and a penchant for heavy eye make-up and ostentatiously dangly earrings. She was wearing a fine, tailored satin suit and red velvet robes. An irascible, strong-minded woman, Preest was nevertheless intensely loyal, although her relationship with Ravenor, and her role as a hired servant of the ordos, had become increasingly strained since the incident at Majeskus. After Bonner's Reach, when the *Hinterlight* had been forced to limp away for repairs a second time, they had parted company, partly through necessity. Ravenor had needed to return to Eustis Majoris urgently, and for that reason, the *Arethusa* was hired. Kys had been privately sure that Preest was glad to see the back of them.

The shipmistress showed no sign of that now. She rose as Nayl brought Kys into the ready room, and gave her a maternal hug.

'How are you, my dear?' she asked, as if she really cared.

'Happier than I was. You'll have to excuse me. I haven't washed or changed my clothes in a fortnight.'

'There will be time for that later,' said Preest. 'Have some amasec to steady yourself. Halstrom? Some amasec?'

Halstrom rose to pour the drink. Kys looked around. The entire situation had a dislocated, dreamy quality. Apart from Preest, Halstrom and Unwerth's band, she saw Angharad seated in a corner. The Carthaen was dressed in a plain brown gown. Her intricate leather body armour was laid out like a shed skin across her lap, and she was diligently repairing it with wire thread, a steel needle and a pair of cutters. She didn't spare Kys a second glance.

A young girl sat near to her, prepubescent, wide eyed and strange. She was playing with a key, and laughing to herself.

Halstrom brought Kys her amasec. 'It's good to see you,' he said, and gave her a peck on the cheek as he handed her the drink. She smiled. She had always been fond of the first officer. He was always reassuring, like the father she had never known.

'Tell me what happened,' she said, sitting down with Nayl. The others looked on.

Nayl told her, as best he could. His explanation lasted a long time, and rambled more than once as details failed to make sense until he backed up and explained them. The workings of the door sounded impossible and insane to Kys's ears, and she asked a lot of questions. Angharad, working and not looking up, interjected several times to correct Nayl's facts.

'Finally, we ended up in this place, Rahjez,' said Nayl at length. Preest had just given him a second amasec. 'We were a long way out by then. The Ultima Segmentum, a thousand years out.'

'A thousand?' Kys breathed. 'Back, or–?'

'Back,' said Nayl.

'A thousand long years, a thousand long years,' the child, Iosob, sang, playing with her key. Everyone looked at her. She didn't notice.

'Gideon was in a bad way by then,' Nayl continued, 'close to death. He tried to hide it, but I knew. He'd worked out how to steer us through the door by using his mind, but his mind wasn't strong enough any more. The door was playing games, I think, being deliberately wilful. He'd asked it for the *Arethusa* in 404, and that's where it took us. Listening Station Arethusa, in 404.M40.'

Kys shook her head. 'Go on.'

'We were locked up, as suspected enemy agents. Ravenor's rosette was no use. No one could confirm we were who we said we were, but I convinced them to help Ravenor. There was a medicae, Bashesvili. We owe her a lot.'

'And?'

'I think Ravenor managed to form some kind of bond with her while she worked on him. He got into her mind,

and showed her the truth. He persuaded her how important
it was for us to get out. He died, technically speaking, several times on her table. Once she had resuscitated him and
got him stable, she was able to show a partial monitor
record of one of his "deaths" to the station commander.
With her key prisoner dead, the commander turned her
attention to other priorities. They were expecting a raid.'

'A raid?'

'There was a war going on. Anyway, it bought Bashesvili enough breathing space to fix up and clean up the
chair, get Ravenor back into it, and spring us. By the time
the station commander noticed her other prisoners were
gone, Bashesvili had got us out of the compound and
into the thorns.'

Kys held up a hand. 'Whoa. The thorns?'

'Ah, sorry,' said Nayl. 'I missed a bit. The Rahjez station
was surrounded by psy-active thorn growth. Ki-kid, they
called it.'

'Ku'kud,' said Angharad from the back of the room.
'Get it right, man.'

'Ku'kud. That was the key, you see? That was what Ravenor had realised.'

'I don't see,' said Kys.

'His mind was too weak by then to operate the door
properly,' said Nayl, 'but the psy-active weed gave him a
boost, an amplifier. He willed us home, and the thorn scrub
magnified the thought. He wanted to go back to his ship.'

'And this Bashesvili woman?'

Nayl sighed. 'She had as much desire to be displaced a
thousand years out of time as we did. She stayed.'

He paused. 'So, we opened the door.'

'I opened the door,' said Iosob with a giggle, holding
up the key. 'That is my function.'

'That's right,' said Nayl. 'Iosob very cleverly opened the
door, and we stepped through, and we weren't on the
Arethusa at all.'

'They gave me a bloody scare, I can tell you,' said Preest.

'You were on the *Hinterlight*?' asked Kys.

'In dry dock anchor, at the Navy Yards at Lenk,' said Preest. 'This blooming door had taken your lord and master literally again. It had brought him to his ship, all right. *My* bloody ship.'

'How long ago?'

'Two weeks ago,' said Nayl.

'I'll tell her this bit,' Preest cut in. 'I was walking the rounds one afternoon. We'd just signed off repairs the month before with the Navy architects. I was considering my options, developing plans to open a trade line down to Caxton, small perishables and quality goods, you know the sort of thing. My dear Patience, the last thing I intended was to get entangled with the Inquisition again.'

'They'd given us some bother,' said Halstrom. He looked at Kys. 'We'd been inspected and interviewed by ordo agents three times. They were aware of our links to your master.'

'The last time was by some high-faluting bitch called – what was it, Halstrom?'

'Inquisitor Lilith,' said Halstrom.

'That's the bitch,' said Preest, clapping her hands.

'That's the bitch, that's the bitch!' Iosob sang out, not looking at them.

'Play with your lovely key, dear,' Preest told her. 'This Lilith, she turned up just a few days before this door did. I became very aware that Gideon was a wanted man. I wondered what the bloody hell he'd been up to. Anyway, I told her we hadn't seen him in months. She searched my darling ship, and buggered off. So I was walking the rounds, as I say, and was just going though the enginarium. I'd given the crew some shore leave, a last hoorah before we disembarked, and there shouldn't have been anyone around. Then this bloody voice says out of nowhere–'

'Hello, Cynia,' said Nayl.

'I nearly wet myself,' said Cynia Preest. 'I turned around, and there was your man Harlon, the little girl, the big lass with the sword, and Gideon in his chair, gasping his last. More importantly, there was a brand new wooden door opening out from the left ventricle of the drive assembly.'

'He'd got you home,' said Kys to Nayl. She sighed. 'You know, Kara never doubted him? Kara said he'd beat the odds, even certain death. I didn't believe her. I should have.'

Nayl shook his head. 'In your place, I wouldn't have. We played the longest shot possible, the odds stacked up against us. We went the long way round. I'm still amazed we made it.'

'Is the door still there?' asked Kys.

Halstrom nodded his head. 'We check on it regularly. Its presence in engineering, the impossibility of it, troubles the crew. If it doesn't disappear in due course, I don't know what we'll do about it.'

Kys rose to her feet. She swayed slightly. 'I'm sorry,' she told them. 'That amasec's gone straight to my head. I haven't eaten much. What I want to know is, after all of that, how in Throne's name did you end up here?'

+Hedgerow birds, pollen and the local constellations.+

'Gideon?' she asked. They could all hear him. Iosob stopped playing, and Angharad looked up sullenly.

+I'm sorry for eavesdropping, and I know I should be resting, but I've come too far to stop now.+

'Birds?' asked Kys.

+Through the door, I met Orfeo Culzean. Remember him? We had a conversation.+

'What kind of conversation?' asked Kys.

+It doesn't matter. We were in a field. I had no idea where, and he wasn't going to tell me, but knew it was wherever he and Molotch had gone to ground. A planet somewhere, in affordable jump distance of Utochre, no more than a subsector or two away at most. There were birds, local flora, evening stars. Once I got here, and the excellent medicae Zarjaran made me comfortable, I started to go back through the records I'd made, comparing them to the *Hinterlight's* extensive database. The asset of having a support chair with perfect recording systems is that you can store things in the most extreme detail, more extreme than a regular mind could remember. I compared star patterns, the cellular detail of crop husks, the patterning of small birds. It took a while, but ultimately, there was no doubt at all.+

'Gudrun,' said Kys.

'We set off immediately,' said Preest. 'I could tell Gideon was in no mood to tarry.'

'Oh Throne, you pinpointed Gudrun by some birds and corn husks?' asked Kys.

+Every planet has its own specific and quite characteristic microculture. And, actually, I didn't pinpoint Gudrun.+

'What then?'

+I pinpointed the Upper Sarre provincial zone of Gudrun, within twenty kilometres of the Kell Massif.+

Kys started to laugh.

'I knew you'd like that,' said Nayl, grinning. 'Now, it's your turn. What happened to you?'

Kys looked at her empty glass and Halstrom refilled it. Then she told them everything that had happened since they had broken free of the dying Wych House.

'ANY RESPONSE FROM Carl or Ballack?'

'Nothing,' said Nayl grimly.

'Not even a hint?' Ravenor's repaired voxponder had a slightly lower, droning quality. They were still getting used to it.

'Wherever they are, they're not answering,' Nayl said.

'We must tread carefully with Ballack,' said Ravenor. 'I'm not sure what he is yet, but he's hiding something.'

'Interrogator Ballack is beyond reproach,' Angharad snapped from the back of the launch's cabin.

'No, he's not,' said Ravenor. 'When I was waring him, I found a Black Dam block.'

'Yes, you do like to 'ware people, don't you?' sneered Angharad. 'Against their will.'

'Shut up,' said Kys. She had showered – for a long time – and was wearing clean clothes, *Hinterlight* crew fatigues that didn't quite fit. She felt ungainly and unfeminine. She imagined that was how Maud Plyton felt much of the time. The thought of Maud made her tense. 'Are you sure you're up to this?' she asked.

'He shouldn't be doing it at all,' said Nayl.

'Well, I am,' Ravenor replied. 'From what you've told me, I haven't got time to sit around and heal. Mister Halstrom?'

'Two minutes to dock,' Halstrom called from the launch's helm position. He had insisted on piloting them.

'Thank you.'

Nayl, Kys and a nervous-looking Unwerth sat in the cabin behind him. Ravenor's chair, repaired but still showing the marks of its damage, sat in the cargo space behind them. Angharad reclined in one of the rear seats. She was wearing her restitched armour, and Iosob had patiently rebraided her hair. None of them had any idea what they should do with the child housekeeper.

Evisorex lay in its scabbard across Angharad's long legs.

'A Black Dam?' asked Kys. 'That's a Cognitae technique.'

'It is,' said Ravenor. 'Our friend Ballack was concealing something, something big. It is possible he is the one hiding Slyte.'

'Nonsense!' Angharad spat.

'I tend to agree with obnoxious sword-girl,' said Kys. 'It's Zael. I have no doubt. He'd got to Frauka somehow, turned him. I know what went on aboard the *Arethusa.*'

'I saw it, in all fair point,' said Unwerth. 'Psychic chaos, the breadth of the warp relapsed. If it wasn't a daemon, I don't know what.'

'We'll see,' said Ravenor.

Halstrom guided the launch expertly into the *Arethusa's* docking bay. Automatic systems clamped them in place and folded the hull doors, equalising pressure.

'We're good,' said Halstrom, taking off his headset, unbuckling his harness and turning to look back at them.

'Mister Halstrom, please stay here. Stand by to leave at a moment's notice.'

'Understood, sir,' said Halstrom.

The others unbuckled their restraints and rose. They clambered down out of the launch's aft hatch into the echoing docking bay. Nayl held a shotgun. Unwerth fumbled with a laspistol that Preest had lent him.

'You may stay with the launch, if you like, Master Unwerth,' said Ravenor as he floated down the ramp.

'Thank you. I will deblige you, however,' said Unwerth. 'I want my ship back.'

They advanced towards the access way. The air, oddly fresh, smelled of cinnamon or fresh-cut grass.

'Do you feel anything?' asked Kys. 'I couldn't lock him down, but I was too afraid to try. You're much stronger than me.'

'Not today,' said Ravenor. 'I may have to rely on all of you. In answer to your question, Patience, not yet. I can feel something. I can hear...'

'What?' asked Kys.

'Sobbing. You hear that?'

They turned down one of the *Arethusa's* empty spinal corridors. The deck lights were still guttering.

Angharad pulled out her sword in a fluid movement. 'Evisorex thirsts,' she said.

'I'm sure it does,' said Ravenor. 'I've got something, something very clear. It feels like... Wystan.'

'How can you feel him?' asked Nayl. 'He's a blunter.'

'He's compromised,' said Kys. 'I said he was.'

'It's Wystan,' said Ravenor, 'or, at least, it's something that wants us to feel it's Wystan.'

Kys shuddered. Unwerth looked up at her and calmly held her hand. She looked down at him, saw his nervous smile, and squeezed his hand.

'How close?' asked Nayl.

'Very close,' Ravenor replied. 'The forward hold.'

They approached the hold hatch. Unwerth let Kys's hand go and scurried forwards to key in a code. The hatch groaned. Tutting, Angharad strode up, put her shoulder to the hatch, and slid it slowly open with a grunt.

'Gotta love her,' said Nayl.

Kys snorted.

They entered the forward hold. It was empty, derelict. Packing cartons, pulped and shredded, littered the floor space.

'I hear sobbing,' said Kys.

They looked up.

Wystan Frauka sat on one of the iron cross beams high up in the hold's roof. How he'd got up there, none of them would ever know. He was sobbing, every breath jagging out of him like a gasp. His upper lip, mouth and chin were wet with blood. It was dripping out of his nose.

'I tried,' he murmured. 'I tried. Protect him you said, and I tried.' He coughed, and blood sprayed from his mouth. Zael hung in his arms like a string-less puppet.

+Wystan?+

'Yes, Gideon?'

+Glory, you can hear me?+

'Yes, Gideon. That's... that's really frigged up, isn't it? I mean, I'm an untouchable, right?'

'Not any more,' said Ravenor.

Frauka sobbed some more. Blood dripped down onto the deck beside them.

+Is he awake?+

'What?' asked Frauka.

+Is Zael awake?+

'No. Yes. In his head, he is. He has been for a long time.'

'I told them! I told them!' Kys exclaimed.

'Sorry about that, Patience, but if he'd known, he would have killed him.'

'Who?'

'Slyte, of course.'

+Wystan...+

'I had to hide for so long, Chair,' said Frauka, hugging the limp body to his chest with both arms. 'For so long. He was here all the time, and I didn't dare look out. He'd have seen me. He'd have killed me as if I was nothing.'

+It's all right.+

'It's not all right!' Frauka barked. 'I was scared. I was tired of hiding, but he was there all the time. Right there. You couldn't hear me, Chair, or you didn't want to.'

+I always wanted to.+

'Huh,' said Frauka. 'Well, I woke up once he'd left the ship. When it was safe. I think I scared the crew a bit. I'm sorry I scared them.'

'What the frig is Frauka babbling about?' Nayl asked.

'It's not Frauka,' said Ravenor, 'it's Zael. He's channelling Zael.'

Nayl looked up at the figures perched in the rafters. 'Zael?'

Patience stepped forwards. +Zael? Hello? I need to know something.+

'Hello, Patience. You're pretty,' said Frauka mindlessly.

+Thank you. Zael, if you're not Slyte, who is?+

'Ballack,' said Ravenor emphatically.

'Ballack's nothing,' said Frauka's mouth. 'Slyte's been with us from the start.'

+Zael?+

'Thonius Slyte. Thonius Slyte, Thonius Slyte,' Frauka cackled.

Incremental terror filled Nayl, Kys and Ravenor simultaneously. Disbelief. Horror.

'Watch above!' Unwerth yelled out.

Frauka had slumped forwards, letting Zael's body go. Both of them dropped like stones from the cross beam and plunged towards the hold deck.

+Kys!+

'I've got them,' she said.

FOUR

CARL THONIUS CLIMBED down out of the cargo-8 they had leased at Dorsay. His boots kicked dust up off the rural track. Behind him, Plyton, Ballack and Belknap got out of the vehicle.

They had parked under a stand of trees on a lonely country road. Evening was closing in across the fields. Ahead of them, two kilometres away, the sudden, grim bulwarks of the Kell Mountains rose like a threat. They were sheathed in mist and storm cover, almost invisible.

The country around was still and quiet. There was a soft breeze, and the evensong of birds heading to roosts in the woods. But there was a persistent ringing, buzzing sound in Carl Thonius's head, like tinnitus. Carl started to breathe deeply, checking the rings on his fingers. *One, two, three–*

'Up there? Is that the place?' asked Belknap, shouldering the worn, ex-Guard issue lasrifle he had brought.

Plyton nodded. 'I'm sure. The lander left the *Allure* in parking orbit and dropped at Dorsay field. Then it came out here.'

'You're sure?' Belknap asked her, dubiously.

'Magistratum skills, Belknap, trust me,' she said. 'I know how to ask around on the sly, and how to track a suspect vehicle. It came here. The flight path was keyed and logged at the field office.'

'I don't think they know we're here,' said Thonius. 'If they suspected we were right behind them, we'd know it.'

He stared up at the almost invisible summit above them. 'I am going to kill Zygmunt Molotch,' he said in a whisper none of the others heard.

Belknap had crossed to the far side of the track and was playing his electro binoculars at the crags ahead. The lenses whirred and clicked. None of them had wanted him to come along; they all considered him a non-combatant. But he had insisted, for Kara's sake, while there was still a hope. None of them could argue with that.

'Big place up there,' Belknap said, squinting through his field glasses, 'like a palace. We'll have to get closer for me to make anything definite.'

'Then let's get closer,' said Thonius.

'I still can't raise the *Arethusa*,' said Ballack, shaking his vox link. 'What the hell's up with that?'

'Atmospherics,' said Thonius. 'There's a storm coming in down the mountains.'

'I couldn't raise them in Dorsay either,' said Ballack.

'Atmospherics,' Thonius repeated. 'They're all right, sitting pretty. What's important is down here. Let's spread out and scope the area.'

They fanned out. Plyton and Belknap followed the track down to fields. Ballack and Thonius followed parallel paths into the creaking woods. They could feel the pressure of the gathering storm. The boughs sighed and groaned as the wind stirred them. Leaves fluttered. The rot-dry husks of wind-felled trees attested to the power that local storms could develop.

Carl Thonius came to a halt in a sighing glade. The others were out of sight. He could see the mountains a little better through the swaying branches ahead of him than from the road. They were a black shape smeared in cloud. Behind them, the sky was clean and ochre, stippled with stars.

The buzzing had grown worse. Thonius realised his right hand was shaking. He forced it to be still. He had come to regret many things in these last days of his human life, and the strangest regret of all was that he hadn't left his right arm in the cattle pen on Flint.

He had been trying so hard for such a long time, but he knew it was beating him. It was just a matter of time. The dark energy within him was like a grotesque pressure. He felt like an over-boiled kettle, rattling on a stove burner. At any moment he could burst.

He'd come close to bursting too many times. At Berynth, when he'd killed the man. Then again, by necessity, when they were trapped on the wrong side of the door and facing the hooked monsters. Letting slip his power had been the only thing that had saved them. At that moment, he'd been just a sliver of willpower away from letting go altogether. Such a terrible glee had filled him, and Throne, such temptation! To just give in, to let himself go to the turmoil inside his soul.

It would be so nice to let it stop. To cave in and surrender, and not have to fight any more. The buzzing would stop, the whispers, the pain.

Two simple thoughts kept him focused. One was that he was an Imperial interrogator. He had fought for that post, worked hard for it. The Carl Thonius part of him wanted to serve, wanted to prove himself true. How odd, he considered, that a man inhabited by a daemon might remain so devoted, give or take the odd little slip. Thonius had a dream, an ambition. He believed he had a power inside him that the whole Imperium could benefit from, but if he showed it to his masters before he could control it, they would execute him. They would exterminate him without hesitation. The buzzing in his head chuckled mockingly every time he dwelt on that ambition.

He could hear it again. *Heh heh heh.*

The other simple thought was that he didn't want to die, Not again, not like before, on Eustis Majoris. He really didn't. However much giving in might appeal, he did not want to die.

There was only one more option left open to him. It was up there, in the sulking mountains, Throne willing: Molotch. If Ravenor couldn't help him nurse and control the entity lodging inside him, then the arch-heretic would find a way. Molotch had skills and knowledge, and Molotch was not bound by the moral constraints and edicts of the ordos.

He would face Molotch, and force him to give up his secrets. Then he would kill him, in an action of sweet vengeance for his beloved master.

And then... and then...

Thonius convulsed. He dropped to his knees. The psychic force of his seizure rocked the trees around him. Loose leaves swirled and fluttered.

'What the hell was that?' Belknap asked over the link. 'Did anyone else feel that?'

'Carl?' Ballack called out through the woods.

Thonius threw up weakly, his last meal splattering across the track as oily liquid. Syncope overtook him and he fell on his side. His vision went. He could hear voices and buzzing.

'Carl? Are you all right?' Plyton's voice echoed from far away.

Eat her, eat her now, eat her up, she's so plump and delicious. Let go and let me go, Carl. I want to be out. I want to be out–

'No,' he moaned. He had never felt so lost. His heart was empty. His soul was sloshing full of black poison. His body ached. His right hand twitched. A ring broke and pinged off. *Fight it, fight it...*

'Carl?'

His vision slowly returned. Thonius sat up, bilious and swimming.

'I'm all right, Maud,' he said into his link hoarsely. 'Just a bad case of ague. It'll pass.'

Leave me alone, Slyte. Leave me alone. I won't let you out, not again. I won't. I will beat you.

He heard mocking laughter, thready and thin, at the back of his mind.

I will beat you. Molotch will know how.

He heard footsteps coming closer. They sounded like the padding footsteps of the fiend itself.

'Throne, Carl, were you sick? Are you all right?'

It was Ballack.

'I'm fine,' said Carl Thonius, rising and wiping his mouth. 'Ague. I always suffer from the ague.'

Ballack placed a comforting arm around Carl's shoulders, and wiped Carl's chin with his handkerchief. 'You'll be all right, my friend. Dry food and boiled water, that's the best remedy for ague.'

'The things you know,' said Thonius.

THEY TRUDGED UP through the farmland towards the Kells. Light was fading fast, and a storm boomed out over the crags ahead of them. Ballack tried the link one last time.

'Absolutely nothing from the *Arethusa*,' he grumbled.

Now they were closer, Belknap fixed the crag with his electro binoculars.

'A thousand-metre cliff. There's definitely some kind of building at the top, a real sprawl.'

'How does anyone get up there?' asked Plyton.

'They land by flier,' said Belknap, lenses whirring. 'I see a flier parked on the lip of the cliff. They've chained it down to weather out the storm. Oh yeah, I can see a winch too, on the east side of the promontory. Heavy duty. A big chain cage they can crank to bring up foot traffic from the fields. It's on the left side of the cliff. See?'

He passed the field glasses to Plyton. 'Like a hoist?' she asked.

'Yeah.'

'I've done enough hoists for this life,' she replied.

'We climb,' said Thonius.

'Up that?' Plyton laughed.

'Yes,' said Thonius.

'We're rushing this,' said Plyton. 'We have no idea what's up there. We should surveil it properly. Maybe get up in the crags to the west there,' she pointed. 'I don't like the idea of just charging in. We need to bed down and watch the place, measure what we're up against.'

'I agree,' said Ballack. 'A few days, and once we're sure–'

'I don't have a few days,' said Thonius.

'What?' asked Ballack, brushing back strands of long white hair that the wind had blown across his face. Thonius realised what he had said.

'We don't have a few days,' said Thonius.

'No, we don't,' said Belknap. He put his field glasses back in their worn case. 'If Kara's alive–'

'Hell with Kara!' snapped Ballack. 'This is too important to–'

Belknap held his rifle out to Plyton.

'Hold this, Maud.'

'Why?'

'Because I'll shoot him otherwise.'

She took the gun. Belknap moved with breathtaking speed. His fist smashed into Ballack's mouth.

'I'll tell you what's important, you bastard,' Belknap said, glaring down at the prone interrogator. 'Kara. Kara, Kara, *Kara*. Stay here, if you like. I'm going up there.'

'Madman!' Ballack coughed, spitting out blood.

'That's enough,' snapped Thonius. Quietly, he was impressed by Belknap's reactions. Quite apart from his speed and power – it was easy to forget that the doctor was a veteran soldier first and a medicae second – Belknap had acted out of loyalty, love and friendship. Those were the only things that mattered any more. Belknap was on his side.

'Let's not fight amongst ourselves,' Thonius said. He held out his right hand to haul Ballack up, and then, at the last moment, proffered his left hand instead. 'Come on.'

'I'm sorry, doctor,' Ballack said as he was helped up. 'I spoke without thinking. Of course Kara is a priority.'

Belknap grunted and took his weapon back from Plyton.

'We go up,' said Thonius. 'I know a few days' surveillance would prepare us better, Maud, but we can't afford it. Kara, bless her soul, can't afford it. If she's alive.'

'She's alive,' said Belknap grimly. Plyton touched his arm reassuringly.

'We can't do this by the book,' said Thonius. 'We can't even call for backup. So we go in tonight.'

Belknap nodded. Plyton sighed.

'Say we do,' said Ballack, fingering his split lip ruefully. 'How? That's a thousand metres sheer.'

'We climb,' said Thonius.

'Again,' snorted Plyton, 'up that?'

'There are several routes,' said Thonius. 'Cliff pathways. I can–'

'You can what?' asked Ballack.

'I can see them,' Thonius replied, pointing. 'There, there, and there.'

Belknap took out his binoculars again and adjusted them. 'Yeah, he's right. Well spotted, Carl. How the hell did you see them?'

Thonius shrugged.

'Pathways?' asked Plyton.

'There are at least three routes up the cliff, east and west,' replied Belknap. 'They're treacherous and steep, but they're a way in. If we survive the climb in the storm that's about to break over us.'

'Big if,' shuddered Plyton.

Belknap looked over at Thonius. 'What's the plan?'

'We go up, we get in. We... I dunno, kill things?' said Thonius. 'Let's get up there first.'

'I think we should–' Ballack began. The other three were already marching off down the field through the enclosing dusk.

'All right,' Ballack said. 'We're going. I get that. Wait for me.'

FIVE

ORFEO CULZEAN OPENED the door to the Alcove. The sounds of a party rang in after him from a terrace high above.

'They're having fun,' said Kara Swole.

'They are, aren't they?' Culzean agreed.

'Now you come for me,' she said. 'More fun?'

He closed the heavy, black door of the room behind him and shut the sounds out. 'Oh, don't be like that. It doesn't have to be like that.'

'You intend to torture me,' said Kara. She was shackled, painfully tight, to a wooden chair. It was the very same chair Culzean had sat on during his conversation with Ravenor in the cornfield.

'Torture is too strong a term,' said Culzean. The Alcove was a dark, dank space in the lower reaches of

Elmingard, more a cell than anything. Culzean believed it had been used by the monks, ages past, when they withdrew to meditate. Experimental seances also suggested that this was the place where the astronomer's servants had locked him on the days when his madness ran particularly wild. Culzean had made it his own, a private sanctum. Not even Molotch was allowed in here. Age-browned specimen skeletons hung from racks, their connective tissues replaced by intricate brass hinges and pins, every bone numbered and serialed in ink. All of the specimens belonged to freaks of nature: a giant, two encephalitic dwarfs, con-joined twins, a canine with a human skull, and other things too misshapen to identify. They were just fused masses of bone and calcification. Fat glass jars sat on shelves full of diseased viscera, tumours, xenotype organs, and pickled animals, blanched white like albinos in the preserving fluids.

Culzean walked over to a chest of drawers and began rifling through the contents.

Kara stared at her captor. 'Let me tell you, Orfeo... you are Orfeo Culzean, aren't you?'

'I am.'

'Uh huh,' she nodded, her lips cut and swollen. 'Look, Orfeo, I understand what you are. I know what you want. I have spent a week being tortured by that animal Siskind. He had Worna's help. He was skilled. I have nothing left to tell.'

'The thing is,' said Culzean, 'I actually believe you. Siskind is third generation Cognitae. He has tremendous invasive skills, and Worna, well, Worna is Worna. I am truly sorry for you, the pains you must have endured, but the thing is, the thing is, I think you might know more than you think you know.'

'I don't. Just kill me,' Kara begged. 'Please don't hurt me any more. In the name of–'

'Kara, I don't intend to,' said Culzean. He drew something out of one of the drawers. 'Do you know what this is?'

'I can't imagine.'

'It's a kinebrach oculous. See?'

He held it out in front of her. He showed her the head brace, and made the coloured lenses flip and exchange.

'Surprisingly timid, the kinebrach, very cautious. Humanoid forms, about so high,' he held out his hand in indication. 'They liked to know what was coming. Of course, they're long dead, so maybe this device has its limits, although I like to think that, through such instruments, they saw their impending doom. Anyway, where was I? Ah yes. You look into this and...'

He paused. 'Kaleidoscopes. I had a kaleidoscope when I was a boy,' he said. 'Did you?'

'I was a girl.'

'Funny, Kara. Did you? A kaleidoscope?'

'Yes.'

'Great, weren't they? The shuffling and the clattering? I loved that. I saw the galaxy through mine. What did you see, Kara?'

'Pretty patterns.'

'A kinebrach oculous is very like that. It doesn't hurt. It just shows you the truth. Pretty patterns of truth.'

Kara made a tiny moan.

Both of them jumped as Culzean's link chimed. Taking it out of his pocket, Culzean looked at Kara and laughed.

'My, my! Tense, aren't we? Must be the storm.' He put the link to his ear. 'Yes, Leyla?'

'We're tracking someone. A warm hit on the crag paths below us.'

'A shepherd, probably.'

'No, Orfeo,' the link crackled. 'I'm waiting for confirmation, but I think we have a genuine bio-sign fix.'

'An identity? Who's coming to call at this late hour, Ley?'

'Try Carl Thonius.'

Culzean blinked. 'Track him. Arm the sentry guns and track him, Leyla. Call me back the moment you have that confirmation.'

'Yes, sir.'

Culzean closed the link. He looked back at Kara Swole.

'You got a message off to your people, didn't you? Oh, you clever girl. You clever, pretty girl... and you hid that from Siskind and Worna so well. What else are you concealing, Kara? Ravenor's real fate, perhaps?'

'No,' she said. 'That part is true.'

'There's something,' said Culzean gently, bending down to peer into her eyes. She could smell his sweet, clean breath and his hair oil. His eyes were almost kind, almost concerned for her wellbeing. 'I can see it in you... something...'

'Nothing.'

He peered closer, until the tips of their noses were almost touching. 'I have been reading the languages of the body, face and eyes for years, far longer than Siskind. He missed this, but I can see it. There's something wrapped up in that head of yours.'

'Please... I swear there's nothing else.'

He rose. With steady, gentle hands, he fitted the kinebrach device around her head, dropping the coloured lenses over her eyes, and arranging them carefully. The iron scalp brace sat like a barbarian's crown on her red hair. He buckled the straps under her chin. Content with the preparations, he stood back and stared at her.

'Relax,' said Culzean. 'Let it do all the work.'

Nothing happened for a moment. Kara sat, stock-still, tensed for the worst. Then she began to twitch her head slightly every few seconds, flinching a little, as if to avoid some flying insect buzzing at her face.

'Kara?'

She murmured something. Her twitching became more accentuated. Her body jumped and jolted, like a blindfolded person tormented by sounds darting about around them.

'Make... make it stop,' Kara said, her voice wobbling.

'Only when we're done,' said Culzean. He placed a hand on her left shoulder to steady her. 'Look directly into it. Stop flinching away.'

'No...'

'Do it, please.'

She began to tremble. The tremble was so spastic, it seemed to be prefiguring a grand mal seizure.

'Oh!' she cried. 'Oh! Oh Throne! Oh Emperor!'

'What do you see?' Culzean asked. She made a choking, gagging sound in her throat, as if she was about to retch. She writhed in the restraints.

'Tell me,' he soothed.

'I remember! I remember!' Kara Swole shrieked. 'Carl!'

Then she began to scream.

ON THE LOWER south terrace of Elmingard, Siskind was celebrating. All of Culzean's people not on duty that night had assembled. There were about twenty-five in all – hired guns, savants and technical experts, and some of the senior domestics. They had taken dinner in the long room over the terrace, and had come out onto the terrace with drinks in their hands to watch the storm begin its slow, lusty tumble down the nightscape of the mountains.

In a half hour or so, conditions would be too fierce and wet for them to remain outside, but just then there were only a few big raindrops in the air, propelled by the gathering wind. The revellers gathered amongst the fluttering taper lights, and enjoyed the building light show of the storm. Lightning, blue-white and vivid, lanced around the crags of the hog's back, fixing its silhouette against the bleak night sky. Sheet electrics, a foggy, blinking radiance, underlit the bunching cloud wall.

Siskind had already drunk too much. In a voice louder than any of the jovial voices on the north terrace, he was regaling some of the staff members with the tale of Ravenor's demise. Worna, a bottle of amasec in his fist, sat aloof at the end of the terrace, regarding the pitch black drop into the flat country below.

Molotch appeared beside him. He was dressed in black with only his head and hands exposed. He loomed, like a spectre.

'A notable night,' Worna rumbled, as if the thunder was speaking through him.

Molotch half nodded.

'An achievement,' Worna added, taking a sip from his bottle. He offered it to Molotch, but Molotch shook his head. Worna shrugged and said, 'I know this is a result you have longed for these many years. Your enemy is dead.'

'Yes,' said Molotch.

'You are pleased, then, sir?' Worna asked.

'I am trying to allow myself a feeling of triumph,' said Molotch quietly. 'I certainly thank you and the shipmaster for your sterling efforts. Ravenor has, as you remark, dogged me for more years than I care to recall. I have wished him dead so many times, yearned for it. I suppose now it is actually true, it feels like an anti-climax. It is often the way with things that are sought after for so long. Compared to the effort, the victory seems barren.'

Worna grunted. 'I know that one. Hunting a mark for months or years, and when you finally get the strike, it feels hollow and empty, but there's more to this, isn't there, if you don't mind me asking?'

Molotch glanced at the ancient bounty hunter and smiled an asymmetrical smile. 'You amuse me, Lucius.

For all your brute demeanour, you exhibit a perceptive mind. Yes, there is more to this.'

Molotch looked away as a particularly violent jag of lightning seared the peaks above. It seemed as if he was unwilling to say anything further.

Then he glanced back at Worna and said. 'There are dark days ahead, you see, Lucius, dark even by our standards. Through Orfeo, I made Ravenor an offer. I have no love for him, you understand, but he was a very capable being. I believed that, together, we might avert the oncoming darkness. Ravenor chose to reject my offer. Now he is dead, and in no position to reconsider it. So, I suppose, I mourn his death as much as I celebrate it.'

Worna shrugged. 'I dunno,' he considered, 'the crippled bastard was the enemy, when all was said and done.'

'There is another enemy,' said Molotch. He looked around. 'Where's Culzean? He usually enjoys this kind of merriment. I haven't seen him since the end of the meal.'

Worna shook his scarred head. He felt awkward. Culzean had ordered him firmly not to tell Molotch about the prisoner, and he found it extremely uncomfortable keeping secrets from Molotch. There were very few things in the forsaken galaxy that Lucius Worna was afraid of, but Zygmunt Molotch made the cut.

'He'll be back, I'm sure,' Worna said. 'He's probably checking something.'

LEYLA SLADE LEANT over Drouet's cogitator post in the security control centre, watching the multiple images drifting and switching on the hololithic projection.

'That's definitely Thonius,' she said.

'Bio-print confirms,' Drouet said.

'Pinpoint, please.'

Drouet adjusted some of the cogitator's controls. 'West flank of the cliffs, between markers thirty-six and thirty-seven,' he replied. 'That's about sixty metres shy of the summit. I've got him painted by three motion and pict scanners. Positive ID. If he continues unchecked, he'll make west low terrace in under ten minutes. I thought he was supposed to be a principal agent, mam?'

'Why do you say that?'

Drouet shrugged. 'He's not exactly moving with any skill or subtlety. It seems to me it's taking all his effort just to climb the cliff. Doesn't he realise we've got him cold?'

Leyla leaned in closer. 'Have we got a gun on him yet?'

'Sentry 18 will acquire him in about three minutes. He must know we can see him, surely? He must realise Elmingard is locked down tight with scanners and trips?'

'Apparently not,' Slade replied. 'I think our friend Thonius has underestimated our capabilities. Load sentry 18. Track and fix, and fire on my command.'

'Yes, mam,' said Drouet.

'Mam?' Tzabo called from his machine. She crossed to him. 'I've found another. Confirmed sensor hit. Eastern side, a little closer than target one.'

'Show me.'

'He's in deep shadow, and partially concealed. I'll punch up night scoping and enhance.'

An image – just a portion of a profile boosted by low-light enhanciles – flickered onto the 'lith projection.

'Know him?' asked Tzabo.

'No, I...' Slade paused. 'Shit, that's Ballack! Frig it, he's supposed to be dead! Molotch killed him on Tancred!'

'Not with any lasting success, it would appear,' said Tzabo.

'Is he ranged?' Slade asked.

'He will be in twenty-five seconds at current rate of advance.'

'Get me–' she began. Her link beeped.

'Slade,' she answered, pulling the device out of her pocket.

'Ley, it's me.' Culzean's voice floated back. There was a strange, muffled yelping sound coming through behind him.

'What's going on?' Slade asked. 'I can hear–'

'Ignore the background fuss,' Culzean replied. 'The lovely Kara just had an epiphany, and she's getting over it. Ley, tell me quickly, have you confirmed Thonius?'

'Bio-trace and visual,' she said. 'Definitive match. Palpable. Get this, we've also got Ballack coming up for a visit.'

'Ballack? Really?'

'I'd wager my reputation, sir.'

'Listen to me, Leyla, and listen carefully. I want them taken alive, especially Thonius.'

'What?'

'I'm deadly serious, Ley. Do this for me, and do it discreetly. Knock your systems back to passive before they realise they're being targeted.'

'Orfeo, that's madness! The sentry guns are seconds away from acquiring them both. I can hose them off the rocks!'

'No! I want Thonius brought in alive, you understand me? Alive. Do it personally, if you have to. Get him into custody, immediately and quietly. Make sure Zygmunt doesn't know anything about it.'

'This has a bad feel to me,' she warned.

'Leyla, I love you, but this is one of those times when you act like a good girl and do exactly what I frigging well tell you. Go passive, shut the system back, get Thonius alive. Ballack too, the silly little fool, but I don't care so much if you have to top him. Are we clear?'

Leyla Slade breathed tightly. 'Totally, sir,' she said.

She clicked off her link, and put it away.

'Cut to passive running,' she told Drouet and Tzabo. 'Turn off the sentries.'

They looked at her. 'Mam, are you sure?' asked Tzabo.

'We've got Throne agents crawling up the rock face,' Drouet added.

'I know what I've been told,' snapped Slade, pulling her handgun out and arming it. 'Do as I say.'

Eyebrows raised, the two security experts obliged, throwing a series of switches that set the Elmingard defences to passive. The powerful sentry gun servitors went to dormant status.

'Now what?' asked Tzabo.

'Get two guns up here to join me. I'm going to greet Master Thonius. Drouet, can you handle Ballack when he shows his face?'

Drouet got to his feet and checked his laspistol. 'Certainly,' he said. 'Alive?'

'If possible,' she said.

SIX

THE RAIN WAS in his face, and the whole world was black. Shuddering with cold and effort, Carl Thonius clambered a few metres more up the steep rock track. It was a sheer climb in places where the path fell away, nothing like the simple ascent he had envisioned. The laughing, buzzing thing in his soul had lied about that.

He hauled himself up over an overhang, straining with arms alone, his legs dangling. The darkness yawned below him. If his numb fingers let go, it would be a long, final drop. Overhead, the breaking storm boomed. The rock was wet.

Heh heh heh.

He pulled himself up onto the overhang and lay there for a moment, panting. Rain fell on his face.

He'd lost touch with the others. At the base of the crag, they'd split up, deciding to optimise their chances. Thonius had gone up the western path he'd identified. Ballack had taken the east face. Plyton and Belknap had chosen to work their way up the ravine behind the Elmingard plateau, to see if they could find a way up from the north.

Thonius resumed his climb. Conditions were awful and getting worse, inside and out. The storm was closing in. His own storm was closing in. Fire and buzzing laughter licked at his mind. He tried to force it back, but it sizzled at his thoughts and burned back his memories. Pain shot through him, making him gag and lose his grip. Nausea yawned. He could hear a voice inside him sniggering at his puny, mortal efforts to survive and stay human. Buzzing, buzzing... *heh heh heh*.

His scanner pad bipped, and he pulled it out to check it. The pad showed him the contact prints of several scanner pods built into the rock face above. They read as passive. That was good. Lucky, in fact. He'd expected serious electronic countermeasures, an active system, probing and stabbing at them as they came up, but a passive system was easy to beat.

Perhaps Molotch was getting slack in his old age. No one was expecting them.

Thonius drew himself up and clambered on.

THE RAIN HAD begun in earnest, driving the partygoers indoors. Out on the lower north terrace, the tapers sputtered and fizzled as the downpour extinguished them. Siskind's first mate, Ornales, closed and bolted the double doors once they were inside.

Siskind was ordering more drinks, and there was laughter in the room. Off in one corner, Molotch had been drawn into deep conversation with two of Culzean's most learned savants. They were ancient, robed individuals, their bald heads like heavy ivory balls.

Worna stayed outside the activity, watching. He had never been one for hellraising and drink, unless it was with his own kind, and the members of his team that he'd managed to pull out of the Utochre mess were all still aboard Siskind's ship. These people were not his type: intellectuals, savants, Culzean's brand of people. Even the hard-bodied men in blue wool suits with silver buttons who acted as security were not Worna's sort. They were good, Worna acknowledged, but they were young. Guard-vets mostly, a few high-end underworld recruits, well drilled and well made. None of them had the grizzled edge of experience that a bounty life provided. They regarded him with curiosity, but he knew they thought he was low-life scum. 'Scum' barely covered what Lucius Worna thought of them.

The only person around that he had the vaguest sense of connection with was Culzean's minder, Slade. He liked her. She hadn't had the same career path as him, but she was good, professional and dedicated. He'd seen her work. She was a kindred spirit, or as close to a kindred spirit as he was likely to find in this blasted house at the end of the world.

He left Siskind's party quietly and slipped out into the draughty corridor. He'd been privately scanning the vox net for the past few minutes, and he'd heard some tantalising stuff on the back and forth. Something was up.

GALL BALLACK HAULED himself up over the lip wall of one of the eastern terraces. The rain was sheeting down, like a white curtain. He was soaked, and chilled to the bone. His long white hair hung lank and wet, and water streamed down his face.

The place was empty and unlit. He could smell wet stone and wet earth, and hear nothing but the hiss of the rain.

He rose, and glanced around. His pad showed no sign of active sensor noise. Parched rosebushes nearby fluttered and shook in the night's wind and rain. He looked up. Several levels above him, in the inner knot of the ancient house, lights glowed behind shuttered windows. He stepped forwards across flagstones so worn and uneven that rainwater had collected in deep, angular puddles.

Another step, another. It looked like there was a staircase ahead, a flight of steps cut in the terrace side, which might afford him access to the next level of the haphazard palace.

'I suggest you stop there,' said Drouet, stepping out of the rain and the shadows behind him, a laspistol raised and aimed.

Ballack froze and slowly, resignedly, raised his hands. 'Throne, you're good. I didn't even hear you,' he said.

Drouet came closer. 'On the ground. Down on the ground, face down,' he instructed sharply. 'Hands where I can see them!'

'Hands?' asked Ballack, bitterly.

'Get down!'

Ballack lay down on his face, smelling the wet rock close up. Rainwater streaked off him.

'I have to see Molotch,' Ballack said.

'Shut up.'

'It's a matter of the most pleasant fraternal confidence,' Ballack tried. It stood to reason that Molotch might employ other Cognitae.

'Whatever you say,' said Drouet. Clearly, he was not of the brotherhood.

'Tell him that, then,' said Ballack. 'Use those exact words, and he'll–'

'Shut up,' Drouet spat, standing over him. He bent down and began to frisk Ballack. The interrogator felt the muzzle of the laspistol poke at the back of his head.

'One move from you I don't like,' Drouet told him, 'you'll be scraping your brains up with a trowel.'

'You paint a vivid picture,' Ballack grunted. Unamused, Drouet pushed harder with the gun and Ballack's face banged into the flags, chipping one of his teeth. The lip cut Belknap had given him began to bleed again.

Drouet found Ballack's weapon, tugged it out, and tossed it away into the rain and darkness over the wall.

'Roll over,' Drouet instructed.

Ballack obeyed. Flat on his back, he stared up into the sheeting downpour at the man standing over him. Ballack blinked the rain away.

'Get me inside,' he said. 'Take me to whoever is in charge.'

'Shut the frig up,' said Drouet, aiming his weapon and taking out his link.

The one-shot las was a small device, just a tube, and Ballack had fitted it to the stump of his wrist, just behind the cuff. It was so small that a cursory pat down wouldn't find it. He swung his arm up, popped the tube forwards on its spring catch with a flex of his forearm, and fired the shot. Its bark was lost in a thump of thunder.

Drouet smacked backwards. The shot had punched in under his chin and gone up through his skull. The entry wound made a neat, fleeting black hole that closed again into a tiny blemish as tissue shock rippled across the flesh of his throat. The back of his head came off in a spray of blood and tissue.

He fell back, slumping against the terrace wall and almost pitching off. Then he fell down heavily. Thick, acrid smoke billowed up from the exit wound in the back of his cranium. What remained of his ruptured brain was still cooking and burning. His limp legs began to spasm and thump.

Ballack got up. He took hold of Drouet, dragged the twitching corpse upright, and then pushed it over the wall into the night.

Drouet plummeted away into the blackness below.

Ballack retrieved Drouet's pistol, and snapped the one-shot back into its holder. I'll recharge it later, he thought as he turned.

A steel fist ploughed him down. It came out of nowhere and piled into the side of his face, smashing most of his teeth. Ballack went over so violently that he almost inverted, his legs flying up. He crunched onto the puddled flagstones.

Gasping, blood pouring from his mouth, he reached out to grab his fallen weapon. The moment his fingers took hold of it, a pearl-armoured boot stamped on it and crushed it to pieces. The laspistol cracked and fractured, its power cell shorting wildly as it met the rain. All the bones in Ballack's remaining hand broke and mashed.

Ballack screamed in agony, aspirating blood out into the drenching downpour.

'Ballack,' said Lucius Worna. 'We meet again.'

'Nyaaaahh!' Ballack wailed as Worna ground his boot down harder to emphasise the point.

'Guess what?' asked Worna, drawing his bolter.

'Hnhhh?'

'End of story.'

CARL THONIUS CLAMBERED over the west wall and dropped two metres onto the flagged yard. The rain was extreme, affording zero visibility. Lightning flashed, brighter than even lightning ought to be. A second later, thunder smashed like a daemon's drum.

Beating for me, beating for me...

He pulled out his weapon. It was going to be a tight call, but he was here. This was where it would play out. Molotch would save him, or Molotch would—

Carl blinked. His gun was no longer in his hand. It had been kicked out of his grip. A woman came at him through the streaming rain. He side-stepped, and they circled one another.

'Hello,' she said, brightly. 'You're Carl, right? Carl Thonius?'

'Who do I have the pleasure of addressing?' he replied, courteous to the end.

'My name is Leyla Slade. I'd like you to come with me, Carl. Quietly.'

'Oh, dear,' he said. 'I might not be able to do that.'

She shrugged and wheeled immediately into a spin kick that almost took his head off.

No wonder his gun had gone flying.

Thonius ducked the kick, and circled again. The woman, Slade, kicked out twice in a rotating one-two, her powerful legs punching like pistons, but he evaded both strikes.

'Come on, Carl,' she taunted. 'I thought you were good?'

'I am,' he answered.

He threw a side-kick feint at her, followed by a lateral jab. She back-stepped out of the former, reading the feint for what it was, and blocked the latter, but he had momentum, and he drove a rapid sequence of killing punches at her. She blocked them all with stinging claps of skin on skin, and managed to wrong-foot him. Pirouetting off the ground, she kicked out a response and caught him square in the chest.

His breath left him in a bark and he staggered backwards. Then he dropped into a quick defensive stance, trying to recover. His chest hurt. He lunged forwards, low and fast, risking a sternum punch.

She met the punch with a high, deflecting kick, and countered with a blade fist, which he barely slapped aside. He switched right with another feint and drove at her throat with a needle fist, but she was too quick for him to catch.

'I think I love you, Leyla Slade,' he panted.

'They all say that,' she retorted. They were circling again.

'I think you should know something,' Thonius added.

'What might that be?'

'Knocking me insensible is probably the last thing you want to do.'

'Why?'

'Because if I'm unconscious, I won't be able to concentrate any more.'

'I'll take my chances,' she said.

They leapt at each other, simultaneously, their attacks clashing and overlapping. There was a meaty crack of flesh and bone as one was successful. Slade landed squarely. Thonius fell hard. His body rolled limply across the rain-slick flagstones.

Breathing hard, Slade opened her link. 'Got him,' she said, over the hissing rain.

Overhead, the thunder roared, as if in approval.

SEVEN

CULZEAN LEFT THE Alcove and hurried out into the drafty gloom of the corridor. 'This way, this way!' he hissed as Slade and Worna approached. Worna had Ballack's body slung over his wide shoulder plate. Slade was dragging Thonius.

'Fine work, my friends,' Culzean said. 'Did anybody see you?'

Slade shook her head.

'Your man Drouet's dead,' Worna grumbled. 'Ballack shot him. Lucky for you, I was close by.'

'Where shall we put them?' Slade asked.

'We can lock Ballack up in the under pantry,' Culzean said. 'First we make Thonius secure. Bring him this way.'

'What's so important about Thonius?' Slade asked.

'Never mind.'

'Why are we hiding this from Molotch?' Worna growled.

'Never mind that either. Come on.'

They moved away down the stone corridor until they were out of sight. The rain beat down, and drools of rainwater seeped into the lower structures of Elmingard. Maud Plyton, a shotgun in her hands, rolled out of hiding as soon as it was quiet.

She ran to the Alcove's door, and tried the handle. It was locked. Muttering an oath, she knelt down and pulled out her picklock bundle. She worked the lock, sweating, jumping at every sound and every boom of thunder.

'Come on!' she spat. 'Oh, come the frig on!'

The door swung open. Raising her weapon, she crept inside, instantly repelled by the skeletal horrors and jarred monstrosities on display in the gloom around her. A woman in a curious head brace sat chained to a wooden chair at the centre of the room, her head bowed.

'Kara?'

Kara Swole looked up, drunkenly, at the sound of Plyton's voice. Her eyes were blinkered by the coloured lenses of the kinebrach device.

'Who?' she sighed.

Plyton moved towards her and began to unfasten the chains. 'It's all right, Kara. It's me, Maud. I'll get you out of this.'

'Maud? Maud, I saw,' Kara murmured.

'It's all right,' Plyton assured her, fighting with the shackles.

'Oh, Throne,' said Kara more clearly, stiffening in her seat.

'Kara? It's all right, just let me–'

'I saw. I remembered. He's here. He's here. He's here.'

'Kara? What are you saying to me?'

Kara shuddered, and then projectile vomited violently.

'Kara!'

Plyton pulled her loose and let the chains fall away with a clatter. She dragged the strange lensed device off Kara's head.

'He's here, Maud. Slyte's here,' Kara gurgled. Hauling her upright, Maud Plyton felt the hairs on her neck rise.

'No, he's not, Kara. We're all right. Stop saying that.'

'He's *here*.'

ELMINGARD'S VAST STONE kitchen smelled of peppers, goose fat and grease. Their work over for the night, the cooks had gone, and a few scullery boys had been left clearing the marble counters and mopping the floor. Pots were being scrubbed, and the ovens were being banked down. Two youngsters, on menial dishwashing duties, began to lark around beside their enamel sinks, throwing soap suds and bottle brushes at one another.

A senior domestic in a floor-length apron marched in from the larders and bellowed at the pair. He took them both by the ear-lobes and dragged them out of the kitchen, ignoring their squeals of protest. The other scullery boys quietly stopped their chores and crept over to the doorway to eavesdrop and giggle at the dressing down the pot washers were receiving outside.

Belknap seized his chance. He slipped down the length of the old kitchen, hugging the shadows and the wall, his rifle clutched to his chest. Old skills, never forgotten. Hug the cover. Stay low.

His pulse raced. If any of the youngsters turned away from the door, they would see him and raise the alarm, but he couldn't stay hidden. He had to find Kara. There was nothing more important in the entire galaxy.

A small part of him stepped back and scoffed at his antics. Belknap had been taking risks all his adult life: six years in the Guard, nine as a community medicae, and then the rest as a back-street, unlicensed doctor. The risks he'd taken had always been about the general good, about service. They had always been measured and rational. This was different. This was stalking into a hornets' nest of first degree sociopaths and heretics, and all for the love of a woman he barely knew, a woman who, in all likelihood, had been dead for over a week.

This was not like him, not at all. He was out of his depth. He was no principal agent like Thonius, Ballack or Kys, or even, Throne rest him, Harlon Nayl. This was not the life he had chosen, nor been recruited for. He was just an ex-soldier who knew his way around a rifle, and had a little training in stealth work and the use of cover.

All he really had was his faith and his passion. He hoped they would be enough.

The scullery boys broke from the doorway and flocked back to their chores as the senior domestic returned, shouting. Belknap had just reached the exit at the far end. He slid into other shadows, breathed out, and headed up a dingy staircase into the rambling house.

Halfway up the stairs, he ducked down as he heard a sound from outside, louder than the din of the storm. What was that?

Thrusters?

'I'D REALLY LIKE to know what's going on,' said Zygmunt Molotch, stepping into the cold, damp under pantry.

He had come out of nowhere. Culzean glanced around, saw him, and quietly cursed. He put on a busy smile and strode towards Molotch. 'Zyg, Zyg, my friend, you don't need to bother yourself with this.' He put a hand gently on Molotch's arm to steer him out of the room, but Molotch shook it off.

'I don't like the idea that you're hiding things from me, Orfeo. Who is that?'

Molotch pushed past Culzean and advanced into the dank under pantry. Worna and Slade reluctantly stood back from their captive.

Culzean knew he had to handle Molotch with more care than ever before. He shrugged, changing his approach. 'All right, Zyg, you got me. It's Ballack. It was supposed to be a surprise.'

'Ballack?' Molotch asked. He peered at the man Slade and Worna had been chaining to a stone block by the pantry's back wall. 'Ballack? The interrogator?'

'It was going to be my gift to you,' Culzean said.

Molotch ignored the facilitator. He knelt down beside Ballack, peering at him.

'I was quite sure I'd killed you,' he said.

Behind him, Culzean shot urgent looks at Worna and Slade. Slade put her hand on the grip of her holstered weapon. Worna drew his bolt pistol quietly. Molotch didn't seem to notice. He stimulated a pressure point in Ballack's neck with the tip of his finger.

Ballack woke up with a splutter. He swung his head around and blinked as his eyes focused. Blood seeped out between his shattered teeth.

'M-Molotch…?'

'Indeed,' said Molotch. 'What are you doing here, Ballack? What possible purpose could have brought you to me?'

'I wanted…' Ballack murmured, his words slurred and malformed by his broken mouth. 'I wanted…'

'What did you want?' asked Molotch.

'Revenge, you bastard. I wanted revenge. You left me to die. We were brothers, Cognitae. I served you in fraternal confidence and you betrayed me.'

Molotch rose to his feet and looked down at Ballack. 'You are a poor excuse for a Cognitae. Diluted fifth or sixth generation, an affront to our tradition. You were an instrument, and I used you without compunction. I owed you nothing.'

Ballack groaned, and thrust at Molotch, but the chains were too tight.

'You came all this way to kill me?' Molotch asked. He looked around at Culzean. 'It rather begs the question how the hell he found me.'

'Zygmunt, we'll work that out in due course,' said Culzean carefully. 'For now–'

'No!' snapped Molotch. 'I want to know what's going on, Culzean! Right now!'

Worna moved forwards rapidly. Molotch made a flicking gesture with his right hand, and Worna's bolt pistol flew out of his grasp. Molotch caught it, turned, and aimed it at Ballack's head.

'Molotch! It's a matter of the most pleasant fraternal confidence!' Ballack slurred. 'Molotch!'

'Shut up,' said Molotch, and pulled the trigger.

Ballack's head exploded. Slade leapt back, spattered with blood. Even Worna flinched.

'Zygmunt...' Culzean growled.

Molotch muttered some dark prayer and turned back to face them. He calmly handed the weapon back to Worna. 'What else are you hiding from me, Orfeo?'

'Nothing,' Culzean declared.

'Let me put it another way,' said Molotch. 'How did Ballack find me? Why is it I hear thrusters?'

'I don't–' Culzean began.

Slade and Worna pulled out their links simultaneously. Both of them had started chiming.

'Incoming vehicle,' said Slade to Culzean.

'You see?' said Molotch. 'I think it's time you stopped lying to me Orfeo, and started telling me plainly what in the name of the Undying Eight is going on here.'

EIGHT

THE CUTTER SKIMMED in low and fast out of the night towards the high perch of Elmingard. The sensor web of Culzean's fastness had been set, by the master's own recent command, to passive, but even that did not explain the way the cutter had come into airspace proximity without any prior detection.

There were three other factors in play. The first was the way the cutter was being flown: ultra fast and ultra low, what Navy pilots called 'crust kissing'. The flight path had hugged the terrain all the way from the Sarre borders. In places, the craft's downwash had parted treetops like a comb, or whipped up corn stooks from the harvested fields. The method of flying kept the craft's profile low and tough to paint. It also required a very experienced and dynamic style of piloting.

The second factor was the way the small craft was obscured. A shield or veil had been employed, its mechanism and type unidentifiable to Tzabo and the other professional experts in Elmingard's security control centre. The cutter was suddenly just there. They heard its thrusters before they saw it on their scopes.

The third factor was the night. The storm was a filthy, howling monster, worse than any they'd known. It straddled the mountaintops like a drunken ogre, roaring at the heavens. The storm's savage electrical pattern flared and sparked and wallowed, creating blinks, false artefacts, phantoms and idiot flashes on the instrumentation. It caused two of the cogitators to short out. Bizarre whines and squeals emerged from the speakers, causing Eldrik, the duty man on station with Tzabo, to tear off his headset.

'This isn't natural,' Eldrik complained.

Tzabo was slow replying. He was staring at his own screen, where the fading after-image of the last lightning ghost had shown an uncanny resemblance to a human skull.

'What?' he asked, distractedly.

'I said this isn't natural. The storm,' said Eldrik.

'No, I don't think it is,' said Tzabo. He shook himself. 'Concentrate on the damn contact. Pull it up for me, sharp.'

'On it,' said Eldrik.

Tzabo lifted his handset and pressed the master channel. Culzean answered.

'Sir,' said Tzabo, 'we have an airborne contact two kilometres out, coming in strong. No marker, no registration, no handshake codes.'

'I can hear it already,' replied Culzean's voice. 'It must be really moving.'

'It is, as I said, sir. I am about to light the house defences and switch to active, with your permission.'

Down in the clammy gloom of the under pantry, the ghastly stink of Ballack's detonated skull still clinging to the air, Culzean glanced at Molotch and then nodded.

'Light them up, Mister Tzabo. Activate all perimeter and surface to air systems. Stand ready to deny them and annihilate them.'

'Hail them first,' Molotch said.

'What?' asked Culzean.

'Hail them. Hail them,' Molotch demanded.

'Zygmunt, they are coming in unauthorised, no codes. They are not ours.'

'They want to be here.'

'Zyg, Zyg, Zyg... it could be an Inquisition raid.'

Molotch laughed. It was a disconcerting sound, because he didn't do it very often. 'Orfeo, if the Inquisition had found us, they'd have called in Battlefleet Scarus and wiped us off the map already. Hail them.'

'No, Zygmunt, this–'

Molotch demonstrated his right arm flick again, and the link sailed out of Culzean's manicured hand. Culzean cursed.

Molotch caught the device neatly and raised it to his ear. 'Tzabo, hail the contact.'

There was a long silence.

'Tzabo?'

'I'm sorry, sir. I only take orders from Master Culzean,' Tzabo's voice said.

Molotch sighed and looked back at Culzean. He handed the link back to him. 'I am ever impressed by the quality of the people you employ, Orfeo.'

Culzean took the link back. 'Mister Tzabo, hail the contact.'

'Yes, sir.'

Culzean lowered the link. He glanced at Slade and Worna. 'Ley, I'd like you up in the centre to take charge.'

'Yes, sir,' Slade said, hurrying out.

'Lucius,' Culzean said, 'you'd be useful up on the landing if this goes arse up.'

Worna nodded, and strode away. Culzean looked over at Molotch.

'We should go up and see what this is.'

Molotch nodded. 'We should. Just to be clear, Orfeo, we're not done, you and me.'

'I know.'

'We're not done.'

'I know.'

Molotch placed a hand on Culzean's arm and gently prevented him from leaving the under pantry.

'What I mean, Orfeo, is that there's a very real possibility that we are about to experience a parting of the ways, and you do not, believe me, want that to happen.'

Culzean looked down and very deliberately took hold of Molotch's hand and removed it from his sleeve. 'Zyg, don't threaten me. I am the last person you should ever threaten.'

Molotch smiled. It was the expression a hyena might wear as it salivated over some newly felled prey.

'Orfeo, there's no one anywhere I would ever be afraid of threatening. Understand that, and our relationship might last a little longer.'

LEYLA SLADE ENTERED Elmingard's security control centre in time to hear Tzabo say, 'Approaching vehicle, approaching vehicle, respond and identify yourself. This is private airspace. Identify yourself, or suffer the consequences of trespass.'

Static fuzzled back.

'Approaching vehicle, approaching vehicle–' Tzabo began again.

Slade took his vox-mic away from him. 'Approaching vehicle,' she said sternly, 'this is Elmingard. Speak now, or we'll hammer you out of the sky with the Emperor's own righteous fury. Respond.'

Static.

'Are the systems active?' Slade asked the duty men.

'Sentries are live. Missiles armed and ranged,' Eldrik replied quickly, clicking brass switches on his desk.

'Approaching vehicle,' Slade began again. She didn't get a further word out. The approaching vehicle interrupted her by answering.

It was not a vox squirt, nor a pict-enabled transmission.

It was a psi-blurt.

+Elmingard. Hold your fire. You do not want to destroy me, because I am not your enemy. Not *this* time.+

HEADING UP THROUGH the Byzantine stairwells of Elmingard, Culzean and Molotch stopped in their tracks.

'Ow!' said Culzean. 'Did you feel that?'

'Yes,' said Molotch. 'It's him.'

'Who?'

'Who the hell do you think? Who else knows us this well? Who else is so powerful a sender?'

'Ravenor?'

Molotch nodded. 'It's Gideon,' he said.

'Ravenor's alive?'

Molotch looked at him in disdain. 'Of course he is. Did you ever doubt it? Oh, grow up, Orfeo.'

IT WAS DARK and cold and wet out in the raw base of the astronomer's broken tower. The wind shrieked in through the gappy stones, and there was no shelter from the rain.

Carl Thonius moaned, pulling at the wrist chain Leyla Slade had shackled him with. The chain was anchored to the heaviest tumbled block in the heart of the tower.

He had heard the voice. In his head, he had heard the voice, despite the buzzing and the chuckling.

Gideon's voice. Gideon was alive.

Thonius felt a sudden, soaring sense of hope. There was regret and shame and pain mixed in with it, but hope was the strongest flavour. He pulled himself upright and looked out into the sheeting rain at the approaching lights. He had strength at last, a force of will. Since that afternoon, in Miserimus, in Formal E of Petropolis, when he'd been stupid enough to look into the flect and let the daemon into his soul in the first place, he hadn't felt this strong. He could do this. He could beat this. He–

He went blind. No, not blind. Deaf. No, not deaf–

Falling. He was falling. There was a pit filled with the darkest smoke of Old Night, and the blemish of forgotten suns, decaying into oblivion, and an ochone moaning that crackled like an untuned vox.

It was there in the darkness, swooping around him as he fell into the infinite, his mouth yelling but making no sound. He knew this. He knew what this was. It had happened before.

The thing in the darkness swooped closer, pale and cold, yet burning. It was anguished and spavined, old and so, so dreadful. It snorted like a beast in Carl's head.

Terrible pressure pushed his eyes back into their sockets. Claws rammed up into his nostrils, and dragged out his tongue until it was tight and stretched. Molten lead poured into his ears, suffocating all sounds. He toppled over, pulling the chain tight, wailing in distress. Black, stinking blood suddenly welled out of his mouth, nostrils and tear ducts. Cramps viced and wrenched at his intestines. His legs exhibited a sudden, palsied tremor.

One by one, the rings he had collected snapped and pinged off the swelling fingers of his right hand.

Carl Thonius screamed. He decided he wanted to die after all, really, properly die, and soon.

He let the buzzing out. The pain had become too much. It had been inside him for so long, wearing him down, wearing him out. A lifetime, so it seemed. Buzzing, buzzing, buzzing.

His vision returned. For a bare instant, he saw Slyte, face to face. Thonius's eyeballs burst and jellied matter dribbled down his cheeks.

The rain pelted down on him. It was the last hour of Carl Thonius's human existence. It would be the most miserable and ghastly sixty minutes anyone would ever endure.

NINE

THEY WALK OUT into the storm to greet us. Gunmen, hireling guards, weapons ready. I count twenty of them. I taste the old, high wall behind them, and find it full of automated weaponry. I fear I am too weak for this, too slow. A different me, a younger me, might have done this. Not any more. Not after the door. Words are all I have left.

I hope they will be enough.

Below me, amongst the armed men, I see Culzean and Molotch, coming out through the wall's gate, their hands raised to fend off my cutter's downwash.

It's a bad night. I've seldom seen a storm this wild.

'Set us down, Master Unwerth,' I say. His flying has been superlative.

'With directness,' he replies.

We drop, thrusters gunning. We settle beside the other lander lashed to the rock-lip landing.

'Thank you, Sholto,' I say as I move towards the hatch.

The hatch folds open. Rain sprays in. It's a really bad night. I hover down outside onto the landing and face Culzean and his waiting troops. Molotch himself hangs back, peering at me. This is a strange moment.

+Hello, Zygmunt.+

'Gideon.'

+There's no time to fight each other, Zygmunt. That goes for you too, Culzean. Slyte is here.+

'Here?' Molotch echoes me. 'How could he be here?'

'That's enough of that,' Culzean cries out, walking forwards to take control of the standoff. There's a small, robed woman beside him. She's a blunter; not a good one, but the best Culzean could afford, and she's good enough to keep my mind back.

'Gideon!' Culzean cries, as if welcoming an old friend. He approaches across the rain-swept rock, arms wide, accompanied by his gunmen and his blunter. 'Gideon! So wonderful to see you! I thought I'd killed you!'

'You came close,' my voxponder crackles back, 'very close.'

'No harm done, then,' he laughs. 'What brings you here?'

'As I said quite plainly, Slyte,' I reply. I see Molotch take a step forwards. In all our encounters up to this point, I've never seen him scared. He's scared now.

'Slyte?' chuckles Culzean. 'Gideon, he's not here.'

'Oh, he most surely is,' I answer. 'I can taste him. Turn off your blunter and feel the truth.'

'Turn off my blunter? Seriously, Gideon, you're an alpha-plus psyker. What makes you think I'd do something as suicidal as that?'

'Self preservation,' I reply. 'My interrogator, Carl Thonius, is hosting Slyte. If he's not here already, he will be soon. You're going to die, Culzean, all of you. The warp is not selective in its predations.'

'Thonius?' asks Molotch, pushing forward through the gang of gunmen. 'Your man, Thonius?'

'Yes, Zygmunt. Carl Thonius. I don't know how or why, but he was the one infected.'

Molotch approaches my chair. He crouches down in the fierce rain and embraces it. It is a strange gesture for a mortal enemy to make, but it is earnest. He is friendless and he is scared. 'Gideon,' he whispers, 'Culzean can't be trusted.'

+Oh, and *you* can be trusted, can you, Zygmunt?+

He leans back and gazes dully at the hull of my chair. 'Of course I can't, Gideon, but this is a different scale of trust. I understand what Slyte means, Culzean doesn't. We need to... we need to be of one mind and one purpose now.'

+I agree.+

'Oh, good, good.'

'Orfeo,' I venture, 'can we reach some compact here? Against a mutually destructive foe?'

Culzean shrugs. A woman with a hard face and close-cropped hair walks out onto the landing behind him and hands him a control wand.

'You sent for this, sir?' she says.

'Thank you, Ley.'

'Last chance, Culzean,' I say. 'I'm agreeing with the proposal you made to me.'

'It's too late,' he says. 'As of about half an hour ago, I got everything I ever wanted.'

He clicks the wand and a void shield suddenly covers him, opaque and fizzling in the rain.

'Kill them,' he says. 'Kill them all. Molotch too.'

The sentry guns clatter. The gunmen raise their weapons.

They open fire.

Culzean, shielded, walks calmly back into the rambling hulk of Elmingard.

* * *

TEN

THE BROADSIDE OF automatic fire hammered down on the landing area. The gunfire was deafening, and the strobe of muzzle flashes blinding. Ravenor's cutter took several punishing hits.

'Get away! Get away, Sholto!' Ravenor yelled.

The cutter took off and dropped away out of sight over the lip of the cliff, wounded and pluming smoke. As the firestorm began, Ravenor had desperately raised a force wall with the last of his strength. The hard rounds and las fire laid down by Culzean's men and the wall defences spanged off it. Ravenor projected the psi barrier wide enough to shield Molotch as well as himself. It seemed odd to be expending precious effort trying to protect a man he had spent a large part of his life trying to kill.

Shells and las-bolts continued to punch against Ravenor's shield, rippling and dimpling the air in brief crater patterns.

'You can't hold this back forever!' Molotch yelled.

'If there's any luck left in this accursed galaxy,' Ravenor replied, 'I won't have to.'

+Now would be a good time!+ he sent with as much willpower as he could spare.

ON THE OTHER side of the monastic wall, more hired guns were massing at Slade's orders to protect the landing. They came running from several directions, arming weapons and running link checks. The gunfire beyond the wall was a rattling, coughing blurt of sound.

'Fan out!' ordered Eldrik, in charge of the support unit. 'Some of you get on the wall top. Heavy weapons to the gate!'

Eldrik paused suddenly. Some of his men ran on past him. 'Where the hell did that come from?' he asked.

There was a door in the lower terrace wall. It was made of wood, a very ordinary old door in a very ordinary frame. It looked as if it had always been there, but Eldrik was quite certain he'd never seen it before.

The door opened. A small girl, barely a teenager, stepped out into the rain and looked around with innocent fascination. She held an ornate key in her hand.

'Hello!' she said to Eldrik with a bright smile.

'Who the hell are you?' asked Eldrik.

'She's with me,' said Angharad Esw Sweydyr.

The towering Carthaen swordswoman came out of the open doorway with such virile speed, Eldrik didn't have time to raise his weapon. His eyes went wide at the sight of her, a goddess in armour.

Evisorex cut him in half.

'Get back, child,' Angharad hissed, and Iosob scooted into the shadows by the door. Angharad became a blur in the rain and lightning, her cloak and her braided hair flying, her sabre flashing. She ripped into the squad Eldrik had been assembling. In the confusion, few of them were able to tell exactly what was happening, although it was patently obvious that they were being slaughtered. A few got off hasty shots. Screams echoed, and lopped limbs spun into the air. Arterial blood squirted up into the torrential rain.

Nayl and Kys followed Angharad out of the door. He wore an armoured bodyglove and carried a Voss-pattern automatic grenade launcher, heavy and pugnacious, with a fat drum magazine. Patience was wearing a dark green bodyglove with long black boots, and a billowing overskirt. The pleats of the skirt contained dozens of concealed kineblades. Four needle blades already circled around her.

They moved fast, following Angharad's trail of destruction. The flagstones were slick with rain and swilling blood. The steam of entrails and opened bodies fumed in the cold air. Nayl fired two rounds from the launcher, lobbing them down the length of the approach. He was rewarded by a meaty fireball that hurled rock chips in all directions. He sent another round over into the gate itself, throwing two of Culzean's gunmen headlong with the blast, and then ran forwards, firing single grenades up at the backs of the sentry pods built into the old wall.

The grenades were magnetic. Each one thumped onto a pod's metal cowling and stuck fast. A sentry gun exploded, blown out of the wall top in a fire shock and a rain of bricks. A second blew out, and then a third. Each pod had been firing on full auto until the moment it was obliterated. Nayl took out a fourth pod, and paused to reload the drum mag. His handiwork had torn holes along the monastic wall, like a gum with the teeth extracted. There was a sharp tang of fycelene in the air. Kys brought down a gunman on the wall steps with her kineblades, and then reached out with her telekinesis into the mouldering bricks and stones of the wall itself. She found the hot, heavy power cables and datawire bundles that fed the rest of the wall's automatic defences. Gritting her teeth, she pulled.

A long, fat snake of armoured trunking tore out of the wall in a shower of plaster and masonry. It came clean out like the spine of a cooked fish and then snapped in two places, sheeting electrical sparks and voltage flashes across the wet stone.

The remaining wall defences went dead.

+Gideon?+

+That's better, thank you.+

Outside, on the gale-swept landing, Ravenor began to move forwards, Molotch close behind him. The ground in front of them had been chewed to smoking pulp by the bombardment that had, until a moment before, been hammering them relentlessly. Ravenor was able to slacken his shield at last, and did so with relief. The only shots coming their way were from the blue-suited gunmen Culzean had left on the landing. Ravenor popped his chair's cannon-pods from their recesses and cut down two of them. The others began to flee back through the gate into Elmingard, firing as they went.

Kys, Nayl and Angharad were waiting for them. By the time Ravenor and Molotch came through the gate, the only gunmen still alive were the ones who had been wise enough to flee up into the banked terraces of the cliff top fastness.

+Start moving. Start searching.+

'Are you sure he's here?' asked Nayl.

+I'm sure. He's hard to read, hard to pinpoint, because he's not really Carl any more, but he's here. I can hear him screaming.+

'What do we do if we find him?' asked Kys.

+Call for me.+

The three of them ran off up the steps onto the terraces. In under a minute, Ravenor and Molotch could hear more shooting, and the ominous crump of Nayl's launcher.

'Iosob, stay here, by the door,' Ravenor told the girl. She nodded.

+Let's follow the others,+ Ravenor sent to Molotch.

'Do you have a plan?' asked Molotch.

+No. This is entirely improvised. I am just hoping we can find Thonius before it's too late.+

'What weren't you telling your people?' Molotch asked.

+I don't know what you mean, Zygmunt.+

'Come on, Gideon, don't try to trick a trickster. What were you keeping from them?'

They moved up a mouldering flight of steps and onto one of the lower terraces. The dark, interlocking bulk of Elmingard rose above them in the storm.

+That it's already too late. This place is radiating a psychic force that's off the scale. I daren't probe it in any detail, because it would burn out my mind. There is no question that Slyte is here.+

'So I return to my original question. Is there a plan?'

+I was hoping you might have some suggestions. Dae-monology is one of your specialties, Zygmunt. I was also hoping that Culzean might have tools or resources to help us.+

'Culzean's playing his own game,' Molotch replied, dis-missively, 'but his house is full of arcane trinkets and talismans. It's possible there might be something that could aid us. However, I've been studying Culzean's col-lection for weeks, and I haven't found anything so far that would do. Believe me, I've searched diligently.' He paused, thoughtfully. 'As for my own talents... I don't know. I have dabbled. I have studied. I have bound cer-tain lesser fiends, and created a daemonhost or two over the years. I understand the basic principles of gate and portal rituals, but Slyte is a Daemonicus Arcana Majoris. I would never try to summon him, because even with the correct rites and wards, he would be too powerful to bind. As it is, he's already here. It's long past the time for prophylactic rituals.'

Thunder splintered the sky.

'The only control a man can ever have over a daemon is by way of transaction,' Molotch said. 'A man provides the daemon with a way into our dimension, and in exchange, the daemon is bound by the terms of that favour. It is a very complex, hazardous thing to do, and takes years of precise preparation to pull off. If a daemon is already here, in our universe, there is no transaction left to hold it to. No terms, Gideon. There's no way of asserting power or command over it, because it owes us nothing and wants nothing from us. It is simply a mate-rial fact, ungoverned by mortal powers.'

+What about banishment?+

Molotch laughed. 'Like binding, it's a complex process. It takes months or years of preparatory study. It also requires the correct time and place.'

+And this isn't the correct time or place?+

'Does it look like it to you?'

+I'm not going to give up. We have to try, while we still have life in our bodies. We have to try something. You know the layout of this place, Molotch. Take me to Culzean's trinkets and help me search for that something.+

CULZEAN'S HIRED GUNS offered resistance to the bitter end. Nayl came up some crumbling stone steps onto a paved terrace several levels above Ravenor and Molotch, and immediately came under renewed fire. Las shots shrieked at him from a large doorway across the terrace, forcing him into cover behind a stone urn that quickly became a shapeless lump.

He, Kys and Angharad had been obliged to fight every step of the way up into Elmingard, and he was down to his last few grenades. He switched to his heavy autopistol, keeping the launcher in reserve.

There was no backup to call for. Kys had split to the left a few minutes earlier, heading into what looked like the domestic quarters. They'd both lost touch with Angharad before that. In her warrior fury, she'd simply stormed ahead, expecting them to keep up. From the screams emanating from a nearby wing of the place, she'd found suitable work to occupy herself.

The rain was getting worse. Nayl had seen lightning strike the roofline of Elmingard at least twice in the last five minutes. A black cloud, blacker than the night itself, whirled like a halo around the upper ramparts of the building. He didn't like to dwell on what might be causing that. Nayl also didn't want to notice the sweet, rancid smell that he kept catching on the wind. Putrefaction, the cloying scent of the warp.

The gunmen at the doorway had him pinned. With a grunt of resignation, Nayl hoisted up his launcher and banged a grenade into the air. It landed in the doorway and detonated in a sheet of fire and grit.

He was up and running at once. Two gunmen lay dead, mangled by the blast. Another staggered, deafened, in the ruin of the doorway. Part of the building facade had collapsed and smoke poured out of the broken door.

Letting his slung launcher bang against his hip as he ran, Nayl drew his autopistol and capped the staggering man as he went in past him. The hall inside was thick with smoke. Another survivor was crawling around on the debris-strewn floor on his hands and knees. Nayl put the wretch out of his misery, and then headed on. The smoke began to clear. He found himself in the door arch of a large room with a high roof. Lightning backlit the large, leaded windows. The room was a dining hall of sorts. It was dominated by a huge refectory table of old, sturdy timber, big enough to seat thirty. There were the chairs to prove it.

Nayl took a step forwards, and two heavy rounds exploded against the wall beside him, blitzing out plaster and stone chips. Nayl hurled himself forwards and rolled across the floor, using the end of the hefty table as cover. Another heavy shot whooshed past. He knew the distinctive sound: a bolt pistol.

From the other end of the chamber, Lucius Worna came out to play. The flashes of lightning outside glinted off his pearly armour. He fired his bolt pistol as he advanced, blasting splintered holes in the table.

'That you, Nayl? Is that you?' he roared.

'Oh, probably,' Nayl replied, crouching under the table end and looking around desperately for an option.

Worna snorted. 'I'm gonna mess you up, Harlon. Don't frig with me. Be a man, and come out and take it.'

'I'm going to say no,' Nayl answered. Another bolt round tore clean through the table top and fractured the floor tiles beside him.

Worna grabbed hold of the long table with his left hand. The fingers of his metal gauntlet sank into the wood. With a whine of power armour, he hurled the huge table right over. It left the ground and crashed down on its side, shattering some of the chairs.

Nayl was left, crouching, on the open tiles, his cover removed.

He looked up at Worna, five metres away.

'Nayl,' Worna growled, a smile crossing his face. 'You know what this is?'

'Yeah. End of story,' said Nayl. He fired the grenade launcher he was clutching against his chest.

The grenade round hit Worna in the sternum, with enough kinetic force to knock him back several steps.

Recovering his balance, the grizzled bounty hunter looked down. The round had magnetically attached itself to his breastplate. Worna scrabbled at it to knock it off.

It exploded.

The blast sent Nayl sprawling along the floor. It threw Worna's mighty, spread-eagled form violently across the chamber in the other direction, demolishing the far doors as he ploughed into them.

Nayl picked himself up and hobbled down the room to the wreckage of the doors. Smoke threaded the air. He could see Worna's corpse on its back, half buried in broken hardwood door panels. The armour of his upper torso was buckled and blackened, and his face was a raw, red mask of burnt flesh.

Nayl peered down at his old partner in crime for a moment. He'd always wondered how this story would end.

The corpse grabbed him by the right ankle. With a whipcrack snap, it jerked Nayl down onto his back. Winded, Nayl tried to struggle, but Worna was already rising, black eyes burning savagely out of the blast-flayed remains of his face. Blood wept from the seared flesh.

Worna picked Nayl up by the throat, and lifted him off the floor. With his left hand, he tore the grenade launcher off Nayl's body and chucked it aside. Then he threw Nayl back into the dining room.

Nayl landed hard, dazed. Worna came to him and picked him up again, with both hands this time. He raised him high, and threw him a second time. Nayl's flailing body hit one of the dining room's grand windows and smashed through it in a blizzard of glass and broken leading. Nayl fell six metres and landed on the grey slates of an annex roof below. His impact shattered some of the slates and made a dent. He lay on the damaged roof in the torrential rain, twisted and unconscious.

Lightning flared. A fork of it struck the ridge of a nearby roof, exploding the heavy tiles and exposing black rafters that began to burn.

Worna turned away from the shattered window, breathing in long, sucking rasps. He walked slowly across the dining room, found his bolt pistol, and picked it up. He returned to the window. Small fragments of glass were still falling out of the remaining twists of leading, tinkling as they hit the ground. Rain blew in, stinging Worna's ruined face.

He slammed a new clip into his bolt pistol, racked it, and leaned out of the window to take aim at Harlon Nayl's helpless form.

ELEVEN

'I HOPE YOU know what the hell you're doing,' Leyla Slade said to Culzean as they advanced briskly up through the northern layers of Elmingard.

'I always know what I'm doing,' he replied jauntily. 'Now, you put him where I told you to put him, didn't you?'

'In the old tower, yes.' Slade looked at Culzean. 'Believe me, if I'd known what he was when I was doing it, I wouldn't have gone near him.'

A squad of six hired guns were escorting them. At her words, they exchanged troubled looks.

'Everything's all right,' Culzean said. 'Everything's all right, gentlemen. Believe me, you'll all be receiving triple pay for tonight's work.'

'We're getting reports, sir,' said Tzabo, leading the fire team. 'The inquisitor's forces have taken the gate and are inside Elmingard. We've lost men. A lot of men.'

'Our distinguished foe won't trouble us much longer,' Culzean said confidently. 'Now come along.' They ran across a courtyard, braving the relentless rain, and entered another wing of the sprawling building.

'Thonius is really Slyte?' Slade asked Culzean as they strode along. She kept her voice low.

'This is what I have learned from the Swole woman, and she was in no position to lie. It's sweet, I think she'd actually been trying to protect him.'

'Orfeo, Slyte is–'

'Slyte is perfect. Slyte is the thing I've spent my life working towards and look, Leyla, he comes to me in the end almost by chance. Ah, the irony!'

'I don't understand what you think you can achieve. Molotch–'

'Zygmunt was a fine enough distraction, but there was no real future in that relationship. I believed for a long time he would be an invaluable asset to my work, but I hadn't taken into account his character. So difficult. So hard to govern.'

'So smart,' said Slade darkly.

'Yes, that too. You must have noticed, these last few weeks, how we were falling out? It was just a matter of time before it turned nasty.'

Slade shuddered. 'I think it's turned nasty already,' she remarked.

'Oh, poo, Ley. You know what I mean. He was so paranoid.'

'Was he?' she asked. 'Or was he the only one who really knew what kind of disaster Slyte represented?'

Culzean stopped and turned to face Slade. The men came to a halt behind them.

'Ley, listen to me. Have I ever let you down? Have I? You've seen some of the shining weapons I have at my disposal. They've taken me years to collect and years to learn how to use. Molotch, for all his smart mind, is just a dabbler. I am a professional in these things. Experienced, informed, detached. Slyte is just another asset for me to exploit. Another shining weapon... albeit the brightest and shiniest I've ever acquired.'

'You think... you think you can control a daemon of the Major Arcana?'

Culzean laughed. 'Oh, I know I can. Control him and bind him. Subjugate him. I sent our savants up to the tower just before Ravenor made his grand entrance. As we speak, they are completing the necessary rituals and enslaving Slyte's power to my command.'

Slade hesitated before responding. 'Sir, I advise caution,' she said, taking out her handgun and fitting it with one of the specially prepared clips. 'I have always admired your ambition−'

'Thank you, Ley.'

'May I ask... what you intend to do?'

'That's just it,' said Orfeo Culzean with a winning smile. 'I can do anything I want. Anything at all. With Molotch as an ally, I might have taken down a government or seized control of a world. But with Slyte... oh, Leyla. The whole Imperium is mine. Start dreaming. I'll soon be able to grant you any heart's desire.'

'Right now,' she replied, 'I'd settle for being somewhere else. What about Ravenor and his people?'

'Slyte will destroy them, at my order. I'd like you to contact the Divine Fratery later tonight. I've kept a line of communication open with Frater Stefoy. They will want

to know of Slyte's birth. They may wish to come and worship him. Encourage them. The Fratery, with their
long-standing knowledge of Slyte, will be useful to have
around, an added guarantee. Now, can we proceed?'

They left the northern wing and stepped out into the
storm. Tzabo's men lit lamp packs. Rain swirled into
their faces as they struggled up the track to the
astronomer's tower. Incandescent lightning boomed like
atomic blasts overhead in the murk.

The ragged tower formed an ominous black shape
through the sheeting rain. They soldiered on, their clothes
drenched, arms raised to protect their faces. Culzean
reignited his void shield for cover against the elemental fury,
and the rain sizzled and steamed off its field.

Then the rain stopped, and there was utter calm.

They stopped outside the tower's base, steam rising off
their soaked clothing. There was shocking peace and
silence.

'Eye of the storm?' Culzean suggested, with a nervous
laugh.

Slade looked back down the track. Ten yards away, the
rain was falling. It was falling like a monsoon deluge all
across the black silhouette of Elmingard. Lightning
jagged the sky. They could hear none of it.

'This is, this is...' one of Tzabo's men said, raising his
weapon.

'Oh, Throne,' said Tzabo, looking up. The sky directly
above the tower was bare of clouds. The black weight of
the thunderhead hung over the mountains, but had
swirled and parted to form a deep chimney of clear air
over the astronomer's broken edifice. Alien stars glittered
high above. They were moving, circling like fireflies,
forming and re-forming constellations and the spirals of
unknown galaxies.

'Let's go back,' said Slade, her voice hollow in the still
air. 'Orfeo, please.'

'It's just the binding,' Culzean told her. 'Our savants have done their work. This area is becalmed because of the rites they have performed. Slyte is bound.'

'What's that stink?' asked Tzabo. A noxious odour oozed out of the black tower, a charnel air.

Slade moved forwards, her weapon aimed. Culzean followed her. They stepped through the doorway into the base of the tower. Rainwater dripped down from the upper levels. Scraps of torn parchment, sodden and limp, littered the floor.

Slade saw the stone block she'd shackled Thonius to an hour before. The remnants of the chain trailed from it, broken and bent.

'Orfeo?'

'What?'

'Orfeo, look.'

The walls around them were decorated with something dark and sticky. It took them a moment to comprehend what they were looking at. Culzean's savants were dead. Their pulverised meat and bones were smeared in a thin, clotting layer onto stone all around the tower. Blood ran down and congealed at the base of the walls.

'Leyla?' Culzean whispered.

She grabbed his hand and dragged him back out of the tower. Tzabo and his men were waiting there.

'We're leaving,' she told them.

'Sir?'

'She's right,' mumbled Culzean, trying to think straight. 'She's right, Tzabo. We're leaving.'

So soon?

They turned.

Something that had once been Carl Thonius stood in the doorway of the tower. He was naked, his clothes burnt off him. A ghastly red light radiated from the core of his being, illuminating him from within. His skin had become transparent and his skeletal structure was revealed like a medicae's scan. His right arm was fleshless from the middle of the upper half. What remained was a scorched bone limb that ended in vast, black talons.

Culzean, he said. When his mouth opened, they could see flames dancing inside.

'Slyte?' stammered Orfeo Culzean. 'Slyte, I command you–'

'Don't be such an idiot!' Slade cried.

The thing's mouth opened. It kept opening. It stretched and distended like a snake's jaw, far wider than any human mouth could ever open. Then it exhaled with a dull, buzzing roar. A wave of wretched vapour streamed out of its maw and engulfed them. Tzabo's men recoiled, gasping and vomiting. All of the silver buttons on their smart blue outfits tarnished and went black. Two of them fell down, overcome with nausea.

Gagging, Slade raised her weapon. 'Run!' she gasped. 'Run, Orfeo!'

She started to fire. Tzabo and his remaining men added their firepower to hers. Their las shots bounced off the daemonic figure, but Slade's special loads had been aimed low, into the soil at its feet. They burst on impact, releasing their contents from their bondage in the specially engraved shells.

Gibbering warp-forms bloomed like unholy flowers, sprouting from the earth. Hooktors and clawbrils and other hideous sub-daemons that Culzean had painstakingly captured and imprisoned over the years manifested as they were released, and struck at Slyte in mindless wrath.

Cackling, Slyte dismembered them, shredding their bodies like wet sacks, spraying ichor and pus in all directions. His black talons ripped through their writhing masses and reduced them to dissolving ectoplasmic sludge.

Slyte stepped forwards through the last of the warp-things. He made a barking sound, like a dog-fox, and the ground split. Insectile vermin, glittering black, some the size of lobsters or small felines, poured out of the ground in a frenetic, clicking flood.

'Run!' Slade screamed.

Culzean started to run. The insects enveloped him, burning and falling away as the void shield threw them back.

Tzabo and his men were engulfed. The seething mass of chittering bodies covered them from head to toe, and stripped them of clothing and meat. Bare skeletons, crawling with black things, collapsed onto the ground and disarticulated. Tzabo was the last to fall. He turned his gun on himself and blew off his own head.

The air was full of flies, buzzing and swarming.

Culzean ran. Slade ran after him, wailing. There were things on her, on her arms and her legs, biting and scurrying.

'Orfeo!'

'Leyla! Protect me!'

She turned, loyal to the end, clapped a fresh clip into her weapon, and faced the burning daemon striding after them. She started to fire.

Culzean ran on regardless. He heard Leyla Slade shrieking, and shuddered when that shrieking cut off abruptly.

He kept running.

IN THE HEART of Elmingard, Siskind and the others heard awful roaring and baying coming from outside. A dire stink suddenly permeated the place.

'That's it,' Siskind told Ornales. 'We're leaving.'

The rest of Culzean's staff and employees were already fleeing. Tables and chairs were overturned in their efforts to exit. There was screaming and shouting. The noises echoed down the hallways.

'Is the flier locked?' Siskind asked his first mate as they hurried along.

'It'll only open to our voice prints,' Ornales assured him. 'What in hell is happening?'

Siskind drew his laspistol. 'I have no idea and no wish to know,' he said. A man slammed into them. The silver buttons of his blue wool clothing had turned black. Siskind saw how every metal surface in the place was tarnished and soiled. The air had gone bad. The stink was everywhere.

'Take me with you! Take me with you, shipmaster!' the man pleaded. Siskind shot him.

'This is madness!' he growled.

Ornales said nothing, but drew his own weapon.

They reached a stairwell that led down into the southern terraces. Scullery boys and domestics ran past them, trying to find a place of refuge. Siskind and Ornales started down the steps.

Plyton appeared on the staircase below them, hauling Kara Swole. She cried out as she saw Siskind.

Siskind started shooting. Plyton dropped Kara and fired her shotgun. The blast took Ornales in the chest and hurled him back up the stairs. He landed, limp, and rolled back down a step or two.

Siskind kept firing. He hit Plyton in the right hip and the left shoulder, and spun her back down the staircase. She screeched in pain as she bounced off the wall and fell on her face. Leaping down two steps at a time, Siskind came to a halt over Kara's body.

She looked up at him, blankly.

'Kara!' Plyton yelled in pain, doubled up and writhing at the base of the stairs. Siskind pointed his hand weapon at Kara Swole.

The first las-shot blew out his spine. The second chopped the back off his head as cleanly as an axe blow. Siskind staggered, gaping, smoke streaming out of his mouth. Blood poured down the back of his expensive coat of Vitrian glass.

He toppled over the stair rail and fell.

Belknap clattered down the staircase to reach Kara, slinging his lasrifle onto his shoulder. He grabbed her, and covered her face with kisses.

'I thought I'd lost you,' he whispered.

'Pat, Patrik...' she moaned. 'Help Maud.'

He looked over her head at Plyton thrashing in anguish on the deck below.

'Yeah,' he said. 'Of course.'

LEANING OUT OF the broken window, Lucius Worna fired his bolt pistol at Nayl on the cratered roof below. Nothing happened.

He glanced at his weapon. It was a trusty tool and had never malfunctioned before. He tried again. He realised that something was preventing his finger from squeezing the trigger.

He turned instinctively. A kineblade impaled him through one eye like an arrow. Two more struck into his chest.

Patience Kys walked towards him across the ruined dining hall, her skirt flowing.

'There's more where that came from,' she promised.

Worna tried to fire at her. She lashed out with the full fury of her telekinesis and grabbed him around the neck, throttling him.

Worna choked.

Kys raised her arms like a sorcerer casting a spell and propelled him up off the floor and out through the window. Advancing, she lifted his struggling bulk up into the sky and suspended him there.

A bolt of lightning slammed into his metal-clad form. A second later, two more monumental lightning strikes hit him.

'End of story?' she asked sarcastically, her hands raised.

'You... wish...' Worna gasped, blood streaming out of his mouth.

Kys determinedly held the bounty hunter in the sky a little longer. Eight more forks of lightning slammed into Worna in rapid succession. His armoured carcass began to burn.

Once it was blazing like a torch, she hurled it away. It arced across the rooftops of Elmingard like a comet, leaving a trail of fire behind it.

Kys leaned out of the window. 'Harlon?' she yelled. 'You alive down there? Harlon?'

TWELVE

THEY HURRIED ACROSS the rose terrace into the solar. Ravenor led the way.

'Of course, I knew it was Thonius all along,' Molotch said.

+What?+

'Oh, not at the time, but now... it all makes sense.'

+How?+

'At Petropolis, Gideon. In the Sacristy. I came so close to my dreams.'

+I know you did.+

'Gideon, you'd have enjoyed them too, admired them. Enuncia was so perfect, so clean.'

+Zygmunt...+

Molotch shrugged. 'At the point of creation, I was interrupted by your people. Kara Swole and Carl Thonius. Of course, I dealt with them quickly. Then Slyte appeared.'

+Slyte was there?+

'Yes, Gideon. Did you not realise what actually thwarted my efforts on Eustis Majoris? Slyte stopped me. Slyte hurt me. But for Slyte, I would have triumphed.'

+Holy Throne.+

'The daemon just appeared, and I was too scared to think. Culzean and his woman helped me escape. But now it's so obvious. Slyte was there because Thonius was there. Thonius was Slyte. He destroyed my plans for Enuncia.'

Ravenor's chair coasted to a halt in the middle of the solar. Rain spattered in through the open doors behind them. +I thought it was me, Zygmunt. I thought I was the one who'd beaten you. Slyte takes the credit for that, does he?+

'Rather, I think, Carl Thonius,' Molotch replied. 'Now let's get on with this.' He started to rummage through the crates Culzean had left stacked in the chamber. 'Come along, Gideon.'

Molotch paused in his search and looked back at the support chair.

'What's the matter?'

+Nothing.+

'You never told me how you found out,' said Molotch.

+A nascent psyker called Zael. He knew it all. I have a feeling he left it too late to tell me.+

'What's the matter?'

+You keep asking me that, Zygmunt.+

'I'll keep asking until you tell me.'

+Very well. Things have changed. I can feel it. The storm's shifting. The magnitude of power has increased. The daemon is on the move, coming closer. I can feel him closing in. He's entered the house. We've only got a few minutes left. Can't you smell him?+

'Then this is all a waste of time,' said Molotch.

The end door of the solar burst open and Culzean scrambled in, his void shield still flickering around him. It was close to failure. He began to ransack the drawers at the far end of the room. His shield blinked out.

Culzean turned, suddenly aware he was not alone. He snatched out an auto-snub and aimed it at Molotch and Ravenor.

'Don't be so silly,' Ravenor said.

'He's coming! He's coming!' Culzean cried. 'He's right behind me! He killed my poor Leyla!'

Molotch flicked his right arm. Culzean's pistol flew out of his hand and tumbled in the air. Molotch caught it, and shot Culzean through the belly. Culzean crashed back into the chest of drawers, and fell down clutching his abdomen. His face went white. There was a look of speechless surprise on his face.

+Was that really necessary?+

'You have no idea,' said Molotch.

Culzean was bleeding out. His agony was tangible, and pressed down on Ravenor's mind like a dead weight. Ravenor was quite sure Molotch had gone for a belly wound because he knew it was an excruciating, lingering way to die. +Culzean, is there anything we can do?+

Culzean groaned and coughed up blood. 'Help me. A doctor...'

+I meant about the daemon.+

The door behind him flew open. Angharad landed like a cat in front of Molotch and sliced the end off his pistol. She was about to gut him. Ravenor threw her back against the wall with psychic force.

+No, Angharad. Leave him.+

'He is the devil!' she sneered.

+There are worse devils abroad tonight.+

Angharad glared at Molotch.

+We will need him if we want to survive.+

Molotch bent over Culzean. 'Orfeo? Orfeo, listen. What were you looking for when you came in here?'

'Something. Anything.' Culzean swallowed hard. 'I wondered if there was something I'd forgotten, something I'd overlooked.'

'Is there? What have you got left? Any shining weapons? Any talismans or incantations that might be efficacious?'

Culzean shook his head. 'Nothing, nothing. I have a few rites of banishment, but I'm certain none would be suitable.'

'Because this isn't the right time or place?' Ravenor asked. 'Show us anyway.'

Culzean gestured weakly at a nearby book case. 'Third shelf, in the green box.'

Molotch rose, slid the box off the shelf, and opened it. He pulled out a thick sheaf of old parchments bound with a cord.

'Banishment rites,' Culzean murmured, pain etched across his face, 'all very old, and from a number of sources. The *Hech'ell Deportation* is the most complete and the most reliable. I've used it before. It works.'

+But?+

'It won't work here. None of them will.'

Molotch was speed-reading the crumbling parchments. 'He's right. It's like I told you. To cast out a daemon, one must choose the right place and time. One must find a location where the walls between dimensions are tissue-thin, a rift or fissure, a place of weakness. There are only a few such places in the entire cosmos and Elmingard isn't one of them. Any banishment rites we try here are a waste of effort.'

He was about to say something else but his voice cut off. Something flickered and blinked in the corner of the solar. It manifested, just a hazy shimmer, like smoke in sunlight.

It was Carl Thonius.

THIRTEEN

THONIUS FLICKERED IN and out of reality. He seemed to be moving too fast, like a speeded up pict sequence.

I told you told you told you

Ravenor, Molotch and Angharad backed slowly towards the terrace doors. The room's lights dimmed and flashed in time to the lightning. Sprawled near to the manifested spectre, Culzean whimpered and tried to drag himself away.

'Slyte...' whispered Molotch.

+No. Slyte's still out there, coming closer. This is an aberration. A random psychic effect, just an echo.+

Gideon Gideon Gid Gideon

+Carl?+

Help me help me help meee

+Throne! Carl?+

The spectre sat down on one of the solar's armchairs. Its form continued to jump and flicker as if it was running at the wrong speed, and repeated and overlapped.

Gideon, please. It it hurts hurts. It hurts. Help me.

+Carl, it's too late.+

Oh, it hurts. I can I can beat this, I can.

+No, Carl, you can't.+

Gideon, I can. If you you you help me. You owe me me owe me owe me. I've been working with you with you all the way. I stopped Molotch at Petropolis. I did that. Did that. Did that. Me, Gideon. I made Kara made Kara Kara well again. I saved you from the creatures behind the door. Behind the door.

+Carl, I realise what you've done. I realise what you've tried to accomplish, but it's too late. You cannot be saved. The daemon has consumed you.+

The spectre blinked and fluttered in front of them. Blow flies began to collect on the insides of the window panes.

Don't say say that, Gideon. Help me beat this. Help me me. When Slyte took me, I thought I thought it was the end the end. But then I realised. I could control it. I could I could I could control it. I could master it. Give give me that chance. Imagine imagine what we could do then, you and me. For the ordos. For the Imperium. For the Imperium. For the Imperium. I could show you how the warp works. The warp warp the warp.

'He's just a phantom! A lie!' Culzean screeched.

I'm not not not.

'We're witnessing the last remains of Carl's being, driven by his will,' said Ravenor. 'We are witnessing an act of formidable determination.'

Gideon.

Ravenor hovered forwards and approached the jumping, bleached out image.

+Carl? If I could help you, I would. Courage such as yours should not go unrewarded, but I cannot help you. You are gone. You were gone the moment Slyte flowed into you. The idea that you can master an entity like Slyte is the sort of misguided radicalism you and I used to scoff at. Your logic has been altered by the corruption inside you. Slyte is feeding you excuses and false hopes to wear you down. What you're talking about cannot be countenanced by the Inquisition. It cannot be countenanced by any rational person. It cannot be countenanced by me.+

Nooo! no no

+Carl. I'm sorry.+

Nooooooooo!

THE SPECTRE LOSES form and control. It quivers, shaking as if caught in a violent earth tremor. I feel the scalding fury of the psi-force inside it. The windows of the solar rattle and panes crack. The swirls of blow flies cascade into the air like soot. The buzzing is everywhere. Culzean screams in undignified terror as books and other totemic objects clatter off the shelves, and pieces of parchment take flight like paper streamers in a parade.

They remind me of the Great Triumph on Thracian Primaris where I was mutilated. I am back there, for a moment, walking in the procession, paper streamers and petals showering down around me. Spatian Gate looms above me through the blizzard of tickertape.

That was a kind of damnation, one that I have never really come to terms with and never will. What awaits us here, tonight, is a more complete kind of damnation.

I call out to Carl, apologising and placating. 'I'm sorry,' I say. 'I'm sorry,' over and over again. Carl's anguished spectre vibrates itself into smoke with a wild frenzy, the last shreds of it burning and discorporating into a thin sludge of acrid mist.

Once he is gone, the solar becalms and falls silent, apart from the buzz of the flies. Outside, the storm rages on, and we can hear other sounds in its cacophony. First, a purring roar, that comes and goes with the incessant thunder, and then an immense grinding sound, as if the hog's back peaks are writhing against one another.

'We've no choice but to flee,' says Molotch.

+I doubt Slyte will let us go. Even if we escaped this rock, where would we run to? Slyte's reach will be considerable.+

Molotch looks at me. I can tell his mind is still racing. I can also tell it is churning nothing but frustration and helplessness.

Angharad turns, raising her sword. Figures are grouped behind us in the terrace doors, framed by the flapping drapes. Belknap and Kara support the wounded Maud Plyton between them.

'Ravenor?' Belknap utters in surprise.

'Oh gods!' Plyton gasps. Her mind is a seething knot of pain, but I feel her intense relief through it. The unexpected sight of me gives her hope for a moment.

'It's good to see you, all three of you,' I say.

A bow-wave of almost unbearable emotion swamps my mind. Kara runs forwards, leaving Belknap to support Plyton, and falls across the front of my chair, hugging it tightly. She is weeping.

+Kara.+

'You're alive!'

+Kara.+

She is inconsolable. I try to soothe her, but someone has hurt her. Someone has imprisoned her and tortured her. My poor Kara. There are so many things in her mind: grief, joy, relief, surprise, love, shame. She believed me to be dead and she can barely deal with the fact that I am not.

+Kara, it's all right. Kara, who did this to you?+

She clutches my chair tighter, her tears leaking out over the metal casing. 'I'm sorry!' she wails. 'I'm sorry!'

+Hush, Kara. It will be all right. Who did this to you?+

I reach into her unguarded, fragile mind to see, to soothe. Culzean had a hand in this. Behind him, I see an older memory of Siskind and Worna, and blanch at the inhuman desecrations they performed.

+I will find Siskind, I promise, Kara, and I will–+

I stop. Behind the toxic memories of Siskind and the brute Worna, other figures lurk: Carl, and Kara herself.

I read her deepest secret self, the white hot centre of her torment.

+Oh, Kara.+

'I'm sorry, Gideon!'

'What is she talking about?' Belknap demands. His love and concern for her burn like a molten ingot in mind space. He sets Plyton down on a couch and comes over. 'Kara? Ravenor? What?'

'I knew it was Carl! I knew it, and I hid it!' she wails.

'Carl blocked your memories,' I say. 'I can see the scars.'

She looks up at me. 'Before that. I knew. I knew and I hid it. He made me promise not to tell you. He made me promise not to tell anyone. He just needed time–' She wails again and becomes incoherent.

'What is she saying?' Belknap asks me.

'When did you know?' I ask. 'Kara, when did you know?'

'Eustis Majoris. At the Sacristy.'

'She was there,' says Molotch softly. 'She must have seen it all.'

'Why did you hide it? Why didn't you tell me?' I ask.

'I owed him so much,' she murmurs. 'He cured my... I was dying. He cured me. He saved me. He begged me to keep his secret for just a few months, to give him time to study, to find a way to beat it. I couldn't say no. He saved me. What kind of daemon does that?'

'The cunning kind,' I reply, 'and that's the only kind there is.'

'But–' she begins.

'You knew?' asks Belknap.

'What?'

'You knew? You knew Thonius was the daemon and you covered for him?'

Belknap takes a step back from us. He is a man of strong, simple emotions. What I read in him now is revulsion and betrayal. It is painful, and total. Everything he is thinking and feeling is driven by his focused devotion to the holy God-Emperor. It is the cruellest and ugliest emotion I believe I have ever read, made crueller and uglier because it is sincere.

'He saved me!' Kara stammers, looking up at Belknap with tear-reddened eyes.

'A daemon saved you?' he replies. For a moment, I fear he is going to strike her. I take no chances. I shove him back with my mind and make him sit down on the couch beside Maud.

'Sit down,' I instruct him. 'I will deal with this.'

'But she–'

'Sit down, Belknap, and shut up!'

'I'd do as he suggests, if I were you,' says Molotch. A smile curls his asymmetric lips. Even now, despite the dire circumstances, he can't stop himself from enjoying the ruin this whole affair has reduced my people to.

'And why the frig would anyone ever listen to anything you have to say, Molotch?'

Eight needle-sharp kine-blades hover in a spread, less than a finger's length from Molotch's pale face. He swallows. The solar's end door is open, and Nayl stands there, aiming his autopistol down the length of the chamber at Molotch. Nayl is battered and hurt, one eye half-closed and swollen. Patience stands beside him, murderous concentration on her face.

'Oh look,' says Molotch, with fake enthusiasm. 'They're all here.'

+Let him be.+

'Gideon?' Kys questions, hesitantly.

+Let him be! Harlon, put away your gun!+

'What's he doing here?' Kys asks.

I pull her kine-blades away from Molotch's face and discard them on the floor. +The same as us, trying to live until tomorrow. We have pooled our resources.+

'I hope the frig you know what you're doing,' says Kys.

She hurries to Kara and holds her, peeling her off my chair. Nayl crosses to Angharad and they embrace, kissing.

'So,' says Plyton from the couch, with an enforced brightness to mask her pain, 'we got a plan yet?'

'No,' Molotch and I answer together.

The mountains shake. Elmingard shudders. A roar comes out of the night, so loud and throaty it bruises our souls. It is part scream, part wail, part howl, part bellow, a drawn-out ululation of huge volume that blots out the fury of the storm.

It is the roar of a predator, the voice of a billion billion-year-old predator that has just woken, and realised it is hungry.

FOURTEEN

KARA ROSE TO her feet, breaking Kys's embrace. She wiped her cheeks. She dared not glance at Belknap for fear of seeing the look in his eyes.

'Get out of here,' she said. 'Get everyone out of here, Gideon.'

'Kara–'

'Get out of here while you still can, all of you. I'll–'

'You'll do what?' Ravenor asked.

'I'll hold him back, as long as I can.'

'How?' asked Kys.

'I'll talk to him. I'll talk to Carl. He trusts me. I can slow him down.'

'No,' said Ravenor. 'I've already spoken to him. Carl is trying his best, but he's lost to us. Any tenuous control he once had has gone. He's dead and Slyte is in control. In full control.'

'Gideon is correct,' mumbled Culzean, propped up against the foot of the chest of drawers, his life's collection of precious papers littered around him, scorched. 'I've seen Slyte. Like a mockery of Thonius, using his form, twisting it. Such power, such radiance.' He brushed flies away from his face. His skin had taken on the pallor of a corpse. He was sitting in a puddle of his own blood.

'That wasn't Slyte,' sneered Molotch. 'That was just Slyte's way in, his harbinger, like a limb extended through a door. Thonius, powers rest his soul, is Slyte's conduit. What we saw in the Sacristy that night, Orfeo, and what you undoubtedly witnessed tonight, was just the tip of the iceberg. You know what an iceberg is, don't you Orfeo?'

'Of course.'

'Thonius is just the gate. The rest is coming through.'

The awful, primordial roar shook the room again. The flies billowed up.

'Listen,' said Molotch, almost enraptured by the sounds of the warp. 'Here it comes.'

'Let me try, Gideon,' said Kara. 'Please, let me try to talk to him.'

'No, Kara,' Ravenor replied.

'Please! Let me–'

Without warning, she went into some kind of shock, and collapsed across the front of his chair, her limbs spasming. Kys tried to hold her steady. Despite himself, Belknap rose to help.

'I've got her,' Kys told him.

Gideon, Kara's mouth said.

Kys pulled back, unnerved. Kara rose, her eyes closed. Ravenor knew at once that someone, some*thing*, was waring her.

Gideon. Please. This is my last chance.

'There is no last chance, Carl,' Ravenor said. 'I've explained this to you. Let Kara go.'

Oh, please, you don't understand. Kara's mouth moved slackly, as if language was an alien, unfamiliar material passing through it. The blow flies settled on her face in increasing numbers, and scurried in and out of her mouth. They covered her eyes like scabs. *I only have a few moments left. I'm hanging on by my fingertips. He's eating me, Gideon, he's eating me up!*

'I can't help you, Carl.'

You bastard! You bastard! Kara Swole's mouth cried. *All the years I served you, and this is how you repay me? Save me! Save me!*

'For Throne's sake!' cried Nayl. 'Do something!'

'Can't you help him, Gideon?' demanded Patience Kys. 'Please!'

'I can't,' said Ravenor simply. 'I can't and I shouldn't, and I won't.'

Everyone stared at him, even Molotch.

Then kill it! Kill me! Banish it! Banish it! Give me peace!

Kara Swole swayed. Crawling flies covered her from head to toe.

'We can't banish it. We haven't the means, and this location is not right for–'

*Don't be such an idiot! Of course you have the means! You
brought a hole in the warp here with you! You can make this
the right time and place!*

Ravenor paused. Revelation seeped through him. He
looked at Thonius's unwilling avatar in grief and grati-
tude. +Oh Carl. The things you know.+

Manic laughter filled the air. As one, the flies lifted off
Kara and she fell heavily onto the solar floor.

'Help her, Patience,' Ravenor voxponded. He turned to
Molotch. +The door. He means the door, Zygmunt. We
can make our own damn rift!+

Wonder crossed Molotch's face. 'Oh, of course,' he said.
Then he frowned. 'You brought that thing here?'

+Yes.+

'There's preparation time, you realise–' Molotch began.

+Get what you need.+

Molotch hurried to the far end of the room and began
a violent search of Culzean's collection. He found a small
leather case and started to fill it with parchments and
other objects.

Ravenor turned to Kys. 'Does your link still work?' he
asked.

'I think so.'

'Call to Sholto and request his aid. If he doesn't want
to come, tell him I understand. We'll do this anyway.'

She nodded.

'Get everyone down onto the landing and tell him, if
he's willing, to meet us there.'

'Let's go!' she cried. She scooped up Kara and headed
for the terrace doors. Belknap gathered Plyton to himself
and, despite her protests of pain, headed out into the
storm.

Nayl, his weapon in his hand, remained beside Ravenor.

'You too, Harlon.'

'I'm fine where I am,' he replied.

'What about me?' Culzean whined.

'Angharad?' Ravenor directed.

'Do I have to?' the Carthaen asked sourly.

'Please.'

Angharad sheathed Evisorex in her cross-shoulder scabbard and walked across to Culzean. He squealed as she lifted him.

'Shut up.'

He didn't. He couldn't. Blood dribbled out of him. She carried him like a leaking sack back towards the terrace doors.

'Molotch?' Ravenor called.

'Almost there, almost.' Molotch stopped riffling through the junk and looked back at Ravenor. 'I know this won't make you very happy, but we'll need blood, human blood.'

Ravenor psyked up an unbroken saucer from the floor and held it under Culzean. It filled quickly.

'Making use of available resources,' Molotch smiled. 'How very practical.'

He paused. He looked up at the end wall of the solar behind him.

'Oh shit–' he started to say.

The windows blew in like grenade blasts. Rain and wind swirled into the room. The lamps went out. The ancient predator roared again, the concussive force of its voice shaking everything. They could all hear the distant, gigantic grinding sound, like cliffs scraping against cliffs.

Molotch staggered backwards, clutching the leather case.

The solar's end door swung open and red light shone in. The thing that had been Thonius entered, naked, lit from within, fire flaring in its mouth. Its bare, black arm swung, weighted by its bunched talons. A carpet of cockroaches and other iridescent black beetles scuttled into the solar around its feet. Backing rapidly away from the daemon, Molotch slipped on the scurrying insects and fell.

Slyte approached him, grinning. Its talons rippled out.

'Move!' Nayl urged, heading for the terrace doors. 'Leave him!'

'We can't go without Molotch! He has everything we need!'

Angharad dropped Culzean on the floor. The facilitator screamed. Sweeping out her sabre, she leapt between the daemon and the fallen heretic. Nayl yelled out her name. He opened fire at the glowing figure. Ravenor's chair started firing at it too. The heavy rounds bounced off the burning, black-taloned thing.

Angharad's sword did not. She took off its head in one stroke. Pressurised black ichor squirted up out of the severed neck with such force it spattered the ceiling. The thing clawed at her with its jet-black hooks. She took its bone arm off, and then cut it entirely in half.

'Evisorex thirsts!' she cried as the daemon fell apart, reducing to dust, its red glow evaporating.

'You see?' Angharad said, cocky with triumph. 'Sometimes a good sword is all you need.'

Behind her, Molotch clambered to his feet. 'You stupid bitch. Weren't you listening? That wasn't Slyte. *That's* Slyte.'

The entire end wall of the solar collapsed, brought down by an advancing cliff of wet beige flesh. Mottled, lumpen tentacles reached out, flapping and snaking, from the gigantic mass. Some ended in sucker mouths, foul beaks of clear cartilage that snapped and yawned. Others were tipped by what looked like grasping human fingers. Vast, oozing orifices opened and closed between the roots of the whipping tentacles, and black-tipped transparent teeth, like giant quills, interlaced and clattered. Fetid gases exhaled through the pulsing orifices. The daemon-bulk stank of spoiled meat and disease.

The solar gradually disintegrated, its walls giving way under the crushing weight.

Angharad slashed her blade at a suppurating wall of daemonic flesh three times her height. She tore huge gouges into the bruised, glistening meat, and sheared off several tusks and tentacles. Wretched brown ichor gushed out of the wounds.

Nayl yelled her name again, firing his weapon. Molotch was already fleeing, Ravenor was backing rapidly out through the collapsing frame of the terrace doors. Culzean, lying in the path of the monster, scrambled helplessly.

He squealed as the first of the dripping worm-limbs found him. They seized him with their beaks and suckers, and constricted around his body. Their touch spread virile corruption. Accelerated decomposition overtook Orfeo Culzean while he was still alive. He rotted in seconds and dissolved into a mass of wriggling worms and maggots.

Another writhing tendril, as fat as a man's arm and as white as a sea-floor mollusc, snapped around Angharad's neck and snatched her off her feet. She was sucked into one of the open maws in a single, gurgling inhalation. The flailing, pallid tentacles around the gulping orifice suddenly flushed bright red.

Evisorex clattered to the floor.

Nayl, in blind rage, ran forwards to where she had been standing a second before. He took up the fallen blade and hacked at the shuddering bulk, as if he could somehow cut it open and drag her back out.

Ravenor had moved clear of the collapsing chamber out onto the terrace. Molotch was with him, holding the leather case to his chest.

'Go, Zygmunt. Make things ready,' Ravenor said.

Molotch nodded and ran off down the terrace steps. Ravenor looked back.

+Harlon!+

Nayl just yowled back in answer, chopping with the sabre. He couldn't see what Ravenor could see.

The towering wall of daemon flesh ploughing through the solar was just a small part of a vast mass manifesting on top of Elmingard, a mountain of infected meat, growing all the time. Towers and roofs collapsed under it. In the sheeting rain, it was hard to define any real detail of the mass except for the black, blistered bulk of it. Jagged tusks, as big as tree trunks, covered its upper flanks like battlements. Vast pseudopods, hundreds of metres long and dozens in girth, rippled and danced up into the sky above from the apex of the mass. The cyclone of storm clouds, many kilometres across, rotated around the dancing limbs like a crown.

Ravenor gazed up at the abomination the warp had disgorged onto Elmingard.

'Oh Throne help us,' he said.

FIFTEEN

'Stop,' pleaded Iosob. 'Stop it. Stop it. It's making my head hurt.'

'Shut up,' said Molotch.

'Stop. Make him stop. Kys, make him stop.'

The girl looked up at Patience. 'Please.'

'Shhhhh...' said Kys. 'It's all right.'

'But he's spoiling my door. He's spoiling it.'

'He has to do this,' Kys told her softly.

Molotch was using a stick of chalk to inscribe runes and patterns on the door and the wall around it. He'd already got Kys to hold one end of a length of twine so that he could measure out distances along the wall and the wet flagstones and mark them out accurately.

He was working furiously, copying certain symbols from sheets of parchment that were beginning to disintegrate in the driving rain. The symbols were ugly. Kys didn't want to look at them. They made her skin crawl. She stayed at his side, however, because the only alternative was to look up at the gargantuan horror bestriding Elmingard, and that was a far more disturbing prospect.

'Are you done yet?' she asked.

'I'm going as fast as I can,' Molotch replied. 'There is a degree of precision required. This can't be rushed. You want it to work, don't you?'

'I'm not sure what I want any more,' said Kys.

Molotch patiently scratched with the tip of his chalk stub. 'This is an art. One rune imprecisely drawn, one sigil out of alignment... that would doom us to failure.'

She didn't reply. Molotch looked up at her. 'I often think of "Lynta", you know.'

'Don't.'

'I was very fond of "Lynta". She was with me for about a year. Yes, I was very fond of her, until I discovered that "Lynta" had infiltrated my team to betray me, and that her actual name was Patience Kys.'

'I won't tell you again. Get on with your work, Molotch.'

'It was Zenta Malhyde. 397.M41. You were very good. Very, very good. The things you did to convince me you were loyal.'

'Shut up,' Kys spat. 'Shut your damn mouth!'

'All your efforts and sacrifices were for nothing,' Molotch smiled. 'Because although you and Thonius, and Kara and Nayl tore my team apart and left me for dead, I survived, as I always survive. I imagine that must have been hard to live with afterwards, "Lynta".'

A kineblade was suddenly hovering, trembling, a thumb's length from his left eye. 'Why?' Kys snarled through clenched teeth. 'Why the hell would you try to goad me like this?'

'My dear, if this all goes wrong, I want to be sure you'll kill me quickly.'

'Finish your work!' she cried. Molotch shrugged and got busy with his chalk stick again. Another primordial roar rent the air. They felt the deep vibration of it in their chests. Iosob yelped. Insect vermin, black and whiskered, had begun to spill down the wall from above. A river of them ran down the nearby steps. Kys pulled Iosob to her. She stamped on a few of the bugs milling around her feet.

Ravenor appeared at last, soaring down the steps to join them. Nayl stumbled after him. Kys could both see and feel that Ravenor was waring Nayl. That was almost unheard of. The wraithbone pendant around Nayl's neck was glowing. He held the Carthaen's sabre in his hands.

'Are we ready?' Ravenor asked.

'Nearly,' Molotch replied.

'Where are the others?'

Kys gestured beyond the monastic wall. Out on the landing, a lander's thrusters growled.

'They're boarding the lander. Sholto came.'

'Good,' said Ravenor.

They all looked up as the bulk of Slyte roared again. It was a deep, atonal blast, like the blaring warhorn of savage gods. The huge, snaking tentacles of the titanic abomination had begun to flop down over the sides of the Elmingard cliffs and reach around. Swelling black flesh bulged over the crushed palace. The smell was intolerable. Terraces crumpled and gave way under Slyte's putrescent folds.

+Harlon, I'm going to release you. Don't be a liability.+

Nayl's figure shivered and hunched slightly as Ravenor's mind let him go. His knuckles whitened around the hilt of Evisorex and he uttered a terrible, heartbreaking moan.

'She's gone. I'm sorry, Harlon,' Ravenor said.

Nayl didn't reply. He was shaking.

'There was nothing we could have done.'

Nayl nodded slowly, as if he understood, but Kys could see nothing left in him of the strong, vital man she knew.

'I'm done,' said Molotch, turning to face them and flicking a cockroach off his sleeve, 'except for the blood, of course.'

The bowl of Culzean's blood had long since been lost in the mayhem.

Harlon Nayl, without hesitation, raised Evisorex. He slid his left hand along its length. Blood ran from his sliced palm.

'Use this,' he told Molotch.

They stood and waited while Molotch anointed the door with Nayl's blood. The red smudges immediately began to dilute in the rain.

'Key, young lady?' Molotch said to Iosob. Pouting reluctantly, she handed it to Molotch, and he fitted it into the lock.

'Now we should leave, if we're ever going to leave,' said Molotch.

They headed out through the wall arch onto the landing. Sholto's craft sat waiting for them, its engines throbbing impatiently. Kys could see Unwerth's concerned face in the glow of the instrumentation, watching for them through the cockpit window.

Kys, Iosob and Nayl clambered aboard.

'Is there not some incantation?' Ravenor asked as he and Molotch stood beside the waiting craft.

'Incantation?' Molotch laughed.

'I don't, I'm happy to say, know much about these things. I assumed there would be some words to speak, some ritual.'

Molotch giggled. 'What a strange notion your kind has of mine, Gideon. You picture us all, sheltered away on our covens, mumbling arcane phrases from decrepit tomes for the adulation of our masters.'

'I'm sorry,' said Ravenor. 'I assumed–'

'Actually, there is,' said Molotch, holding out a shred of parchment, 'and I want you to say it.'

SIXTEEN

RAVENOR SPOKE THE words, reading them from the paper Molotch held out in front of him. The blasphemy of them choked him, and polluted him. Every word was a taste of venom. He allowed Molotch this moment of triumph.

'That wasn't so hard now, was it?' Molotch asked.

'It was the hardest thing I've ever done,' Ravenor replied, truthfully. 'You are an irredeemable bastard, Molotch. I think I might leave you here.'

'That would just be unsporting,' said Molotch.

'It simply delays the inevitable.'

'Then let's delay it. Who knows, there may not be an inevitable anything.'

They boarded and closed the hatch. 'Master Unwerth,' Ravenor called, 'if you please!'

THE LANDER LIFTED, jets straining, into the night. Wind shear punished them, and threatened to dash them into the cliff or the surrounding mountains. Unwerth cursed, fighting the stick. Kys moved into the cockpit, and used her telekinetic strength to help him lever back the controls.

They rose into the storm, ailing and wrenching. Behind them, Elmingard had gone. Occupying its clifftop site like a nest, the vast, rugose mass of black flesh and flailing pseudopods roared and quivered.

'Now!' Molotch yelled over the wall of the struggling thrusters. 'It has to be now!'

'We're still too close,' Ravenor replied.

'Better too close than too late,' said Molotch.

Ravenor lashed out with his mind. He reached back down into the filthy hell pit, his mind blistering and curdling as it was forced to extend into the warping maelstrom. It was like dipping his arm into a boiling cauldron to reach something at the bottom. He yelled out in pain.

He saw the door. The pustular folds of Slyte's distending form had almost crushed it. The old monastic wall had toppled, pushed out by the daemon's stinking girth. Ravenor lunged for the door, for the key in the lock.

It was white-hot. He screamed again. It wouldn't turn.

The lander jolted violently as a flailing tentacle struck it. They dipped and almost inverted. Dozens of alarm warnings began to shrill. Unwerth cried out with rage as he fought to right them again.

He brought them true, the thrusters maxing out at the limit of their power. Ice caked the front ports. Blow flies hatched from nowhere in their thousands and buzzed around the compartment. Iosob shrieked. Every metallic surface and object in the lander blackened and tarnished. The wounds Plyton and Nayl had taken suddenly began to bleed again. Belknap tried to staunch them. Kara's nostrils spurted blood, and she fell back in her seat.

'Damn it, and we were so close,' Molotch said, flapping the flies away from his face.

'The Emperor protects,' said Ravenor.

He took hold of the key. He turned it. The door opened.

The door opened into a bright, cold, white void that was somehow more hideous and terrible than the blackness and the daemon, and the storm. The light poured out, alien and sterile. The marks Molotch had painstakingly inscribed around the doorway lit up like phosphorescent flares, burning down into the stone despite the rain. Straight lines of dazzling white power linked them together like las beams, shooting from one to another until a geometric web of frosty light surrounded the open door.

The old wooden door caught fire. Its frame combusted and burned. As it came apart in flames, the awful white light on the other side escaped, fracturing beyond the destroyed doorway and then out past the geometric web itself. A jagged white gash tore across the ground and up through the wall. It spread and split, faster and wider and longer.

A vast fissure of cold white light opened across the black rock of Elmingard.

There was a second of silence followed by a nuclear blink and a false dawn brighter than the sun.

The Kell Mountains ceased to be. They were sucked back into nothingness as the warp engulfed them and dragged them in. The gigantic storm was swallowed up along with them like ink in water, spinning down a drain. The night side of Gudrun lit up as clear as day.

A shockwave front two kilometres deep slammed out from the event across the countryside of Sarre.

It caught the tiny craft struggling to escape its wrath and hurled it, tumbling, from the sky.

AFTER

Thracian Primaris, 405.M41

I SIT IN the shadows of the cloister outside the hearing rooms. They will call me again soon, for the next round of questioning. I have lost count of the days now: thirty-one, thirty-two? My pardoner will know.

The court appointed him to me. His name is Culitch, an aspiring interrogator. He is reasonably efficient. As I go over the details with him in our briefings, his eyes widen as if I am telling him tall stories. He marks my comments down on his data-slate and wonders how he is going to recount them in open court without ridicule.

I wish him good luck.

My Lord Rorken still refuses to talk to me. I can understand his anger, although I had hoped he would affirm my actions without recourse to a formal hearing. His advisors privately assure me this is just for show, and that Lord Rorken is obliged to follow correct process. I am not so sure.

So, I sit in the chilly cloisters of the Palace of the Inquisition day after day. I have become used to its menacing, shadowy halls and unforgiving black marble floors. Inquisitorial guardsmen in burgundy armour, carrying their double-handed powerblades upright before them, stalk past from time to time, escorting solemn men and women in grim robes. They pretend not to look at me. They know who I am.

The rogue, the radical who saved Eustis Majoris by crippling it, and who spared Gudrun by wasting an entire province. Rogue, rogue, *rogue*.

I sit and wait for the next session to begin. My elders and betters will determine my fate. I trust they will make a good decision.

Footsteps approach. I assume it's Culitch, but then I recognise the limp and the clack of the walking stick.

'Hello,' says Maud, sitting down on the stone bench beside me. She leans her stick against the armrest. She is young and strong, and still healing. Her arm is in a sling. There is a smile on her face.

'How are we today?' she asks breezily.

'Fine. Did you find it?'

She nods. She has papers in her hand. 'At last. Took me ages. The archives are immense, and I was going back a long way. The prefects thought I was mad to be searching for something so distant and insignificant.'

'But you found it?'

'Of course I did. Say what you like about the Munitorum, but they keep the most thorough records. Besides, I'm a detective. What was that, was that a laugh?'

'Yes.'

'All right then. Sometimes your voice box makes damn funny sounds.'

'I laughed, Maud.'

It's good to have her with me. I appreciate her loyalty. Most of my friends are gone now, some for ever. Nayl said his goodbyes to me two weeks ago. He was bound for Carthe, intending to return Evisorex to the clan. He was brooding and quiet. I doubt he will ever return.

Zael and Frauka left last week, in the care of Inquisitor Lilith. She took Iosob with her too. They will all be tested and processed. I think Lilith will be compassionate, but I entertain no real hopes of seeing any of them again.

Kara, my dear Kara, remains under arrest. They are keeping her here, somewhere. Her hearing will follow mine, and I hope by the Emperor's grace I will be there to testify for her. She doesn't deserve this.

Belknap took passage to Eustis Majoris while we were still on Gudrun, the day before I turned myself over to Lilith. There was nothing to be said. He was a noble man, but his heart was broken by the strength of his faith.

As for Unwerth and Preest, I have had no word from either of them. I wish them well in whatever voyages they undertake.

And Kys. Kys haunts the dining houses of the hive, loitering quietly, waiting for me to be exonerated. I have no idea what she will do if the Inquisition demands my incarceration or death. I wish she would come and see me.

'So d'you want to hear this or not?' Plyton asks, 'after all the bloody effort I went to.'

'Tell me, please.'

She shuffles the papers. 'Rahjez, Fantomine sub. 404, M.40.'

'Go on.'

'Listening Station Arethusa. Service personnel. Service records for Bashesvili, Ludmilla. It... uhm... it lists her as deceased that year.'

'Was there a raid?'

'No. No actions reported until 405. The records suggest she was—'

'Executed,' I finish.

'For treason, I think.'

The ku-kud bristles and whispers. Iosob has opened the door.

'Will you come with us?' I ask.

Bashesvili shivers. 'Oh, no, Gideon, I don't think so. The far future frightens me. I think I'll be safer here.'

'I owe you everything. If this works, the far future you're so unsure of will owe you a great debt too.'

'Go and do what you have to do, Gideon. It sounds important.'

'Goodbye, Ludmilla.'

I HEAR FOOTSTEPS. It is Culitch. 'Sir, the hearings are about to recommence. Are you ready?'

'Yes, young man.'

He walks towards the heavy doors and waits for me to join him. A session bell is ringing

'I'm coming,' I tell him. 'Thank you for your work, Maud. I needed to know.'

Plyton rises, leaning on her stick.

'I'll wait here until you get out,' she says.

THEN

Sarte Province, Gudrun, 404.M41

THE LANDER WAS a broken, buckled mass of wreckage. It had impacted in a bare field eighteen kilometres away from the epicentre, cutting itself a sixty-metre long gouge in the earth before coming to rest.

Steam and smoke rose from the crumpled shape. Right until the last moment, Unwerth had fought to bring them in safely. His skills had prevented them from simply crashing into the ground. Even so, it had not been a comfortable touchdown.

Most of the passengers were unconscious. Vapour hissed, and lubricant dripped from torn hoses.

Molotch clambered out onto the dry straw of the field. The crash had broken several of his ribs, and they ground together as he moved.

'Ow,' he said. 'Ow, shit. That hurts.'

He began to stagger away across the parched fields. The sky was a threaded grey of pre-dawn. To the north, where

413

the Kells had once stood, an immense pall of black
smoke hung like a shadow.

RAVENOR CAUGHT UP with him several fields away, near a
small wood. The trees in the wood had been stripped of
their leaves by the aftershock. Molotch had come to a
halt, leaning against the bars of a broken gate. He was
breathing hard and clutching his ribs. His face was drawn
and bloodless.

He looked up as Ravenor glided towards him, and
laughed sadly. Laughing made him wince.

'I can't run any more,' he said, pain colouring his voice.

'That's good. I'm tired of chasing you.'

Molotch nodded. 'This is the inevitable bit we were
talking about, isn't it?'

'It is,' said Ravenor, and reached out into Molotch's
mind. Zygmunt Molotch did not put up a fight.

When the others caught up with them, Molotch was
lying on the ground beside the gate. Ravenor felt Kys
approaching, with Kara close behind her. Behind them, a
little further off, Nayl was limping across the stubbled
field.

They drew close and halted, staring at the corpse
beside the gate. In death, Molotch seemed a pathetic and
insignificant thing, not at all the sort of being that should
have required decades of devotion, sacrifice and effort to
bring down.

+I told you closure was overrated.+

Kara nodded. 'It's still closure,' she said.

ABOUT THE AUTHOR

Dan Abnett lives and works in Maidstone, Kent, in England. Well known for his comic work, he has written everything from Mr Men to the X-Men. His work for the Black Library includes the best-selling Gaunt's Ghosts novels, the Inquisitor Eisenhorn and Ravenor trilogies, and the Horus Heresy novel, *Horus Rising*. He's also worked on the Darkblade novel series (with US author **Mike Lee**).